Richard Hildreth

THE WHITE SLAVE

Another Picture
of
Slave Life in America

Elibron Classics
www.elibron.com

Elibron Classics series.

© 2006 Adamant Media Corporation.

ISBN 0-543-91904-8 (paperback)
ISBN 0-543-91903-X (hardcover)

This Elibron Classics Replica Edition is an unabridged facsimile
of the edition published in 1852 by George Routledge and Co., London

THE

WHITE SLAVE.

ANOTHER PICTURE

OF

SLAVE LIFE IN AMERICA.

BY

R. HILDRETH,

AUTHOR OF "THE HISTORY OF THE UNITED STATES."

All men are by nature equally free and independent, and have certain
ENT RIGHTS, of which, when they enter into society, they cannot by any
:t deprive or divest their posterity; namely, the enjoyment of life and
, with the means of acquiring and possessing property, and pursuing
ess and safety."—*Virginia Bill of Rights, Art. I.*

FIRST ENGLISH EDITION.

LONDON:
GEORGE ROUTLEDGE AND CO., FARRINGDON STREET.
1852.

THE WHITE SLAVE.

CHAPTER I.

YE who would know what evils man can inflict upon his fellow without reluctance, hesitation, or regret; ye who would learn the limit of human endurance, and with what bitter anguish and indignant hate the heart may swell, and yet not burst,—peruse these Memoirs!

Mine are no silken sorrows, nor sentimental sufferings; but that stern reality of actual woe, the story of which may perhaps touch even some of those who are every day themselves the authors of misery the same that I endured. For however the practice of tyranny may have deadened every better emotion, and the prejudices of education and interest may have hardened the heart, humanity will still extort an involuntary tribute; and men will grow uneasy at hearing of those deeds, of which the doing does not cost them a moment's inquietude.

Should I accomplish no more than this; should I be able, through the triple steel with which the love of money and the lust of domination has encircled it, to reach one bosom,—let the story of my wrongs summon up, in the mind of a single oppressor, the dark and dreaded images of his own misdeeds, and teach his conscience how to torture him with the picture of himself, and I shall be content. Next to the tears and the exultations of the emancipated, the remorse of tyrants is the choicest offering upon the altar of liberty!

But perhaps something more may be possible; not likely, but to be imagined; and it may be, even faintly to be hoped. Perhaps within some youthful breast, in which the evil spirits of avarice and tyranny have as yet failed to gain unlimited control, I may be able to rekindle the smothered and expiring embers of humanity. Spite of habits and prejudices inculcated and fostered from his earliest childhood, spite of the enticements of wealth and political distinction, and the still stronger enticements of indolence and ease, spite of the pratings of hollow-hearted priests, spite of the arguments of time-serving sophists, spite of the hesitation and terrors of the weak-spirited and wavering; in spite of evil precept and evil example, he dares—that generous and heroic youth!—to cherish and avow the feelings of a man.

Another Saul among the prophets, he prophesies terrible things in the ear of insolent and luxurious tyranny; in the midst of tyrants he dares to preach the good tidings of liberty; in the very school of oppression, he stands boldly forth the advocate of human rights!

He breaks down the ramparts of prejudice; he dissipates the illusions of avarice and pride; he repeals the enactments, which, though wanting every feature of justice, have sacrilegiously usurped the sacred form of law! He snatches the whip from the hand of the master; he breaks for ever the fetter of the slave!

B

In place of reluctant toil, drudging for another, he brings in smiling industry to labour for herself! All nature seems to exult in the change! The earth, no longer made barren by the tears and the blood of her children, pours forth her treasures with redoubled liberality. Existence ceases to be torture; and to live is no longer, to millions, the certainty of being miserable.

Chosen Instrument of Mercy! Illustrious Deliverer! Come! come quickly!

Come!—lest, if thy coming be delayed, there come in thy place, he who will be at once DELIVERER and AVENGER!

CHAPTER II.

THE county in which I was born was then, and for aught I know, may still be, one of the richest and most populous in eastern Virginia. My father, Colonel Charles Moore, was the head of one of the most considerable and influential families in that part of the country; and family, however little weight it may have in other parts of America, at the time I was born was a thing of no slight consequence in lower Virginia. Nature and education had combined to qualify Colonel Moore to fill with credit the station in which his birth had placed him. He was a finished aristocrat; and such he showed himself in every word, look, and action. There was in his bearing a conscious superiority which few could resist, softened and rendered even agreeable by a gentleness and suavity, which flattered, pleased, and captivated. In fact, he was familiarly spoken of among his friends and neighbours, as the faultless pattern of a true Virginian gentleman—an encomium by which they supposed themselves to convey, in the most emphatic manner, the highest possible praise.

When the war of the American Revolution broke out, Colonel Moore was a very young man. By birth and education he belonged, as I have said, to the aristocratic party, which being aristocratic, was, of course, conservative. But the impulses of youth and patriotism were too strong to be resisted. He espoused with zeal the cause of liberty, and by his political activity and influence contributed not a little to its success.

Of liberty indeed he was always a warm and energetic admirer. Among my earliest recollections of him, is the earnestness with which, among his friends and guests, he used to vindicate the cause of the French Revolution, then going on. Of that revolution, throughout its whole progress, he was a most eloquent advocate and apologist; and though I understood little or nothing of what he said, the spirit and eloquence with which he spoke could not fail to affect me. *The rights of man* and the *rights of human nature* were phrases which, although at that time I was quite unconscious of their meaning, I heard so often repeated, that they made an indelible impression upon my memory, and in after years frequently recurred to my recollection.

But Colonel Moore was not a mere talker; he had the credit of acting up to his principles, and was universally regarded as a man of the greatest good nature, honour, and uprightness. Several promising young men, who afterwards rose to eminence, were indebted for their first start in life to his patronage and assistance. He settled half the differences in the county, and never seemed so well pleased as when by preventing a lawsuit or a duel, he hindered an accidental and perhaps trifling dispute from degenerating into a bitter, if not a fatal, quarrel. The tenderness of his heart, his ready, active benevolence, and his sympathy with misfortune, were traits in his character spoken of by everybody.

Had I been allowed to choose my own paternity, could I possibly have selected a more desirable father? But by the laws and customs of Virginia, it is not the father, but the mother, whose rank and condition determine that of the child; and, alas! my mother was a concubine, and a slave!

Yet those who beheld her for the first time, would hardly have imagined, or would willingly have forgotten, that she was connected with an ignoble and degraded race. Humble as her station might be, she could at least boast possession of the most brilliant beauty. The trace of African blood, by which her veins were contaminated, was distinctly visible; but the tint which it imparted to her complexion only served to give a peculiar richness to the blush that mantled over her cheek. Her long black hair, which she understood how to arrange with an artful simplicity, and the flashing of her dark eyes, which changed their expression with every change of feeling, corresponded exactly to her complexion, and completed a picture which might perhaps be matched in Spain or Italy, but for which, it would be in vain to seek a rival among the pale-faced and languid beauties of eastern Virginia.

I describe her more like a lover than a son. But in truth, her beauty was so uncommon, as to draw my attention while I was yet a child; and many an hour have I watched her, almost with a lover's earnestness, while she fondled me on her lap, and tears and smiles chased each other alternately over a face, the expression of which was ever changing, yet always beautiful. She was the most affectionate of mothers; the mixture of tenderness, grief, and pleasure, with which she always seemed to regard me, gave a new vivacity to her beauty; and it was probably this which so early and so strongly fixed my attention.

But I was very far from being her only admirer. Her beauty was notorious through all that part of the country; and Colonel Moore had been frequently tempted to sell her by the offer of very high prices. All such offers, however, he had steadily rejected; for he especially prided himself upon owning the swiftest horse, the handsomest wench, and the finest pack of hounds in the "Ancient Dominion."

Now it may seem odd to some people, in some parts of the world, that Colonel Moore, being such a man as I have described him, should keep a mistress and be the father of illegitimate children. Such persons, however, must be totally ignorant of the state of things in the slaveholding states of America.

Colonel Moore was married to an amiable woman, whom I dare say he loved and respected; and in the course of time she made him the happy father of two sons and as many daughters. This circumstance, however, did not hinder him, any more than it does any other American planter, from giving, in the mean time, a very free indulgence to his amorous temperament among his numerous slaves at Spring-Meadow,— for so his estate was called. Many of the young women occasionally boasted of his attentions; though generally, at any one time, he did not have more than one or two acknowledged favourites.

My mother was for several years distinguished by Colonel Moore's very particular regard, and she brought him no less than six children, all of whom, except myself, who was the eldest, were lucky enough to die in infancy.

From my mother I inherited some imperceptible portion of African blood, and with it, the base and cursed condition of a slave. But though born a slave, I inherited all my father's proud spirit, sensitive feelings, and ardent temperament; and as regards natural endowments, whether of mind or body, I am bold to assert that he had more reason to be proud of me than of either of his legitimate and acknowledged sons.

CHAPTER III.

THAT education is the most effectual which commences earliest— a maxim well understood in that part of the world in which it was my misfortune to be born. As it sometimes happens there, that one half of a man's children are born masters and the other half slaves, it has become sufficiently obvious how necessary it is to begin by times the course of discipline proper to train them up for these very different situations. It is, accordingly, the general custom, that young master, almost from the hour of his birth, has allotted to him some little slave near his own age, upon whom he begins, from the time he can go alone, to practise his apprenticeship of tyranny. It so happened that within less than a year after my birth, Colonel Moore's wife presented him with her second son, James; and while we both slept unconscious in our cradles, I was duly assigned over and appointed to be the body-servant of my younger brother. It is in this capacity, of Master James's boy, that, following back the traces of memory, I first discover myself.

The natural and usual consequences of giving one child absolute authority over another may be easily imagined. The love of domination is perhaps the strongest of our passions, and it is surprising how soon the veriest child will become perfect in the practice of tyranny. Of this, Colonel Moore's eldest son, William, or Master William, as he was called at Spring-Meadow, was a striking instance. He was the terror and bugbear, not only of Joe, his own boy, but of all the children on the place. That unthinking and irrational delight in the exercise of cruelty, which is sometimes displayed by a wayward child, seemed in him almost a passion; and this passion, by perpetual indulgence, was soon fostered into a habit. When any delinquent slave was to be punished, he contrived if possible to find it out, and to be present at the infliction; so that he soon became an adept in all the horrible practices and disgusting slang of an overseer. He always went armed with a whip, twice as long as himself, and upon the least opposition to his whims and caprices, was ready to show his skill in the use of it. All this he took some little pains to conceal from his father; who, however, was pretty careful not to see what he could by no means approve, but what, at the same time—indulgent father as he was—he would have found it very difficult to prevent or cure.

Master James, to whose service I was particularly appointed, was a very different boy. Sickly and weak from his birth, his temper was gentle and his mind effeminate. He had an affectionate disposition, and soon conceived a fondness for me, which I very thankfully returned. He protected me from the tyranny of Master William by his entreaties, his tears, and what had much more weight with that amiable youth, by threats of complaining to his father, and making a complete exposure of his brutal and cruel behaviour.

I soon learned to put up with and to pardon an occasional pettishness and ill humour, for which Master James's bad health furnished a ready excuse; and by flattery and apparent obsequiousness, for a child learns and practises such arts as readily as a man, I presently came to have a great influence over him. He was the master and I the slave; but while we were both children, this artificial distinction had less potency, and I found little difficulty in maintaining that actual pre-eminence, to which my superior vigour both of body and mind so justly entitled me.

When Master James had reached the age of five years, it was judged expedient by his father, that he should be initiated into the rudiments of learning. To learn the letters was a laborious undertaking enough, —but for putting them into words, my young master seemed to have no genius whatever. He was not destitute of ambition; he was indeed very desirous to learn; it was the ability—not the inclination—that was wanting. In this difficulty he had recourse to me, who was on all occasions his chief counsellor. By putting our heads together we soon hit upon a plan. My memory was remarkably good, while that of my poor little master was very miserable. We arranged, therefore, that the family tutor should first teach me the letters and the abs, which my strong memory, we thought, would enable me easily to retain, and which I was gradually, and between plays, as opportunity served, to instil into the mind of Master James. This plan we found to answer admirably. Neither the tutor nor Colonel Moore made any objection to it; for all that Colonel Moore desired was, that his son should learn to read; and the tutor was very willing to shift off the most laborious part of his task upon my shoulders.

As yet, no one had dreamed of those barbarous and detestable laws—unparalleled in any other codes, and destined to be the everlasting disgrace of America—by which it has been made a *crime*, punishable with fine and imprisonment, to teach a slave to read.

It is not enough that custom and the proud scorn of unfeeling tyranny unite to keep the slave in hopeless and helpless ignorance, but the laws too have openly become a party to this accursed conspiracy! Yes, I believe they would tear out our very eyes,—and that too by virtue of a regularly enacted statute—had they ingenuity enough to invent a way of enabling us to drudge and delve without them!

I soon learned to read, and before long I made Master James almost as good a reader as myself. As he was subject to frequent fits of illness, which confined him to the house, and disabled him from indulging in those active sports to which boys are chiefly devoted, his father obtained for him a large collection of books adapted to his age, which he and I used to read over together, and in which we took great delight.

In the further progress of my young master's studies I was still his associate; for though the plan of teaching me first, in order that I might afterwards teach him, was pursued no longer, yet as I had a desire to learn, as well as a quick apprehension, I found no difficulty in extracting every day from Master James the substance of his lessons. Indeed, if there was any difficulty in them, he was in the constant habit of appealing to me for assistance. In this way I acquired some elementary knowledge of arithmetic and geography, and even a smattering of Latin.

These acquisitions, however, I took great pains to conceal, since even the fact that I could read, though it increased my consequence among the servants, exposed me to a good deal of ridicule, to which I was very sensitive. I was not looked upon, as I suppose they now look upon a slave, who knows how to read, and who exhibits some marks of sense and ability, as a dreadful monster breathing war and rebellion, and plotting to cut the throats of all the good people in America; I was regarded rather as a sort of prodigy—like a three-legged hen, or a sheep with four eyes; a thing to be produced and exhibited for the entertainment of strangers. Frequently at a dinner-party, after the Madeira had circulated pretty freely, I was set to read paragraphs in the newspapers, to amuse my master's tipsy guests, and was puzzled, perplexed, and tormented, by all sorts of absurd, ridiculous, and impertinent questions, which I was obliged to answer under penalty of having a wine-glass, a bottle, or a plate flung at my head. Master William especially, as he was prevented from using his whip upon me, as freely as he wished, strove to indemnify himself by making me the butt of his wit. He took great pride in the nick-name of the "learned nigger," which he had invented, and always applied to me—though, God knows, that my cheek was little less fair than his, and I cannot help hoping that, at least, my soul was whiter.

These, it may be thought, were trifling vexations. In truth they were so; but it cost me many a struggle before I could learn to endure them with any tolerable patience. I was compensated in some measure, by the pleasure I took in listening, as I stood behind my master's chair, to the conversation of the company,—I mean their conversation before they set regularly in to drinking; for every dinner-party was sure to wind up with a general frolic.

Colonel Moore kept an open house, and almost every day, he had some of his friends, relatives, or neighbours, at his table. He was himself an eloquent and most agreeable talker; his voice was soft and musical, and he always expressed himself with a great deal of point and vivacity. Many of his guests were well-informed men; and though politics was always the leading topic of conversation, a great variety of other subjects were occasionally discussed. Colonel Moore, as I have already observed, was himself a warm democrat—republican was then the phrase—for democrat, however fond the Americans have since become of the name, was at that time regarded as an epithet of reproach. The greater part of those who frequented Colonel Moore's house entertained the same liberal opinions on political subjects. I listened to their conversation with eagerness and pleasure; and when I heard them talk of equal rights, and declaim against tyranny and oppression, my heart would swell with emotions of which I scarcely understood the meaning. All this time, I made no personal application of what I heard and felt. It was only the abstract beauty of liberty and equality of which I had learned to be enamoured. It was the French republicans with whom I sympathised; it was the Austrian and English tyrants against whom my indignation was roused; it was John Adams and his atrocious gag-law. I had not yet learned to think about myself. What I saw around me I had always been accustomed to see, and it appeared, as it were, the fixed order of nature. Though born a slave, I had, as yet, experienced scarcely anything of the miseries of that wretched condition. I was singularly fortunate in my young master, to whom I was, in many respects, as much a companion as a servant. By his favour, and through means of my mother, who still continued a favourite with Colonel Moore, I enjoyed more indulgences than any other servant on the place. Comparing my situation with that of the field hands, I might pronounce myself fortunate indeed; and though exposed to occasional mortifications, enough to give me already a foretaste of the bitter cup which every one who lives a slave must swallow, my youth and the buoyant vivacity of my temper as yet sustained me.

At this time I did not know that Colonel Moore was my father. That gentleman was indebted for no inconsiderable part of his high reputation, to a very strict attention to those conventional observances which so often usurp the place of morals. Some observances of this sort, which prevail in America, are sufficiently remarkable. It is considered, for instance, no crime whatever for a master to be, if he chooses, the father of every infant slave born upon his plantation. Yet it is esteemed a very grave breach of propriety, indeed almost an unpardonable crime, for such a father ever, in any way, to acknowledge or take any notice, of any of his unfortunate children. Imperious custom demands that he should treat them, in every respect, like his other slaves. If he drive them into the field to labour, if he sell them at auction to the highest bidder, it is all well. But if he audaciously undertake to exhibit towards them, in any way, the slightest indication of paternal tenderness, he may be sure that his character will be assailed by the tongue of universal slander; that his every weak point and unjustifiable action will be carefully sought out, malignantly magnified, and ostentatiously exposed; that he will be compelled to run a sort of moral gauntlet, and will be represented among all the *better sort of people*, as everything that is infamous, base, and contemptible.

Colonel Moore was far too wise a man to entertain the slightest idea of exposing himself to anything of that sort. He had always kept the best society,—and though he might be a democrat in politics, he was certainly very much of an aristocrat and an exclusive in his feelings. Of course, he had the same sort of indescribable horror, at the thought of violating any of the settled proprieties of the society in which he moved, that a modern belle has of cotton lace, or a modern dandy of an iron fork. This being the case, nobody will wonder—so far at least as Colonel Moore had any control over the matter—that I was still ignorant who my father was.

But though a secret to me, it certainly was not so to Colonel Moore's friends and visitors. If nothing else had betrayed it, the striking resemblance between us would certainly have done so; and although that same *regard to propriety*, which prevented Colonel Moore from ever noticing the relationship, also tied up the tongues of his guests, yet, after I had learned the secret, there immediately occurred to my mind the true explanation of certain sly jests and distant allusions, which had sometimes been dropped towards the end of a dinner, by some of those guests whom deep potations had inspired at once with wit and veracity. These brilliancies, of which I had never been able to understand the meaning, were always ill received by Colonel Moore, and by all the soberer part of the company, and were frequently followed by a command to me and the other servants to quit the room; but why or wherefore, till I became possessed of the key above mentioned, I was always at a great loss to determine.

The secret which my father did not choose, and which my mother did not dare to communicate, I might easily have obtained from my fellow-servants. But at this time, like most of the lighter-complexioned slaves, I felt a sort of contempt for my duskier brothers in misfortune. I kept myself as much as possible at a distance from them, and scorned to associate with men a little darker than myself. So ready are slaves to imbibe all the ridiculous prejudices of their oppressors, and themselves to add new links to the chain which deprives them of their liberty!

But let me do my father justice; for I do not believe that he was totally destitute of a father's feelings. Though he never made the slightest acknowledgment of the claims which I had upon him, yet I am sure, in his own heart, he did not totally deny their validity. There was a tone of good-natured indulgence whenever he spoke to me—an air of kindness, which, though he always had it, seemed toward me to have in it something peculiar. At any rate, he succeeded in captivating my affections; for though I regarded him only as my master, I loved him very sincerely.

CHAPTER IV.

I WAS about seventeen years old, when my mother was attacked by a fever, which proved fatal to her. She early had a presentiment of her fate; and before the disorder had made any great progress, she sent me word that she desired to see me. I found her in bed. She begged the woman who nursed her to leave us together, and bade me sit down by her bed-side. Having told me that she feared she was going to die, she could not think it kind to me, she said, to leave the world, without first telling me a secret, which possibly I might find hereafter of some consequence. I begged her to go on, and waited with impatience for the promised information. She began with a short account of her own life. Her mother was a slave; her father was a certain Colonel Randolph—a scion of one of the great Virginian families. She had been raised as a lady's maid, and on the marriage of Colonel Moore, had been purchased by him and presented to his wife. She was then quite a girl. As she grew older and her beauty became more noticeable, she found much favour in the eyes of her master. She had a neat little house, with a double set of rooms—an arrangement as much for Colonel Moore's convenience as her own; and though some light tasks of needlework were sometimes required of her, yet as nobody chose to quarrel with master's favourite, she lived, henceforward, a very careless, indolent, but as she told me, a very unhappy life.

For a part of this unhappiness she was indebted to herself. The air of superiority she assumed in her intercourse with the other servants made them all hate her, and induced them to improve every opportunity of vexing and mortifying her; and to all sorts of feminine mortifications she was as sensitive as any belle that ever existed. But though vain of her beauty and her master's favour, she was not ill-tempered; and the foolish pride from which she suffered, sprung in her, as a similar feeling did in me, from a groundless, though common prejudice. Indeed, our situation was so superior to that of most of the other slaves, that we naturally imagined ourselves, in some sort, a superior race. It was doubtless under the influence of this feeling that my mother, having told me who my father was, observed with a smile and a self-complacent air, which even the tremors of her fever did not prevent from being apparent, that both on the father's and the mother's side, I had running in my veins the best blood of Virginia—the blood, she added, of the Moores and the Randolphs!

Alas! she did not seem to recollect that though I might count all the nobles of Virginia among my ancestors, one drop of blood imported from Africa—though that, too, might be the blood of kings and chieftains—would be enough to taint the whole pedigree, and to condemn me to perpetual slavery, even in the house of my own father!

The information which my mother communicated made little impression upon me at the moment. My principal anxiety was for her; for she had always been the tenderest and most affectionate of parents. The progress of her disorder was rapid, and on the third day she ceased to live. I lamented her with the sincerest grief. The sharpness of my sorrow was soon over; but my spirits did not seem to regain their former tone. The thoughtless gaiety, which till now had shed a sort of sunshine over my life, seemed to desert me. My thoughts began to recur very frequently to the information which my mother had communicated. I hardly know how to describe the effect which it seemed to have upon me. Nor is it easy to tell what were its actual effects, or what ought to be ascribed to other and more general causes. Perhaps that revolution of feeling, which I now experienced, should be attributed in a great measure to the change from boyhood to manhood, through which I was passing. Hitherto things had seemed to happen like the events of a dream, without touching me deeply or affecting me permanently. I was sometimes vexed and dissatisfied; I had my occasional sorrows and complaints. But those sorrows were soon over, and as after summer showers the sun shines out the brighter, so my transient sadness was soon succeeded by a more lively gaiety, which, as soon as immediate grievances were forgotten, burst forth, unsubdued either by reflections on the past, or anxieties for the future. In that gaiety there was indeed scarcely anything of substantial pleasure; it originated rather in a careless insensibility. It was like the glare of the moonbeams, bright, but cold. Such as it was, however, it was far more comfortable than the state of feeling by which it now began to be succeeded. My mind seemed to be filled with indefinite anxieties, of which I could divine neither the causes nor the cure. There was, as it were, a heavy weight upon my bosom, an unsatisfied craving for something, I knew not what, a longing which I could do nothing to satisfy, because I could not tell its object. I would be often lost in thought, but my mind did not seem to fix itself to any certain aim, and after hours of apparently the deepest meditation, I should have been very much at a loss to tell about what I had been thinking.

But sometimes my reflections would take a more definite shape. I would begin to consider what I was and what I had to anticipate. The son of a freeman, yet born a slave! Endowed by nature with abilities, which I should never be permitted to exercise; possessed of knowledge, which already I found it expedient to conceal! The slave of my own father, the servant of my own brother, a bounded, limited, confined, and captive creature, who did not dare to go out of sight of his master's house without a written permission to do so! Destined to be the sport of I knew not whose caprices; forbidden in anything to act for myself, or to consult my own happiness; compelled to labour all my life at another's bidding; and liable every hour and instant to oppressions the most outrageous, and degradations the most humiliating!

These reflections soon grew so bitter that I struggled hard to suppress them. But that was not always in my power. Again and again, in spite of all my efforts, these hateful ideas would start up and sting me into anguish.

My young master still continued kind as ever. I was changing to a man, but he still remained a boy. His protracted ill health, which had checked his growth, appeared also to retard his mental maturity. He seemed every day to fall more and more under my influence; and every day my attachment to him grew stronger. He was, in fact, my sole hope. While I remained with him I might reasonably expect to escape the utter bitterness of slavery. In his eyes I was not a mere servant. He regarded me rather as a loved and trusted companion. Indeed, though he had the name and prerogatives of master, I was much less under his control than he was under mine. There was between us something of a brotherly affection, at least of that kind which may exist between foster brothers, though neither of us ever alluded to our actual relationship, and he, probably, was ignorant of it.

I loved Master James as well as ever; but towards Colonel Moore, my feelings underwent a rapid and a radical change. While I considered myself merely as his slave, his apparent kindness had gained my affections, and there was nothing I would not have done or suffered for so good-natured and condescending a master. But after I had learned to look upon myself as his son, I began to feel that I might justly claim as a right what I had till now regarded as a pure gratuity. I began to feel that I might claim much more—even an equal birth-right with my brethren. Occasionally I had read the Bible, and I now turned with new interest to the story of Hagar the bond-woman, and Ishmael her son; and as I read how an angel came to their relief, when the hard-hearted Abraham had driven them into the wilderness, there seemed to grow up within me a wild, strange, uncertain hope, that in some accident, I knew not what, I too might find succour and relief. At the same time, with this irrational hope, a new spirit of bitterness burst in upon my soul. Unconsciously I clenched my hands, and set my teeth, and fancied myself, as it were, another Ishmael, wandering in the wilderness, every man's hand against me, and my hand against every man. The injustice of my unnatural parent stung me deeper and deeper, and all my love for him was turned into hate. The atrocity of those laws which made me a slave—a slave in the house of my own father—seemed to glare before my too prophetic eyes in letters of blood. Young as I was, and as yet untouched, I trembled for the future, and cursed the country and the hour that gave me birth!

I endeavoured as much as possible to conceal these new feelings with which I was tormented; and as deceit is one of those defences against tyranny of which a slave early learns to avail himself, I was not unsuccessful. My young master would sometimes find me in tears; and sometimes, when I would be lost in thought, he complained of my inattention. But I put him off with plausible excuses; and though he suspected there was something which I did not tell him, and would frequently say to me, "Come Archy, boy, let me know what it is that troubles you,"—I made light of the matter, and laughed off his suspicions.

I was now about to lose this kind master, in whose tenderness and affection I found the sole palliative that could make slavery tolerable. His health, which had always been bad, grew rapidly worse, and confined him first to his chamber and then to his bed. I nursed him during his whole illness with a mother's tenderness and assiduity. Never was master more faithfully served;—but it was the friend, not the slave, who rendered these attentions. He was not insensible to my services; he did not seem to like that any one but I should be about him, and it was only from my hand that he would take his physic or his food. But it was not in the power of physician or of nurse to save him. He wasted daily, and grew weaker every hour. The fatal crisis soon came. His weeping friends were collected about his bed,—but the tears they shed were not as bitter as mine. Almost with his last breath he recommended me to the good graces of his father; but the man who had closed his heart to the promptings of paternal tenderness was not likely to give much weight to the request of a dying son. He bade his friends farewell,—he pressed my hand in his; and, with a gentle sigh, he expired in my arms.

CHAPTER V.

THE family of Colonel Moore knew well how truly I had loved, and how faithfully I had served my young master. They respected the profound depth of my grief, and for a week or two, I was suffered to weep on unmolested. My feelings were no longer of that acute and piercing kind which I have described in the preceding chapter. The temperament of the mind is for ever changing. That state of preternatural sensibility, of which I have attempted to give an idea, had disappeared when my attention became wholly occupied in the care of my dying master. It was succeeded by a dull and stupid sorrow. Apparently I now had increased cause for agitation and alarm. That which I then dreaded had happened. My young master, upon whom all my hopes were suspended, lived no longer, and I knew not what was to become of me. But the fit of fear and anxious anticipation was over; and I now waited my fate with a sort of stupid and careless indifference.

Though not called upon to do it, I continued as usual to wait upon my master's table. For several days, I took my place instinctively near where Master James's chair ought to have stood; till the sight of the vacant place drove me in tears to the opposite corner. In the mean time, nobody called upon me to do anything, or seemed to notice that I was present. Even Master William made an effort to suppress his habitual insolence.

But this could not last long. Indeed it was a stretch of indulgence, which no one but a favourite servant could have expected; since slaves, in general, are thought to have no business to be sorry—if it makes them unable to work.

One morning, after breakfast, Master William, having discussed his toast and coffee, began by telling his father that, in his opinion, the servants at Spring-Meadow were a great deal too indulgently treated. He was by this time a smart, dashing, elegant young man, having returned upwards of a year before from college, and quite lately, from Charleston, in South Carolina, whither he had been to spend a winter, and, as his father expressed it, to wear off the rusticity of the schoolroom. It was there, perhaps, that he had learned the new precepts of humanity which he was now preaching. He declared that any tenderness towards a servant only tended to make him insolent and discontented, and was quite thrown away on the ungrateful rascals. Then looking about, as if in search of some victim upon whom to practise a doctrine so consonant to his own disposition, his eye lighted upon me. " There's that boy Archy—I'll bet a hundred to one I could make him one of the best servants in the world. He's a bright fellow naturally, and nothing has spoiled him, but poor James's over indulgence. Come, father, just be good enough to give him to me, I want another servant most devilishly."

Without stopping for an answer, he hastened out of the room, having, as he said, two jockey races to attend that morning; and what was more, a cock-fight into the bargain. There was nobody else at table. Colonel

Moore turned towards me. He began with commending very highly
my faithful attachment to his poor son James. As he mentioned his
son's name the tears stood in his eyes, and for a moment or two he was
unable to speak. He recovered himself presently, and added—" I hope
now you will transfer all this same zeal and affection to Master William."
These words roused me in a moment. I knew Master William to be
a tyrant, from whose soul custom had long since obliterated what little
humanity nature had bestowed upon him; and to judge from what he
had let drop that morning, he had of late improved upon his natural
inclination for cruelty, and had proceeded to the final length of reducing
tyranny into a system and a science. I knew, too, that from childhood
he had entertained a particular spite against me; and I dreaded lest he
was already devising the means of inflicting upon me with interest all
those insults and injuries from which the protection of his younger
brother had hitherto shielded me.

It was with horror and alarm, that I found myself in danger of falling
into such hands. I threw myself at my master's feet, and besought him,
with all the eloquence of grief and fear, not to give me to Master William.
The terms in which I spoke of his son, though I chose the mildest I could
think of, and the horror I expressed at the thoughts of becoming his
servant, though I endeavoured as much as possible to save the father's
feelings, seemed to make him angry. The smile left his lip, and his brow
grew dark and contracted. I began to despair of escaping the wretched
fate that awaited me; and my despair drove me to a very rash and
foolish action. For emboldened by the danger of becoming the slave of
Master William, I dared to hint—though distantly and obscurely—as
the information which my mother had communicated on her death-
bed; and I even ventured something like a half appeal to Colonel
Moore's *paternal* tenderness. At first he did not seem to understand
me; but the moment he began to comprehend my meaning, his face
grew black as a thunder cloud, then became pale, and immediately was
suffused with a burning blush, in which shame and rage were equally
commingled. I now gave myself up for lost, and expected an instant
out-break of fury;—but, after a momentary struggle, Colonel Moore
seemed to regain his composure; even the habitual smile returned to his
lips; and without taking any notice of my last appeal, or giving any
further signs of having understood it, he merely remarked, that he did
not know how to refuse Master William's request, nor could he comprehend the meaning of my reluctance. It was mighty foolish; still he
was willing to indulge me so far as to allow me the choice of entering
into Master William's service, or going into the field. This alternative
was proposed with an air and a manner which was intended to stop my
mouth, and allow me nothing but the bare liberty of choosing. It was
indeed no very agreeable alternative. But anything, even the hard
labour, scanty fare, and harsh treatment, to which I knew the field
hands were subjected, seemed preferable to becoming the sport of Master
William's tyranny. I was piqued, too, at the cavalier manner in which
my request had been treated, and I did not hesitate. I thanked Colonel
Moore for his great goodness, and at once made choice of the field. He
seemed rather surprised at my selection, and with a smile which
bordered close upon a sneer, bade me report myself to Mr. Stubbs.

An overseer is regarded, in all those parts of slave-holding America
with which I ever became acquainted, very much in the same light in
which people, in countries uncursed with slavery, look upon a hangman;
and as this latter employment, however useful and necessary, has never
succeeded in becoming respectable, so the business of an overseer is

likely, from its nature, always to continue contemptible and degraded. The young lady who dines heartily on lamb has a sentimental horror of the butcher who killed it; and the slave-owner who lives luxuriously on the forced labour of his slaves has a like sentimental abhorrence of the man who holds the whip and compels the labour. He is like a receiver of stolen goods, who cannot bear the thoughts of stealing himself, but who has no objection to live upon the proceeds of stolen property. A thief is but a thief; an overseer but an overseer. The slave-owner prides himself upon the honourable appellation of a planter; and the receiver of stolen goods assumes the character of a respectable shop-keeper. By such contemptible juggle do men deceive not themselves only, but oft-times the world also.

Mr. Thomas Stubbs was overseer at Spring-Meadow, a person with whose name, appearance, and character I was perfectly familiar, though hitherto I had been so fortunate as to have had very little communication with him.

He was a thick-set, clumsy man, about fifty, with a little bullet head, covered with short tangled hair, and stuck close upon his shoulders. His face was curiously mottled and spotted, for, what with sunshine, what with whisky, and what with ague and fever, brown, red, and sallow, seemed to have put in a joint claim to the possession of it, without having yet been able to arrive at an amicable partition. He was generally to be seen on horseback, leaning forward over his saddle, and brandishing a long thick whip of twisted cow-hide, which, from time to time, he applied over the head and shoulders of some unfortunate slave. If you were within hearing, his conversation, or rather his commands and observations, would have appeared a string of oaths, from the midst of which it was not very easy to disentangle his meaning. Some such exclamations were pretty sure to begin every sentence, and others to end it. It was, however, only when Mr. Stubbs had sole possession of the field, that he sprinkled his orders with his strong spice of brutality;—for when Colonel Moore or any other gentleman happened to be riding by, he could assume quite an air of gentleness and moderation, and what appears very surprising, was actually able to express himself, with not more than one oath to every other sentence.

Mr. Stubbs in his management of the plantation, did not confine himself to hard words. He used his whip as freely as his tongue. Colonel Moore had received a European education; and like every man educated anywhere—except on a slave estate—he had a great dislike to all *unnecessary* cruelty. He was usually made very angry, about once a week, by some brutal act on the part of his overseer. But having satisfied his outraged feelings by declaring himself very much offended, and Mr. Stubbs's proceedings to be quite intolerable, he ended with suffering things to go on just as before. The truth was, Mr. Stubbs understood making crops; and such a man was too valuable to be given up, for the mere sentimental satisfaction of protecting the slaves from his tyranny.

It was a great change to me, after having been accustomed to the elegance and propriety of Colonel Moore's house and the gentle rule and light service of Master James to pass under the despotic control of a vulgar, ignorant, and brutal blackguard. Besides, I had never been accustomed to severe and regular labour; and it was trying indeed to submit at once to the hard work of the field. However, I resolved to make the best of it. I was strong, and use would soon make my tasks more tolerable, I knew well enough that Mr. Stubbs was totally destitute of all humane feelings, but I had no reason to suppose that he entertained towards me any of that malignity which I had so much dreaded in Master William. From what I had known of him, I did not judge him to be a very bad-tempered man; and I took it for granted that he cursed and whipped, not so much out of spite and ill-feeling, but as a mere matter of business. He seemed to imagine, like every other overseer, that it was impossible to manage a plantation in any other way. My diligence, I hoped might enable me to escape the lash; and Mr. Stubb's vulgar abuse, however provoking the other servants might esteem it, I thought I might easily despise.

Mr. Stubbs listened to my account of myself very graciously, all the time rolling his tobacco from one cheek to the other, and squinting at me with one of his little twinkling grey eyes. Having cursed me to his satisfaction for a "blunder-head," he bade me follow him to the field. A large clumsy hoe, with a handle six feet long, was put into my hands, and I was kept hard at work all day.

At dark, I was suffered to quit the field, and the overseer pointed out to me a miserable little hovel, about ten feet square, and half as many high, with a leaky roof, and without either floor or window. This was to be my house, or rather I was to share it with Billy, a young slave about my own age.

To this wretched hut I removed a chest, containing my clothes and a few other things, such as a slave is permitted to possess. By way of bed and bedding, I received a single blanket, about as big as a large pocket-handkerchief; and a basket of corn and a pound or two of damaged bacon, were given me as my week's allowance of provisions. But as I was totally destitute of pot, kettle, knife, plate, or dish of any kind,—for these are conveniences which slaves must procure as they can,—I was in some danger of being obliged to make my supper on raw bacon. Billy saw my distress and took pity on me. He helped me to beat my corn into hominy, and lent me his own little kettle to cook it in; so that about midnight I was able to break a fast of some sixteen or twenty hours. My chest, being both broad and long, served tolerably well for bed, chair, and table. I sold a part of my clothes, which were indeed much too fine for a field hand; and having bought myself a knife, a spoon, and kettle, I was able to put my house-keeping into tolerable order.

My accommodations were as good as a field-hand had a right to expect; but they were not such as to make me particularly happy; especially as I had been used to something better. My hands were blistered with the hoe; and coming in at night completely exhausted by a sort of labour to which I was not accustomed, it was no very agreeable recreation to be obliged to beat hominy, and to be up till after midnight preparing food for the next day, with the recollection, too, that I was obliged to turn into the field with the first dawn of the morning. But this labour, severe as it was, had been in a manner, my own choice. In choosing it, I had escaped a worse tyranny and a more bitter servitude. I had avoided falling into the hands of Master William.

As I shall not have occasion to mention that amiable youth again, I may as well finish his history here. Some six or eight months after the death of his younger brother, he became involved in a drunken quarrel, at a cock-fight. This quarrel ended in a duel, and Master William fell dead at the first fire. His death was a great stroke to Colonel Moore, who seemed for a long time almost inconsolable. I did not lament him, either for his own sake or his father's. I knew well that in his death I had escaped a cruel and vindictive master; and I felt a stern and bitter pleasure in seeing the bereavements of a man who had dared to trample upon the sacred ties of nature.

CHAPTER VI.

I HAD the same task with those who had been field-hands all their lives; but I was too proud to flinch or complain. I exerted myself to the utmost, so that even Mr. Stubbs had no fault to find, but, on the contrary, pronounced me, more than once, a "right likely hand."

The cabin which I shared with Billy had a very leaky roof, and as the weather was rainy, we found it by no means comfortable. At length, we determined one day to repair it; and to get time to do so, we exerted ourselves to get through our tasks at an early hour.

We had finished about four o'clock in the afternoon, and were returning together to the *town*, — for so we called the collection of cabins in which the servants lived. Mr. Stubbs met us, and having inquired if we had finished our tasks, he muttered something about our not having half enough to do, and ordered us to go and weed his garden. Billy submitted in silence, for he had been too long under Mr. Stubbs's jurisdiction to think of questioning his commands. But I ventured to say, in as respectful a manner as I could, that as we had finished our regular tasks, it seemed very hard to give us this additional work. This put Mr. Stubbs into a furious passion, and he swore twenty oaths, that I should both weed the garden and be whipped into the bargain. He sprang from his horse, and catching me by the collar of my shirt, the only dress I had on, he began to lay upon me with his whip. It was the first time, since I had ceased to be a child, that I had been exposed to this degrading torture. The pain was great enough; the idea of being whipped was sufficiently bitter; but these were nothing in comparison with the sharp and burning sense of the insolent injustice that was done me. It was with the utmost difficulty that I restrained myself from springing upon my brutal tormentor, and dashing him to the ground. But alas!—I was a slave. What in a freeman is a most justifiable act of self-defence, becomes in a slave unpardonable insolence and rebellion. I griped my hands, set my teeth firmly together, and bore the injury the best I could. I was then turned into the garden, and the moon happening to be full, I was kept there weeding till near midnight.

The next day was Sunday. The Sunday's rest is the sole and single boon for which the American slave is indebted to the religion of his master. That master tramples under foot every other precept of the Gospel without the slightest hesitation, but so long as he does not compel his slaves to work on Sundays, he thinks himself well entitled to the name of a Christian. Perhaps he is so,—but if he is, a title so easily purchased can be worth but little.

I resolved to avail myself of the Sunday's leisure to complain to my master of the barbarous treatment I had experienced the day before at the hands of Mr. Stubbs. Colonel Moore received me with a coolness and distance, quite unusual in him, for generally he had a smile for everybody, especially for his slaves. However, he heard my story, and even condescended to declare that nothing gave him so much pain as to have his servants unnecessarily or unreasonably punished, and that he never would suffer such things to take place upon his plantation. He then bade me go about my business, having first assured me that in the course of the day he would see Mr. Stubbs and inquire into the matter. This was the last I heard from Colonel Moore. That same evening Mr. Stubbs sent for me to his house, and having tied me to a tree before his door, gave me forty lashes, and bade me complain at the house again if I dared. "It's a hard case indeed," he added, "if I can't lick a cursed nigger's insolence out of him without being obliged to give an account of it."

Insolence!—the tyrant's ready plea!

If a poor slave has been whipped and miserably abused, and no other apology for it can be thought of, the rascal's "insolence" can be always pleaded,—and when pleaded, is enough in every slaveholder's estimation to excuse and justify any brutality. The slightest word, or look, or action that seems to indicate the slave's sense of any injustice that is done him, is denounced as *insolence*, and is punished with the most unrelenting severity.

This was the second time I had experienced the discipline of the lash; but I did not find the second dose any more agreeable than the first. A blow is esteemed among freemen the very highest of indignities; and low as their oppressors have sunk them, it is esteemed an indignity among slaves. Besides—as strange as some people may think it—a twisted cowhide, laid on by the hand of a strong man, does actually inflict a good deal of pain, especially if every blow brings blood.

I will leave it to the reader's own feelings to imagine, what no words can sufficiently describe, the bitterness of that man's misery, who is every hour in danger of experiencing this indignity and this torture. When he has wrought up his fancy,—and let him thank God, from the very bottom of his heart, that in his case it is only fancy,—to a lively idea of that misery, he will have taken the first step towards gaining some notion, however faint and inadequate, of what it is to be a slave!

I had now learned a lesson, which every slave early learns,—I found that I did not enjoy even the privilege of complaining; and that the only way to escape a reiteration of injustice was to submit in silence to the first infliction. I did my best to swallow this bitter lesson, and to acquire a portion of that hypocritical humility so necessary to a person in my unhappy condition. Humility, and whether it be real or pretended, they care but little, is esteemed by masters the great and crowning virtue of a slave; for they understand by it, a disposition to submit, without resistance or complaint, to every possible wrong and indignity; to reply to the most opprobrious and unjust accusations with a soft voice and a smiling face; to take kicks, cuffs, and blows as though they were favours; to kiss the foot that treads you to the dust!

This sort of humility was a virtue with which, I must confess, nature had but scantily endowed me; nor did I find it so easy as I might have desired, to strip myself of all the feelings of a man. It was like quitting the erect carriage which I had received at God's hand, and learning to crawl on the earth like a base reptile. This was, indeed, a hard lesson; but an American overseer is a stern teacher, and if I learned but slowly it was not the fault of Mr. Stubbs.

CHAPTER VII.

It would be irksome to myself, and tedious to the reader, to enter into a minute detail of all the miserable and monotonous incidents that made up my life at this time. The last chapter is a specimen, from which it may be judged what sort of pleasures I enjoyed. They may be summed up in a few words; and the single sentence which embraces this part of my history might suffice to describe the whole lives of many thousand Americans. I was hard worked, ill fed, and well whipped. Mr. Stubbs, having once begun with me, did not suffer me to get over the effects of one flogging before he inflicted another; and I have some marks of his about me which I expect to carry to the grave. All this time he assured me that what he did was only for my own good: and he swore that he would never give over till he had lashed my cursed insolence out of me.

The present began to grow intolerable; and what hope for the future has the slave? I wished for death; nor do I know to what desperate counsels I might have been driven, when one of those changes to which a slave is ever exposed, but over which he can exercise no control, afforded me some temporary relief from my distresses.

Colonel Moore, by the sudden death of a relation, became heir to a large property in South Carolina. But the person deceased had left a will, about which there was some dispute, which had every appearance of ending in a lawsuit. The matter required Colonel Moore's personal attention; and he had lately set out for Charleston, and had taken with him several of the servants. One or two also had recently died; and Mrs. Moore, soon after her husband's departure, sent for me to assist in filling up the gap which had been made in her domestic establishment.

I was truly happy at the change. I knew Mrs. Moore to be a lady who would never insult or trample on a servant, even though he were a slave, unless she happened to be very much out of humour, an unfortunate occurrence, which in her case did not happen oftener than once or twice a week—except, indeed, in the very warm weather, when the fit sometimes lasted the whole week through.

Besides, I hoped that the recollection of my fond and faithful attachment to her younger son, who had always been her favourite, would secure me some kindness at her hands. Nor was I mistaken. The contrast of my new situation, with the tyranny of Mr. Stubbs, gave it almost the colour of happiness. I regained my cheerfulness and my buoyant spirits. I was too wise, or rather this new influx of cheerfulness made me too thoughtless, to trouble myself about the future; and, satisfied with the temporary relief I experienced, I ceased to brood over the miseries of my condition.

About this time Miss Caroline, Colonel Moore's eldest daughter, returned from Baltimore, where she had been living for several years with an aunt, who superintended her education. She was but an ordinary girl, without much grace or beauty; but her maid Cassy,* who had formerly been my playfellow, and who returned a woman, though she had left us a child, possessed a high degree of both.

I learned from one of my fellow servants that she was the daughter of Colonel Moore, by a female slave, who for a year or two had shared her master's favour jointly with my mother, but who had died many years since, leaving Cassy an infant. Her mother was said to have been a great beauty, and a very dangerous rival of mine.

So far as regarded personal charms, Cassy was not unworthy of her parentage, either on the father's or the mother's side. She was not tall, but the grace and elegance of her figure could not be surpassed; and the elastic vivacity of all her movements afforded a model, which her indolent and languid mistress, who did nothing but loll all day upon a sofa, might have imitated with advantage. The clear soft olive of her complexion

* Cassandra.

C

brightening in either cheek to a rich red, was certainly more pleasing
than the sickly, sallow hue, so common, or rather so universal, among
the patrician beauties of lower Virginia; and she could boast a pair
of eyes, which, for brilliancy and expression, I have never seen surpassed.

At this time, I prided myself upon my colour as much as any Virginian of them all; and although I had found by a bitter experience that
a slave, whether white or black, is still a slave, and that the master,
heedless of his victim's complexion, handles the whip with perfect im-
partiality, still, like my poor mother, I thought myself of a superior
caste, and would have felt it a degradation to put myself on a level with
those a few shades darker than myself. This silly pride had kept me
from forming intimacies with the other servants, either male or female;
for I was decidedly whiter than any of them. It had too, justly enough,
exposed me to an ill-will, of which I had more than once felt the
consequences, but which had not yet wholly cured me of my folly.

Cassy had perhaps more African blood than I; but this was a point,
however weighty and important I had at first esteemed it, which, as I
became more acquainted with her, seemed continually of less consequence, and soon disappeared entirely from my thoughts. We were
much together; and her beauty, vivacity, and good humour, made
every day a stronger impression upon me. I found myself in love before
I had thought of it; and presently I discovered that my affection was
not unrequited.

Cassy was one of nature's children, and she had never learned those
arts of coquetry, often as skilfully practised by the maid as the mistress,
by which courtships are protracted. We loved; and before long we
talked of marriage. Cassy consulted her mistress; and the answer was
favourable. Mrs. Moore listened with equal readiness to me. Women
are never happier than when they have an opportunity to dabble in
match-making; nor does even the humble condition of the parties
quite deprive the business of its fascination.

It was determined that our marriage should be a little festival among
the servants. The coming Sunday was fixed on as the day; and a
Methodist clergyman, who happened to have wandered into the neighbourhood, readily undertook to perform the ceremony. This part of his
office, I suppose, he would have performed for anybody; but he undertook it the more readily for us, because Cassy, while at Baltimore, had
become a member of the Methodist society.

I was well pleased with all this; for it seemed to give to our union
something of that solemnity which properly belonged to it. In general,
marriage among American slaves is treated as a matter of very little
moment. It is a mere temporary union, contracted without ceremony,
not recognized by the laws, little or not all regarded by the masters, and
of course, often but lightly esteemed by the parties. The recollection
that the husband may, any day, be sold into Louisiana, and the wife
into Georgia, holds out but a slight inducement to draw tight the bonds
of connubial intercourse; and the certainty that the fruits of their
marriage, the children of their love, are to be born slaves, and reared to
all the privations and calamities of hopeless servitude, is enough to
strike a damp into the hearts of the fondest couple. Slaves yield to the
impulses of nature, and propagate a race of slaves; but, save in a few
rare instances, servitude is as fatal to domestic love as to all the other
virtues. Some few choice spirits indeed will still rise superior to their
condition, and when cut off from every other support, will find within
their own hearts the means of resisting the deadly and demoralizing

influences of servitude. In the same manner, the baleful poison of the plague or yellow fever—innocent indeed and powerless in comparison!—while it rages through an infected city, and sweeps its thousands and tens of thousands to the grave, finds, here and there, an iron constitution, which defies its total malignity, and sustains itself by the sole aid of nature's health-preserving power.

On the Friday before the Sunday which had been fixed upon for our marriage, Colonel Moore returned to Spring-Meadow. His arrival was unexpected; and by me, at least, very much unwished for. To the other servants who hastened to welcome him home, he spoke with his usual kindness and good nature; but though I had come forward with the rest, all the notice he took of me was a single stare of dissatisfaction. He appeared to be surprised, and that too not agreeably, to see me again in the house.

The next day I was discharged from my duties of house servant, and put again under the control of Mr. Stubbs. This touched me to the quick; but it was nothing to what I felt the day following, when I went to the house to claim my bride. I was told that she was gone in the carriage with Colonel Moore and his daughter, who had ridden out to call upon some of the neighbours; and that I need not take the trouble of coming again to see her, for Miss Caroline did not choose that her maid should marry a field hand.

It is impossible for me to describe the paroxysm of grief and passion which I now experienced. Those of the same ardent temperament with myself will easily conceive my feelings; and to persons of cooler temper, no description can convey an adequate idea. My promised wife snatched from me, and myself exposed to the hateful tyranny of a brutal overseer —and all so sudden too—and with such studied marks of insult and oppression!

I now felt afresh the ill effects of my foolish pride in keeping myself separate and aloof from my fellow servants. Instead of sympathizing with me, many of them openly rejoiced at my misfortune; and as I had never made a confidant or associate among them, I had no friend whose advice to ask, or whose sympathy to seek. At length, I bethought myself of the Methodist minister, who was to come that evening to marry us, and who had appeared to take a good deal of interest in the welfare of Cassy and myself. I was desirous not only of seeking such advice and consolation as he could afford me, but I wished to save the good man from a useless journey, and possibly from insult at Spring-Meadow; for Colonel Moore looked on all sorts of preachers, and the Methodists especially, with an eye of very little favour.

I knew that the clergyman in question held a meeting about five miles off; and I resolved, if I could get leave, to go and hear him. I applied to Mr. Stubbs for a pass, that is, a written permission, without which no slave can go off the plantation to which he belongs, except at the risk of being stopped by the first man he meets, horsewhipped, and sent home again. But Mr. Stubbs swore that he was tired of such gadding; and he told me that he had made up his mind to grant no more passes for the next fortnight.

To some sentimental persons it may seem hard, after the slave has laboured six days for his master, and the blessed seventh at length gladdens him with its beams, that he cannot be allowed a little change of scene, but must still be confined to the hated fields, the daily witnesses of his toils and his sufferings. Yet many thrifty managers and good disciplinarians are, like Mr. Stubbs, very much opposed to all gadding; and they pen up their slaves, when not at work, as they pen up their cattle, to keep them, as they say, out of mischief.

At another time, this new piece of petty tyranny might have provoked me; but now, I scarcely regarded it, for my whole heart was absorbed by a greater passion. I was slowly returning towards the servants' quarter, when a little girl, one of the house servants, came running to me, almost out of breath. I knew her to be one of Cassy's favourites, and I caught her in my arms. As soon as she had recovered her breath, she said she had been looking for me all the morning, for she had a message from Cassy; that Cassy had been obliged, much against her inclination, to go out that morning with her mistress, but that I must not be alarmed or down-hearted, for she loved me as well as ever.

I kissed the little messenger, and thanked her a thousand times for her news. I then hastened to my house. It was quite a comfortable little cottage, which Mrs. Moore had ordered to be built for Cassy and myself, but of which I expected every moment to be deprived. The news I had heard excited new commotions in my bosom. I had no sooner sat down, than I found it impossible to keep quiet. My heart beat violently; the fever in my blood grew high. I left the house, and walked about within the limits of my gaol-yard,—for so I might justly esteem the plantation; I used the most violent exercise, and tried every means I could think of to subdue the powerful emotions of mixed hope and fear with which I was agitated, and which I found more oppressive than even the certainty of misery.

As evening drew on, I watched for the return of the carriage; and at length its distant rumbling caught my ear. I hastened towards the house, in the hope of seeing Cassy, and perhaps of speaking with her. The carriage stopped at the door, and I was fast approaching it; but, at the instant, it occurred to me, that it would be better not to risk being seen by Colonel Moore, who, I was now well satisfied, entertained a decided hostility towards me, and whom I believed to be the author of the cruel repulse I had that morning met with. This thought stopped me, and I drew back and returned home, without catching a glimpse or exchanging a word.

I threw myself upon my bed; but I turned continually from side to side, and found it impossible to compose myself to rest. Hour after hour dragged on; but I could not sleep. It was past midnight, when I heard a slight tap at the door, and a soft whisper, which thrilled through every nerve. I sprung up; I opened the door; I clasped her to my bosom. It was Cassy; it was my betrothed wife.

She told me that since Colonel Moore's return, every thing seemed changed at the house. Miss Caroline had told her that Colonel Moore had a very bad opinion of me, and was very much displeased to find that during his absence I had been again employed as one of the house servants. She added that, when he was told of our intended marriage, he had declared that Cassy was too pretty a girl to be thrown away upon such a scoundrel, and that he would undertake to provide her with a much better husband. So her mistress had bidden her to think no more of me; but, at the same time, had told her not to cry, for she would never leave off teasing her father till he had fulfilled his promise; "and if you get a husband," the young lady added, "that, you know, is all that any of us want." So thought the mistress; the maid, I have reason to suppose, was rather more refined in her notions of matrimony.

I was not quite certain how to interpret this conduct of Colonel Moore's. I was strongly inclined to consider it only as a new out-break of that spite and hostility which I had been experiencing ever since my useless and foolish appeal to his fatherly feelings. It occurred to me, however, as possible, that his opposition to our marriage might spring from other motives. Whatever I might imagine, I kept my own counsel. One motive which occurred to me, I could not think of myself, with the slightest patience; and still less could I bear to shock and distress poor Cassy by the mention of it. Another motive, which I thought might possibly have influenced Colonel Moore, was less discreditable to him, and would have been flattering to the pride of both Cassy and myself. But this, I could not mention without leading to disclosures, which I did not see fit to make.

Cassy knew herself to be Colonel Moore's daughter; but early in our acquaintance I had discovered that she had no idea that I was his son. I have every reason to believe that Mrs. Moore was perfectly well informed as to both these particulars; for they were of that sort which seldom or never escape the eagerness of female curiosity, and more especially the curiosity of a wife.

Whatever she might know, she discovered in it no impediment to my marriage with Cassy. Nor did I; for how could that same regard for the *decencies of life,*—such is the soft phrase which justifies the most unnatural cruelty,—that refused to acknowledge our paternity, or to recognize any relationship between us, pretend at the same time, and on the sole ground of relationship, to forbid our union?

But I knew that Cassy felt, rather than reasoned; and, though born and bred a slave, she possessed great delicacy of feeling. Besides, she was a Methodist, and though as cheerful and gay-hearted a girl as I ever knew, she was very devout in all the observances of her religion. I feared to put our mutual happiness in jeopardy; I was unwilling to harass Cassy with what I esteemed unnecessary scruples. I had never told her the story of my parentage, and every day I grew less inclined to tell it. Accordingly, I made no other answer to what she told me, except to say, that however little Colonel Moore might like me, his dislike was not my fault.

A momentary pause followed;—I pressed Cassy's hand in mine, and in a faltering voice, I asked what she intended to do.

"I am your wife;—I will never be anybody's but yours," was the answer. I clasped the dear girl to my heart. We knelt together, and with upraised hands invoked the Deity to witness and confirm our union. It was the only sanction in our power; and if twenty priests had said a benediction over us, would that have made our vows more binding, or our marriage more complete?

CHAPTER VIII.

IT was impossible for my wife to visit me except by stealth. She slept every night upon the carpet in her mistress's room; for a floor is esteemed in America a good enough bed for a slave, even for a favourite and a woman. She was liable to be called upon in the night, at the caprice of a mistress, who was, in fact, a mere spoiled child; and she could only visit me at the risk of a discovery, which might have been attended with very unpleasant consequences; for if these clandestine visits had been detected, I fear that not all Cassy's charm,—whatever poets may have fabled of the power of beauty,—could have saved her from the lash.

Yet short and uncertain as these visits were, they sufficed to create and to sustain a new and singular state of feeling. My wife was seldom with me, but her image was ever before my eyes, and appeared to make me regardless of all beside. Things seemed to pass as in a happy dream. The labour of the field was nothing; the lash of the overseer was scarcely felt. My mind became so occupied, and, as it were, filled up with the pleasure which I found in our mutual affection, and by the anticipated delights of each successive interview, that it seemed to have no room for disagreeable emotions. Strong as was my passion, there was nothing in it uneasy or unsatisfied. When I clasped the dear girl to my bosom, I seemed to have reached the height of human fruition. I was happy; greater happiness I could not imagine, and did not desire.

The intoxication of passion is the same in the slave and in the master; it is exquisite, and, while it lasts, all-sufficient in itself. I found it so. With almost everything to make me miserable, still was I happy,—for the excess of my passion rendered me insensible to anything save its own indulgence.

But such ecstasies are unsuited to the human constitution. They are soon over, and perhaps are ever purchased at too dear a price; for they are but too apt to be succeeded by all the anguish of disappointed hope and all the bitterness of deep despair. Still I look back with pleasure to that time. It is one of the bright spots of my existence, which eager memory discovers in her retrospections, scattered and scarcely visible,— tiny islets of delight, surrounded on all sides by a gloomy and tempestuous ocean.

We had been married about a fortnight. It was near midnight, and I was sitting before my door, waiting for my wife to come. The moon was full and bright; the sky was cloudless. I was still at the height and flood of my intoxication; and as I watched the planet, and admired her brightness, I gave thanks to heaven that the base tendencies of a servile condition had not yet totally extinguished within me all the higher and nobler emotions of man's nature.

Presently, I observed a figure approaching. I should have known her at any distance, and I sprang forward and caught my wife in my arms. But as I pressed her to my heart, I felt her bosom to be strangely agitated; and when I brought her face to mine, my cheek was moistened with her tears.

Alarmed at these unusual indications, I hurried her into the house, and hastily inquired the cause of her agitation. My inquiries appeared to increase it. She sunk her head upon my breast, burst into sobs, and seemed wholly incapable of speaking. I knew not what to think, or what to do. I exerted myself to compose her; I kissed off the tears that trickled fast down her cheeks; I pressed my hand against her beating heart, as if, in that way, I could have checked its palpitations. At length she grew more calm; but it was by slow degrees, and in broken sentences, that I learned the origin of her terror.

It seemed that Colonel Moore, ever since his return, had distinguished her by particular kindness. He had made her several little presents; had sought frequent occasions to talk with her, and was ever, half-jocosely, complimenting her beauty. He had even dropped certain hints, which Cassy could not help understanding, but of which she thought it best to take no notice. He was not to be repelled in that way; but proceeded to words and actions, of which it was not possible for her to affect to misunderstand the meaning. Her native modesty, her love for me, her religious feelings, were all alarmed; and the poor girl began to tremble at the fate that seemed to await her; but, as yet, she kept her terrors to herself. She was reluctant to torture me with the story of insults, which, however they might pierce my heart, I had no power to repel.

That day, Mrs. Moore and her daughter had gone to visit one of the neighbours, and Cassy was left at home. She was employed on some needlework in her mistress's room, when Colonel Moore entered. She rose up hastily, and would have gone away; but he bade her stop, and listen to what he had to say to her. He did not seem to notice her agitation, and appeared perfectly self-possessed himself. He told her that he had promised her mistress to provide her with a husband, in place of that scoundrel Archy; that he had looked about, but did not see anybody who was worthy of her; and, on the whole, he had concluded to take her himself.

This he said with a tone of tenderness, which no doubt he meant to be irresistible. To many women in Cassy's situation it would have been so. They would have esteemed themselves highly honoured by their master's notice, and would have felt not a little flattered by the delicate terms under which he concealed the real character of his proposal. But she, poor child, heard him with shame and dread; and was ready, she told me, to sink into the earth with terror and dismay. In relating it, she blushed—she hesitated—she shuddered—her breathing became short and quick—she clung to me, as if some visible image of horror were present before her, and bringing her lips close to my ear, she exclaimed in a trembling and scarcely audible whisper—" Oh, Archy!—and he my father ! "

Colonel Moore, she believed, could not have misunderstood the feelings with which she listened to his offer. But if so, he disregarded them; for he proceeded to enumerate all the advantages she would derive from this connexion, and strove to tempt her by promises of idleness and finery. She stood with her eyes upon the floor, and only answered him by sobs and tears, which she strove in vain to suppress. Upon this, Colonel Moore, in a tone of pique and displeasure, told her " not to be a fool;" and catching one of her hands in his, he threw his arm about her waist, and bade her not provoke him by a useless resistance; she uttered a scream of surprise and terror, and sunk at his feet. At that moment, the sound of the carriage wheels fell, she said, like heavenly music on her ear. Her master heard it too, for he let go his grasp, and muttering something about another time, hastily left the room. She remained almost senseless on the floor, till the sound of her mistress's footsteps in the passage, recalled her to herself. The rest of the afternoon and evening she had passed she hardly knew how. Her head, she told me, was dizzy; a cloud swam before her eyes; and she had hardly been sensible of anything but a painful feeling of languor and oppression. She had not dared to leave her mistress's room, and had waited with impatience for the hour that would permit her to throw herself into the arms of her husband, her natural protector.

Her natural protector !—alas, of what avail is the natural right of a husband to protect his wife against the assaults of a villain, who is at once her owner and his?

Such was Cassy's story; and strange as it may seem, I heard it quite unmoved. Although I held the panting, trembling, weeping narrator in my arms, I listened to her story with far less emotion than I have since experienced in recounting it. In truth, I was prepared for it; I had anticipated it; I expected it.

I knew well that Cassy's charms were too alluring not to excite a voluptuary, in whom a long indulgence had extinguished all the better feelings and rendered incapable of controlling himself; and to whom, neither the fear of punishment nor the dread of public indignation supplied the place of conscience. What else could be reasonably expected of a man who knew well, let him proceed to what extremities he might, not only that the law would justify him, but that anybody who might think of calling him to account before the bar of public opinion would be denounced by the public voice as an impertinent intermeddler in the affairs of other people ?

Little of paternal tenderness as Colonel Moore ever showed to me, at least from the moment that he found I knew him to be my father, I have too much of filial respect to entertain the wish of misrepresenting him. Though he was of a warm and voluptuous temperament, he was naturally a good-natured man ; and his honour was, as I have said, unquestioned. But honour is of a very diverse character. There is honour among gentlemen, and honour among thieves; and though both these codes contain several excellent enactments, neither can fairly claim to be regarded· as a perfect system of morality. Of that code in which he had been educated, Colonel Moore was a strict observer. To have made an attempt on the chastity of a neighbour's wife or daughter, he would have esteemed, and so the honorary code of Virginia esteems it, an offence of the blackest dye; an offence, he well knew, to be expiated only by the offender's life. But beyond this, he did not dream of prohibition or restraint. Hardened and emboldened by certain impunity, provided the sufferer were a slave, he regarded the most atrocious outrage that could be perpetrated upon the person and feelings of a woman rather as a matter of jest, a thing to be laughed at over the fourth bottle, than a subject of serious and sober reprehension.

Of all this I was well aware. I had from the first foreseen that Cassy would be devoted by her master to the same purposes which had been fulfilled by my mother and her own. It was from these intentions, as I had all along believed, that his opposition to our marriage had originated. In imagining that it might spring from another cause, I had done him an honour to which, as was now too evident, he had not the slightest title. What I had just now heard, I had daily expected to hear. I had expected it ; yet such had been my intoxication, that even anticipations terrible as this had not been able to alarm or distress me ; and now that anticipation was changed into reality, still I remained unmoved. The ecstasy of passion still sustained me ; and as I pressed my wretched trembling wife to my bosom, I still rose superior to the calamity that assailed me ; even yet, I was happy.

This seems incredible !—

Love then as I did; or if that suit your temperament better, hate with the same intensity with which I loved. Be absorbed in any passion, and while the fit continues, you will find yourself endowed with a surprising and almost superhuman energy.

My mind was already made up. The unhappy slave has but one way of escaping any threatening infliction ; a poor and wretched resource, to which he recurs always at the imminent risk of redoubling his miseries. That remedy is flight.

Our preparations were soon made. My wife returned to the house, and gathered up a little bundle of clothing. In the mean time I employed myself in collecting such provisions as I could readiest lay my hands on ; a couple of blankets, a hatchet, a little kettle, and a few other small articles, completed my equipments; and by the time my wife returned, I was ready for a start. We set out, with no other companion but a faithful dog. I did not wish to take him, for fear that somehow or other he might lead to our detection; but he would not be driven back, and I was afraid to tie him, lest his howlings might give an alarm, and lead to an immediate pursuit.

Lower Virginia had already begun to feel the effects of that blight, which has since lighted so heavily upon her, and which, in truth, she has so well deserved. Already her fields were beginning to be deserted; already impenetrable thickets had commenced to cover plantations, which, had the soil been cultivated by freemen, might still have produced a rich and abundant harvest. There was a deserted plantation about ten miles from Spring-Meadow. I had formerly visited it several times, in company with my young master, James, who, when he was well enough to ride about, had a strange taste for wandering into out-of-the-way places. It was thither that, in the hurry of the moment, I resolved to go.

The by-road which had formerly led to this estate, and the fields on both sides, were grown over with small scrubby pines, so close and tangled as to render the thicket almost impenetrable. I contrived, however, to keep on in the right direction. But the difficulties of the way were so great, that the morning had dawned before we reached the plantation buildings. They were still standing; but in a most dilapidated condition. The great house had been a structure of large size, and considerable pretensions. But the windows were gone, the doors had dropped from their hinges, and the roof was partly fallen in. The court-yard was completely grown up with young trees. Wild vines were creeping over the house; and all was silent, desolate, and deserted. The stables, and what had been the servants' quarter, were mere heaps of ruins, overgrown with weeds and grass.

At some distance behind the house there was a rapid descent, which formed one side of a deep ravine; and near the bottom of this hollow a fine bubbling spring burst from under the hill. It was now half-choked with leaves and sand, but its waters were pure and cool as ever. Near the spring was a little low building of brick, which perhaps had been intended for a dairy, or some such purpose. The door was gone, and half the roof had tumbled in. The other half still kept its position, and the vacancy occasioned by the part that had fallen served well enough to admit the light and air, and to supply the place of windows, which had formed no part of the original construction. This ruinous little building was shaded by several large and ancient trees; and was so completely hidden by a more recent growth, as to be invisible at the distance of a few paces. It was by mere accident that we stumbled upon it, as we were searching for the spring, of which I had drank upon my former visits, but the situation of which I did not exactly recollect. It struck us at once, that this was the place for our temporary habitation; and we resolved forthwith to clear it of the rubbish it contained, and to turn it into a dwelling.

CHAPTER IX.

I KNEW that the place where we now were was very seldom visited by anybody. The deserted house had the reputation of being haunted; and this, as well as its seclusion from the road, and the almost impenetrable thickets by which it was surrounded, would serve to protect us against intruders. There were several plantations about it; for it occupied the highest ground between two rivers, which flowed at no great distance apart, and of which the low grounds were still in cultivation. But there were no cultivated fields nearer than four or five miles; and no houses nearer than Spring-Meadow, which, I have said, was some ten or twelve miles distant. I judged that for the present we might remain secure in this retreat; and it seemed our best policy to suffer the search for us to be pretty well over before we attempted to continue our flight.

In the mean time we exerted ourselves to make things as comfortable as possible. It was the height of summer, and we anticipated but little inconvenience from the openness of our habitation. A heap of pine straw, in one corner of our ruinous hovel, formed our bed; and sweeter slumbers, not down itself could have ensured. Out of such materials as the wainscoting of the deserted house supplied, I made two rude stools, and something that served for a table. The spring furnished us with water; our principal concern was to provide ourselves with food. The woods and thickets produced some wild fruits; and the peach-orchard near the house, though choked and shaded by a more recent growth, still continued to bear. I was an adept in the art of snaring rabbits, and such other small game as the woods supplied. The spring which furnished us with water was one of the heads of a little branch or brook which discharged, at a short distance, into a larger stream. In that stream there were fish. But our chief resource was in the neighbouring corn-fields, which already furnished roasting ears, and from which I did not scruple to draw a plentiful supply.

On the whole,—though we were both quite unaccustomed to so wild a livelihood,—we passed our time very agreeably. Those who are always idle can never know the true luxury of idleness, the real pleasure with which he who has been pushed to work against his will relaxes his strained muscles, and delivers himself up to the delight of doing nothing. I used to lie for hours, in a dreamy sort of indolence, outstretched upon the shady slope, enjoying the sweet consciousness of being my own master, and luxuriating in the idea that I need come or go at no one's bidding, but might work or be idle as suited my own good will. No wonder that emancipated slaves are inclined to indolence. It is to them a new pleasure. Labour, in their minds, is indissolubly associated with servitude and the whip; and *not to work*, they have ever been taught to look upon as the badge and peculiar distinction of freedom.

The present was passing pleasantly enough; but it was necessary to be thinking about the future. We had always regarded our present place of refuge as temporary only; and it was now time to think of leaving it. I should have esteemed it delightful indeed to pass a whole life of solitude and seclusion with Cassy, where, if we had lacked the pleasures of society, we might have escaped its ten-fold greater ills. But this was not possible. The American climate was never meant for hermits. Our present station would answer well enough for a summer retreat; but the winter would render it untenable; and before long, winter would be approaching. Our hope was to escape into the free states, —for I knew that north of Virginia there was a country where there were no slaves. If we could once get away from the neighbourhood o. Spring-Meadow, where I was well known, we should enjoy one great advantage during the remainder of our flight. Our complexions would not betray our servile condition; and we should find no great difficn⁴⁻ we thought, in passing ourselves as free citizens of Virginia. Col Moore had, no doubt, filled the country round with advertisement. which our persons were accurately described, and every peculiarity each of us carefully noted. It was therefore necessary to use great caution; and I considered it essential to our escape that Cassy should adopt some disguise. What this should be, or where we should get it, was now the question.

We finally determined to assume the character of persons travelling to the north to seek our fortunes; and we arranged that Cassy should adopt a man's dress, and accompany me in the character of a younger brother. The night on which we had left Spring-Meadow I had brought away my best suit, one of the last gifts of poor Master James, and such as would well enough enable me to play the part of a travelling Virginian. But I had neither hat nor shoes; nor any clothes whatever, that could properly serve as a disguise for Cassy.

Luckily I had a small sum, the accumulated savings of Master James's liberality, which I had always kept in reserve, in the hope and expectation that I should some time have a use for it. This money I had been careful to take with me; and it was now our sole reliance, not only for the expenses of the road, but for procuring the means, without which we could not start at all.

But though we had the money, how could we make any use of it, without running a very serious risk of detection?

There lived, about five or six miles from Spring-Meadow, and near the same distance from us, one Mr. James Gordon. He kept a little store, and his principal customers were the slaves of the neighbouring plantations. Mr. James Gordon, or Jemmy Gordon, as he was familiarly called, was one of those *poor white men* of whom the number in Lower Virginia is or was very considerable, and who are spoken of even by the slaves themselves with a sort of contempt. He had neither lands nor servants, for his father before him had been a poor white man. He had been educated to no trade, for where every planter has his own mechanics on his own plantation a free workman can expect no encouragement. The only resource for a man in Jemmy Gordon's situation is to find employment as an overseer for some of his richer neighbours. But in Virginia there are more persons who desire to be overseers than there are plantations to oversee; besides, Mr. Gordon was one of those careless, easy, good-natured, indolent sort of men who are generally pronounced good for nothing. He never could bring himself to that ever-watchful scrutiny and assiduous oversight which is so necessary among slaves, whose maxim it is to work as little as possible and to plunder all they can. He was apt enough to get into a passion, and cut and slash right and left without discrimination, but he was incapable of that regular severity and systematic cruelty by which other overseers gained the reputation of excellent disciplinarians. Moreover, on a certain plantation of which he had been the manager some large vacancies had occurred in the corn-crib, which were never very clearly accounted for. How far this was occasioned by negligence, or how far by dishonesty, was never, so far as I know, satisfactorily determined; all I can say is, that Mr. Gordon was dismissed from his employment, and found it so difficult to get a new situation, that he gave up the search in despair, and resolved to turn trader. He had nothing to begin upon, and of course traded in a very small way; he dealt principally in whisky, but in addition kept shoes and such articles of clothing as slaves are in the habit of purchasing to eke out the miserable and insufficient supply which they receive from their masters. He took money in payment, but likewise corn and other produce, without any strict inquiry how his customers came into possession of it.

It is this class of men against whom the legislators of Virginia have exercised all their ingenuity in the construction of penal statutes, and against whom they have exerted all the severity which they have dared to use towards men who might still claim the title and demand the rights of "free white citizens." But these penal enactments have failed in a great measure of their object. Though the trade with slaves is dangerous and disgraceful, and the traders in consequence are desperate and reckless, their number is still so great as to furnish the planters with an inexhaustible topic of declamation and complaint, and to supply the slaves with numerous little comforts and luxuries which they might in vain have expected from the indulgence or humanity of their masters.

These traders are no doubt the receivers of plunder, and no small proportion of what they sell is paid for in that way. It is in vain that tyranny fences itself about with the terrors of the law; it is in vain that the slaveholder flatters himself with the hope of appropriating to his own sole use the entire fruits of the forced labours of his fellow-men. The slave cannot resist the compulsion with which the law has armed the hand of his master. The lash is an ensign of authority and of torture, to which the stoutest heart and the most stubborn will is soon compelled to yield. But fraud is the natural counterpart to tyranny, and cunning is ever the defence of the weak against the oppressions of the strong. Can the unhappy slave, who has been compelled to plant in the daytime for his master's benefit, be blamed if he strives in the night to gather some gleaning of the crop for his own use?

Blame him you who can! Join if you will in the clamour of the master against the cursed knavery of his slaves! That same master who thinks it no wrong to rob those slaves of their labour, their sole possession, their only property! He to talk about theft! he—the slaveholder—who has carried the art of pillage to a perfection of which robbers and pirates never dreamed! They are content to snatch such casual spoils as chance may offer; but the slaveholder, whip in hand, extorts from his victims a large, a regular, an annual plunder! Nay, more, he sells for money, he has inherited from his father, and he hopes to transmit to his children, the privilege of continuing this systematic pillage!

I had once saved Mr. Gordon's life, and for this piece of service he had always expressed the greatest gratitude. This had happened several years before. He was fishing on the river not far from Spring-Meadow, when a sudden squall upset his boat. It was no great distance from the shore, but Mr. Gordon was no swimmer, and was in the greatest danger. Master James and myself happened to be walking along the bank; we saw a man struggling in the water, and I plunged in after him, and caught him as he was sinking the third time. This service Mr. Gordon was in the habit of acknowledging by occasional little presents, and I flattered myself with the hope that he would not refuse his aid in my present circumstances. My plan was, to get from Mr. Gordon a hat and shoes for myself, a man's dress for Cassy, and such information as he could give us about the route we ought to follow. A great many difficulties presented themselves to my mind in the prosecution of the journey. I resolved, however, not to afflict myself with borrowed trouble, but to leave the future to take care of itself.

The first thing was, to see Mr. Gordon, and find out how far he was disposed to assist me. His house and store, both under the same roof, were in a lonely part of the country, near the crossing of two roads, and out of sight of any other buildings. I did not think it safe to trust myself upon the highway earlier than midnight, and it was considerably past that hour before I approached Mr. Gordon's house. When I came within sight of it I hesitated, and more than once came to a halt; I did not like to trust my liberty and all my hopes of happiness to the unsure guardianship of any man's gratitude, and least of all such a man as Mr. Gordon. The risk seemed too great, and my heart sunk within me when I called to mind how frail was the prop on which depended, if not my life, every thing certainly that made life desirable.

I was on the point of turning back, but I recollected that this was my only resource. Mr. Gordon must help us to escape, or our chance was worth nothing. This thought pushed me on. I plucked up courage and approached the door. Three or four dogs which kept watch about the house immediately opened in full chorus, but though they barked loud enough, they gave no signs of any intention to attack me. I knocked again, and pretty soon Mr. Gordon thrust his head from the window, bade his dogs be quiet, and inquired who I was, and what I wanted. I begged him to open the door and let me in, for I had business with him. Expecting, perhaps, to drive a profitable trade with some midnight customer, he hastened to do as I had requested. He opened the door; the moonlight as I entered fell upon my face, and he recognised me at once.

"What! Archy, is it you?" and he spoke it with an air of the greatest surprise, "where, in the devil's name, did you spring from? I hoped you were clear out of the neighbourhood a month ago." And with these words he drew me into the house and shut the door.

I told him that I had a place of concealment near by, and that I had come to get a little assistance from him in making my escape.

"Anything in reason, Archy; but if I were caught helping off a runaway, it would ruin me for ever. There's Colonel Moore, your master, and Major Pringle, and Captain Knight, and a half dozen more, were over here, it's only yesterday, and they swore, if I did not leave off trading with the hands, they'd pull my house down about my ears, and ride me on a rail out of the county; and now, if I were caught helping you, fact, Archy, 'twould do my business for me with a witness. I'm not quite such a fool as all that."

I used tears, and flatteries, and entreaties. I reminded Mr. Gordon how often he had wished for an opportunity to serve me; I told him that all I wanted was a few articles of dress, and some directions about the road I ought to follow.

"True, Archy, true. You saved my life, boy; I can't deny it; and one good turn deserves another. But this business of yours is an ugly, bad business at the best. What the devil must you and that wench be running away for? I never knew any mischief in my life, that a woman wasn't at the bottom of it. It's that tattling babbler, widow Hinkley, that brought Colonel Moore and the rest of 'em over here yesterday;—curse the envious old jade, she wants to drive me out of the neighbourhood, and get all the custom for herself."

I knew that Mr. Gordon had no turn for sentiment, and that it would be casting pearls before swine's feet to waste any upon him. So I told him it was too late to talk about our reasons for running away,—run away we had,—and the only thing now was to avoid being taken.

"Ay, ay, boy, I understand you. Its a damned silly business, and you begin to be ashamed of it already. You had better make up your minds now to go in, take your whippings, and make the best of it. It's the loss of the wench that Colonel Moore is most angry about; and I dare say, if you were to go in, Archy, and make a merit of telling where he could find her, you might get off mighty easy, and shift all the blame upon her shoulders."

I concealed the indignation which this base proposal excited. Such treachery to one another is too common among slaves, and is always promoted and rewarded by the masters. I could not expect Mr. Gordon to rise very far above the level of current morals. So I passed by his proposal in silence. I only said that I had made up my mind to undergo anything rather than return to Spring-Meadow. If he was resolved not to assist me, I would be off as soon as possible, trusting to his honour to say nothing about this visit. As a last resource, I hinted that I had the money to pay for all I wanted, and that I should not dispute about the price.

Whether it was this last hint, or some more generous motive, or the combined effect of both, I shall not undertake to determine; but certain it is that Mr. Gordon began to exhibit a more favourable disposition.

"As to money, Archy, between friends like us, there is no need of speaking about that. And if you will have your own way, considering what has happened between us, 'twould be mighty unkind in me not to let you have the things you're wanting. But you'll never get off—mind now what I tell you—you'll never get off. Why, boy, the colonel swears he'll spend five thousand dollars but what he'll catch you. He's got printed handbills stuck up all through the country, with *Five Hundred Dollars Reward*, at the head of 'em. Come into the store here, and I'll show you one. Five hundred dollars!—somebody is to pocket that money, I reckon."

I did not like the tone in which this was spoken. The emphasis with which Mr. Gordon dwelt on the five hundred dollars was rather alarming. The idea of this reward was evidently taking strong hold upon his imagination.

Mr. Gordon's establishment consisted of but two rooms, of which one was his parlour, bed-room, and kitchen, and the other his store. All this time we had been in the bed-room, with no light but that of the moon. I now followed him into the store. He struck a light, kindled a piece of light wood, and holding it up to a large handbill posted opposite the door, I read, to the best of my recollection, pretty much as follows :—

"FIVE HUNDRED DOLLARS REWARD.

"Ran away from the subscriber, at Spring-Meadow, on Saturday evening last, two servants, Archy and Cassy, for whose apprehension the above reward will be paid.

"They are both very light-coloured. Of the two, Cassy is a shade the darker. Archy is about twenty-one years of age, five feet eleven inches high, and a stout muscular frame. He has a firm erect walk, and is a very likely fellow. Smiles when spoken to. His hair is a light brown, and curls over his head; he has blue eyes and a high forehead. Said boy was raised in my family, and has always been kindly treated. It is not known what clothes he wore away.

"Cassy is about eighteen, five feet three inches, or thereabouts, and a handsome face and figure. She has long dark hair, and a bright black eye. When she smiles there is a dimple in her left cheek. She has a good voice, and can sing several songs. No other marks particularly recollected, except a mole on her right breast. She has been raised a lady's maid, and she took a variety of good clothing with her. Said slaves have gone off in company as is supposed.

"Whoever will return them to me, or lodge them in any gaol, so that

I can get them, shall be paid the above reward; or one half for either separately.   CHARLES MOORE.

"N.B. I suspect they have taken the road to Baltimore, as Cassy formerly lived in that city. No doubt they will attempt to pass for white people."

While I was reading this advertisement, Mr. Gordon looked over my shoulder, and added his comments upon each sentence of it. Neither his remarks, nor the advertisement itself, were calculated to make me feel very comfortably. Perhaps Mr. Gordon observed it; for he handed me a glass of whisky, and bade me keep up my spirits. He swallowed one himself; and drank to my escape. This reassured me a little,—for, to tell the truth, I was a good deal startled at Mr. Gordon's very evident hankering after the five hundred dollars. The whisky he drank,—and he was not content with a single glass,—seemed to rekindle his gratitude. He swore he would run any risk to serve me, and told me to pick out such articles as I wanted.

I fitted myself with hat and shoes, and selected the same for Cassy. But it was necessary to have a man's dress for her. Mr. Gordon did not deal in ready-made clothing, but he had some cloth, which I thought would answer our purpose; and he undertook to get the suit made up for me. I gave him the measure by guess, and was to return in three days, by which time he promised to have the clothes finished. I had much rather have completed the business at once, and have started directly on our journey; but that was impossible. A disguise for Cassy was absolutely necessary; it would have been foolish to have attempted an escape without it. I pressed him to be sure and have the clothes finished at the time appointed, for a reward of five hundred dollars, and the chance of making friends with Colonel Moore, and rising in the world by his assistance, was a temptation to which I wished to keep Mr. Gordon exposed for as short a time as possible. I now inquired what I had to pay for my various purchases. Mr. Gordon took his slate and began to figure it up. He proceeded very diligently for a few minutes, and then suddenly came to a full stop. He looked at the goods I had selected and then at the slate. For a moment he hesitated; then looking at me, "Archy," he said, "you saved my life,—you are welcome to them 'ere things."

I knew well how to value this instance of generosity. Whatever money Mr. Gordon got was pretty sure to go in gambling and dissipation. Of course he was not only poor, but often distressed and tormented to get the means of indulging his propensities. Money was to him what whisky is to the lips of the drunkard. For such a person to be generous is hard indeed; and I ceased at once to distrust a man who gave so substantial a proof of his inclination to assist me. I bade him good night, and set out on my return home, with a heart much lightened.

Mr. Gordon put me some questions about the place of my retreat, to which, however, I thought it best to return a somewhat equivocal reply. Though greatly reassured, I still could see no good purpose to be answered by too great confidence; and at setting out from Mr. Gordon's, I was careful to take a direction quite wide of the true one. Once or twice I thought I was followed. The moon was now setting, and her light was scanty and uncertain. My path led through a scattered growth of stunted trees and bushes. A pursuer might easily have concealed himself; but when I stopped to listen all was silent, and I soon dismissed my fanciful fears.

Taking a considerable circuit, I struck into the direction of the deserted plantation, and arrived there about daybreak. Cassy came out to meet me. It was the first time we had been so long separated since our escape from Spring-Meadow. I felt as overjoyed to see her as if I had returned after a year's absence; and the eagerness with which she flew into my arms and pressed me again and again to her bosom satisfied me that I was not alone in the feeling. We spent the three days in making preparations, starting and answering difficulties, and sometimes in pleasing ourselves with anticipations of future happiness.

At the appointed time I set off for Mr. Gordon's. I approached the house, not trembling and hesitating as before, but with the confident step with which one hastens to the dwelling of a tried friend. I knocked. In a moment Mr. Gordon opened the door; he caught me by the arm, and would have drawn me into the house; but the door half opened enabled me to discover that there were others there beside himself.

I snatched myself from his grasp, and starting back, I said in a whisper, "Heavens! Mr. Gordon, who have you in the house?"

He returned me no answer; but almost while I spoke, I heard Stubbs's grum voice growling, "Seize him—seize him!"—and that moment I knew I was betrayed. I ran; but very soon I felt somebody grasping at my shoulder. Luckily I had a thick stout stick in my hand, and turning short about, with one blow I struck my pursuer to the ground. It was the traitor Gordon. I was tempted to stop and renew the blow, but that moment a pistol ball whizzed by my head, and looking round I saw Stubbs and another man, with pistols in their hands, close upon me. There was no time to lose. I sprang forward, and ran for my life. Two or three shots were fired in quick succession, but without effect; and presently I reached a thicket, where I felt myself more safe. It was soon evident that I was much the fleetest of the party: for before long I was out of sight and hearing of my pursuers. I kept on for near half an hour; when, almost exhausted, I sunk upon the ground; and strove to recover my breath and to collect my thoughts. There was no moon; the starlight was obscured by a thin mist; and I did not well know where I was. Having determined, as well as I was able, the probable direction of the deserted plantation, I again set forward. In the race I had sprained one of my ankles. This I had scarcely observed at the moment; but it now became painful, and I moved with difficulty. However, I kept on the best I could, and flattered myself with the hope of getting back before daylight. I passed for a considerable distance through fields and thickets, with which I was not acquainted: but presently I reached a brook which I knew. I quenched my thirst, and pushed forward with greater alacrity. I was still five or six miles from the deserted plantation, and was obliged to take a very circuitous route. I kept on as fast as I was able; but the sun was up some hours before I arrived at the spring. Cassy was anxiously watching for me. She had become exceedingly alarmed at my delay; nor did the disorder of my dress and my appearance of hurry and fatigue tend to reassure her.

I hastened towards the spring, and was stooping to drink, when Cassy gave a loud shriek. I looked up, and saw two or three men rushing down the side of the hollow. I sprang upon my feet; but immediately felt myself seized from behind. Two other men had rushed down the hollow, upon the other side, and while I was preparing to give battle to those I had first seen, before I was aware of my danger, I found myself in the grasp of their confederates.

CHAPTER X.

I. LEARNED afterwards that when Mr. Stubbs and his companions, who were waiting for me at Gordon's, had failed to bring me down with their pistols, discovering that I ran too fast for them, they soon gave over the chase and returned to the store. They sent off immediately for assistance; and were presently joined by two men, and what was of more importance, by a dog, named Jowler, and celebrated throughout the county for his skill in tracking out runaways.

Jowler had no sooner arrived than they tied a string about his neck, the other end of which one of the party held in his hand. The dog was then put upon my trail, and trotted slowly forward with his nose to the ground, followed by Mr. Stubbs and the rest of the party. All the latter part of the way I had walked quite slowly, and Jowler and his company had gained so fast upon me that they reached the spring almost as soon as I did. Having discovered my retreat, they resolved to make everything certain; and dividing into two parties, they rushed down both sides of the hollow at the same time, and secured me in the manner I have related.

Poor Cassy was seized at the same instant; and almost before we knew what had happened we found our hands tied, and ourselves connected by a stout chain, the ends of which were made fast about our necks. This was sad business for Cassy; and the poor girl, when she felt the iron around her neck, wept bitterly. I do not believe the chain was drawn much tighter than was necessary; yet when I saw the tears of my poor wife, I could not help feeling a choking sensation about my throat. What aggravated my distress and my indignation, was the brutal jests of our captors. It was well my hands were fast, for had they been free, I verily believe I should have found the means to finish one or another of the scoundrels. Mr. Gordon was one of the party. His head was bound up in a bloody handkerchief; but instead of joining in the jests of his companions, he tried to keep them from vexing and insulting us.

"I'll tell you what Stubbs, you nasty, infernal blackguard, let that gal Cassy be. Ain't it I who've taken them? Ain't it I who am to have the reward? Let them be, I say; I tell you they are under my protection."

"Indeed! a fine sort of protector they've found in you," answered Stubbs, with a loud laugh, in which he was joined by his companions,— "No question, they're mightily obliged to you. The deuce take your nonsense and yourself into the bargain; I'll say what I please to the gal, and do what I please too. Ain't I the overseer?"—and here he broke out with a fresh string of ribaldry, addressed to poor Cassy.

It was only by a promise to treat his companions to a quart of whisky, that Mr. Gordon could prevail on them to let us alone. The word "whisky" worked like a charm, and by the influence of it, he persuaded the others to drop a little behind, and to give him a chance, as he expressed it, to have some private conversation with me. He had no objection to their hearing what he said to me, but he did not want to be interrupted.

I was a good deal surprised at all this. Mr. Gordon had betrayed me; —and after doing me so base and irreparable an injury, what could he

D

mean by these little marks of good-will? Mr. Gordon was, as I have described him, a good-natured fellow. He had not been able to resist the temptation of five hundred dollars, and all the other advantages, which he expected to gain by betraying me;—but for all that, he had not forgotten that I had saved his life. He walked up beside me, and stammering and hesitating, he attempted to enter into conversation.

"That was a deuced hard blow you struck me, Archy," he began.

"I am sorry it was not harder," was my answer.

"Come, come now, don't be in such a devilish savage humour. Why, boy, I thought I might as well get the five hundred dollars, as to let it slip through my fingers, and all for nothing too. I knew right well you were sure to be taken,—and for all you pout so about it, I've made better terms for you than anybody else would have done. Come, boy, cheer up, and I'll tell you how it all was. You see, when you left me t'other night, I could not sleep a wink for thinking. Says I to myself, that's a damned foolish project of Archy's. He is sure to be caught; and then it will be coming out as how I helped him, and then there will be the devil and all to pay. He'll be whipped, and I'll be fined and sent to gaol, and for anything I know, ridden on a rail out of the county, as Colonel Moore and them others threatened me; and then,—to make a bad matter worse,—somebody else will get the reward. Now that boy Archy, said I, saved my life—there's no denying that, any how,—and if I can save him a whipping, and at the same time put five hundred dollars into my pocket, it will be a mighty pretty business for both of us.

"So the next morning, I got up early and started off for Colonel Moore's; and a mighty fluster I found the colonel in, to be sure,—for he could hear no news of you nowhere. So says I, 'Colonel,' says I, 'I hear as how you've offered five hundred dollars reward to anybody that'll catch them 'ere runaways of yours.' 'Yes,' says the Colonel, 'cash down;'—and he looked me in the face, as though he thought I knew where to find you.

"'Just so, Colonel,' says I; 'and perhaps I might, if you'll promise me something, in the first place.'

"'Promise you something,' said the colonel, 'haven't I promised five hundred dollars already? what is it you mean?'

"Says I, 'Colonel, it isn't the reward I was thinking about,—the reward is handsome, a very pretty reward, surely. Pay me four hundred and fifty dollars, colonel, and promise me not to whip Archy, when you get him, and I'll not ask for the other fifty.'

"'Pshaw, nonsense,' says the Colonel. 'Pray, Mr. Gordon, what is it to you how much I whip the scoundrel, provided you get your money?'

"Says, I, 'Colonel, Jemmy Gordon isn't the chap to forget a favour. That boy, Archy, saved my life, it's three years ago this very month; and if you'll promise me, upon your honour, not to punish him for running away, I will undertake to hunt him up for you; and not otherwise.'

"The colonel higgled and haggled a good deal; but he found he couldn't get round me no how,—he promised all I had asked him. So I told him how you had been at my house, and how you were coming again; and he sent Stubbs and them other fellows to help me to take you,—and that's the long and the short of the whole matter. So don't be sulky, Archy, but cheer up and take it kindly. You see, I meant to do what was best for us both."

"I wish you much joy, Mr. Gordon, of your part of the bargain; and may you lose your five hundred dollars the next time you play cards, and that will be before you are twelve hours older."

" You're in a passion, Archy, or you wouldn't talk in that way. Well, boy, to tell the truth, I don't much wonder at it. But, by-and-by, you'll think better of it. I should think you might be content with having broken my head; my eyes, Archy, but it aches, as though it would split." So saying, Mr. Gordon broke off the conversation and joined his companions.

Little reason as I have to speak well of him, I am bold to say there are a great many men in the world not much better than Jemmy Gordon. Five hundred dollars was a great temptation to him. Besides, he hoped to secure the good graces of Colonel Moore, and expected by his assistance to get into the way of gaining a living respectably,—at least, as respectably as any poor man can in that country. He not only quieted his conscience with the idea that, if he did not betray me, somebody else would, but he had made terms with Colonel Moore for my benefit, and actually seemed to have flattered himself into the notion that he was doing me a favour by betraying me.

There is many a *gentleman* in slave-holding America,—for, anti-republican as it may seem, in no part of the world is the distinction between *gentlemen* and the *common people* more distinctly marked,—who would consider it an insult to be compared with Jemmy Gordon, but whose whole life is a continued practice of the very principles upon which that man acted, when he made up his mind to play the traitor. Many is the gentleman in slave-holding America who knows full well,—and, in the secret recesses of his own soul, most unequivocally acknowledges,—that to keep his fellow-men in bondage is a gross, flagrant, high-handed violation of the first and clearest principles of justice and equity, —a practice, abstractly considered, fully more criminal than piracy or highway robbery. Slavery, in the abstract, he acknowledges to himself and to others to be totally indefensible. But then his slaves are his estate,—and he cannot live *like a gentleman* without them. Besides, he treats his servants particularly well,—so very well, that he does not hesitate to argue that they are much happier as slaves, than freedom, under any form, could possibly make them !

When men of sense and education can satisfy themselves with such wretched sophistry as this, let us learn to have some charity for poor Jemmy Gordon.

CHAPTER XI.

It was past noon before we arrived at Spring-Meadow, where Colonel Moore had been for some time impatiently expecting us. But as he happened to have a large party to dine with him, he was too busy in entertaining his company to pay any immediate attention to us. Yet, no sooner had he received notice of our arrival, than he sent out Mr. Gordon's five hundred dollars. It was a large roll of bank notes; the fellow's eye kindled up at the sight of it, and he snatched it eagerly. I was looking steadily at him, and his eyes met mine. The change was sudden. He blushed and grew pale by turns;—shame, remorse, and self-contempt were painted in his face. He thrust the money hastily into his pocket, and walked away without speaking a word.

Cassy and myself were driven to the stables, and locked up in a close, narrow, dark room, which served sometimes as a corn-crib, and some-times as a sort of dungeon for refractory slaves. We sat down upon the floor,—for there was nothing else to sit upon,—and poor Cassy sunk into my arms. Her grief and terror seemed to burst out afresh, and she wept bitterly. I kissed away her tears, and tried to console her. But she would not be comforted; and little, indeed, was the comfort I had to offer. The more I said to her, the more she wept; and she clung to me closer and closer, till her embrace became almost convulsive. "He will kill us: he will separate us for ever," she murmured, in a low, inarticulate voice; and it was the only reply she made to all I could say to her.

Our situation was, indeed, pitiable. Had we fallen into the hands of an ordinary pirate or robber, there might have been some room for hope. The consciousness of his own violence might, perhaps, alarm him; the fear of avenging justice might stay his hand. At the worst, death, and that, too, a speedy and an easy one, would be the farthest limit of his malice. But we, unhappy creatures, could flatter ourselves with no such prospect. We were runaway slaves who had fallen again into the hands of their master,—a master, whom the very recollection that he *owned* us inspired with rage at our insolence, in daring to run away from him; and who knew well, that both the law and public opinion would amply justify him in the infliction of any tortures not likely to result in immediate death.

It is true that we had fled from the greatest outrage that can be inflicted upon a wife and a husband. But that was no excuse, not even the slightest palliation. Slaves are not permitted to fly at all. It is their duty,—alas! that such a word should be so prostituted!—to submit without a murmur to all the insults, outrages, and oppression of their masters.

I clasped my wife to my bosom, with almost the same trembling earnestness with which she clung to me. I felt, as she did, that it was the last time,—and this idea sunk into my heart with a bitterness which all my late ecstasies served only to aggravate. I almost stifled her with eager kisses; but the fever that glowed in her cheek was not the flush of pleasure; and those deep sighs she heaved, they could not be mistaken for the pantings of delight. The speedy separation that threatened us, was not only terrible in anticipation, but it seemed to destroy all our capacity for present enjoyment. But for that, with Cassy in my arms, what should I have cared for chains and a dungeon! Dreading that, her lips lost all their sweetness, her bosom was an uneasy pillow, and though I could not leave her, every embrace seemed to increase both her distress and mine.

We passed several hours in this way without any interruption. We had not tasted food that day, and nobody brought us even a cup of cold water. The heat and closeness of the room, into which the air had no admission, aggravated the fever in our blood, and made our thirst almost intolerable. How I longed for the cool spring, the balmy air, the freedom we had lost!

Towards evening, we heard somebody approaching, and I soon recognized the voices of Colonel Moore and his overseer. They opened the door, and bade us come out. At first, the light dazzled my eyes so that I could scarcely distinguish one object from another; but in a little while I was enabled to see that our visitors were accompanied by Peter, a tall fellow, with a very suspicious smile, the spy and tell-tale of the place, the detestation of all the servants, but the especial favourite of Mr. Stubbs, and his regular assistant on all occasions.

Colonel Moore's face was a good deal flushed, and I judged that he had been drinking. This was a practice very unusual with him. For though every dinner at his house was pretty sure to end by putting the greater part of the guests upon the floor, Colonel Moore generally passed the bottle, under the plea that his physician had forbidden its use, and commonly rose up the only sober man from his own table. It was too plain, that, on the present occasion, he had forgotten his accustomed sobriety. He spoke not a word to me, and I found it impossible to catch his eye; but turning to his overseer, he said, in an under tone, and with the air of being a good deal irritated, " It was a damned blunder, Mr. Stubbs, to shut them up together. I thought you understood my orders better."

The overseer mumbled out some unintelligible apology, of which Colonel Moore took no notice; and without further preface or explanation, he ordered Mr. Stubbs to tie me up.

The padlock by which the chain was fastened about my neck was undone. They stripped me almost naked. Mr. Stubbs produced a piece of rope, with one end of which he bound my hands, and the other end he made fast, with Peter's assistance, to a beam over my head; not, however, till he had drawn it so tight as almost to lift me from the floor.

Colonel Moore then ordered them to free Cassy from the chain. He put a heavy whip into her hand, and pointing to me, " Take care, my girl," he said, " that you lay it on to some purpose."

Poor Cassy looked about in utter amazement. She did not understand him; she had no idea of such refined cruelty, such ferocious revenge.

He repeated his commands, with a tone and a look that were frightful. " If you wish to save your own carcass, see that you bring blood at every blow. I'll teach you—both of you—to trifle with me."

She now comprehended his brutal purpose; and giving one look of mingled horror and despair, sunk senseless to the ground. Peter was sent for water. He dashed it in her face, and she soon revived. They placed her on her feet, and Colonel Moore again put the whip into her hand and repeated his orders.

She threw it down, as if the touch had stung her; and looking him full in the face, the tears, all the while, streaming from her eyes, she said in a tone firm, but full of entreaty, " Master, he is my husband!"

That word *husband* seemed to kindle Colonel Moore into a new fury, which totally destroyed his self-command. He struck Cassy to the ground with his fists, trampled on her with his feet, and snatching up the whip which she had thrown down, he laid it upon me with such violence, that the lash penetrated my flesh at every blow, and the blood ran trickling down my legs and stood in little puddles at my feet. The torture was too great for human endurance; I screamed with agony. " Pshaw," said my executioner, " his noise will disturb the house; and drawing a handkerchief from his pocket, he thrust it into my mouth, and rammed it down my throat with the butt-end of his whiphandle. Having thus effectually gagged me, he renewed his lashes. How long they were continued I do not know; a cloud began to swim before my eyes; my head grew dizzy and confused; and a fortunate fainting-fit soon put me beyond the reach of torture.

CHAPTER XII.

WHEN I recovered my senses, I found myself stretched upon a wretched pallet, which lay upon the floor, in one corner of a little, old, and ruinous hovel. I was very weak and hardly able to move; and I afterwards learned that I had just passed through the paroxysm of a fever. A deaf old woman, too much superannuated to be fit for anything but a nurse, was my only companion. I recognized the old lady, and forgetting that she could not hear me, I put her a thousand questions in a breath. I dreaded, yet I wished to learn the fate of poor Cassy; and it was to her that most of my questions related. But to all my inquiries the old woman returned no answer. I might scream myself deaf, she said, and she could not hear a word. Besides, she told me, I was too sick and weak to talk.

I was not to be silenced in that way, and only bawled the louder, and added signs and gestures, to enable the old woman to understand me. But it was plain that Aunt Judy had no intention to gratify my curiosity; for when she found she could not quiet me, she went out, and locking the door after her, left me to my own meditations. These were not very agreeable. As yet, however, my thoughts were so confused, and my head so dizzy, that I could scarcely be said to reflect at all.

I learned afterwards, that it was more than a week that I had remained delirious, the effect of the violent fever into which I had been thrown, and which threatened a speedy termination to my miserable existence. But the crisis was now past. My youth and the vigour of my constitution had carried me through it, and had preserved me for new sufferings.

I recovered rapidly, and was soon able to walk about. Lest I should make an undue use of my returning strength, and attempt another escape, I was presently accommodated with fetters and handcuffs. My fetters were taken off once a day, for about an hour, and under Peter's supervision I was allowed to breathe the fresh air, and to take a short walk about the plantation. It was in vain that I attempted to get from Peter any information concerning my wife. He could not, or he would not, tell me anything about her.

I thought that, perhaps, he might sell the information which he refused to give; and I promised to make him a present of some clothes, if he would allow me to visit my former house. We went together. This house I had been enabled, in anticipation of my marriage, and through the bounty of Mrs. Moore and her daughter, to fit up quite comfortably. It was furnished with a variety of things, seldom seen in a slave's cabin. But I found it stripped and plundered; every article of furniture was gone, and my chest was broken open and all my clothes taken away. For this I was no doubt indebted to my fellow-servants. The strongest, or almost the strongest, impulse of the human mind, is the desire of acquisition. This passion the slave can only gratify by plunder. Besides, such is the baneful effect of slavery, that it almost destroys the very germ of virtue. If oppression makes the wise man mad, it too often makes the honest man a villain. It embitters the feelings and hardens and brutifies the heart. He who finds himself plundered from his birth, of his liberty and his labour—his only inheritance—becomes selfish, reckless, and regardless of everything save the immediate gratification of the present moment. Plundered of everything himself, he is ready to plunder in his turn, even his brothers in misfortune.

Finding my house stripped, and my clothes stolen, it put me in mind to feel in my pockets for my money. That was gone too. Indeed I soon recollected, that, when surprised and seized by Mr. Gordon and his assistants, Mr. Stubbs had searched my pockets, and transferred their contents to his own. This, of course, was the last that I expected to see of my money. According to the Virginian code of morals, Mr. Stubbs was a very respectable man, who did what was perfectly proper. Certainly, it was highly dangerous to trust a rogue and a runaway with the possession of a considerable sum of money. But, according to the same code, the servants who had stolen my clothes were a set of outrageous thieves, who richly deserved a whipping. So Mr. Stubbs declared, whom we happened to meet, as we were returning, and to whom I complained that my house had been plundered. That honest gentleman worked himself quite into a passion, and swore roundly that if he could catch the thieves he would make them smart for it. Notwithstanding this outburst of virtuous indignation, Mr. Stubbs said nothing about returning my money, and I judged it safest not to introduce the subject myself.

In two or three weeks I had nearly recovered my strength, and the gashes with which my back had been scored were quite healed, over. I was beginning to wonder what Colonel Moore intended to do with me; when, one evening, I received a message from Mr. Stubbs, to be up by sunrise the next morning, and ready for a journey. Where we were going, or what was to be the object of our travels, he did not condescend to inform me; nor did I feel much curiosity to know. I had now one great consolation. Do what they pleased, it was impossible to render me any more miserable. It was this idea which sustained me and enabled me to regard the future with a sort of careless and stupid indifference, at which, when I reflect upon it, I am myself surprised.

In the morning Mr. Stubbs came for me. He was on horseback, whip in hand, as usual. He undid my fetters, but allowed me to retain my handcuffs. He tied a piece of rope about my neck, and fastened the other end of it to his own waist. Thus guarded against escapes, he mounted his horse, and bade me walk beside him. I was still rather weak, and sometimes my pace flagged a little; but a stroke from Mr. Stubbs's whip soon quickened me into vigour. I inquired where we were going. "You'll know when you get there," was the answer.

That night we lodged at a sort of tavern. We both occupied one room—he the bed, and I the floor. He took the cord from my neck and bound my legs with it. It was drawn so tight, and caused me so much pain, that I could not sleep. Several times I complained to Mr. Stubbs; but he ordered me to go to sleep quietly, and not be troubling him with foolish complaints. The next morning when he came to untie me, he found my ankles a good deal swollen. He seemed sorry that he had paid no more attention to my appeals, but excused himself by saying, that we were all such a devilish pack of liars, there was no telling when to believe us; and he did not want to be at the trouble of getting up for nothing.

The next day we continued our journey; but I was so broken down by the fatigues of the day previous, and by the want of sleep, that nothing but the frequent application of Mr. Stubbs's whip could stimulate me into the necessary exertion. My spirits and that stubbornness of soul, which hitherto had sustained me, seemed to fail at the same time with my strength, and I wept like a child. At last, we reached our journey's

end. Late that evening, we entered the city of Richmond. I am not
able to describe the town; for I was hurried off to gaol, and there locked
up for safe keeping.

I was now told why we had come. Colonel Moore, according to
Mr. Stubbs's account, was sick of such an unruly fellow, and had determined to sell me. I had not seen him since the day I had fainted under
the energy of his paternal discipline. Nor did I ever see him afterwards. A strange parting that, between a son and a father!

CHAPTER XIII.

THE next day I was to be sold. There was to be a public sale of
slaves, and several besides myself were to be disposed of. I was fettered
and handcuffed, and taken to market. The rest of the merchandise was
already collected; but it was some time before the sale began, and I
occupied the interval in looking about me. Several of the groups
attracted my particular attention. .

The first that caught my eye was an old man whose head was completely white, and a pretty little girl, his granddaughter, as he told me,
about ten or twelve years old. Both the old man and the little girl had
iron collars about their necks, which were connected by a heavy chain.
One would have imagined, that the old age of the man, and the youth
of the girl, would have made such savage precautions unnecessary. But
their master, so far as I could learn, had resolved to sell them in a fit of
passion, and the chains, perhaps, were intended more for punishment
than security.

A man and his wife, with an infant in her arms, stood next to the old
man and his daughter. The man and wife were quite young, and
apparently fond of each other; at least they seemed very much distressed
at the idea of falling into the hands of different purchasers. The
woman now; and then would address some one or other of the company, who seemed to indicate an intention of buying. She would beg
them to purchase herself and her husband; and she ran over, with great
volubility, the good qualities of both. The man looked on the ground,
and preserved a moody and sullen silence.

There was another group of eight or ten men and women, who seemed
to regard the sale with as much unconcern as if they were merely spectators. They laughed, and talked, and jested with one another with as
much gaiety as any of the company. An apologist for tyranny would,
no doubt, rejoice in such a spectacle, and would be emboldened to argue,
that, after all, being sold at public auction is not so terrible a thing as
some weak people are apt to imagine. The argument would be quite as
sound as any that the slave-holder ever uses; and for ingenuity and con-
clusiveness, deserves to be compared with that of the philosopher, who
having seen through the grates of a prison a parcel of condemned
criminals laughing and jesting together, concluded that the expectation
of being hung must have something in it very exhilarating.

The truth is, that the human mind, in its eager, though too often unavailing struggle after happiness, will still make the most of its means;
and even in the valley of despair, or under the ribs of death itself, still
strives to create some matter of enjoyment. Even the slave will sing at
his task; he can laugh too, though he find himself sold like an ox in the

market. The tyrant discovers that all his wrongs and oppressions have not been able to extinguish in the soul of his victim the capability of enjoyment; and he points you to these outbursts of a nature not yet totally subdued, and dares to boast of the happiness he causes!

But to be sold is not always a laughing matter. The first bargain which the auctioneer offered to the company was a man apparently about thirty, with a fine, open, prepossessing countenance. He had no expectation of being sold, till the moment he was placed upon the table; for it appeared that his master, who lived near the city, had lured him to town under the delusive pretext of an intention to hire him out to some one of the citizens. When the poor fellow found that he was actually to be sold, he was seized with such a trembling that he could scarcely support himself. He shook from head to foot; and his face indicated the greatest terror and distress. The two principal bidders—and they seemed to enter into a pretty warm competition—were a gentleman of the neighbourhood, who appeared to know the poor fellow on sale, and a dashing, buckish young man, who, it was said, was a slave-trader from South Carolina, who had come to purchase slaves for that market.

As the sale proceeded, it was curious, but at the same time most distressing, to observe the anxiety of the unhappy slave. When the slave-trader took the lead, his jaw fell, his eyes rolled wildly, aud he seemed the very picture of despair; but when the Virginian bid higher, a gleam of pleasure shot across his face, the tears ran down his cheeks, and his earnest "God bless you, master!" was enough to touch the hardest heart. He interrupted the sale by his cries and vociferations, and not even the whip could keep him still. He called upon his favourite bidder by name, and entreated him to persevere, by every motive he could think of. He promised to serve him faithfully to the last minute of his life, and work himself to death in his service, if he would only buy him, only save him from being wholly separated from his wife and children, and sent away—he knew not whither—from the place where he was born and raised, and where, as he said, he had always behaved well, and borne a good character. Not that he had any particular objections to the other gentleman either—for the poor fellow began to see the danger of offending a man who was likely to become his master; no doubt he was a very fine gentleman too; but he was a stranger, and would take him out of the country, and carry him far away from his wife and children; and as he mentioned them, his voice sunk, choked and interrupted, to an inarticulate sobbing.

The bidders kept up the contest with much spirit. The man was evidently a first-rate hand. Aside from this, the Virginian seemed touched by the poor fellow's entreaties, and dropped some hints about slave-traders, which put his opponent into a violent passion, and came near ending in a quarrel. The interposition of the by-standers kept the competitors apart; but the slave-trader, whose passions were roused, swore that he would have the "boy," cost what he might, if it were only to teach him a little good manners. One or two of the company cried shame, and called upon the slave-trader to leave off bidding, and suffer the poor fellow to remain in the country. He replied with an oath and a sneer, that he was not fool enough to be bamboozled by any such nonsense; and immediately rose fifty dollars on the last bid. This was more than the Virginian could afford to sacrifice to a fit of good nature, and piqued and chagrined, he yielded up the contest. The auctioneer knocked off the purchase; and the man, more dead than alive, was delivered into the hands of the slave-trader's attendants, who received orders to give him twenty lashes on the spot, for his "cursed ill-mannerly Virginian insolence."

The sneering emphasis with which this was spoken created no little sensation among the by-standers; but as the slave-trader strutted about with his hand on his dirk-handle, and as two pistols might plainly be seen sticking out of his pockets, nobody saw fit to question this provoking exercise of "his sacred right of property," and the sale proceeded as before.

At length came my turn. I was stripped half naked, the better to show my joints and muscles, and placed upon the table or platform, on which the subject of the sale was exposed to the examination of the purchasers. I was whirled about, my limbs were felt, and my capabilities discussed, in a slang much like that of a company of horse-jockeys. Various were the remarks that were made upon me. One fellow declared that I had "a savage, sullen look;" another swore that my eye was "devilish malicious;" a third remarked that these light-coloured fellows were all rascals;—to which the auctioneer replied, that he never knew a slave of any smartness who was not a rogue.

Abundance of questions were put to me, as to where I was raised, why I was sold, and what I was fit for. To all these inquiries I made the shortest and most indefinite answers. I was not in a humour to gratify this curiosity; and I had none of that ambition to bring a high price, so common among slaves, the last and lowest form in which is displayed that love of superiority, which exercises so principal an influence over the feelings and the actions of men.

Mr. Stubbs kept in the background, and said nothing. He had his own reasons, I suppose, for this reserve. The auctioneer did his best. According to his account, there was not a stronger, more laborious, docile and obedient servant to be bought in all the States. Notwithstanding all these praises, a suspicion seemed to spread itself that my master had some reasons for selling me, which he did not think fit to avow. One suggested that I must be consumptive; another thought it likely I was subject to fits; while a third expressed the opinion that I was an unruly fellow and "mighty hard to manage." The scars on my back tended to confirm these suspicions; and I was knocked off, at last, at a very low price, to a portly, smiling old gentleman, by name Major Thornton.

No sooner had the auctioneer's hammer struck upon the table, than my new master spoke kindly to me, and ordered my irons to be taken off. Against this, Mr. Stubbs and the auctioneer remonstrated very earnestly; and assured the purchaser that if he unchained me, he did it at his own risk. "I know it," replied my new master, "the risk is mine,—but I will never own a servant who wants to run away from me."

CHAPTER XIV.

WHEN my new master learned that I had but just recovered from a fever, and that my strength was not yet entirely restored, he procured a horse for me, and we set out together for his plantation. He lived a considerable distance west of Richmond, in that part of the state known as Middle Virginia. During the ride he entered into conversation with me, and I found him a very different person from any one I had ever met with before.

He told me that I might consider myself lucky in falling into his hands, for he made it a point to treat his servants better than anybody in the neighbourhood. "If they are discontented, or unruly, or apt to run away," he added, "I sell them at once, and so get rid of them. I don't want any such fellows about me. But as my servants know very well, that they stand no chance to better themselves by changing their master, they are very cautious how they offend me. Be obedient, my boy, and do your task, and I will ensure you plenty to eat, enough clothes, and more indulgence than you will be likely to get from any other master." Such was the amount of Major Thornton's lecture, which it took him, however, some five or six hours to get through with.

It was late in the evening before we arrived at Oakland—for that was the name of Major Thornton's property. The house was of brick, with wooden porticoes. It was not large, but neat, and very handsome, and presented many more appearances of substantial comfort than are to be found about most of the houses of Virginia. The grounds around it were prettily laid out, and ornamented with flowers and shrubbery,—a thing quite uncommon, and which I had seldom seen before. At a distance, on a fine swell, were the servants' cabins, built of brick, neat and substantial; not placed in a straight line, but clustered together in a manner that had something picturesque about it. They were shaded by fine large oaks; no underbrush nor weeds were suffered to grow about them; and altogether, they presented an appearance of neatness and comfort as new and singular as it was pleasing. The servants' cabins, on all the plantations I had ever seen before, were a set of miserable, ruinous hovels, with leaky roofs and clay floors, almost buried in a rank growth of weeds, and as dirty and ill-kept as they were uncomfortable.

The children, who were playing about the cabins, furnished a new occasion of surprise. I had been accustomed to see the children of a plantation running about stark naked, or dressed—if dressed at all—in a shirt of dirty osnaburgs, hanging in tatters about their legs, and never washed after it was once put on. But the children at Oakland were neatly and comfortably clothed, and presented nothing of that squalid, pinched, neglected, and half-starved appearance to which my eye was so well accustomed. Their merry faces and boisterous sports called up no idea of juvenile wretchedness. I observed, too, that the hands, who were just coming in from their work, were all well clothed. I saw none of those patched, tattered, ragged, and filthy garments so common on other plantations.

Major Thornton was not a planter; that is to say, he did not make tobacco, and he chose to call himself a farmer. His principal crop was wheat; and he was a great advocate for the clover system of cultivation, which he had adopted and pursued with much success. He owned some thirty or forty working hands; the children and superannuated made his entire stock of slaves upwards of eighty. He kept no overseer, but managed for himself. Indeed, it was a maxim with him, that an overseer was enough to ruin any man. He was naturally stirring and industrious, and agriculture was his hobby—a hobby which he rode to some purpose.

In all these things, and many others, he was the perfect contrast of all his neighbours; and for that reason very little liked by any of them. He carefully avoided horse-racing, cock-fights, political meetings, drinking, gambling, and frolicking of every sort. His money, he used to say, cost him too much to make it to be thrown away upon a bet; and as to frolics, he had neither time nor taste for any such nonsense. His neighbours revenged themselves for this contempt of their favourite sports, by pronouncing him a mean-spirited money-making fellow. They went further, and accused him of being a bad citizen and a dangerous neighbour. They complained most bitterly, that his excessive indulgence to his servants made all the slaves in the neighbourhood uneasy and discontented; and at one time some of them went so far as to talk about giving him warning to move out of the county.

But Major Thornton was a man of spirit. He understood his own rights;—he knew well the people among whom he lived, and what sort of reasoning would influence them most. He contrived to get hold of an offensive remark of one of the busiest of his ill-disposed neighbours, and sent him a challenge. It was accepted; and his antagonist was shot through the heart at the first fire. Henceforward—though his neighbours liked him no better than before—they took very good care how they talked about him, and allowed him to go on in his own way without any interference.

Major Thornton had not been bred a planter, and this perhaps was the reason why he departed so much from the ordinary routine, and managed things so very differently from all his neighbours. He was born of a good family, as they say in Virginia, but his father died when he was a mere boy, and left but a very scanty property. He began life, in a small way, in a country store. His shrewdness, economy, and attention to his business, enabled him, in the course of a few years, to lay up a considerable sum of money. In Virginia, trade is hardly looked upon as respectable, at least such was the case at the time of which I am speaking, and every one who desires to be anybody, aims at becoming a landed proprietor. About the time that Major Thornton had made enough to think of changing his store for a plantation, the proprietor of Oakland, having already wasted two good estates on dogs, horses, and wild debauchery, became so pressed for money as to be obliged to bring his remaining property under the hammer. Major Thornton became the purchaser; but the place he bought was very different from Oakland as I saw it. The buildings, which were old and ugly, were all out of repair, and just tumbling to the ground; and the land was nearly ruined by that miserable, thriftless system of cultivation, so universal throughout the slave-holding states of America.

In a few years after the property had passed into the hands of Major Thornton, everything was changed. The old houses were torn down and new ones built. The grounds about the house were enclosed and ornamented; and the land, under skilful management, was fast regaining its original fertility. Those who had been born and bred planters, and whose estates were very much in the same way in which Oakland had been before it fell into the hands of Major Thornton, looked at what was going on there with astonishment and envy, and wondered how it could possibly happen. Major Thornton was always ready to tell them; for he was extremely fond of talking, particularly about himself and his system of farming. But though he had explained the whole matter at least ten times to every one of his neighbours, he never could make a single convert. He had three favourite topics; but he was equally unsuccessful upon all of them. He never could persuade any one of his neighbours that a clover lay was the true cure for sterile fields; that the only way to have a plantation well managed, was to manage it one's self; or that to give servants enough to eat, was a sure method to prevent them from plundering the corn-fields and stealing sheep.

But though Major Thornton could gain no imitators, he still persevered in farming according to his own notions. In no respect was he more an innovator than in the management of his slaves. A merciful man, he used to say, is merciful to his beast; and not having been raised on a plantation, he could not bear the idea of treating his servants worse than his horses. "It may do very well for you, colonel," he said one day, to one of his neighbours, "to tie a fellow up and give him forty lashes with your own hand; you were born and bred to it, and I dare say you find it very easy. But as odd as you may think it, I had much rather be flogged myself than to flog one of my servants; and though sometimes I am obliged to do it, it is a great point with me to get along with as little whipping as possible. That's a principal reason why I keep no overseer, for a cowhide and a pair of irons are the only two things those fellows have any notion of. They have no wish, and if they had they have not the sense, to get along in any other way; —the devil take the whole generation of them. Everybody, you know, have their oddities. For my part, I hate to hear the crack of a whip on my plantation, even though it be nothing more than a cart-whip."

The above speech of Major Thornton's contained a brief summary of his system. He was, what every other slaveholder is, and from the very necessity of his condition must be, a tyrant. He felt no scruple in compelling his fellow-men to labour, in order that he might appropriate the fruits of that labour to his own benefit, and in this certainly, if in anything, the very essence of tyranny consists. But though a tyrant, as every slaveholder is and must be, he was a reasonable, and, as far as possible, a humane one,—which very few slaveholders either are or can be. He had no more thought of relinquishing what he and the laws called his property in his slaves, than he had of leaving his land to be occupied by the first comer. He would have been as ready as any of his neighbours, to have denounced the idea of emancipation, or the notion of limiting his power over his servants, as a ridiculous absurdity, and an impertinent interference with his "most sacred rights." But though in theory he claimed all the authority and prerogatives of the most unlimited despotism, he displayed, in his practice, a certain share of common sense and common humanity, two things which, so far as relates to the management of his slaves, it is extremely uncommon for a slaveholder to have, or, if he has them, very difficult for him to exercise.

These unusual gifts led him to a discovery which at the time was entirely new in his neighbourhood; though I hope before now it has become general. He discovered that men cannot work without eating; and that so far as the capability of labour is concerned, there is the same policy in attending to the food, shelter, and comfort of one's slaves, as in spending something on corn and stabling for one's horses. "Feed well and work hard," was Major Thornton's motto and practice,—a motto and a practice which, in any other country than America, would never have subjected him to the charge of unreasonable and superfluous humanity.

As to whipping, Major Thornton, to use his own phrase, could not bear it. Whether he felt some qualms of conscience at the barefaced, open tyranny of the lash,—which I do not think very probable, for I once heard him tell a Methodist parson, who ventured to say something to him on that delicate subject, that he had as much right to flog his slaves as to eat his dinner,—or whether it was the influence of that instinctive humanity which is wanting only in brutal tempers, and which, till evil custom has worn it out, will not permit us to inflict pain without feeling ourselves a sympathetic suffering; or whatever might be the reason, unless Major Thornton was put into a passion—to which he was but seldom liable—he certainly had a great horror at using the whip.

But this was not all. Another man might have detested it as much as he did; but the practice of a year or two in planting, and the apparent impossibility of dispensing with its use, would have taught him to get rid of so inconvenient a squeamishness. There are very few men indeed—and of all men in the world, very few planters—whose good sense and knowledge of human nature would enable them to manage their slaves by any other means. Major Thornton, however, contrived to get on wonderfully well; and in all the time that I lived with him, which was nearly two years, there were not more than half a dozen whippings on the place. If one of his servants was guilty of anything, which, in a slave, is esteemed especially enormous, such as running away, repeated theft, idleness, insolence, or insubordination, Major Thornton sent him off to be sold. By a strange but common inconsistency, this man of feeling, who could not bear to whip a slave, or to see him whipped, or even to have him whipped on his own plantation, felt no scruples at all at tearing him from the arms of his wife and children, and setting him up at public sale, to fall into the hands of any ferocious master who might chance to purchase him!

This dread of being sold was ever before our eyes, and was as efficacious as the lash is on other plantations, in forcing us to labour and submission. We knew very well, that there were few masters like Major Thornton; and the thought of exchanging our nice, neat cottages, our plentiful allowance, our regular supply of clothing, and the general comfort and indulgence of Oakland, for the fare and the treatment to be expected from the common run of masters, was more terrible than a dozen whippings. Major Thornton understood this well; and he took care to keep up the terrors of it, by making an example of some delinquent once in a year or two.

Then he had the art of exciting our emulation by little prizes and presents; he was very scrupulous never to exact anything beyond the appointed task; and he kept us in good humour, by allowing us, when not at work, to be very much our own masters, and to go where, and do what we pleased. We were rather cautious, though, how we visited the neighbouring plantations; for with a magnanimity worthy of slaveholders, some of Major Thornton's neighbours were in the habit of gratifying their spite against him, by improving every opportunity that offered to abuse his servants. And here I may as well relate an incident that happened to myself, which will serve, at once, as a curious illustration of Virginian manners, and a proof of what I believe will be found to be true all the world over,—that where the laws aim at the oppression of one half the people of a country, they are seldom treated with much respect by the other half.

Captain Robinson was one of Major Thornton's nearest neighbours, and a person with whom he had frequent altercations. I was passing along on the public road one Sunday, at a little distance from Oakland, when I met Captain Robinson on horseback, followed by a servant. He bade me stop and inquired if I was the fellow whom that "damned scoundrel Thornton" sent to his house yesterday with an insolent message about his lower-field fences. I answered that I had been sent yesterday with a message about the fence, which I had delivered to his overseer.

"A mighty pretty message it was—mighty ! I'll tell you what, boy, if my overseer had known his business, he would have tucked you up on the spot and given you forty lashes."

I told him that I had only delivered the message which my master had sent me with, and it seemed hard to blame me for that.

"Don't talk to me, don't talk to me, you infernal scoundrel—I'll teach both you and your master what it is to insult a gentleman. Lay hold of him, Tom, while I dust that new jacket of his a little."

Having received these orders from his master, Captain Robinson's man Tom jumped off his horse, and laid hold of me; but as I struggled hard, and was the stronger of the two, I should soon have got away, if the master had not dismounted, and come to the aid of his servant. Both together, they were too strong for me; and having succeeded in getting me down, they stripped off my coat, and bound my hands. Captain Robinson then mounted his horse, and beat me with his whip till it was quite worn out. Having thus satisfied his rage, he rode off, followed by Tom, without taking the trouble to loose my hands. They had no sooner left me, than I began to look about for my hat and coat. Both were missing; and whether it was the captain or his servant that carried them off, I never could discover. I suppose, though, it was the servant—for I recollect very well seeing Tom, a few Sundays after, strutting about at a Methodist meeting, with a blue coat on, which I could almost have sworn to be mine.

When I got home, and told my master what had happened, he was in a towering passion. At first, he was for riding at once to Captain Robinson's, and calling for an explanation. But presently he recollected that the county court was to meet the next day, at which he had business. This would give him an opportunity to consult his lawyer; and after a little reflection, he thought it best not to move in the affair till he had legal advice upon it.

The next day he took me with him. We called upon the lawyer; I told what had happened to me, and Major Thornton inquired what satisfaction the law would afford me.

The lawyer answered, that the law in this case was very clear, and the remedy it provided, all-sufficient. "Some people," he said, "who know nothing about the matter, have asserted that the law in the slave-holding States, does not protect the person of the slave against the violence of the free, and that any white man may flog any slave at his own good pleasure. This is a very great mistake, if not a wilful falsehood. The law permits no such thing. It extends the mantle of its protection impartially over bond and free. In this respect, the law knows no distinction. If a freeman is assaulted, he has his action for damages against the assailant; and if a slave is assaulted, the master of that slave, who is his legal guardian and protector, can bring his action for damages. Now, in this case, Major Thornton, it is quite plain that you have good ground of action against Captain Robinson; and the jury, I dare say, will give you a swinging verdict. I suppose you are able to prove all these facts?"

"Prove them—to be sure," answered my master; "here is Archy himself, who has told you the whole story."

"Yes, my good sir; but you do not seem to remember that a slave cannot be admitted to testify against a white man."

"And pray tell me, then," said Major Thornton, "what good the law you speak of is going to do me? Did not Robinson catch Archy alone, and abuse him, as he has told you! You don't suppose he was fool enough to call in a white man, on purpose to be a witness against him. Why, sir, notwithstanding the protection of the law, which you commend so highly, every servant I have may be beaten by this Robinson every day in the week, and I not be able to get the slightest satisfaction. The devil take such law, I say.

"But, my dear sir," answered the lawyer, "you must consider the great danger and inconvenience of allowing slaves to be witnesses."

"Why yes," said my master, with a half smile, "I fancy it would be rather dangerous for some of my acquaintances; quite inconvenient, no doubt. Well, sir, since you say the law can't help me in this matter, I must take care of myself. I cannot allow my servants to be abused in this way. I'll horsewhip that scoundrel Robinson at sight."

With these words my master left the office, and I followed behind him. We had gone but a little way down the street when he had an unexpected opportunity of carrying his threat into execution,—for as it chanced, we met Captain Robinson, who had business, it seemed, at the county court as well as Major Thornton. My master did not waste many words upon him, but began striking him over the shoulders with his riding whip. Captain Robinson drew a pistol; my master threw down his whip and drew a pistol also. The captain fired, but without effect; Major Thornton then levelled his weapon, but Robinson called out that he was unarmed, and begged him not to fire. Major Thornton hesitated a moment, and then dropped his hand. By this time quite a crowd had collected about us, and some friend of Captain Robinson's handed him a loaded pistol. The combatants renewed their aim, and fired together. Captain Robinson fell desperately wounded. His ball missed my master, but passed through the body of a free coloured man, who was the only person of all the company who made any attempt to separate the parties. The poor fellow fell dead; and the people about declared that it was good enough for him, for what right had " a cursed free fellow" like him to be interfering between gentlemen?

Captain Robinson's friends lifted him up and carried him home. Major Thornton and myself walked off the field in triumph, and so the affair ended. Such affrays are much talked about, but the grand jury very seldom hears anything of them; and the conqueror is pretty sure to rise in the public estimation.

CHAPTER XV.

SOME persons perhaps may think that having fallen into the hands of such a master as Major Thornton I had now nothing to do but to eat, to work, and to be happy.

Had I been a horse or an ox there would be good ground for this idea; but unfortunately I was a man; and the animal appetites are by no means the only motive of human action, nor the sole sources of human happiness or misery.

It is certainly true that several of Major Thornton's servants, born perhaps with but little sensibility, and brutalized by a life of servitude, seemed very well content with their lot. This was the sort of servant which Major Thornton especially admired. In this particular he did not differ much from his neighbours. The more stupid a field hand is, the more he is esteemed; and a slave who shows any signs of capacity is generally set down as certain to be a rogue and a rascal.

I soon discovered my master's fondness for stupid fellows; and I took care to play the fool to his entire satisfaction. In a short time I made myself quite a favourite; and my master having taken a fancy to me, I was more indulged, perhaps, than any servant on the place. But this could not make me happy.

Human happiness—with some very limited exceptions—is never in fruition, but always in prospect and pursuit. It is not this, that, or the other situation that can give happiness. Riches, power, or glory are nothing when possessed. It is the pleasure of the pursuit and the struggle, it is the very labour of their attainment, in which consists the happiness they bring.

Those moralists who have composed so many homilies upon the duty of contentment betray an extreme ignorance of human nature. No situation, however splendid, in which one is compelled to remain fixed and stationary, can long afford pleasure; and on the other hand, no condition, however destitute or degraded, out of which one has a fair prospect, or anything like a sufficient hope of rising, can justly be considered as utterly miserable. This is the constitution of the human mind; and in it we find the explanation of a thousand things, which, without this key to their meaning, seem full of mystery and contradiction.

Though all men have not the same objects of pursuit, all are impelled and sustained by the same hope of success. Nothing can satisfy the lofty desires of one man, but influence, fame, or power, the myrtle wreath or laurel crown; another aims no higher than to rise from abject poverty to a little competency, or, if his ambition is of another sort, to be the chief person in his native village, or the oracle of a country neighbourhood. How different are these aims!—and yet, the impulse that prompts them is the same. It is the desire of social superiority. He whom circumstances permit to yield to this impulse of his nature, and to pursue—successfully or not, it matters little—but to pursue, with some tolerable prospect of success, the objects which have captivated his fancy, may be regarded as having all the chance for happiness which the lot of humanity allows; while he, whom fate, or fortune, or whatever malignant cause, compels to suppress and forego the instinctive impulses and wishes of his heart—whatever in other respects may be his situation —is a wretch condemned to sorrow, and deserving pity. To the one, toil is itself a pleasure. He is a hunter whom the sight of his game fills with delight, and makes insensible to fatigue. Desire sustains him, and hope cheers him on. These are delights the other never knows; for him, life has lost its relish; rest is irksome to him, and labour is intolerable.

This is no digression. He who has taken the pains to read the preceding paragraph will be able to understand how it happened, that even with such a master as Major Thornton, I was neither happy nor content.

It is true I was well fed, well clothed, and not severely worked; and in these particulars,—as my master was fond of boasting, and as I have since found to be the case,—my situation was far superior to that of very many freemen. But I lacked one thing which every freeman has; and that one want was enough to make me miserable. I wanted liberty; the liberty of labouring for myself, not for a master; of pursuing my own happiness, instead of toiling at his pleasure, and for his gain. This liberty can lighten the hardest lot. He knows but little of human nature who has not discovered, that to all who rise one step above the brutes, it is far pleasanter to starve and freeze after their own fashion, than to be fed and clothed and worked upon compulsion.

I was wretched,—for I had no object of hope or rational desire. I was a slave; and the laws held out no prospect of emancipation. All the efforts in the world could not better my condition; all the efforts in the world could not prevent me from falling—perhaps to-morrow—into the hands of another master, as cruel and unreasonable as evil passions and hard-heartedness could make him. The future offered only the chance of evils. I might starve with cold and hunger as well as another; I might perish by gun-shot wounds, or the torture of the lash; or be hung up, perhaps, without judge or jury. But of bettering my condition, I had neither chance nor hopes. I was a prisoner for life; at the present moment not suffering for food or clothing, but without the slightest prospect of liberation; and likely enough at any moment to change my keeper, and under the discipline of a new gaoler, to feel the pinchings of cold and hunger, and to tremble daily beneath the whip. I was cut off and excluded from all those hopes and wishes, which are the chief impulses of human action. I could not aim to become the master of a little cottage, which, however humble, I might call my own: to be the lord of one poor acre, which, however small or barren, might still be mine. I could not marry—alas, poor Cassy!—and become the father of a family, with the fond hope, that when age should overtake me, I might still find pleasure and support in the kindness of children and the sympathy of a wife. My children might be snatched from the arms of their mother, and sold to the slave-trader; the mother might be sent to keep them company,—and I be left old, desolate, uncomforted. Motives such as these, motives which strengthen the freeman's arm and cheer his heart, were unfelt by me. I laboured;—but it was only because I feared the lash. The want of willingness unnerved me, and every stroke cost a new effort.

It is even true, that Major Thornton's humanity, or to speak more correctly, his sense of his own interest, while it preserved his servants from the miseries of hunger and nakedness, at the same time exposed those among them, whom slavery and ignorance had not completely brutalized, to other and more excruciating miseries. Had we been but half fed and half clothed, like the servants on several of the neighbouring plantations, we should, like them, have enjoyed the excitement of plunder. We should have found some exercise for our ingenuity, and some object about which to interest ourselves, in plans and stratagems for eking out our short allowance by the aid of theft.

As it was, stealing was but little practised at Oakland. The inducement was too small, and the risk too great; for detection was certain to result in being sold. Money was no object to us; we could only spend it on food and clothes, and of these we had enough already. Whisky was the only luxury we wanted; and we could make enough to purchase that without the necessity of theft. Mr. Thornton allowed each of us a little piece of ground. That was customary; but what was quite contrary to custom, he allowed us time to cultivate it. He endeavoured to stimulate our industry by the promise of buying all we could produce, not at a mere nominal price, as was the fashion on other plantations, but at its full value.

I am sorry to say it, but it is not the less true, that Major Thornton's people, like all slaves who have the means and the opportunity, were generally drunkards. Our master took good care that whisky did not interfere with our work. To be drunk before the task was finished was a high misdemeanour. But after the day's labour was over we were at liberty to drink as much as we pleased; provided always that it did not prevent us turning out at daylight the next morning. Sunday was generally a grand Saturnalia.

Hitherto I had scarcely been in the habit of drinking; but now I began to be eager for anything which promised to sustain my sinking spirits, and to excite my stagnant soul. I soon found in whisky a something that seemed to answer the purpose. In that elevation of heart which drunkenness inspires, that forgetfulness of the past and the present, that momentary halo with which it crowns the future, I found a delight which I hastened to repeat, and knew not how to forego. Reality was to me a blank, dark and dreary. Action was forbidden; desire was chained; and hope shut out. I was obliged to find relief in dreams and illusions. Drunkenness, which degrades the freeman to a level with the brutes, raises, or seems to raise, the slave to the dignity of a man. It soon became my only pleasure, and I indulged it to excess. Every day, as soon as my task was finished, I hastened to shut myself up with my bottle. I drank in solitude—for, much as I loved the excitement of drunkenness, I could not forget its beastliness and insanity, and I hated to expose my folly to the sight of my fellow-servants. But my precautions were not always successful. In the frenzy of excitement I sometimes forgot all my sober precautions, undid the bolts I had carefully fastened, and sought the company I most desired to shun.

One Sunday, I had been drinking till I was no longer the master of my own actions. I had left my house, and gone to seek some boon companions with whom to protract the revel and increase its zest. But I was unable to distinguish one object from another; and after straggling off for some distance, I sunk down, almost insensible, upon the carriage way which led towards Major Thornton's house.

I had grown a little more sober, and was endeavouring to rally my thoughts and to recollect where I was, and what had brought me there, when I saw my master riding up the road with two other gentlemen They were all on horseback; and as drunk as I was, I saw at a glance, that my master's two companions were very much in the same predicament. The manner in which they reeled backward and forward in their saddles was truly laughable; and I expected every moment to see them fall. I made these observations as I lay upon the road, without once thinking where I was, or recollecting the danger I was in of being ridden over. They had come quite near before they noticed me. By this time I was sitting up, and my master's drunken companions took it into their heads to jump their horses over me. Major Thornton did his best to prevent them; one he succeeded in stopping, but the other evaded his attempt to seize the bridle, swore that the sport was too pretty to be lost, put spurs to his horse, and brought him up to the leap.

But the horse had no fancy for this sort of sport. When he saw me before him, he started back, and his drunken rider came tumbling to the ground. The others dismounted, and went to his assistance. Before he was well upon his feet, he begged Major Thornton's attention, and forthwith commenced a very grave lecture on the indecency of allowing servants to get drunk, and to lie about the plantation,—particularly across the roads, frightening gentlemen's horses, and putting the necks of their riders into jeopardy. "Especially you, Major Thornton, who pretend to be a pattern for all of us. Yes, sir, yes, if you did as you ought to do, every time one of the rascal fellows had the insolence to get drunk, you would tie him up and give him forty lashes. That's the way I do on my plantation."

My master was so very fond of setting forth his method of farming, and his plan of plantation discipline, that he did not always stop to consider whether his auditors were drunk or sober. The present opportunity was too good to be lost, and, rubbing his hands together, he answered, with a half smile, and a very sagacious look,—" But, my dear sir, you must know it is a part of my plan to let my servants drink as much as they please, so that it does not interfere with their tasks. Poor fellows! it serves to keep them out of mischief, and soon makes them so stupid they are the easiest creatures in the world to manage." Here he paused a minute, and assuming the look which a man puts on who thinks he is going to urge an unanswerable argument—" Besides," he added, "if one of these drinking fellows happens to take a huff, and runs away, the very first thing he does is to get drunk, so that you seldom have any difficulty in catching him."

Though I was still too much under the influence of whisky to be capable of much muscular motion, I had so far recovered my senses as to comprehend perfectly all that my master was saying; and no sooner had he finished, than, drunk as I was, I made a resolution to drink no more. I was not yet so far lost as to be able to endure the idea of being myself the instrument of my own degradation. My resolution was well kept, for I have seldom tasted spirits since that day.

CHAPTER XVI.

IT is the lot of the slave to be exposed, in common with other men, to all the calamities of chance and all the caprices of fortune. But, unlike other men, he is denied the consolation of struggling against them. He is bound hand and foot; and his sufferings are aggravated tenfold by the bitter idea that he is not allowed to help himself, or to make any attempt to escape the blow which he sees impending over him. This idea of utter helplessness is one of the most distressing in nature; it is twin-sister to Despair.

Major Thornton, by over-exertion and imprudent exposure, brought on a fever, which in a short time assumed a very unfavourable aspect. It was the first time he had been sick for many years. The alarm, and even terror, which the news of his danger excited at Oakland was very great. Every morning and evening we collected about the house to learn how our master did; and mournful were the faces, and sad the hearts, with which we heard the bitter words, "no better." The women at Oakland had always been treated with peculiar indulgence, such as their sex and weakness demands,—but demands so often without obtaining it. Major Thornton's illness gave an instance how full of gratitude is the female heart, and at what a trifling expense one may purchase its most zealous affection. All the women on the place were anxious to be employed in some way in ministering to the comfort of their suffering master. The most disagreeable duties were eagerly performed; and if ever man was tenderly and assiduously nursed, it was Major Thornton. But all this care, all our sympathy, our sorrow, and our terrors, were of no effect. The fever raged with unabated fury, and seemed to find new fuel in the strength of the patient's constitution. But that fuel was soon exhausted, and in ten days our master was no more.

When his decease became known, we looked upon each other in silent consternation. A family of helpless orphans, from whom death had just snatched their last surviving parent, could not have felt a greater destitution. Tears rolled down the cheeks of the men; and the lamentations of the women were violent and wild. His old nurse, in particular, wept, and would not listen to any consolation. She had good reason. At his father's death she had been sold, with the other property, to satisfy the creditors. But Major Thornton had repurchased her, out of his very first earnings; he had made her the head servant of his household, and had always treated her with great tenderness. The old woman loved him like her own child, and lamented her "dear son Charley," as she called him, with all the pathetic energy of a widowed and childless mother.

We all attended the funeral, and followed our dead master to the grave. The hollow sound of the earth as it fell upon the coffin was echoed back from every bosom; and when this last sad office was finished, we stood over the spot, and wept together. Doubt not the sincerity of of our sorrow! It was for ourselves we were lamenting.

Major Thornton was never married; and he left no children whose rights the laws acknowledged. If he had intended to make a will, his sudden death prevented him; and his property passed to a troop of cousins, for whom, I suspect, he did not entertain any great affection. At all events, I had never seen any of them at Oakland, nor could I learn from the other servants that either of them had ever made a visit there. It was thus that we became the property of strangers, who had never seen us, and whom we had never seen.

These heirs-at-law were poor as well as numerous, and seemed very eager to turn all the property into money, so as to get their several shares with the least possible delay. An order of court, or whatever the legal process might be called, was soon obtained; and the sale of the slaves was advertised to take place at the county court-house. The agent to whom the care of the estate was intrusted made the necessary preparations. Of course, it was not thought expedient that we should know what was going on, or what our new owners intended to do with us. The secret was carefully kept, lest some of us should run away.

The day before that which had been appointed for the sale we were collected together. The able-bodied men and women were handcuffed and chained in a string. A few old grey-headed people and the younger children were carried in a cart. The rest of us were driven along like cattle—men, women, and children together. Three fellows on horseback, with the usual equipment of long whips, served at once as guards and drivers.

I shall not attempt to describe our affliction. It would be but the repetition of an oft-told tale. Who has not read of slave-traders on the coast of Africa? Whose heart has not ached at picturing the terrors and despair of the kidnapped victims? Our case was much the same. Many of us had been born and reared at Oakland, and all looked upon it as a home; nay more, as a city of refuge, where we had always been safe from gratuitous insults and aggressions. From this home we were now snatched away, without a moment's warning; and were driven chained to the slave-market to be sold to the highest bidder.

Is it strange that we were reluctant to go? Had we been setting out, of our own accord, to seek our fortunes, we could not have broken, all at once, all the ties that bound us to Oakland without some throbs of natural grief. What, then, must have been our anguish to leave it as we did?

But the tears of the men, the sobs of the women, and the cries and errors of the poor children, availed us nothing. Our conductors cracked their whips, and made a jest of our lamentations. Our sorrowful procession moved slowly on; and many a sad lingering look we cast behind us. We said nothing; and our melancholy reflections were only interrupted by the curses, shouts, and loud laughter of our drivers.

We lodged that night by the road side; our drivers sleeping and keeping watch by turns. The next day we reached the county courthouse, and at the appointed hour the sale began. The company was not very numerous, and the bidders seemed extremely shy. Many of our late master's neighbours were present. One of them remarked that several of us were fine stout fellows, but, for his part he should be afraid to buy any of the Thornton hands, for we had been so spoiled by our late master's foolish indulgence, that one of us would be enough to spread discontent through a whole neighbourhood. This speech was received with evident applause, and it had its intended effect. The auctioneer did his best, and harangued most eloquently upon our healthy, sound, and plump condition. "As to the over-indulgence that gentleman speaks about," he added, "a good cow-hide and strict discipline will soon bring them into proper subordination; and from what I have heard of that gentleman's own management, he is the very person who ought to buy them." A slight titter ran through the company at this sally of the auctioneer's, but it did not seem to make the bidding much brisker. We went off at very moderate prices. Most of the younger men and women and a large proportion of the children were bought by a slave-trader, who had come on purpose to attend the sale. It was very difficult to get a bid for several of the old people. Mr. Thornton's nurse, who, as I have mentioned, had been his housekeeper, and a person of no little consequence at Oakland, was knocked off for twenty dollars. She was bought by an old fellow well known in the neighbourhood for his cruelty to his servants. He shook his head as the auctioneer's hammer struck the table, grinned a significant smile, and said he believed the girl was yet able to handle a hoe; any how, he would get one summer's work out of her. The old lady had scarcely held up her head since the death of her master; but she forgot all her sorrows, she forgot even to deplore the lot that seemed to await her, in her anger at being sold at so small a price. She turned to her purchaser, and with an indignant air told him that she was both younger and stronger than folks thought for, and assured him that he had made the best bargain of any of the company. The old fellow chuckled, but said nothing. It was easy to read his thoughts. He was evidently resolving to hold the old woman to her word.

Some of the old and decrepit slaves could not be sold at all. They were not worth purchasing, and nobody would make an offer. I do not know what became of them.

The slave-dealer who had purchased most of the children declined buying such of the mothers as were past the age of child-bearing. The parting of these mothers from their children was a new scene of misery and lamentation. The poor things, snatched a little while before from the home of their birth and their infancy, and now, torn from the mothers that bore and nursed them, clasped their little hands, and shrieked with all the unrestrained vehemence of infant agony. The mothers wept too; but their grief was more subdued. There was one old woman, the mother, she said, of fifteen children. One little girl, about ten or twelve years old, was all that remained to her. The others had been sold and scattered, she knew not whither. She was now to part from her youngest and only remaining child. The little girl clung to her mother's dress with all the terror of one who was about to be kidnapped, and her screams and cries might have touched a heart of stone. Her new master snatched the child away, hit her a cut with his whip, and bade her hold her "cursed clatter." A slave-trader, however he may have the exterior of a gentleman, is in fact the same ferocious barbarian, whether on the coast of Guinea or in the heart of the "Ancient Dominion."

When our new master had completed his purchases he prepared to set out with his drove. He was one of a slave-dealing firm, whose head-quarters were at the city of Washington, the seat of the federal government, and the capital of the United States of America. It was to this place that he intended to carry us. The whole purchase was about forty head, consisting in nearly equal proportions of men, women, and children. We were joined in couples by iron collars about our necks, which were connected by a link of iron. To these connecting-links a heavy chain was fastened, extending from one end of the drove to the other. Besides all this, the right and left hands of every couple were fastened together by hand-cuffs, and another chain passed along these fastenings. The collars about our necks, with their connecting-chain, might have been thought, perhaps, under ordinary circumstances, a sufficient security; but as our new master had heard from Major Thornton's neighbours, who were present at the sale, that we were "a set of very dangerous fellows," he thought it best, as he said, to omit no *reasonable* means of security.

The drove was presently put in motion. Our purchasers, with two or three assistants, rode beside us on horseback, armed with whips, as usual. The journey was slow, sad, and wearisome. We travelled without any goodwill; the poor children harassed with the weight of their chains, and unaccustomed to fatigue; and all of us faint for want of food—for our new master was an economist, who spent as little on the road as possible.

I will not dwell upon the tedious monotony of our sufferings and our journey. Suffice it to say, that after travelling for several days, we crossed the noble and wide-spreading Potomac, and late at night began to enter the federal city. Perhaps I ought to say, the place where the federal city was to be,—for Washington, at that time seemed only a straggling village, scattered over a wide extent of ground, and interspersed with deserted fields, overgrown with bushes. There were some indications, however, of the future metropolis. The Capitol, though unfinished, was rearing its spacious walls in the moonlight, and gave promise of a magnificent edifice. Lights gleamed from the windows. The Congress perhaps was in session. I gazed at the building with no little emotion. "This," said I to myself, "is the head-quarters of a great nation, the spot in which its concentrated wisdom is collected, to devise laws for the benefit of the whole community—the just and equal laws of a free people and a great democracy!" I was going on with this mental soliloquy, when the iron collar about my neck touched a place from which it had rubbed the skin; and as I started with the pain, the rattling of chains reminded me, that "these just and equal laws of a free people and a great democracy" did not avail to rescue a million* of bondmen from hopeless servitude; and the cracking of our drivers' whips told too plainly that

---

* The slaves in the United States are now near three millions and a half. It ought perhaps to be added, that by the federal constitution the general government has no right to interfere with the question of slavery in the States. The legislature of each State is the sole judge of that question, within its own limits.

within a stone's throw of the Temple of Liberty—nay, under its very porticos—the most brutal, odious, and detestable tyranny, found none to rebuke, or to forbid it. What sort of liberty is it whose chosen city is a slave-market?—and what that freedom, which permits the bravado insolence of a slave-trading aristocracy to lord it in the very halls of her legislation?

We passed up the street which led by the Capitol, and presently arrived at the establishment of Savage, Brothers and Co., our new masters. Half an acre of ground, more or less, was enclosed with a wall some twelve feet high, well armed at the top with iron spikes and pieces of broken bottles. In the centre of the enclosure was a low brick building of no great size, with a few narrow grated windows, and a stout door, well secured with bars and padlocks. This was the establishment used by Messrs. Savage, Brothers and Co. as a warehouse, in which they stowed away such slaves as they purchased from time to time, in the neighbouring country, to be kept till they were ready to send them off in droves, or to ship them to the south. In common with all the slave-hunting gentry, Messrs. Savage, Brothers, and Co. had the free use of the city prison; but this was not large enough for the scale on which they carried on operations; so they had built a prison of their own. It was under the management of a regular gaoler, and was very much like any other gaol. The slaves were allowed the liberty of the yard during the day-time; but at sunset they were all locked up promiscuously in the prison. This was small, and ill-ventilated; and the number that was forced into it was sometimes very great. While I was confined there the heat and stench were often intolerable; and many a morning I came out of it with a burning thirst and a high fever.

The states of Maryland and Virginia claim the honour of having exerted themselves for the abolition of the African slave-trade. It is true they were favourable to that measure,—and they had good reasons of their own for being so. They gained the credit of humanity by the same vote that secured them the monopoly of a domestic trade in slaves, which bids fair to rival any traffic ever prosecuted on the coast of Africa. The African traffic they have declared to be piracy, while the domestic slave-trade flourishes in the heart of their own territories, a just, legal, and honourable commerce!

The district of Colombia, which includes the city of Washington, and which is situated between the two states above mentioned, has become, from the convenience of its situation, and other circumstances, the centre of these slave-trading operations,—an honour which it shares, however, with Richmond and Baltimore, the chief towns of Virginia and Maryland. The lands of these two states have been exhausted by a miserable and inefficient system of cultivation, such as ever prevails where farms are large and the labourers enslaved. Their produce is the same with the productions of several of the free states north and west of them; and they are every day sinking faster and faster under the competition of free labour, to which they are exposed.

Many a Virginian planter can only bring his revenue even with his expenditures, by selling every year a slave or two. This practice, jocularly, but at the same time significantly known as "eating a negro"

Slavery, however, is still tolerated within the district of Columbia, which includes the city of Washington, over which Congress has an exclusive right of legislation. It is to be hoped that the people of the free States will not be deterred by the insolent and ferocious spirit of the slave-holders from doing themselves the justice to abolish slavery wherever it is within their power.—ED.

—a phrase worthy of slave-holding humanity—is becoming every day more and more common. A very large number of planters have ceased to raise crops with the expectation of profit. They endeavour to make the produce of their lands pay their current expenses; but all their hopes of gain are confined to the business of raising slaves for the southern market; and that market is as regularly supplied with slaves from Virginia as with mules and horses from Kentucky.

But the slave-trade in America, as well as in Africa, carries with it the curse of depopulation; and, together with the emigration which is constantly going on, has already unpeopled great tracts of country in the lower part of Virginia, and is fast restoring the first seats of Anglo-American population to all their original wildness and solitude. Whole counties almost are grown up in useless and impenetrable thickets, already retenanted by deer and other wild game, their original inhabitants.

CHAPTER XVII.

WE were driven into the prison-yard, through a stout gate well studded with iron nails. The heavy padlocks of the prison-door were unfastened, and we were thrust in, without further ceremony. A faint glimmer of moonlight stole in at the narrow and grated windows of the prison; but it was some time before I was able to distinguish one object from another. When at length my eyes had accommodated themselves to the faintness of the light, I found myself crowded into the midst of perhaps a hundred human beings,—most of them young men and women between the ages of eighteen and twenty-five,—closely packed on the bare floor.

A considerable number started up at our entrance, and began to crowd about us, and to inquire who we were, and whence we came. They seemed glad of anything to break the monotony of their confinement. But wearied and fatigued, we were in no humour for talking; and sinking down upon the floor of our prison, notwithstanding the poisonous stench, and the confined and impure atmosphere, we were soon buried in profound slumbers. Sleep is the dearest solace of the wretched; and there is this sweet touch of mercy in it, that it ever closes the eyes of the oppressed, more willingly than those of the oppressor. I hardly think that any member of the firm of Savage, Brothers, and Co. slept so soundly that night, as did the most unquiet of their newly purchased victims.

Day came—the prison-door was unlocked, and we were let out into the inclosure about it. The scanty allowance of corn-bread which the penuriousness of our wealthy but economical masters allowed us, was doled out to each. My meal finished, I sat down upon the ground, and observed the scene about me. With a few exceptions, the prisoners were collected in groups, some containing two or three, and others a much larger number. The men were more numerous than the women, though the females had received a considerable addition from our party. The acquaintance of these new comers was eagerly sought for, and they were constantly receiving solicitations to enter into temporary unions, to last while the parties remained together. Most of the women whom we found in the prison had already formed connections of this sort.

These courtships, if so they should be called, were still going on, when a tall young fellow, with a very quizzical face, produced a three-stringed fiddle, and after preluding for a few moments, struck up a lively tune. The sound of the music soon drew a large group about him, who provided themselves with partners and began a dance. As the fiddler warmed to his business, he played faster and faster; and the dancers, amidst laughs and shouts and boisterous merriment, did their best to keep up with the tune.

It is thus that men, whenever their natural sources of enjoyment fail them, betake themselves to artificial excitements. Too often, we sing and dance, not because we are merry, but in the hope to become so; and merriment itself is seldomer the expression and the evidence of pleasure, than the disguise of weariness and pain, the hollow echo of an aching heart.

But the entire company did not join the dancers. As it happened, it was Sunday; and a part of them seemed to entertain conscientious scruples about dancing on that, and for aught I know, upon any other day. The more sober part of the company gradually collected together in the opposite corner of the prison-yard; and a sedate young man, with a handsome and intelligent face, mounted upon the head of an empty barrel which happened to be standing there, and taking a hymn-book from his pocket, struck up a Methodist psalm. His voice was sweet and clear, and his singing far from disagreeable. He was soon joined by several others; and as the chorus swelled, the sound of the psalmody almost drowned the scraping of the fiddle and the laughter of the dancers. I observed, too, that several of the dancing party cast their eyes from time to time wistfully towards the singers; and before the psalm was half finished several of the females had stolen softly away, and mingled in the group collected about the preacher. The singing being ended, he began to pray. His hands were clasped and raised, and he spoke with a ready fluency and a natural earnestness and unction not always heard from a regular clergyman in a cushioned pulpit. Tears ran down many a face, and sighs and groans almost drowned the voice of the speaker. These perhaps were mere practised responses, as artificial and as little sincere as the drawl of the parish clerk in the English church service. And yet in some cases they had every appearance of being genuine bursts of natural feeling,—an involuntary tribute to the eloquence and fervour of the speaker.

Next followed the exhortation. The text was from Job; and the preacher began upon the trite subject of patience. But like all ignorant and illiterate speakers, he soon deserted his original topic, and ran on from one thing to another with very little of method or connection. Now and then some sparks of sense were struck out; but they were speedily quenched in a flood of absurdity. It was a strange farrago; but it was delivered with a volubility, an earnestness, and a force, which produced a strong effect upon the hearers. It was not long before he had worked them up to a pitch of excitement which far surpassed that of the dancers in the opposite corner. Indeed, the dancing group grew thinner and thinner, and the squeak of the fiddle sounded weaker and weaker, till at last the fiddler threw down his instrument, and with his remaining adherents hastened to swell the audience of a performer whose powers so much out-matched his own.

As the sermon proceeded, the groans and cries of mercy and amen grew louder and more frequent, and several, overcome by their feelings, or wishing, or affecting to be so, fell flat upon the ground, and screamed and shouted as if they were possessed by evil spirits. So strong was the contagion, and so powerful the sympathetic infectiousness of this spiritual intoxication, that I, a mere looker-on, felt a strong impulse to rush among the crowd, and to shriek and shout with the rest. The paroxysm was now at its height, and the speaker was almost exhausted by his vehement gesticulation, when, stamping his foot with more than common energy, he burst in the head of the barrel and tumbled headlong among his auditors.

This unlucky accident instantly converted the cries and groans of his hearers into shouts of irrepressible laughter, and they seemed to pass all at once from a state of the utmost terror and solemnity into outrageous and uncontrollable merriment. The fiddler crept out from amidst the hurly-burly, caught up his fiddle, and struck up a lively air,—I forget the name of it, but I recollect very well that it contained some allusion to the disaster of his rival. The dance was renewed, while the preacher, with a few of his more attached hearers, slunk away mortified and disheartened. The dancers grew more boisterous, and the fiddler played his best, till at last the party had fairly tired themselves out, and were too much exhausted to keep it up any longer.

Men born and bred in slavery are not men, but children; their faculties are never permitted to unfold themselves, and it is the aim of their masters, and the necessary effect of their condition, to keep them in a state of perpetual imbecility. Tyranny is ever hostile to every species of mental development, for a state of ignorance involves of necessity a state of degradation and of helplessness.

I soon made myself acquainted with a number of my fellow-prisoners, and entered into conversation with them. Some of them had been in the jail a fortnight, and others longer. I presently discovered that they considered their confinement as a sort of holiday. They had nothing to do; and not to be compelled to work seemed for them the supreme idea of happiness. As to being confined within the walls of a prison, they had the liberty of the yard, and it was just as agreeable being shut up within four brick walls as to be prisoner on a plantation, forbidden to go beyond the line of its zig-zag fences. Then they had no overseer to harass them, and nothing to do but to dance and sleep; nothing was wanted but a little whiskey, and even that was not always wanting. They seemed anxious to drown all memory of the past and all dread of the future, and to bask without concern in the sunshine of their present felicity.

CHAPTER XVIII.

I HAD been in the jail ten days or a fortnight, when Messrs. Savage, Brothers, and Co., selected from among their chattels a cargo of slaves for the Charleston market. I was one of the number, and with some fifty others was loaded on board a small vessel bound for that port. The captain's name was Jonathan Osborne; he was a citizen of Boston, and the vessel, the brig Two Sallys, belonged to that port, and was the property of a rich and respectable merchant.

The people of the northern states of the American Union talk finely upon the subject of slavery, and express a very proper indignation at its horrors; yet while the African slave-trade was permitted their merchants carried it on, and these same merchants do not always refuse to employ their vessels in the domestic slave-trade, a traffic not one iota less base and detestable.

Northern statesmen have permitted slavery where no constitutional objections prevented them from abolishing it; the courts and lawyers of the north scrupulously fulfil to the utmost letter, the constitutional obligation to restore to the southern master the victim who has escaped his grasp, and fled to the "free states," in the vain hope of protection; whilst the whole north looks calmly on, and tamely suffers the southern slave-holders to violate all the provisions of that same constitution, and to imprison, torture, and put to death, the citizens of the north without judge or jury, whenever they imagine that such severities can contribute in the slightest degree to the security of their slave-holding tyranny. Nay, more; many of the northern aristocrats, in the energy of their hatred of democratical equality, seem almost ready to envy, while they affect to deplore, the condition of their southern brethren. And yet the northern states of the union dare to assert that they are undefiled by the stain of slavery. It is a vain, false boast. They are partners in the wrong. The blood of the slave is on their hands, and is dripping in red and gory drops from the skirts of their garments.

Before leaving the prison, we were supplied with handcuffs, those usual badges and emblems of servitude, and having reached the wharf, we were crammed together into the hold of the vessel, so close that we had hardly room to move, and not room enough either to lie or sit with comfort. The vessel got under way soon after we came on board, and proceeded down the river. Once or twice a-day we were suffered to come on deck, and to breathe the fresh air for a few minutes; but we were soon remanded to our dungeon in the hold. The mate of the vessel seemed to be a good-natured young man, and disposed to render our condition as comfortable as possible; but the captain was a savage tyrant, worthy of the business in which he was engaged.

We had been on our voyage a day or two, and had already cleared the river, and were standing down the bay, when I became excessively sick. A burning fever seemed raging in my veins. It was after sunset; the hatches were closed down; and the heat of the narrow hold in which we were confined, and which was more than half filled up with boxes and barrels, became intolerable. I knocked against the deck, and called aloud for air and water. It was the mate's watch. He came forward to ascertain what was the matter, and bade the men unfasten the hatches and lift me upon deck. I snatched the basin of water which he gave me, and though brackish and warm, it seemed to my feverish taste the most delicious of drinks. I drained it to the bottom and called for more; but the mate, who feared perhaps that excessive drinking might aggravate my disorder, refused this request. I wanted air as much as water. This he did not refuse me; and I was lying on the deck, imbibing at every pore the cool breeze of the evening, when the captain came up the companion-way.

He no sooner saw the hatches off, and me lying on the deck, than he stepped up to his mate, with a clenched fist, and a face distorted with passion, and addressed him with "How dare you, sir, take off the hatches after sundown, without my orders?"

The mate attempted an apology, and began with saying that I was taken suddenly sick, and had called for assistance; but without waiting to hear him out, the brutal captain rushed by, and hitting me a kick, precipitated me headlong into the hold, upon the heads of my companions. Without stopping to inquire whether or not my neck was broken, he bade his men replace and secure the hatches. Luckily I sustained but little injury; though I came within an inch of having my skull broken against one of the beams. The water I had drank, and the cool air I had breathed, abated my fever, and I soon began to grow better.

In the course of the next day, we passed the capes of the Chesapeake, and entered the great Atlantic. We stood to the southward and eastward, and were making rapid way, when it came on to blow a furious gale. The tossing and pitching of the ship was terrible indeed to us poor prisoners confined in the dark hold, and expecting, at every burst of thunder, that the vessel was breaking in pieces. The storm continued to increase. The noise and tumult on deck, the creaking of the rigging, the cries of the seamen, and the sound of cracking spars and splitting canvas, added to our terror. Pretty soon we found that the hold was filling with water, and an alarm was given that the vessel had sprung a leak. The hatches were opened, and we were called on deck. Our handcuffs were knocked off, and we were set to work at the pumps.

I could not tell whether it were night or morning; for the gale had now lasted a good while, and since it began, we had not been suffered to come on deck. However it was not totally dark. A dim and horrid glimmer, just sufficient to betray our situation, and more terrible perhaps than total darkness, was hovering over the ocean. At a distance, the huge black waves, crested with pale blue foam, seemed to move on like monsters of the deep; nor when nearer did they lose any of their terrors. Now we sunk into a horrid gulf, between two watery precipices, which swelled on either side, black and frowning, and ready to devour us; and now, lifted on the top of a lofty wave, we viewed all around, a wild and fearful waste of dark and stormy waters. It was a terrible sight for one who had never seen the sea before; and as I gazed upon it, half stupified with terror, little did I think that this same fierce and raging element was to prove hereafter my best and surest friend.

The brig was almost a total wreck. Her foremast was gone by the board, and she was lying-to on the starboard tack, under a close-reefed main-top-sail. These are terms which at that time I had never heard. It was long afterwards that I learned to use them. But the whole scene remains as distinct upon my memory as if it had been painted there.

Notwithstanding all our efforts, the leak gained upon us; and the captain soon made up his mind that it would be impossible to keep the vessel afloat. Accordingly, he made his preparations for quitting her. He and his mates were armed with swords and pistols; and cutlasses were put into the hands of two or three of the crew. The long boat had been washed overboard; but they had succeeded in securing the jolly boat, which they now lowered away and dropped into the water, under the vessel's lee. The crew were already embarking, before we well understood what they were about; but as soon as we comprehended that they were going to desert the ship, we rushed franticly forward, and demanded to be taken on board. This they had expected, and they were prepared for it. Three or four pistol shots were fired among us, and several of us were severely wounded by the sailors' cutlasses. At the same time, they cried to us to stand back, and they would take us on board as soon as all things were ready. Terrified and confused, we stood a moment doubting what to do. The sailors improved this interval to jump on board,—"Cast off," shouted the captain,—the seamen bent to their oars, and the boat was fast quitting the vessel before we had recovered from our momentary hesitation.

We raised a shout, or rather a scream of terror, at finding ourselves thus deserted; and three or four poor wretches, on the impulse of the moment, sprang into the water, in the hope of reaching the boat. All but one sunk instantly in the boiling surge; he, a man of herculean frame, springing with all the effort of a death-struggle, was carried far beyond the rest, and rising through the billows, found himself just behind the boat. He stretched out his hand and caught the rudder. The captain was steering. He drew a pistol and fired it at the head of the swimmer. We heard a scream above all the noise of the tempest. It was only for a moment; he sunk, and we saw him no more.

It is impossible to convey any adequate idea of the terror and confusion which now prevailed on board. The women, now screaming, now praying, were frantic with fear. Four or five poor fellows lay about the deck bleeding and desperately wounded. Death seemed to ride upon the storm, and to summon his victims. The vessel still lay with her head to windward; but the spray dashed over her continually, and every now and then she shipped a sea, which set the decks afloat; and drenched us in salt water. It occurred to me, that unless the pumps were kept going, the vessel would soon fill and carry us to the bottom. I called about me such of the men as seemed to be most in their senses, and endeavoured to explain to them our situation; but they were stupified with terror, and would not, or could not, understand me. As a last resource, I rushed forward, crying—"Pump, my hearties, pump, for your lives!" This was the phrase which the captain and his mates had continually repeated, as they stood over us and directed our labour. The poor creatures seemed to obey, as if instinctively, this voice of command. They collected about me and began to work the pumps. If it had no other good effect, at least it served to call off our attention from the horrors with which we were surrounded. We plied our work till one of the pumps was broken, and the other choked and rendered useless. By this time the storm had abated, and the vessel, notwithstanding all our fears to the contrary, still rode the waves.

It grew lighter by degrees. Presently, the clouds began to break away, and to drive in huge, misty masses along the sky. Occasionally the sun broke out; and, after a considerable dispute whether it were rising or setting, we concluded it must be some four or five hours past sunrise.

As soon as the women had recovered from the first paroxysm of their terror, they gave such care as they could to the poor sufferers, who had been wounded. They had bound up their wounds, and had collected them together on the quarter-deck. One poor fellow, who had been shot through the body with a pistol-ball, was much worse hurt than the others. His wife was supporting his head on her lap, and was trying to prevent the pitching of the vessel from aggravating his sufferings. She had been standing by him, or rather clinging to him, at the moment he was wounded. She had caught him in her arms as he fell, had dragged him from the press, and from that moment seemed to forget all the horrors of our situation, in her incessant efforts to soothe his pains. Her affectionate care had proved of little avail. The struggle was now almost over. In a little while he expired in her arms. When she found that he was dead, her grief, which she had controlled and suppressed so long, burst forth in all its energy. Her female companions gathered about her; but the poor woman was beyond the reach of consolation.

Some of us now ventured below, and took the liberty of overhauling the steward's stores. Everything was more or less damaged with salt water; but we lighted upon a cask or two of bread, which was tolerably dry, and which sufficed to furnish us a sumptuous repast.

We had not finished it before we discovered a vessel standing towards us. As she approached, we waved fragments of the tattered sails, and shouted for assistance. Having run down pretty near us, she hove to, and sent a boat on board. When the boat's crew had mounted over the brig's side, they seemed utterly amazed at the scene which her decks presented. I stepped forward, and explained to the officer the nature of our situation; that we were a cargo of slaves bound from Washington to Charleston, and that the vessel and her lading had been deserted by the crew; that contrary to every expectation, we had succeeded in keeping her afloat, but that the pumps were out of order and she was again filling.

The mate hastened back to his own ship, and soon returned with the captain and the carpenter. After examining and consulting together, they determined to put a part of their own crew on board the brig, and to navigate her into Norfolk, to which port they were bound, and which was the nearest harbour. The carpenter was put to work stopping her leaks and repairing her pumps. Her new crew set up a jury foremast out of such materials as they found on board. She was soon in sailing order, and they shook the reefs out of her maintopsail and put her before the wind.

The vessel which had rescued us was the "Arethusa," of New York, Charles Parker, master; and lest we might need assistance, she slackened sail and kept us company. Before night we made the land, and a pilot came on board. The next morning we entered the harbour of Norfolk. The vessel had scarcely touched the wharf, before we were hurried away, and locked up in the city gaol for safe keeping.

CHAPTER XIX.

WE remained in gaol some three weeks before anybody condescended to inform us why we were kept there, or what was to become of us. We now learned that Captain Parker and his crew had libelled the Two Sallys and her cargo for salvage, and that the court had ordered the libelled property to be sold at auction, for the joint benefit of the owners and salvors. This was all Greek to us. I had not the most distant idea what was meant by "libelling for salvage," and I hardly think that any of the others understood it better than I. Nobody took the trouble to explain it to us; it was enough for us to understand that we were to be sold; the why and the wherefore, it was thought of no consequence for slaves to know.

As I had already been twice sold at public auction, the thing had lost its interest and its novelty. I was tired of the confinement of the prison; and as I knew that I must be sold at last, I was as ready to take my chance now as ever.

The sale was much like other sales of slaves. There was only one circumstance about it that seemed worthy of particular notice. The wounded men, though they were not yet cured, indeed two of the four were hardly thought out of danger, were to be sold among the rest. " Damaged articles," the auctioneer observed, " which he was willing to dispose of at a great discount." The four were offered in one lot,— " Like so many broken frying-pans," said one of the spectators; " but for my part I have no fancy for speculating, either in broken frying-pans, wounded slaves, or sick horses." A physician who was present was advised to purchase. "If they should happen to die," said his adviser, "they would be quite useless to anybody else, but you might find some use for their dead bodies." Various other jests equally brilliant and pointed were thrown out by others of the company, and were received with shouts of laughter that, contrasted a little harshly with the sad woe-begone faces and low moans of the wounded men, who were brought to the place of sale on little pallets, and who lay upon the ground the very pictures of sickness and distress.

This jocular humour had reached a high pitch, when it was rather suddenly checked by a tall fine-looking man, who had more the air and manners of a gentleman than the greater part of the company. He observed, with a tone and a look of some severity, that, in his opinion, selling men upon their deathbeds was no laughing matter. He immediately made a bid quite beyond anything that had been offered, and the auctioneer pronounced him to be the purchaser. I hoped this same gentleman might have purchased me also; but as soon as he had given some directions about the removal of the wounded men, he left the place of sale. Perhaps I had no reason to regret it. This gentleman, for aught I could tell, had acted as a hundred other slave-buyers might have done, from a momentary impulse of humanity, which disgusted him, it is true, with the brutality of the rest of the company, but which in all likelihood was neither strong nor steady enough to render his treatment of his servants much different from that of his neighbours. Such temporary fits of humanity and good nature are occasionally felt by everybody; but they are no guarantee whatever against an habitual disregard of the rights and feelings of those who are not allowed to protect themselves, and who are protected neither by the laws nor by public opinion.

I was purchased by an agent of Mr. James Carleton, of Carleton Hall, in one of the northern counties of North Carolina, and was presently sent off, with two or three of my companions, for the plantation of our new master.

After a journey of four or five days we arrived at Carleton Hall. It was like the residences of so many other American planters, a mean house, with no great signs about it either of ornament or comfort. At a short distance from the house was the servants' quarter, a miserable collection of ruinous cabins, crowded together without any order, and almost concealed in the vigorous growth of weeds that sprung up around and among them.

Soon after our arrival we were carried into the presence of our new master, who examined us one by one, and inquired into our several capabilities. Having learned that I had been raised a house-servant, and being pleased, as he said, with my manners and appearance, he told me he would take me into the house to supply the place of his man John, who had become so confirmed a drunkard that he had been obliged to turn him into the field.

I was well enough pleased with this arrangement; for, in general, those slaves who are house-servants are infinitely better off than those who are employed in field labour. They are better fed, and better clothed, and their work is much lighter. They are sure of the crumbs that fall from their master's table; and as the master's eyes and those of his guests would be offended by a display of dirt and rags in the dining-room, house-servants are comfortably clothed, not so much, it is true, on their own account as for the gratification of their owner's vanity. As it is a matter of ostentation to have a house full of servants, the labour becomes light when divided among so many. Sufficient food, comfortable clothing, and light work, are not to be despised; but the circumstance which principally contributes to make the condition of the houseservant more tolerable than that of the field hand is of a different description. Men, and especially women and children, cannot have anything much about them, be it a dog, a cat, or even a slave, without insensibly contracting some interest in it and regard for it; and it thus happens that a family servant often becomes quite a favourite, and is at length regarded with a feeling that bears some faint and distant resemblance to family affection.

This is the most tolerable—in fact, the only tolerable point of view—in which slavery can be made to present itself; and it has been, by steadily fixing their eyes on a few cases of this sort, and as steadily closing them to all its intrinsic horrors and enormities, that some bold sophists have mustered courage to make the eulogium of slavery.

Yet this best condition of a slave,—that I mean of a household servant,—is often almost too miserable for endurance. If there are kind masters and good-natured mistresses, it happens too frequently that the master is a capricious tyrant and the mistress a fretful scold. The poor servant is exposed, every hour of his life, to a course of harsh rebukes and peevish chidings, which are always threatening to end in the torture of the lash, and which to a person of any spirit or sensibility are more annoying than even the lash itself. And all this is without hope or chance of remedy. The master and the mistress indulge their bad humour without restraint. No fear of " warning " puts any curb upon them. The slave is theirs; and they can treat him as they please. He cannot help himself, and there is no one to help him.

Mr. Carleton, while he entertained most of the notions of his brotherplanters, differed from the greater part of them in one striking particular. He was a zealous Presbyterian, and very warm and earnest in the cause of religion. Had any one told him that to hold men in slavery was a high-handed offence against religion and morality, what would have been his answer? Would his heart have responded to the truth of a sentiment so congenial to every more generous emotion and better feeling? I am much afraid it would not. I fear he would have answered much like those of his brother-slaveholders who made no pretensions whatever to peculiar piety. With a secret consciousness of his criminality, but with a fixed determination never to admit it, he would have worked himself into a violent passion; talked of the " sacred rights of property,"—more sacred in a slaveholder's estimation than either liberty or justice; and declaimed against impertinent interference in the affairs of other people,—a topic, by the way, which is very seldom much insisted upon, except by those whose *affairs* will hardly bear examination.

Mr. Carleton, though a zealous Presbyterian, had, as I have said, most of the feelings and notions of his brother-planters. It thus happened that his character, his conversation, and his conduct were full of strange contrasts, and were for ever presenting an odd, incongruous mixture of the bully and the puritan. I use the word bully for want of a better, not exactly in its most vulgar sense, but intending to signify by it a certain spirit of bravado and violence, a disposition to settle every disputed point by the pistol, so common, I might almost say universal, in the southern States of America. Mr. Carleton, with all his piety, talked as familiarly of shooting people as if he had been a professed assassin.

As I had the honour of waiting upon Mr. Carleton's table, and the pleasure and advantage of listening every day to his conversation, I soon came

to understand his character perfectly,—as perfectly at least as it was possible for anybody to understand so very inconsistent a character. He had
family prayers, night and morning, with the most punctilious regularity.
He prayed long and fervently, and on his bended knees. He was particularly earnest in his petitions for the universal spread of the gospel;
he asked most devoutly that as all men were creatures of the same God
they might speedily become children of the same faith. Yet not only
the plantation slaves were never invited to join in this family worship,
but even the house-servants were excluded. The door was shut, and at
the very moment when the devout Mr. Carleton professed to prostrate
himself in the dust before his Creator he felt too strongly the sense of
his own superiority to permit even his household servants to participate
in his devotions!

But for all this Mr. Carleton evidently had the cause of religion very
much at heart, and seemed ready to spend and be spent in the service.
There were very few clergymen in the part of the country in which he
resided, and his zeal frequently led him to supply the gap, by acting as
an exhorter. Indeed, there was scarcely a Sunday that he did not hold
forth somewhere in the neighbourhood. Within ten miles of Carleton
Hall, in different directions, there were as many as three churches,—
wretched, ruinous, little buildings, that looked more like deserted barns
than places of public worship. All of these Mr. Carleton had caused to
be repaired, principally at his own expense, and in each of them he
preached occasionally. But he did not consider a church as indispensable to an exhortation. During the summer he frequently held meetings in some shady grove, or by the side of some cool spring, and in the
winter sometimes in his own house, and sometimes in the houses of his
neighbours; he was generally pretty sure of a considerable audience.
That part of the country was thinly inhabited, and the people had but
few amusements; they were glad of any occasion of assembling together, and seemed to care very little whether it were a preaching or a
frolic. Besides, Mr. Carleton was really an agreeable speaker; and the
earnestness and vehemence of his manner were well calculated to attract an audience.

A very considerable proportion of his hearers were slaves, for though
he did not judge it expedient to allow them to become partakers in his
private devotions, he had no objection to their swelling his audience,
and giving a sort of éclat to his public performances. Indeed, towards
the end of his discourses he would often condescend to introduce a few
sentences for their particular benefit. The change which took place in
his manner when he came to that part of his sermon was sufficiently
obvious. The phrase "dear brethren," which in the earlier part of it
he was for ever repeating, was now suddenly dropped; the preacher assumed a condescending, patronizing air, and briefly and drily informed
those of his hearers, "whom God had appointed to be servants," that
their only hope of salvation was in patience, obedience, submission, diligence, and subordination. He warned them earnestly against thieving
and lying, their "easily besetting sins;" and enforced at some length
the great wickedness and folly of being discontented with their condition. All this was applauded by the masters as very orthodox doctrine,
and very proper to be preached to servants; the servants themselves
received it with an outward submission, to which their hearts gave the
lie. Nor is it very strange, considering the doctrines which he preached
to them, that the greater part of Mr. Carleton's converts among the
slaves were hypocritical fellows, who made their religion a cloak for
their roguery. There was in fact much truth in the observation of one

of Mr. Carleton's neighbours, that most of the slaves in that part of the country had no religion at all, and that those who pretended to have any were worse than the others. And how could it be otherwise, when in the venerable name of religion they had preached to them a doctrine of double-distilled tyranny—a doctrine which, not content with now and then a human victim, demanded the perpetual sacrifice of one-half the entire community?

Alas, Christianity! What does it avail,—thy concern for the poor, thy tenderness for the oppressed, thy system of fraternal love and affection! The serpent knows how to suck poison from the harmless nature of the dove. The tyrants of every age and country have succeeded in prostituting Christianity into an instrument of their crimes, a terror to their victims, and an apology for their oppressions! Nor have they ever wanted time-serving priests and lying prophets to applaud, encourage, and sustain them!

However little the slaves might relish Mr. Carleton's doctrines,—of which, indeed, their own hearts instinctively made the refutation,—they were very fond of attending upon his performances. It was some relief to the eternal monotony of their lives; and it gave them an opportunity of getting together after the meeting was over, and having a frolic among themselves. This recreation which it afforded to the servants was, in my opinion, the best effect of Mr. Carleton's labours; though certain gentlemen, who dreaded every assembly of slaves as a source of discontent and conspiracy, were very earnest in the condemnation of his meetings, under the hypocritical pretence of being shocked at the violations of the Sabbath, of which they furnished the occasion !

Mr. Carleton was president of a Bible Society, and was very anxious and earnest about the universal diffusion of the Bible. I soon found out, however, that besides myself, there was not a single slave on his plantation, nor, indeed, in all the neighbourhood, who knew how to read : and what was more, I learned that Mr. Carleton was extremely unwilling to have any of them taught.

There is connected with this subject a point of view, in which the system of domestic slavery that prevails in America exhibits itself as out-braving all other tyrannies, and betraying a demoniac spirit almost too horrid to be thought of. Mr. Carleton believed, and the immense majority of his fellow-countrymen believe also, that the Bible contains a revelation from God, of things essential to man's eternal welfare. In this belief, and animated by a lofty spirit of philanthropy, they have formed societies,—and of one of these Mr. Carleton was president,—and contribute their money,—as Mr. Carleton did very liberally,—to disseminate the Bible through the world, and to put this divine and unerring guide into the possession of every family. But while they are so zealous to confer this inestimable treasure upon all the world beside, they sternly withhold it from those, of whom the law has made them the sole guardians. They withhold it from their slaves, of whom, to use their own favourite phrase, God has appointed them the natural protectors; and in so doing, by their own confession, they voluntarily and knowingly expose those slaves to the danger of eternal punishment ! To this awful danger they voluntarily and knowingly expose them, lest, should they learn to read, they might learn, at the same time, their own rights and the means of enforcing them.

What outrage upon humanity was ever equal to this? Other tyrannies have proceeded all lengths against man's temporal happiness, and in support of their evil dominion have hazarded every extreme of temporary cruelty; but what other tyrants are recorded in all the world's

history, who have openly and publicly confessed that they prefer to
expose their victims to the imminent danger of eternal misery, rather
than impart a degree of instruction which might, by possibility, endanger
their own unjust and usurped authority? Can any one calmly consider
the cool diabolism of this avowal, and believe it is men who make it?
Men, too, who seem in other matters not destitute of the common feelings
of good-will; men who talk about liberty, virtue, and religion, and who
speak even of justice and humanity!

Were I inclined to superstition, I should believe they were not men,
but rather demons incarnate;—evil spirits who had assumed the human
shape, and who falsely put on a semblance of human feelings, in order
the more secretly and securely to prosecute their grand conspiracy
against mankind. I should believe so, did I not know that the love of
social superiority, that very impulse of the human heart, which is the
main-spring of civilization and the chief source of all human improvement, is able, when suffered to work on, uncontrolled by other more
generous emotions, to corrupt man's whole nature, and to drive him to
acts the most horrid and detestable. When to the corruptest form of
this fierce passion is joined a base fear, at once cowardly and cruel, what
wonder that man becomes a creature to be scorned and hated? To be
pitied rather; the maniac can hardly be held accountable for the enormities to which his madness prompts him, even though that madness be
self-created.

However diabolical the tyranny may be esteemed, which, to secure its
usurped authority, is ready to sacrifice both the temporal and eternal
happiness of its victims, it is no doubt well adapted to accomplish the
end at which it aims;—namely, its own perpetuation. But it is necessary to go one step further. The slave-holders ought to recollect, that
all knowledge is dangerous, and that it is impossible to give the slaves
any instruction in Christianity without imparting to them some dangerous ideas. It matters not that the law prohibits the teaching them to
read. Oral instruction is as dangerous as written; and the catechism is
nothing but a Bible in disguise. Let them go on then, and bring their
work to a glorious completion. Let them prohibit at once all religious
instruction. They must come to this at last. Let me tell them that the
time is past, in which Mr. Carleton's doctrine of passive obedience is all
that a religious teacher has to utter. There is another spirit abroad;
and that spirit will penetrate wherever religious instruction opens the
way for it. Now-a-day, it is impossible to hail the slave as a Christian
brother without first acknowledging his rights as a fellow-man.

CHAPTER XX.

I HAD not been long in Mr. Carleton's service before I discovered
that a pretty sure way of getting into his good graces was, to be a great
admirer of his religious performances, and a devout attendant upon such
of them as his servants might attend. There never was a person less
inclined by nature to hypocrisy than myself. But craft and cunning
are the sole resource of a slave; and I had long ago learned to practise a
thousand arts, which, at the same time that I despised them, I often
found extremely useful.

For these arts I now had occasion; and I plied my flattery to such purpose, that I soon gained the good-will of my master, and before long was duly established in the situation of confidential servant. This was a station of very considerable respectability; and next to the overseer, I was decidedly the most consequential person on the place. It was my duty to attend specially upon my master, to ride about with him to meetings, carry his cloak and Bible, and take care of his horse; for among other matters Mr. Carleton was a connoisseur in horses, and he did not like to trust his to the usual blundering negligence of his neighbour's grooms.

Pretty soon my master found out my accomplishments of reading and writing; for I inadvertently betrayed a secret which I had determined to keep to myself. At first he did not seem to like it; but as he could not unlearn me, he soon determined to turn these acquirements of mine to some account. He had a good deal of writing of one sort or another; and he set me to work as copier. In my character of secretary, I was often called upon, when my master was busy, to write passes for the people. This raised my consequence extremely, and my fellow-servants soon began to look upon me as second only to "master" himself.

Mr. Carleton was naturally humane and kind-hearted; and though his sudden outbreaks of impatience and fretfulness were often vexatious enough, still if one humoured him they were generally soon over; and as if he reproached himself for not keeping a better guard upon his temper, they were often followed by an affability and indulgence greater than usual. I soon learned the art of managing him to the best advantage, and every day I rose in his favour.

I had a good deal of leisure; and I found means to employ it both innocently and agreeably. Mr. Carleton had a collection of books very unusual for a North Carolina planter. This library must have contained between two and three hundred volumes. It was the admiration of all the country round, and contributed not a little to give its owner the character of a great scholar, and a very learned man. My situation of confidential servant gave me free access to it. The greater part of the volumes treated of divinity, but there were some of a more attractive description; and I was able to gratify occasionally and by stealth—for I did not like to be seen reading anything but the Bible—that taste for knowledge which I had imbibed when a child, and which all the degradations of servitude had not utterly extinguished. All things considered, I found myself much more agreeably situated than I had been at any time since the death of my first master.

I wish, both for their sakes and his own, that all the rest of Mr. Carleton's slaves had been as well off and as kindly treated as myself. The house servants, it is true, had nothing to complain of, except, indeed, those grievous evils which are inseparable from a state of servitude, and which no tenderness or indulgence on the part of the master can ever do away. But the plantation hands—some fifty in number—were very differently situated. Mr. Carleton, like a large proportion of American planters, had no knowledge of agriculture, and not the slightest taste for it. He had never given any attention to the business of his plantation; his youth had been spent in a course of boisterous dissipation, and since his conversion he had been entirely devoted to the cause of religion. Of course his planting affairs and all that related to them were wholly in the hands of his overseer, who was shrewd, plausible, intelligent, and well acquainted with his business, but a severe taskmaster, bad-tempered, and, if all reports were true, not very much overburdened with honesty. Mr. Warner, for this was the overseer's name, was engaged on terms which however ruinous to the planter and his plantation, were very common in Virginia and the Carolinas. Instead of receiving a regular salary in money, he took a certain proportion of the crop. Of course, it was his interest to make the largest crop possible, without any regard whatever to the means used to make it. What was it to him though the lands were exhausted, and the slaves worn out with heavy tasks and unreasonable labours? He owned neither the lands nor the slaves, and if in ten or twelve years,—and for something like that time he had been established at Carleton-Hall,—he could scourge all their value out of them, the gain was his, and the loss would be his employer's. This desirable consummation he seemed pretty nearly arrived at. The lands at Carleton-Hall were never cultivated, it is likely, with any tolerable skill; but Mr. Warner had carried the process of exhaustion to its last extremity. Field after field had been "turned out," as they call it— that is, left uncultivated and unfenced, to grow up with broom-sedge and persimmon bushes, and be grazed by all the cattle of the neighbourhood. Year after year new land had been opened, and exposed to the same exhausting process which had worn out the fields that had been already abandoned; till at last there was no new land left upon the plantation.

Mr. Warner now began to talk about throwing up his employment, and it was only by urgent solicitations and a greater proportion of the diminished produce that Mr. Carleton had prevailed upon him to remain another year.

But it was not the land only that suffered. The slaves were subjected to a like process of exhaustion; and what with hard work, insufficient food, and an irregular and capricious severity, they had become discontented, sickly, and inefficient. There never was a time that two or three of them, and sometimes many more, were not runaways, wandering in the woods; and hence originated further troubles and fresh severity.

Mr. Carleton had expressly directed that his servants should receive an allowance of corn, and especially of meat, which in that part of the world was thought extremely liberal; and I believe, if the allowance had been faithfully distributed, the heartiest man upon the place would have received about half as much meat as was consumed by Mr. Carleton's youngest daughter, a little girl some ten or twelve years old. But if the slaves were worthy of belief, neither Mr. Warner's scales nor his measure were very authentic; and according to their story, so much as he could plunder out of their weekly allowance went to increase his share in the yearly produce of the plantation.

Once or twice complaints of this sort had been carried to Mr. Carleton, but, without deigning to examine into them, he had dismissed them as unworthy of notice. Mr. Warner, he said, was an honest man and a Christian,—indeed, it was his Christian character that had first recommended him to his employer; and these scandalous stories were only invented out of that spite which slaves always feel against an overseer who compels them to do their duty. It might be so; I cannot undertake positively to contradict it. Yet I know that these imputations upon Mr. Warner's honesty were not confined to the plantation, but circulated pretty freely through the neighbourhood; and if he was not a rogue, Mr. Carleton, by an unlimited, unsuspicious, and unwise confidence, did his best to make him so.

Whether the slaves were cheated or not of their allowance, there is no dispute that they were worked hard and harshly treated. Mr. Carleton always took sides with his overseer, and was in the habit of maintaining that it was impossible to get along on a plantation without frequent whipping and a good deal of severity; and yet, as he was naturally good-natured, it gave him pain to hear of any very flagrant instance of it. But he was much from home, and that kept him ignorant, to a great degree, of what was going on there; and for the rest, the overseer was anxious to save his feelings, and had issued very strict orders, which he enforced with merciless severity, that nobody should run to the house with tales of what was done upon the plantation. By this ingenious device, though a very common one, Mr. Warner had everything in his own way. In fact, Mr. Carleton had as little control over his plantation as over any other in the county; and he knew just as little about it.

When my master was a young man, he had betted at horse-races and gambling-tables, and spent money very freely in a thousand foolish ways. Since he had grown religious he had dropped these expenses, but he had fallen into others. It was no small sum that he spent every year upon Bibles, church repairs, and other pious objects. For several years his income had been diminishing; but without any corresponding diminution of his expenses. As a natural consequence, he had become deeply involved in debt. His overseer had grown rich, while he had been growing poor. His lands and slaves were mortgaged, and he began to be plagued by the sheriff's officer. But these perplexities did not cause him to forego his spiritual labours, which he prosecuted, if possible, more diligently than before.

I had now being living with him some six or seven months, and was completely established in his favour, when one Sunday morning we set off together for a place about eight miles distant, where he had not preached before, since I had been in his service. The place appointed for the meeting was in the open air. It was a pretty place though, and well adapted to the purpose, being a gentle swell of ground over which were thinly scattered a number of ancient and wide-spreading oaks. Their outstretched limbs formed a thick shade, under which there were neither weeds nor undergrowth, but something more like a grassy lawn than is often to be seen in that country. Near the top of the swell, somebody had fixed up some rude benches; and partly supported against one of the largest trees was a misshapen little platform, with a chair or two upon it, which seemed intended for the pulpit.

Quite a troop of horses, and as many as ten or twelve carriages, were collected at the foot of the swell; and the benches were already occupied by a considerable number of people. The white hearers, however, were far outnumbered by the slaves, who were scattered about in groups, most of them in their Sunday dresses, and many of them very decent-looking people. A few, however, were miserably ragged and dirty; and there was quite a number of half-grown children from the adjoining plantations, without a rag to hide their nakedness.

My master seemed well pleased with the prospect of so large an audience. He dismounted at the foot of the hill, if a rise so gentle deserved the name, and delivered his horse into my charge. I sought out a convenient place in which to tie the horses; and as I knew the services would not begin immediately, I sauntered about, looking at the equipages and the company. While I was occupied in this way, a smart carriage drove up. It stopped. A servant jumped from behind, opened the door and let down the steps. An elderly lady, and another about eighteen or twenty, occupied the back seat. On the front seat was a woman whom I took to be their maid, though I could not see her distinctly. Something called off my attention, and I turned another way. When I looked again, the two ladies were walking up the hill and the maid was on the ground, with her back towards me, taking something from the carriage. A moment after, she turned round, and I knew her. It was Cassy,—it was my wife.

I sprang forward and caught her in my arms. She recognized me at the same moment; and uttering a cry of surprise and pleasure, she would have fallen had I not supported her. She recovered herself directly, and bade me let her go, for she had been sent back for her mistress's fan, and she must make haste and carry it to her. She told me to wait, though, for if she could get leave she would come back again immediately. She tripped up the hill and overtook her mistress. I could see, by her gestures, the eagerness with which she urged her request. It was granted, and in a moment she was again at my side. Again I pressed her to my bosom, and again she returned my embrace. Once more I felt what it was to be happy. I took her by the hand and led her to a little wood on the opposite side of the road. Here was a thick young growth, where we could sit screened from observation. We sat down upon a fallen tree, and while I held her hands fast locked in mine, we asked and answered a thousand questions.

The first emotions and agitation of our meeting over, Cassy required of me a detailed narrative of my adventures since our separation. With what a kindling eye and heaving bosom did she listen to my story; at every painful incident of it the fast-flowing tears chasing each other down her cheeks, now pale, now flushed; at every gleam of ease or comfort, a tender, joyous, sympathizing smile beaming upon me, breathing new life into my soul! You who have loved as we loved,—you who have parted as we parted, with no hope ever to meet again,—you who have met as we met, brought together by accident or by Providence,—you, and only you, may imagine the emotions that swelled my heart as I pressed the hand, and felt the presence, and basked in the sympathy of a woman, and a wife, as dear to me, slave though I was, slave though she was—as dear to me as the wife of his bosom is to the proudest freeman of you all.

My story finished, again Cassy clasped me in her arms, and claimed me as her husband; tears, but tears of joy, again fast flowing down her cheeks. There for a short while she sat, silent, seeming as if lost in a sort of reverie, or indeed, almost as if doubting whether all that she had just heard,—whether the very husband whom she saw before her,—whether our whole unexpected meeting was anything more than a treacherous dream. But with a kiss or too I recalled her attention, and made her understand that I was no less anxious to hear her story than she had been to hear mine.

CHAPTER XXI.

It seemed to be with the greatest reluctance that the poor girl carried back her recollection to that terrible day which had separated us, as we then thought, for ever. She hesitated, and seemed half ashamed, and almost unwilling to speak of what had followed after that separation. I pitied her; and great as was my curiosity, if my feelings on that occasion deserve so trifling a name, I could almost have wished her to pass over the interval in silence. Distressing doubts and dreadful apprehensions crowded upon me, and I almost dreaded to hear her speak. But she hid her face in my bosom, and murmuring in a voice half choked with sobs, "My husband must know it," she began her story.

She was already, she told me, more than half dead with fright and horror, and the first blow that Colonel Moore struck, beat her senseless to the ground. When she came to her senses, she found herself lying on a bed, in a room which she did not recollect ever to have seen before. She rose from the bed as well as her bruises would allow her; for she did not move without difficulty. The room was prettily furnished; the bed was hung with curtains, neat and comfortable; a dressing-table stood in one corner; and there was all the usual furniture of a lady's bedchamber, but it was not like any room in the house at Spring-Meadow.

She tried to open the doors, of which there were two, but both were fastened. She endeavoured to get a peep from the windows, in the hope that she might know some part of the prospect. But she could only discover that the house seemed to be surrounded by trees; for the windows were guarded on the outside by close blinds, which were fastened in some way she did not understand, so that she could not open them. This fastening of the doors and windows satisfied her that she was held a prisoner, and confirmed all her worst suspicions.

As she passed by the dressing-table, she caught a look at the glass. Her face was deadly pale; her hair fell in loose disorder over her shoulders, and looking down she saw stains of blood upon her dress, but whether her own or her husband's she could not tell. She sat down on the bedside; her head was dizzy and confused, and she scarcely knew whether she were awake or dreaming.

Presently one of the doors opened, and a woman entered. It was Miss Ritty,* as she was called among the servants at Spring-Meadow, a pretty, dark-complexioned damsel, who enjoyed at that time the station and dignity of Colonel Moore's favourite. Cassy's heart beat hard, while she heard some one fumbling at the lock. When the door opened she was glad to see that it was only a woman, and one whom she knew. She ran towards her, caught her by the hand, and begged her protection. The girl laughed, and asked what she was afraid of. Cassy hardly knew what answer to make. After hesitating a moment, she begged Miss Ritty to tell her where she was, and what they intended to do with her.

"It is a fine place you're in," was the answer, "and when master comes, you can ask him what is to be done with you." This was said with a significant titter, which Cassy knew too well how to interpret.

Though Miss Ritty had evaded a direct answer to her inquiry, it now occurred to her where she must be. This woman, she recollected, occupied a small house, the same that once had been inhabited by Cassy's mother and by mine, at a considerable distance from any other on the plantation. It was surrounded by a little grove which almost hid it from view, and was very seldom visited by any of the servants. Miss Ritty looked upon herself, and was in fact regarded by the rest of us, as a person of no little consequence; and though she sometimes condescended to make visits, she was not often anxious to have them returned. Cassy, however, had been once or twice at her house. There were two little rooms in front, into which she was freely admitted; but the apartment behind was locked; and it was whispered among the servants, that Colonel Moore kept the key, so that even Miss Ritty herself did not enter it except in his company. This perhaps was mere scandal; but Cassy recollected to have noticed that the windows of this

* Henrietta.

room were protected against impertinent curiosity by close blinds on the outside, and she no longer doubted where she was.

She told Miss Ritty as much, and inquired if her mistress knew of her return.

Miss Ritty could not tell.

She asked if her mistress had got another maid in her place.

Miss Ritty did not know.

She begged for permission to go and see her mistress; but that, Miss Ritty said, was impossible.

She requested that her mistress might be told where she was, and that she wished very much to see her.

Miss Ritty said that she would be glad to oblige her, but she was not much in the habit of going to the house, and the last time she was there Mrs. Moore had spoken to her so spitefully that she was determined never to go again, unless she were absolutely obliged to.

Having thus exhausted every resource, poor Cassy threw herself upon the bed, hid her face in the bedclothes, and sought relief in tears.

It was now Miss Ritty's turn. She patted the poor girl on the shoulder, bade her not to be down-hearted, and unlocking a bureau which stood in the room, she took out a dress which she pronounced to be " mighty handsome." She bade Cassy get up and put it on, for her master would be coming presently. This was what Cassy feared; but she hoped, if she could not escape the visit, at least to defer it. So she told Miss Ritty that she was too sick to see anybody; she absolutely refused to look at her dresses, and begged to be allowed to die in peace. Miss Ritty laughed when she spoke of dying; yet she seemed a little alarmed at the idea of it, and inquired what was the matter.

Cassy told her that she had seen and suffered enough that day to kill anybody, that her head was sick, and her heart was broken, and the sooner death came to her relief the better. She then mustered courage to mention my name, and endeavoured to discover what had become of me. Miss Ritty again shook her head and declared that she could give no information.

At that moment the door opened, and Colonel Moore came in. He had a haggard and guilty look. The flush which overspread his face, when she had last seen him, was wholly gone; his countenance was pale and ghastly. She had never seen him look so before, and she trembled at the sight of him. He bade Ritty begone; but told her to wait in the front room, as, perhaps, he might need her assistance. He bolted the door, and sat down on the bed by Cassy's side. She started up in terror, and retired to the farthest corner of the room. He smiled scornfully, and bade her come back and sit down beside him. She obeyed; for however reluctant she could do no better. He took her hand and threw one arm about her waist. Again she shrank from him, and would have fled; but he stamped his foot impatiently, and in a harsh tone bade her be quiet.

For a moment he was silent; then, changing his manner, he summoned up his habitual smile, and began in that mild, gentle, insinuating tone, in which he was quite unsurpassed. He plied her with flattery, soft words, and generous promises. He reproached her, but without any harshness, for her attempts to evade the kindness he intended her. He then spoke of me; but no sooner had he entered on that subject than his voice rose, his face became flushed again, and he seemed in manifest danger of losing his temper.

She interrupted him, and besought him to tell her how I did, and what had become of me. He answered that I was well enough; much better than I deserved to be; but she need give herself no further thought or trouble on that score, for he intended to send me out of the country as soon as I was able to travel; and she need not hope nor expect ever to see me again.

She most earnestly besought and begged that she might be sent off and sold with me. He affected to be greatly surprised at this request, and inquired why she made it. She told him that, after all that had happened, it were better that she should not live any longer in his family; beside, if she were sold at the same time, the same person might buy her that bought her husband. That word, husband, put him into a violent passion. He told her that she had no husband, and wanted none; for he would be better than a husband to her. He said that he was tired of her folly, and, with a significant look, he bade her not be a fool, but to leave off whining and crying, be a good girl, and do as her master desired; was it not a servant's duty to obey her master?

She told him that she was sick and wretched, and begged him to leave her. Instead of doing so, he threw his arms about her neck, and declared that her being sick was all imagination, for he had never seen her look half so handsome.

She started up;—but he caught her in his arms, and dragged her towards the bed. Even at that terrible moment her presence of mind did not forsake her. She exerted her strength, and succeeded in breaking away from his hateful embraces. Then summoning up all her energies, she looked him in the face, as well as her tears would allow her, and striving to command her voice, "Master,—Father!" she cried, "what is it you would have of your own daughter?"

Colonel Moore staggered as if a bullet had struck him. A burning blush overspread his face; he would have spoken, but the words seemed to stick in his throat. This confusion was only for a moment. In an instant he recovered his self-possession, and without taking any notice of her last appeal, he merely said, that if she were really sick, he did not wish to trouble her. With these words he unbolted the door, and walked out of the room.

She heard him talking with Miss Ritty; and he had been gone but a few moments before she entered. She began with a longstring of questions about what Colonel Moore had said and done; but when Cassy did not seem inclined to give her any answer, she laughed, and thanked her, and told her she need not trouble herself, for she had been peeping and listening at the keyhole the whole time. She said she could not imagine why Cassy made such a fuss. In a very young girl it might be excusable; but in one as old as she was, and a married woman too, she could not understand it. Such is the morality, and such the modesty to be expected in a slave!

The poor girl was in no humour for controversy, so she listened to this ribaldry without making any answer to it. Yet even at that moment a faint ray of hope began to display itself. It occurred to her, that if Miss Ritty could be made sensible of the risk she ran in aiding to create herself a rival, she would not be pleased at the prospect of being perhaps supplanted in a situation which she seemed to find so very agreeable. This idea appeared to offer some chance of gaining over Miss Ritty to aid her in escaping from Spring-Meadow, and at once she resolved to act upon it. It was necessary to be cautious and to feel her way, lest by piquing the girl's pride she might deprive herself of all the advantage to be gained from working upon her fears.

She approached the subject gradually, and soon placed it in a light in which it was plain her companion had never viewed it. When it was first suggested to her, she expressed a deal of confidence in her own beauty, and affected to have no fears; yet it soon became obvious that notwithstanding all her boasting she was a good deal alarmed. Indeed it was quite impossible for her to look her anticipated rival in the face, and not to perceive the danger. Cassy was well pleased to see the effect of her suggestions; and began to entertain some serious hopes of once more making her escape.

It was, to be sure, a miserable, and most probably an ineffectual resource, this running away. But what else could she do? What other hope was there of escaping a fate which all her womanly and all her religious feelings taught her to regard with the utmost horror and detestation? This was her only chance; she would try it, and trust in God's aid to give her endeavours a happy issue.

She now told Miss Ritty distinctly how she felt, what she intended, and what assistance she wanted. Her new confederate applauded her resolution. "Certainly, if Colonel Moore was really her father, that did make a difference; and her being a Methodist might help to account for her feelings, for she knew that sort of folks were mighty strict in all their notions."

But though Miss Ritty was ready enough to encourage and applaud, she seemed very reluctant to take any active part in aiding and abetting an escape, which, though apparently it tended to promote her interests, might end, if her agency in it were discovered, in bringing her into danger and disgrace.

Several plans were talked over, but Miss Ritty had some objection to all of them. She preferred anything to the risk of being suspected by her master of plotting to defeat his wishes. As they found great difficulty in fixing upon any feasible plan, it was agreed at last, in order to gain time, to give out that Cassy was extremely sick. This indeed was hardly a fiction,—for nothing but the very critical nature of her situation had enabled the poor girl to sustain herself against the shocks and miseries of the last four and twenty hours. Ritty undertook to persuade her master, that the best thing he could do was to let her alone till she got better. She would promise to take her into training in the mean time, and was to assure Colonel Moore, that she did not doubt of being soon able to convince her, that it was both her interest and her duty to comply with her master's wishes.

So far things went extremely well. They had hardly arranged their plan before they heard Colonel Moore's step in the outer room. Ritty ran to him, and succeeded in persuading him to go away without any attempt to see Cassy. He commended her zeal, and promised to be governed by her advice. The next day a circumstance happened which neither Cassy nor Ritty had anticipated, but which proved very favourable to their design. Colonel Moore was obliged to set off for Baltimore without delay. Some pressing call of business made his immediate departure indispensable. Before setting out, however, he found time to visit Ritty, and to enjoin upon her to keep a watchful eye upon Cassy, and to take care and bring her to her senses before his return.

If Cassy was to escape at all, now was the time. She soon hit upon a scheme. Her object was to screen Ritty from suspicion as much as to favour her own flight. Luckily the same arrangement might be made to accomplish both purposes. Cassy could only escape through the door or out of the windows. Escaping through the door was out of the question, because Ritty had the key of it, and was supposed to be sleeping, or watching, or both together, in the front room. The escape then must be by the windows. These did not lift up, as is commonly the case, but opened upon hinges on the inside. The blinds by which they were guarded on the outside were slats nailed across the window-frames, and not intended to be opened. These must be cut or broken, and as they were of pine, this was a task of no great difficulty. Ritty brought a couple of table-knives, and assisted in cutting them away, though, according to the story she was to tell her master, she was sleeping all the time, most soundly and unsuspiciously, and Cassy must have secretly cut away the slats with a pocket-knife.

Early in the evening of Colonel Moore's departure, every thing was ready, and Cassy was to sally forth as soon as she dared to venture. Ritty agreed not to give any notice of her escape till late the next day. This delay she could account for by the plea of not being able to find the overseer, and by a pretended uncertainty as to whether it would be Colonel Moore's wish that the overseer should be informed at all about the matter. At all events, they hoped that no very vigorous pursuit would be made until Colonel Moore's return.

Cassy now made ready for her departure. She felt a pang at the idea of leaving me; but as Ritty could not or would not tell her what had become of me, and as she knew, that separated and helpless as we were, it was impossible for us to render each other any assistance, she rightly judged that she would best serve me, and best comply with my wishes, by adopting the only plan that seemed to carry with it any likelihood of preserving herself from the violence she dreaded.

Cassy had supplied herself from Ritty's allowance with food enough to last for several days. It was now quite dark, and time for her to go. She kissed her hostess and confederate, who seemed much affected at dismissing her on so lonely and hopeless an adventure, and who freely gave her what little money she had. Cassy was a good deal touched at this unexpected generosity. She let herself down from the window, bade Ritty farewell, and summoning up all her resolution and self-command, she took the nearest way across the fields towards the high road. This road was little travelled except by the people of Spring-Meadow and one or two other neighbouring plantations, and at this hour of the evening there was little danger of meeting anybody, except, perhaps, a night-walking slave, who would be as anxious as herself to avoid being seen. There was no moon, but the glimmer of the star-light served to guide her steps. She felt no apprehension of losing her way, for she had frequently been in the carriage with her mistress, as far as the little village at the court-house of the county; and it was hither that, in the first instance, she determined to go.

She arrived there, without having met a single soul. As yet there were no signs of morning. All was still save the monotonous chirpings of the summer insects, interrupted now and then by the crowing of a cock, or the barking of a watch-dog. The village consisted of a dilapidated court-house, a blacksmith's shop, a tavern, two or three stores, and half-a-dozen scattered houses. It was situated at the meeting of two roads. One of these she knew led into the road that ran towards Baltimore. She had flattered herself with the idea of reaching that city, where she had many acquaintances, and where she hoped she might find protection and employment. Her chance of ever getting there was very small. Baltimore was some two or three hundred miles distant; and she did not even know which of the roads that met at the court-house she ought to take. She could not inquire the way, beg a cup of cold water, or even be seen upon the road, without the risk of being taken up as a runaway, and carried back to the master from whom she was flying.

After hesitating for some time, she took one of the roads that offered themselves to her choice, and walked on with vigour. The excitement of the last day or two seemed to give her an unnatural strength; for, after a walk of some twenty miles, she felt fresher than at first. But the light of the morning dawn, which began to show itself, reminded her that it was no longer safe to pursue her journey. Close by the roadside was a friendly thicket, the shrubs and weeds all dripping with the dew. She had gone but a little way among them, when she found them so high and close as to furnish a sufficient hiding-place. She knelt down, and destitute as she was of human assistance, she besought the aid and guardian care of Heaven. After eating a scanty meal—for it was necessary to husband her provisions—she scraped the leaves together into a rude bed, and composed herself to sleep. The three preceding nights she had scarcely slept at all; but she made it up now, for she did not wake till late in the afternoon.

As soon as evening closed in, she started again, and walked as vigorously as before. The road forked frequently; but she had no means of determining which of the various courses she ought to follow. She took one or the other, as her judgment, or rather as her fancy decided; and she comforted herself with the notion, that whether right or wrong in her selections, at all events she was getting further from Spring-Meadow.

In the course of the night she met several travellers. Some of them passed without seeming to notice her. She discovered some at a distance, and concealed herself in the bushes till they had gone by. But she did not always escape so easily. More than once she was stopped and questioned, but luckily she succeeded in giving satisfactory answers. Indeed, there was nothing in her complexion, especially in the uncertain light of the evening, that would clearly indicate her to be a slave; and in answering the questions that were put to her, she took care to say nothing that would betray her condition. One of the men who questioned her shook his head, and did not seem satisfied; another sat on his horse and watched her till she was fairly out of sight; a third told her that she was a very suspicious character; but all three suffered her to pass. She was the less liable to interruption, because in Virginia the houses of the inhabitants are not generally situated along the public roads. The planters usually prefer to build at some distance from the highway; and the roads, passing along the highest and most barren tracts, wind their weary length through a desolate, and what seems almost an uninhabited country. When morning approached again, she concealed herself as before, and waited for the return of night to pursue her journey.

She proceeded in this way for four days, or rather nights, at the end of which time her provisions were entirely exhausted. She had wandered she knew not whither; and the hope of reaching Baltimore, which at first had lightened her fatigue, was now quite gone. She knew not what to do. To go much further without assistance was scarcely possible. Yet should she ask anywhere for food or guidance, though she stood some chance, perhaps, of passing for a free white woman, still her complexion, and the circumstance of her travelling alone, might cause her to be suspected as a runaway, and very probably she would be stopped, put into some gaol, and detained there till suspicion was changed into certainty.

She was travelling slowly along, the fifth night, exhausted with hunger and fatigue, and reflecting upon her unhappy situation, when descending a hill, the road came suddenly upon the banks of a broad river. There was no bridge; but a ferry-boat was fastened to the shore, and close by was the ferry-house, which seemed also to be a tavern.

Here was a new perplexity. She could not cross the river without calling up the ferry people or waiting till they made their appearance, and this would be exposing herself at once to that risk of detection which she had resolved to defer to the very last moment. Yet to turn back and seek another road seemed to be an expedient equally desperate. Any other road which did not lead in a direction opposite to that which she wished to follow, would be likely to bring her again upon the banks of the same river ; and as she could not live without food, she would be soon compelled to apply somewhere for assistance, and to face the detection she was so anxious to avoid.

She sat down by the roadside, resolved to wait for the morning, and to take her chance. There was a field of corn near the house, and the stalks were covered with roasting ears. She had no fire, nor the means of kindling one ; but the sweet milky taste of the unripe kernels served to satisfy the cravings of hunger.

She had chosen a place where she could observe the first movements about the ferry-house. The morning had but just dawned when she saw a man open the door and come out of it. He was black, and she walked boldly up to him, and told him that she was in great haste and wished to be taken across the ferry immediately. The fellow seemed rather surprised at seeing a woman, a traveller, alone, and at that hour of the morning ; but after staring at her a minute or two, he appeared to recollect that here was an opportunity of turning an honest penny, and muttering something about the earliness of the hour, and the ferry-boat not starting till after sunrise, he offered to take her across in a canoe for half a dollar. This price she did not hesitate to pay ; and the fellow, no doubt, put it into his own pocket without ever recollecting to hand it over to his master, or to mention a word to him about this early passenger.

They entered the boat and he paddled her across. She did not dare to ask any questions lest she should betray herself ; and she did her best to quiet the curiosity of the boatman, who, however, was very civil and easily satisfied. Having landed on the opposite shore, she travelled on a mile or two further. By this time it was broad daylight, and she concealed herself as usual.

At night she set out again. But she was faint with hunger, her shoes were almost worn out, her feet were swollen and very painful, and altogether her situation was anything but comfortable. She seemed to have got off the highway, and to be travelling some cross-road, which wound along through dreary and deserted fields, and appeared to be very little frequented. All that night she did not meet a single person or pass a single house. Painful as was the effort, she still struggled to drag along her weary steps ; but her spirits were broken, her heart was sinking, and her strength was almost gone. At length the morning dawned, but the wretched Cassy did not seek her customary hiding-place. She still kept on in hopes of reaching some house. She was now quite subdued, and chose to risk her liberty and even to hazard being carried back to Spring-Meadow, and subjected to the fearful fate from which she was flying, rather than perish with hunger and fatigue. Sad indeed it is that the noblest resolution and the loftiest stubbornness of soul is compelled so often to yield to the base necessities of animal nature, and from a paltry and irrational fear of death, of which tyrants have ever known so well to take advantage, to sink down from the lofty height of heroic virtue to the dastard submissiveness of a craven and obedient slave !

She had not gone far before she saw a low mean-looking house by the road side. It was a small building of logs, blackened with age, and not a little dilapidated. Half the panes or more were wanting in the two or three little windows with which it was provided, and their places were supplied by old hats, old coats, and pieces of plank. The door seemed dropping from its hinges; and there was no enclosure of any kind about the house, unless that name might properly be given to the tall weeds with which it was surrounded. Altogether it showed most manifest signs of thriftless and comfortless indolence.

She knocked softly at the door; and a female voice, but a rough and harsh one, bade her come in. There was no hall or entry; the out-door opened directly into the only room; and on entering, she found it occupied by a middle-aged woman, barefooted, and in a slovenly dress, with her uncombed hair hanging about a haggard and sunburnt face. She was setting a ricketty table, and seemed to be making preparations for breakfast. One side of the room was almost wholly taken up by an enormous fire-place. A fire was burning in it, and the corn-cakes were baking in the ashes. In the opposite corner was a low bed, on which a man, the master of the family most likely, lay still asleep, undisturbed by the cries and clamours of half-a-dozen brats, who had been tumbling and bawling about the house, unwashed, uncombed, and half naked, but who were seized with sudden silence, and slunk behind their mother, at the sight of a stranger.

The woman pointed to a rude sort of stool or bench, which seemed the only piece of furniture in the nature of a chair which the house contained, and asked Cassy to sit down. She did so; and her hostess eyed her sharply, and seemed to wait with a good deal of curiosity to hear who she was, and what she wanted. As soon as Cassy could collect her thoughts, she told her hostess that she was travelling from Richmond to Baltimore to see a sick sister. She was poor and friendless, and was obliged to go on foot. She had lost her way, and had wandered about all night, without knowing where she was, or whither she was going. She was half dead, she added, with hunger and fatigue, and wanted food and rest, and such directions about the road as might enable her to pursue her journey. At the same time she took out her purse, in order to show that she was able to pay for what she wanted.

Her hostess, notwithstanding her rude and poverty-stricken appearance, seemed touched with this pitiful story. She told her to put up her money; she said she did not keep a tavern, and that she was able to give a poor woman a breakfast, without being paid for it.

Cassy was too faint and weak to be much in a humour for talking; besides, she trembled at every word, lest she might drop some unguarded expression that would serve to betray her. But now that the ice was broken, the curiosity of her hostess could not be kept under. She overwhelmed her with a torrent of questions; and every time Cassy hesitated, or gave any sign of confusion, she turned her keen gray eyes upon her, with a sharp and penetrating expression that increased her disorder.

Pretty soon the ash-cakes were baked, and the other preparations for breakfast were finished, when the woman shook her good man roughly by the shoulder, and bade him bestir himself. This connubial salutation roused the sleeper. He sat up on the bed, and stared about the room with a vacant gaze; but the redness of his eyes, and the sallow paleness of his face, seemed to show that he had not quite slept off the effects of the last night's frolic. The wife appeared to know what was wanting; for she forthwith produced the whisky-jug, and poured out a large dose of the raw spirit. Her husband drank it off with a relish, and with a trembling hand, returned the broken glass to his wife, who filled it half full, and emptied it herself. Then turning to Cassy, and remarking, that "a body was fit for nothing till they had got their morning bitters," she offered her a dram, and seemed not a little astonished at its being declined.

The good man then began leisurely to dress himself: and had half finished his toilet before he seemed to notice that there was company in the house. He now came forward and bade the stranger good morning. His wife immediately drew him aside, and they began an earnest whispering. Now and then they would both look Cassy in the face, and as she was conscious that she must be the subject of their conversation, she began to feel a good deal of embarrassment, which she was too little practised in deceit to be able to conceal. This matrimonial conference over, the good woman bade Cassy draw up her stool and sit down at the breakfast table. The breakfast consisted of hot corn cakes and cold bacon, a palatable meal enough in any case, but which Cassy's long starvation made her look upon as the most delicious she had ever eaten. Sweet indeed ought to be that mess of pottage for which one sells the birthright of freedom!

She ate with an appetite which she could not restrain; and her hostess seemed a good deal surprised and a little alarmed at the rapidity with which the table was cleared. Breakfast being finished, the man of the house began to question her. He asked her about Richmond, and whether she knew such and such persons, who, as he said, were living there. Cassy had never been in Richmond, and knew the town only by name. Of course, her answers were very little to the purpose. She blushed and stammered and held down her head, and the man completed her confusion by telling her, that it was very plain she had not come from Richmond, as she pretended; for he was well acquainted with the place, and it was clear enough, from her answers, that she knew nothing about it. He told her that it was no use to deny it—her face betrayed her; and he "reckoned," if the truth was told, she was no better than a runaway. At the sound of this word, the blood rushed into her face, and her heart sunk within her. It was in vain that she denied, protested, and entreated. Her terror, confusion, and alarm only served to give new assurance to her captors, who seemed to chuckle over their prize, and to amuse themselves with her fright and misery, very much as a cat plays with the mouse it has caught.

He told her that if she were in fact a free woman, there was not the slightest ground for alarm. If she had no free papers with her, she would only have to lie in gaol till she could send to Richmond and get them. That was all!

But that was more than enough for poor Cassy. No proofs of freedom could she produce; and her going to gaol would be almost certain to end in her being restored to Colonel Moore, and becoming the wretched victim of his rage and lust. That fate must be deferred as long as possible, and there seemed but one way of escaping it.

She confessed that she was a slave, and a runaway; but she positively refused to tell the name of her master. He lived, she said, a great way off; and she had run away from him, not out of any spirit of discontent or disobedience, but because his cruelty and injustice were too great to be endured. There was nothing she would not choose rather than fall into his hands again; if they would only save her from that—if they would only let her live with them, she would be their faithful and obedient servant as long as she lived.

The man and his wife looked at each other, and seemed pleased with the idea. They walked aside and talked it over. Nothing appeared to deter them from accepting her proposal at once, but the fear of being detected in harbouring and detaining a runaway. Cassy did her best to quiet these apprehensions; and after a short struggle, avarice and the dear delight of power triumphed over their fears, and Cassy became the property of Mr Proctor—for so the man was named. His property, as he might speciously argue, by her own consent; a ten times better title than the vast majority of his countrymen could boast.

To prevent suspicions among the neighbours, it was agreed that Cassy should pass for a free woman, whom Mr. Proctor had hired; and as that gentleman had been so fortunate as to have been initiated into the art and mystery of penmanship—an accomplishment somewhat rare among the "poor white folks" of Virginia—in order that Cassy might be prepared to answer impertinent questions, he gave her free-papers, which he forged for the occasion.

It was a great thing to have escaped returning to Spring-Meadow. But for all that, Cassy soon discovered that her present situation would not prove very agreeable. Mr. Proctor was the descendant and representative of what, at no distant period, had been a rich and very respectable family. The frequent division of a large estate, which nobody took any pains to increase, while all diminished it by idleness, dissipation, and bad management, had left Mr. Proctor's father in possession of a few slaves and a considerable tract of worn-out land. At his death, the slaves had been sold to pay his debts, and the land being divided among his numerous children, had made Mr. Proctor the possessor of only a few barren acres. But though left with this miserable pittance, he had been brought up in the dissipated and indolent habits of a Virginian gentleman; the land he owned, which was so poor and worthless that none of his numerous creditors thought it worth their while to disturb him in the possession of it, still entitled him to the dignity of a freeholder and a voter; and he felt himself as much above, what is esteemed in that country, the base and degraded condition of a labourer, as the richest aristocrat in the whole state. He was as proud, as lazy, and as dissipated as any of the nabobs, his neighbours; and, like them, he devoted the principal part of his time to gambling, politics, and drink.

Luckily for Mr. Proctor, his wife was a very notable woman. She boasted no patrician blood; and when her husband began to talk, as he often did, about the antiquity and respectability of his family, she would cut him short by observing, that she thought herself full as good as he was; but for all that, her ancestors had been "poor folks" as far back as anybody knew anything about them. If the question between aristocracy and democracy were to be settled by the experience of the Proctors, the plebeians, most undoubtedly, would carry the day; for while her husband did little or nothing but frolic, drink, and ride about the country, Mrs. Proctor ploughed, planted, and gathered in the crop. But for her energy and industry, it is much to be feared that Mr. Proctor's aristocratic habits would have soon made himself and his family a burden upon the county.

Cassy's services were a great accession to this establishment. Her new mistress seemed resolved to make the most of them; and the poor girl before long was almost completely broken down by a degree and a kind of labour to which she was totally unaccustomed. Two or three times a week at least Mr. Proctor came home drunk; and on these occasions he blusterered about, threatened his wife, and beat and abused his children without any sort of mercy. Cassy could hardly expect to come off better than they did; indeed his drunken abuse would have become quite intolerable if the energetic Mrs. Proctor had not known how to quell it. At first she used mild measures, and coaxed and flattered him into quiet; but when these means failed, she would tumble him into bed by main strength, and compel him to lie still by the terror of the broomstick.

It was nothing but the wholesome authority which Mrs. Proctor exercised over her husband that protected Cassy against what she dreaded even more than Mr. Proctor's drunken rudeness. Whenever he could find her alone he tormented her with solicitations of a most distressing kind; and nothing could rid her of his importunities except the threat of complaining to Mrs. Proctor. But her troubles did not end even here. Mrs. Proctor listened to her complaints, thanked her for the information, and said she would speak to Mr. Proctor about it. But she could not imagine that a slave could possibly be endowed with the slightest particle of that virtue of which the free women of Virginia boast the exclusive possession. Full of this notion, she judged it highly improbable, whatever merit Cassy might pretend to claim, that she had actually resisted the importunities and solicitations of so very seducing a fellow as Mr. Proctor; and filled with all the spite and fury of female jealousy, she delighted herself with tormenting the object of her suspicions. Mrs. Proctor, with all her merit, had one little foible, which most likely she had adopted out of compliment to her husband,—she thought a daily dram of whisky necessary to keep off the fever and ague; and when through inadvertence, as sometimes would happen, she doubled the dose, it seemed to give a new edge to the natural keenness of her temper. On these occasions she plied both words and blows with a fearful energy; and though perhaps it were difficult to say which of the two was most to be dreaded, both together they were enough to exhaust the patience of a saint.

Poor Cassy could discover no means of delivering herself from this complication of miseries, under which she was ready to sink, when she was most unexpectedly relieved by the unsolicited interference of a couple of Mr. Proctor's neighbours. They were men of leisure, like him,—like him, too, they were of good families, and one of them had received an excellent education, and was more or less distantly connected with several of the most distinguished people in the state. But a course of reckless dissipation had long ago stripped them of such property as they had inherited, and reduced them to live by their wits, which they exercised in a sort of partnership, principally on the race-course and at the gaming-table.

These two speculating gentlemen were on terms of intimacy with Mr. Proctor, and they knew that he had a free woman, for such they supposed Cassy to be, living at his house. In common with most Virginians, they considered the existence of a class of freed people as a great social annoyance, and likely enough in the end seriously to endanger those "sacred rights of property" in defence of which there is nothing which a true-born son of liberty ought not to be proud to undertake. Instigated doubtless by such patriotic notions, these public-spirited persons judged that they would be rendering the state a service, to say nothing of the money they might put into their own pockets, by applying to this great political evil, so far at least as Cassy was a party to it, a remedy which the doctrines of more than one of the Virginian statesmen, and the spirit of more than one of the Virginian statutes, would seem fully to sanction. In plain English, they resolved to seize Cassy and sell her for a slave!

The business of kidnapping is one of the natural fruits of the American system of slavery, and is as common and as well organized in several parts of the United states as the business of horse-stealing is in many other countries. When they take to stealing slaves, the operations of these adventurers become very hazardous, but while they confine themselves to stealing only free people, they can pursue their vocation with comparatively little danger; they may perhaps inflict some trifling personal wrong, but, according to the doctrines of some of the most popular among the American politicians, they are doing the public no inconsiderable service, since, in their opinion, nothing seems to be wanting to render the slave-holding states of America a perfect paradise, except the extermination of the emancipated class. It was no doubt by some such lofty notions of the public good that Cassy's friends were actuated. At all events, those sophistries which tyranny has invented to justify oppression are as much an apology for them as for any one else.

As far as Cassy could learn, their scheme was pretty much as follows: —They invited Mr. Proctor to a drinking frolic, and as soon as the whisky had reduced him to a state of insensibility, a message was sent to his wife that her husband was taken dangerously ill, and that she must instantly come to his assistance. Notwithstanding a few domestic jars, Mr. and Mrs. Proctor were a most loving couple, and the good woman, greatly alarmed at this unexpected news, immediately set out to visit her husband. The conspirators had followed their own messenger, and were concealed in a thicket close to the house watching for her departure. She was hardly out of sight before they rushed into the field where Cassy was at work, bound her hand and foot, put her into a sort of covered wagon or carry-all, which they had provided for the occasion, and drove off as fast as possible. They travelled all that day and the following night. Early the next morning they reached a small village, where they met a slave-trader with a gang of slaves on his way to Richmond. The gentlemen-thieves soon struck up a bargain with the gentleman slave-trader; and having received their money, they delivered Cassy into his possession.

He seemed touched with her beauty and her distress, and treated her with a kindness which she hardly expected from one of his profession. Her shoes and clothes were nearly worn out. He bought her new ones; and as she was half-dead with fatigue, terror, and want of sleep, he even went so far as to wait a day at the village, in order that she might recover a little before setting out on the journey to Richmond.

But she soon found that she was expected to make a return for these favours. When they stopped for the night, at the end of the first day's journey, she received an intimation that she was to share the bed of her master; and directions were given to her how and when to come there. These directions she saw fit to disregard. In the morning her master called her to account. He laughed in her face when she spoke of the wickedness of what he had commanded, and told her he did not want her to be preaching any of her sermons to him. He would excuse her disobedience this time; but she must take very good care not to repeat it.

The next evening she received directions similar to those which had been given the day before; and again she disobeyed them. Her master, who had been drinking and gambling half the night, with some boon companions whom he found at the tavern, enraged at not finding her in his room as he had expected, sallied forth in pursuit of her. Luckily he was too drunk to know very well where he was going. He had gone but a few steps from the tavern door before he stumbled over a pile of wood, and injured himself very seriously. His cries soon brought some of the tavern people to his assistance. They carried him to his room, bound up his bruises, and put him to bed.

It was late the next morning before he was able to rise; but he was no sooner up than he resolved to take ample vengeance for his disappointment and his bruises. He came hobbling to the tavern door, with a crutch in one hand and a whip in the other. He had all his slaves paraded before the house, and made two of the stoutest fellows among them hold Cassy by the arms while he plied the whip. Her cries soon collected the idlers and loungers, who seem to constitute the principal population of a Virginian village. Some inquired the cause of the whipping, but without seeming to think the question of consequence enough to wait for an answer. It seemed to be the general opinion that the master was tipsy, and had chosen this way to vent his drunken humours; but whether drunk or sober, nobody thought of interfering with his " sacred and unquestionable rights." On the contrary, all looked on with unconcern, if not with approbation; and the greater number seemed as much pleased with the sport as so many boys would have been with the baiting of an unlucky cat.

Just in the midst of this proceeding a handsome travelling carriage drove up to the door. There were two ladies in it; and they no sooner saw what was going on than, with that humanity so natural to the female heart that not even the horrid customs and detestable usages of slave-holding tyranny can totally extinguish it, they begged the brutal savage to leave beating the poor girl, and tell them what was the matter.

The fellow reluctantly dropped the lash, and answered in a surly tone, that she was an insolent, disobedient baggage, not fit to be noticed by two such ladies, and that he was only giving her a little wholesome correction.

However, this did not seem to satisfy them; and in the mean time the carriage steps were let down and they got out. Poor Cassy was sobbing and crying, and scarcely able to utter a word; her hair had fallen down over her face and shoulders, and her cheeks were all stained with tears. Yet, even in this situation, the two ladies seemed struck with her appearance. They entered into conversation with her, and soon found that she had been bred a lady's maid, and that her present master was a slave-trader. These ladies, it seemed, had been travelling at the north, and while on their journey had lost a female servant by a sudden and violent attack of fever. They were now on their return to Carolina; and the younger of the two suggested to her mother—for such their relation proved to be—to buy Cassy to supply the place of the maid they had lost. The mother started some objections to purchasing a stranger, about whom they knew nothing, and who had been sold by her former owner, they knew not for what reasons. But when Cassy's tears, prayers, and supplications were added to the entreaties of her daughter, she found herself quite unable to resist; and she sent to ask the man his price. He named it. It was a high one. But Mrs. Montgomery—for that was the lady's name—was one of those people who, when they have made up their minds to do a generous action, are not easily to be shaken from their purpose. She took Cassy into the house with her, ordered the trunks to be brought in, and told the man to make out his bill of sale. The purchase was no sooner completed than her new mistress took Cassy upstairs, and soon fitted her with a dress better becoming her new situation than did the coarse gown and heavy shoes for which she was indebted to the disinterested generosity of her late master.

Cassy was dressed, the bill of sale was delivered, and the money paid, when Mrs. Montgomery's brother and travelling companion rode up.

He rallied his sister not a little on what he called her foolish propensity to interfere between other people and their servants; he took her to task rather severely for the imprudence of her purchase and the high price she had paid; and he told her with a smile and a shake of the head, that one time or other her foolish confidence and generosity would be her ruin. Mrs. Montgomery took her brother's raillery all in good part; the carriage was ordered, and they proceeded together on their journey.

The ladies with whom Cassy had come to the meeting were Mrs. Montgomery and her daughter. They lived some ten miles from Carleton-Hall. So near had Cassy and myself been to each other for six long months or more, without knowing it. Cassy spoke of her mistress with the greatest affection. Her gratitude was unbounded; and she seemed to find a real pleasure and enjoyment in serving a benefactress who treated her with a gentle and uniform kindness, not often exerted even by those who are capable of momentary acts of the greatest generosity.

As Cassy finished her story, she threw her arms about my neck, leaned her head upon my bosom, and looking me in the face, while the tears were streaming from her eyes, she heaved a sigh, and whispered that she was too, too happy! With such a mistress, and restored so unexpectedly to the arms of a husband whom, fondly as she loved him, she feared to have lost for ever, what more could she desire!

Alas, poor girl! she forgot that we were slaves, and that the very next day might again separate us, subject us to other masters, and renew her sufferings and my miseries!

CHAPTER XXII.

BEFORE we had half finished what we had to say to each other, the movement of the people on the hill-side informed us that the morning's religious services were over. Never before had one of my master's sermons seemed so short to me. We hastened towards the spot; I to receive my master's orders, and Cassy to attend upon her mistress. As we came near the rural pulpit I observed Mr. Carleton in conversation with two ladies, who proved to be Mrs. Montgomery and her daughter. We stopped at a little distance from them. Miss Montgomery looked around, and seeing us standing together, she beckoned to Cassy, and pointing to me, she inquired if that was the husband who had put her into such a flutter that morning? This question drew the notice of the other two; and my master seemed a little surprised at seeing me in this new character. "What's this, Archy," he said; "what is the meaning of all this? It is the first I ever heard of your being married. You don't pretend to claim that pretty girl there for your wife?

I replied that she was indeed my wife, though it was now some two years or more since we had seen or known anything of each other. I added, that I had never mentioned my marriage to him because I had despaired of ever seeing my wife again; and now it was nothing but the merest accident that had brought us together.

"Well, Archy, if she is your wife, I don't know how I can help it, though I suppose I shall have you spending half your time at Poplar Grove. Is not that what your place is called, Mrs. Montgomery?"

She said it was ; and after a moment's pause observed, that too little respect, she feared, was often paid to the matrimonial connections of servants. For her part she could not but regard them as sacred; and if Cassy and myself were really married, and I was a decent, civil fellow, she had no objection to my visiting Poplar Grove as often as Mr. Carleton would permit.

My master undertook to answer for my good behaviour; and turning to me, he bade me bring up the horses. I made all the haste I could; but before I returned Mrs. Montgomery was gone, and Cassy with her. We mounted, and had already taken the road to Carleton Hall when my master seemed to recollect that I had just found a wife from whom I had been long separated; and it began to occur to him that possibly we might take some pleasure in being indulged with a little of one another's company. He gave me joy of my discovery with an air half serious, half jocose, as if in doubt whether a slave were properly entitled to a master's serious sympathy; and remarked, in a careless tone, that perhaps I would like to spend the remainder of the day at Poplar Grove.

As I knew that Mr. Carleton had much real goodness of heart, I had long since learned to put up with his cavalier manner; and however little I might be pleased with the style in which he made the offer, the matter of his present proposal was so much to my fancy that I eagerly caught at it. He took his pencil from his pocket and wrote me a pass; I asked and received such directions as he could give me about the way, and putting spurs to my horse I soon overtook Mrs. Montgomery's carriage, which I followed to Poplar Grove.

This was one of those pretty and even elegant country seats which are sometimes seen, though very seldom, in Virginia and the Carolinas; and which may serve to prove that the inhabitants of those states, notwithstanding their almost universal negligence of such matters, are not totally destitute of all ideas of architectural beauty and domestic comfort. The approach to the house was through a broad avenue of old and venerable oaks. The buildings had the appearance of considerable antiquity; but they were in perfect repair, and the grounds and fences were neat and well kept.

As the ladies left the carriage I came up. I told Mrs. Montgomery that my master had given me leave to visit my wife, and I hoped she would have no objection to my spending the afternoon there.

Mrs. Montgomery answered, that Cassy was too good a girl to be denied any reasonable indulgence; and as long as I behaved well she would never make any objection to my coming to see her. She put me several questions about our marriage and separation; and the softness of her voice and the unassuming gentleness of her manner satisfied me that she was an amiable and kind-hearted woman.

No doubt, through the broad extent of slave-holding America there are many amiable women and kind-hearted mistresses. Yet how little does their kindness avail! It reaches only here and there. It has no power to alleviate the wretchedness or to diminish the sufferings of myriads of wretches, who never hear a voice softer than the overseer's, and who know no discipline milder than the lash.

The house servants at Poplar Grove were treated with kindness and even with indulgence, and were much attached to the family; but as happens in so many other cases, the situation of the field hands was extremely different. Some three years before, Mrs. Montgomery, by her husband's death and the will which he left, became the owner and sole mistress of the estate. Upon this occasion her good nature and her sense of justice prompted her to extend the same humane system to the management of the plantation, which she had always acted upon in the government of her own household. During her husband's life the servants' quarter had been three miles or more from the house; and as the slaves were never allowed to come there unless they were sent for, Mrs. Montgomery saw scarcely anything of them, and knew very little of their wants and grievances, and next to nothing of the general management of the estate. Indeed, she spent the greater portion of every year in visiting her relations in Virginia or in trips to the northern cities; and when at home, her husband's manifest disinclination to her having anything to do with those matters had always prevented her from meddling in any way with the plantation affairs.

But when her husband was dead, and the plantation and slaves had become her own property, she could not reconcile herself to the idea of taking no thought, concern, or care for the welfare and well-being of more than a hundred human creatures, who toiled from morning to night for her sole benefit. She resolved upon a total change of system; and ordered the servants' quarter to be removed near the house, so that she might be able to go there daily, and have an opportunity of inspecting and relieving the wants and grievances of her servants.

She was shocked at the miserable pittance of food and clothing which her husband had allowed them, and at the amount of labour which he had exacted. She ordered their allowances to be increased, and their tasks to be diminished. Several instances of outrageous severity having reached her ears, she dismissed her overseer, and procured a new one. The servants no sooner discovered that their mistress had interested herself in their welfare, than she was overwhelmed with petitions, appeals, and complaints. One wanted a blanket, another a kettle, and a third a pair of shoes. Each asked for some trifling gift, which it seemed very hard to refuse: and every request that was granted was followed by a half-a-dozen others, equally trifling and equally reasonable. But before the end of the year these small items amounted to a sum sufficient to swallow up half the usual profits of the plantation. Scarcely a day passed that Mrs. Montgomery was not pestered with complaints about the severity of her new overseer; and the servants were constantly coming to her to beg off from some threatened punishment. Two or three instances in which the overseer was checked for the tyrannical manner in which he exercised his authority only nerved to increase this annoyance. She was perplexed with continual appeals, as to which she found it next to impossible to get at the truth—since the overseer always told one story, and the servants another. The second overseer was dismissed; a third threw up his place in disgust; and a fourth, who resolved to humour the indulgent disposition of his employer, suffered the hands to take their own course, and to do pretty much as they pleased. Of course, they did not care to work, while they had the choice of being idle. Every season since Mrs. Montgomery had commenced her experiments, the crop had fallen lamentably short; but that year, there was scarcely any crop at all.

Her friends now thought it time to interfere. Her brother, whom she loved, and for whose opinion and advice she entertained a high regard, had all along remonstrated against the course she was pursuing. He now spoke in a more decided tone. He told her that the silly notions she had taken up about the happiness of her slaves would certainly ruin her. Where was the need of being more humane than her neighbours?—and what folly could be greater than to reduce herself and her children to beggary, in the vain pursuit of a sentimental and impracticable scheme?

Mrs. Montgomery defended herself and her conduct with great earnestness. She pleaded her duty towards those unhappy beings whom God had placed in her power and under her protection. She even went so far as to hint at the injustice of living in luxury upon the fruits of forced labour; and she spoke with much feeling of the savage brutality of overseers, and the torture of the lash. Her brother replied that such talk was very pretty, and generous, and philanthropic, and all that; and while it went no further than talk, he had not the least objection to it. But pretty and philanthropic as it was, it would not make either corn or tobacco. She might talk as she pleased; but if she expected to live by her plantation, she must manage it like other people. Everybody who knew anything about the matter would tell her, that if she wished to make a crop, she must keep a smart overseer, put a whip into his hands, and give him unlimited authority to use it. If she would do this, she might justly call herself the mistress of the plantation; but as long as she followed her present plan, she would be no better than the slave of her own servants; and her philanthropy would end in their being sold for debt, and in her being left a beggar.

These warm remonstrances made a deep impression upon Mrs. Montgomery. She could not deny that the plantation had produced scarcely anything since she had come into possession of it; and she was conscious that after all her labours in their behalf, her servants were discontented, idle, and insubordinate. However, she did not feel inclined to yield the point. She still maintained that her ideas on the mutual relation of master and servant were the obvious dictates of justice and humanity, which no one could despise or overlook who made any pretensions to virtue or to conscience. She argued that the system which she was attempting to introduce was a good one; and that nothing was wanting except an overseer who had sense enough to carry it into judicious operation. Possibly, there was something of truth in this. If she could have found a man like Major Thornton, and made an overseer of him, she might perhaps have succeeded. But such men are seldom found anywhere, and in slave-holding America, very seldom, indeed. Take the American overseers together, and they are the most ignorant, intractable, stupid, obstinate, and self-willed race that ever existed. What could a woman do, who could only act through assistance of this sort, and who had the prejudices of the whole neighbourhood actively excited against her? Things went on from bad to worse. The ready money which her husband had left was all spent, and her affairs soon became so entangled and embarrassed, that she was obliged to call upon her brother for assistance. He refused in the most positive manner to have anything to do with the business, unless she would surrender to him the sole and exclusive management of her affairs. To these hard terms, after a short and ineffectual struggle, she was obliged to consent.

He immediately took the plantation into his own hands. He removed the cabins to their former situation; revived the old rule that no servant should ever go to the house unless especially sent for; reduced them to their former allowance of food and clothing; and engaged an overseer on the express condition that Mrs. Montgomery should never listen to any complaints against him, or intermeddle, in any way, with his management of the plantation.

Within the first month after this return to the old system, near one-third of the working hands were runaways. Mrs. Montgomery's brother told her that this was no more than might be expected; for the rascals had been so spoiled and indulged, as to render them quite impatient of the necessary and wholesome severity of plantation discipline. After long searching, and a good deal of trouble and expense, the runaways, except one or two, were finally recovered; and Poplar-Grove, under its new administration, passed by degrees to its ancient routine of whipping and hard labour. Once in a while, notwithstanding all the pains that were taken to prevent it, some instance of severity wonld reach the ear of Mrs. Montgomery; and, in the first burst of indignant feeling, she would sometimes declare that the narrowest poverty would be far better than the wealth and luxury for which she was indebted to the whip of the slave-driver. But these exclamations of generous passion were scarcely uttered, before she acknowledged to herself, that to think of giving up the luxury to which she had been accustomed from her infancy was out of the question. She strove to escape from the knowledge, and to banish the recollection of injustice and cruelty, which her heart condemned, but which she lacked the power, or rather the spirit, to remedy. She fled from a home where she was for ever haunted by the spectre of that delegated tyranny, for which, however she might attempt to deny or disguise it, she could not but feel herself responsible; and while her slaves toiled beneath the burning sun of a Carolina summer, and smarted under the lash of a stern and relentless overseer, she attempted to drown the remembrance of their wrongs in the dissipations and gaieties of Saratoga or New York.

But she was obliged to spend a part of the year at Poplar-Grove; and with all her care she could not always save her feelings from some rude brushes. Of this I had a striking instance on my first visit. One of her plantation hands had been so far indulged by the overseer, who, by the way, was a very rigid Presbyterian, as to receive a pass to attend Mr. Carleton's meeting. After the meeting was over, his mistress happened to see him there; and as she wished to send a message to one of her neighbours, she called him to her, and sent him with it. It so happened that Mrs. Montgomery's overseer was at this neighbour's when the servant arrived there with his mistress's message. The overseer no sooner saw him than he inquired what business he had to come there, when his pass only allowed him to go to the meeting and back again. It was in vain that he pleaded his mistress's orders. The overseer said that made no difference whatever, for Mrs. Montgomery had nothing at all to do with the plantation hands; and to impress this fact upon his memory, he gave him a dozen lashes on the spot.

The poor fellow was bold enough to come to the house, and make his complaint to Mrs. Montgomery. Nothing could exceed her anger and vexation. But her agreement with her brother left her without a remedy. She made the servant a handsome present; told him that he had been very unjustly punished; and begged him to go home, and say nothing about it to anybody. She submitted to the mortification of making this request, in hopes of saving the poor fellow from a second punishment. But by some means or other, as I learned afterwards, the overseer found out what had been going on; and, to vindicate his supreme authority, and keep up the discipline of the plantation, he inflicted a second whipping more severe than the first.

Such is the malignant nature and disastrous operation of the slaveholding system, that in too many instances the sincerest good-will and best intended efforts in the slave's behalf end only in plunging him into deeper miseries. It is impossible to build any edifice of good upon so evil a foundation. The whole system is totally and radically wrong. The benevolence, the good-nature, the humanity of a slave-holder, avail as little as the benevolence of the bandit, who generously clothes the stripped and naked traveller in a garment plundered from his own portmanteau. What grosser absurdity than the attempt to be humanely cruel and generously unjust! The very first act in the slave's behalf, without which all else is useless, and worse than useless, is—to make him free!

CHAPTER XXIII.

I HAVE before observed that Sunday is the slave's holiday. Where intermarriages are allowed between the slaves of different plantations, this is generally the only occasion on which the scattered branches of the same family are indulged with an opportunity of visiting each other. Many planters, who pride themselves upon the excellence of their discipline, forbid these intermarriages altogether; and if they happen to have a superabundance of men-servants, they prefer that one woman should have a half-a-dozen husbands rather than suffer their slaves to be corrupted, by gadding about among other people's plantations.

Other managers, just as good disciplinarians, and a little more shrewd than their neighbours, forbid the men only to marry away from home. They are very willing to let their women get husbands where they can. They reason in this way. When a husband goes to see his wife who lives upon another plantation, he will not be apt to go empty-handed. He will carry something with him, probably something eatable, plundered from his master's fields, that may serve to make him welcome, and render his coming a sort of festival. Now, everything that is brought upon a plantation in this way is so much clear gain, and, so far as it goes, it amounts to feeding one's people at the expense of one's neighbours!

Sunday, as I have said, is the day upon which are paid the matrimonial visits of the slave. But Sunday was no holiday to me; for I was generally obliged on that day to attend my master upon his ecclesiastical excursions. To make up for this, Mr. Carleton allowed me Thursday afternoons, so that I was able to visit Cassy at least once a week.

The year that followed was the happiest of my life; and with all the inevitable mortifications and miseries which slavery, even under its least repulsive form, ever carries with it, I still look back to that year with pleasure,—a pleasure that yet has power to warm a heart, saddened and embittered by a thousand painful recollections.

Before the end of the year Cassy made me a father. The infant boy had all his mother's beauty; and only he who is a father, and as fond a husband, too, as I was, can know the feelings with which I pressed the little darling to my heart.

No!—no one can know my feelings,—no one, alas, but he who is, as I was, the father of a slave. The father of a slave!—And is it true, then, that this child of my hopes and wishes, this pledge of mutual love, this dear, dear infant, of whom I am the father, is it true he is not mine? Is it not my duty and my right, a right and duty dearer than life, to watch over his helpless infancy, and to rear him with all a father's tenderness and love to a manhood, that will, perhaps, repay my care, and in turn sustain and cherish me, a tottering, weak old man?

My duty it may be, but it is not my right. A slave can have no rights. His wife, his child, his toil, his blood, his life, and everything that gives his life a value, they are not his; he holds them all but at his master's pleasure. He can possess nothing; and if there is anything he seems to have, it is only by a sufferance which exists but in his owner's will.

This very child, this very tender babe, may be torn from my arms, and sold to-morrow into the hands of a stranger, and I shall have no right to interfere. Or if not so; if some compassion be yielded to his infancy, and if he be not snatched from his father's embraces and his mother's bosom while he is yet all unconscious of his misery, yet what a sad, wretched, desolate fate awaits him! Shut out from every chance or hope of anything which it is worth one's while to live for;—bred up a slave!

A slave!—That single word, what volumes it does speak! It speaks of chains, of whips and tortures, compulsive labour, hunger, and fatigues, and all the miseries our wretched bodies suffer. It speaks of haughty power and insolent commands; of insatiate avarice, of pampered pride and purse-proud luxury; and of the cold indifference and scornful unconcern with which the oppressor looks down upon his victims. It speaks of crouching fear and base servility; of low, mean cunning, and treacherous revenge. It speaks of humanity outraged, manhood degraded, the social charities of life, the sacred ties of father, wife, and child trampled underfoot; of aspirations crushed; of hope extinguished; and the light of knowledge sacrilegiously put out. It speaks of man deprived of all that makes him amiable or makes him noble; stripped of his soul, and sunk into a beast.

And thou, my child, to this fate thou art born! May heaven have mercy on thee, for man has none!

The first burst of instinctive and thoughtless pleasure with which I had looked upon my infant boy was dissipated for ever the moment I had recovered myself enough to recollect what he was born to. Various and ever changing, but always wretched and distressing were the feelings with which I gazed at him as he slept upon his mother's bosom, or waking, smiled at her caresses. He was indeed a pretty baby—a dear, dear child;—and for his mother's sake I loved him, how I loved him! Yet, struggle as I might, I could not for a moment escape the bitter thought of what his fate must be. Full well I knew that did he live to be a man, he would repay my love, and justly, with curses, curses on the father who had bestowed upon him nothing but a life incumbered and made worse than worthless by the inheritance of slavery.

I found no longer the same pleasure in Cassy's society which it used to afford me; or rather the pleasure which I could not but take in it was intermingled with much new misery. I did not love her less, but the birth of that boy had infused fresh bitterness into the cup of servitude. Whenever I looked upon him my mind was filled with horrid images. The whole future seemed to come visibly before me. I saw him naked, chained, and bleeding under the lash; I saw him a wretched, trembling creature, cringing to escape it; I saw him utterly debased, and the spirit of manhood extinguished within him; already he appeared that worthless thing,—a slave contented with his fate!

I could not bear it. I started up in a phrenzy of passion, I snatched the child from the arms of his mother, and, while I loaded him with caresses, I looked about for the means of extinguishing a life which, as it was an emanation from my existence, seemed destined to be only a prolongation of my misery.

My eyes rolled wildly, I doubt not, and the stern spirit of my determination must have been visibly marked upon my face, for, gentle and unsuspicious as she was, and wholly incapable of that wild passion which tore my heart, my wife, with a mother's instinctive watchfulness, seemed to catch some glimpse of my intention. She rose up hastily, and, without speaking a word, she caught the baby from my feeble and trembling grasp, and, as she pressed it to her bosom, she gave a look that told me all that she feared, and told me, too, that the mother's life was bound up in that of the child.

That look subdued me,—my arms dropped powerless, and I sunk down in a sort of sullen stupor. I had been prevented from accomplishing my purpose, but I was not satisfied that in foregoing it I did a father's duty to the child. The more I thought upon it—and it so engrossed me that I could scarcely draw my thoughts away—the more was I convinced that it were better for the boy to die. And if the deed did peril my own soul, I loved the child so well, I did not shrink even at that!

But then his mother?

I would have reasoned with her, but I knew how vain would be the labour to array a woman's judgment against a mother's feelings; and I felt that one tear stealing down her cheek, one look of hers like that she gave me when she snatched the child away, would, even in my own mind, far outbalance the weightiest of my arguments.

The idea of rescuing the boy, by one bold act, from all the bitter miseries that impended over him, had shot upon my mind like some faint struggling star across the darkness of a midnight storm. But that glimmer of comfort was now extinguished. The child must live,—the life I gave him I must not take away. No! not though every day of it would draw new curses on my devoted head, and those, too, the curses of my child. This, this, alas! is the barbed arrow that still is sticking in my heart,—the fatal, fatal wound, that nought can heal.

CHAPTER XXIV.

ONE Sunday morning, when the boy was about three months old, two strangers unexpectedly arrived at Carleton-Hall. In consequence of their coming some urgent business occupied my master's attention, so that he found himself obliged to give up the meeting which he had appointed for that day. I was not sorry for it, for it left me at liberty to visit my wife and child.

It was the autumn. The heat of summer had abated, and the morning was bright and balmy; there was a soothing softness in the air, and the woods were clothed in a gay variety of colours, that almost outvied the foliage of the spring. As I rode along towards Poplar-Grove, the serenity of the sky and the beauty of the prospect seemed to breathe a peaceful pleasure to my heart. It was the more needed, for I had been a good deal irritated by some occurrences during the week, and every new indignity to which my situation exposed me, I now seemed to suffer twice over,—once in my own person, and a second time, in anticipation for my child. I had set out in no very agreeable frame of mind; but the ride, the prospect, and the fine autumnal air, had soothed me into a cheerful alacrity of spirit, such as I had hardly felt for some weeks before.

Cassy welcomed me with a ready smile, and those caresses which a fond wife bestows so freely on the husband whom she loves. Her mistress the day before had given her some new clothes for the child, and she had just been dressing him out to make the little fellow fit, she said, to see his father. She brought the boy and placed him on my knee. She praised his beauty; and with her arm about my neck she tried to trace his father's features in the baby's face. In the full flow of a mother's fond affection she seemed unconscious and forgetful of the future; and by a thousand tender caresses, and all the little artifices of a woman's love, she sought to make me forget it too. She had but little success. The sight of that poor, smiling, helpless, and unconscious child brought back all my melancholy feelings. Yet I could not bear to disappoint my wife's hopes and efforts, and to make her think herself successful I strove to affect a cheerfulness I did not feel.

The beauty of the day tempted us abroad. We walked among the fields and woods, carrying the child by turns. Cassy had a hundred little things to tell me of the first slight indications of intelligence which the boy was giving. She spoke with all a mother's fluency and fervour. I said but little; indeed I hardly dared to speak at all. Had I once begun I could not have restrained myself from going on; and I did not wish to poison her pleasure by an outpouring of that bitterness which I felt bubbling up at the bottom of my heart.

The hours stole away insensibly, and the sun was already declining. I had my master's orders to be back that night; and it was time for me to go. I clasped the infant to my heart. I kissed Cassy's cheek and pressed her hand. She seemed not satisfied with so cold a parting, for she threw her arms about my neck and loaded me with embraces. This was so different from her usual coy and timid manner that I was at a loss to understand it. Is it possible that she felt some instinctive presentiment of what was going to happen? Did the thought dart across her mind that this might be our last, our final parting?

CHAPTER XXV.

WHEN I got back to Carleton-Hall, I found everything in the greatest confusion. It was not long before I was made acquainted with the cause. It seemed that some twelve months previous Mr. Carleton had found himself very much pressed for money. This had obliged him to look a little into his affairs. He found himself burdened with a load of debt of which before he had no definite idea; and as his numerous creditors, who had been too long put off with promises, were beginning to be very clamorous, he saw that some vigorous remedy was necessary. To borrow seemed the most certain means of relief from the immediate pressure of his debts; and he succeeded in obtaining a large loan from some Baltimore money-lenders, of which he secured the repayment by a mortgage upon his slaves, including even the house servants, and myself among the number. This money he expended in satisfying several executions which had already issued against him; and in stopping the mouths of the most clamorous of his creditors. The money was borrowed for a year, not with any expectation on Mr. Carleton's part of being able to repay it in that time out of any funds of his own; but in the hope that before the year's end, he might succeed in obtaining a permanent loan, and so be enabled to cancel the mortgage.

In this expectation he had been hitherto disappointed; and he was yet negotiating with the persons from whom he expected to borrow, when the time of repayment, mentioned in the mortgage, expired. This happened about a month previous; and when I got back to Carleton-Hall I found that the strangers who had arrived that morning were the agents of the Baltimore money-lenders, who had been sent to take possession of the mortgaged property. They had already caught as many of the slaves as they could find; and I no sooner entered the house than I was seized and put under a guard. These precautions were thought necessary to prevent the slaves from running away or concealing themselves from the agents of their new owners.

My poor master was in the greatest distress and embarrassment that could be imagined. It was in vain that he begged for delay, and proposed various terms of accommodation. The agents declared that they had no discretion in the matter; they were instructed to get either the money or the slaves; and in case the money was not forthcoming, to proceed with the slaves to Charleston, in South Carolina, which, at that time, was esteemed the best market for disposing of that commodity.

As to paying the money at once, that was out of the question; but Mr. Carleton hoped that he might be able in the course of a few days, if not to obtain the loan for which he was negotiating, at least to get such temporary assistance as would enable him to discharge the mortgage. The agents agreed to give him twenty-four hours, but refused to wait any longer. Mr. Carleton despaired of doing anything in so short a time; and did not think it worth his while to attempt it. The plantation hands must go; there did not seem to be any remedy for that; but he was very desirous to save his house servants from the slave-market, and he begged the agents not to leave him without a servant to make his bed or cook his dinner.

The agents replied that they were truly sorry for the disagreeable situation in which he found himself; but that, since the mortgage was made, several of the slaves included in the schedule were dead; that some of the others seemed hardly worth the sum at which they had been valued; that the price of slaves had fallen considerably since the mortgage was made, and seemed likely to fall more; and that, everything considered, they thought it more than doubtful whether the mortgaged property would be sufficient to satisfy the debt. However, they were desirous to oblige him as far as their duty to their principals would allow; and if he would pay the value of such of the slaves as he wished to retain, they had no objections to receive the money instead of the servants.

Mr. Carleton had not fifty dollars in the house; but he immediately started off to see what he could borrow in the neighbourhood. Wherever he went he found that the news of what had happened had preceded him. Besides this Baltimore mortgage, he was known to owe many other debts; and his neighbours generally looked upon him as a ruined man. Of course, the greater part of them felt no inclination to lend him their money; and, in fact, very many of them were not so much better off than Mr. Carleton as to have much money to lend. After riding about the greater part of the day, he succeeded in borrowing a few hundred dollars, on condition, however, that he should secure the repayment by a mortgage of such slaves as he should redeem. He had returned to the house a little before I did, and was already considering with himself which of his slaves he should retain. He told me that I had been a good and trustworthy servant; and that he was very unwilling to part with me. But he had not money enough to redeem us all; and his old nurse and her family were entitled to be retained in preference to any of the rest of us. Not only were their services the most essential to him, but the mother had long been a favourite servant, her children were born and bred in his family, and he considered it a matter of conscience to keep them, at all events. The agents released those of the servants whom he selected. The rest of us were kept confined, and received notice to be ready for a start early the next morning.

I had yet one hope. I thought if Mrs. Montgomery could be informed of my situation she would certainly buy me. I mentioned it to my master. He told me not to flatter myself too much with that idea, for Mrs. Montgomery already had more servants about her house than she had any kind of use for. However, he readily undertook to write her a note explaining my situation. It was despatched by a servant, and I waited with impatient hope for the answer.

At last the messenger returned. Mrs. Montgomery and her daughter had gone that morning to visit her brother, who lived some ten miles from Poplar-Grove, and they were expected to be absent three or four days. I believe I had heard something of this in the morning; but in my hurry, confusion, and excitement, it had escaped my memory.

My last hope was now gone, and as it went, the shock I felt was dreadful. Till that moment I had concealed from myself the misery of my situation. I had been familiar with calamity, but this exceeded anything I had ever suffered. It is true, I had once before been separated from my wife; but my bodily pains, my delirium, and fever, had helped to blunt the agony of that separation. Now, I was torn from both wife and child!—and that, too, without anything to call off my attention, or to deaden the torture of conscious agony. My heart swelled with impotent passion, and beat as though it would leap from my bosom. My forehead glowed with a burning heat. I would have wept; but even that relief was denied me. The tears refused to flow; the fever in my brain had parched them up.

My first impulse was to attempt making my escape. But my new masters were too well acquainted with the business of legal kidnapping, to give me an opportunity. We were all collected in one of the out-houses, and carefully secured. With many of the plantation hands, this was quite an unnecessary precaution. A large proportion of them were so sick and weary of the tyranny of Mr. Carleton's overseer, that they were glad of any change, and when their master made them a farewell visit, and began to condole with them upon their misfortune, several of them were bold enough to tell him that they thought it no misfortune at all ; for whatever might happen, they could not be worse treated than they had been by his overseer. Mr. Carleton seemed not well pleased at this bold disclosure, and took his leave of us rather abruptly; and certainly this piece of information could not have been very soothing to his feelings.

At early dawn we were put into travelling order. A waggon carried the provisions and the younger children. The rest of us were chained together, and proceeded in the usual fashion.

It was a long journey, and we were two or three weeks upon the road. Considering that we were slaves driven to market, we were treated, on the whole, with unexpected humanity. At the end of the third or fourth day's journey, the women and children were released from their chains; and two or three days later, a part of the men received the same indulgence. Those of us of whom they were more suspicious were still kept in irons. Our drivers seemed desirous to enhance our value by putting us into good condition. Our daily journey was quite moderate; we were all furnished with shoes, and were allowed plenty to eat. At night, we encamped by the road-side, kindled a large fire, cooked our hominy, and made a hut of branches to sleep under. Several of the company declared that they were never so well treated in all their lives; and they went along laughing and singing more like men travelling for pleasure, than like slaves going to be sold. So little accustomed is the slave to kindness or indulgence of any sort, that the merest trifle is enough to put him into ecstacy. The gift of a single extra meal is sufficient to make him fall in love even with a slave-driver.

The songs and laughter of my companions only served to aggravate my melancholy. They observed it, and did their best to cheer me. There never was a kinder-hearted company, and I found some relief even in their rude efforts at consolation; for there is more power in the sympathy of the humblest human creature than the haughty children of luxury are apt to believe. I was a favourite among the servants at Carleton-Hall, because I had taken some little pains to be so; for I had long since renounced that silly prejudice and foolish pride, which, at an earlier period, had kept me aloof from my fellow-servants, and had justly earned me their hatred and dislike. Experience had made me wiser, and I no longer took sides with our oppressors by joining them in the false notion of their own natural superiority,—a notion founded only in the arrogant prejudice of conceited ignorance, and long since discarded by the liberal and enlightened; but a notion which is still the orthodox creed of all America, and the principal, I might almost say the sole, foundation which sustains the iniquitous superstructure of American slavery. I had made it a point to gain the good-will and affection of my fellow-servants, by mixing among them; taking an interest in all their concerns; and rendering them such little services as my favour with Mr. Carleton put in my power. Once or twice, indeed, I had over-stepped the mark, and got myself into very serious trouble by letting my master know what severities his overseer inflicted. But though my attempts at serving them were not always successful, their gratitude was not the less on that account.

When my companions observed my melancholy, they stopped their songs, and having run through their few topics of condolence, they continued their conversation in a subdued and moderated tone, as if unwilling to irritate my feeling by what might seem to me un-seasonable merriment. I saw, and in my heart acknowledged, the kindness of their intention; but I did not wish that my sadness should cast a shade over what they enjoyed as a holiday,—the only holiday perhaps which their miserable fate would ever allow them. I told them that nothing would be so likely to cheer me as to see them merry; and though my heart was aching and ready almost to burst, I forced a laugh, and started a song. The rest joined in it; the chorus rose again loud as ever; the laugh went round; and the turbulence of their merriment soon allowed me to sink again into a moody silence.

I had the natural feelings of a man; I loved my wife and child. Had they been snatched from me by death, or had I been separated from them by some fixed, inevitable, natural necessity, I should have wept, no doubt, but my feelings would have been those of simple grief, un-mixed with any more bitter emotion. But that the dear ties of husband

and father, ties so twined about my inmost heart, should be thus violently severed, without a moment's warning, and at a creditor's caprice, —and he, too, the creditor of another;—to be thus chained up, torn from my home and driven to market, there to be sold to pay the debts of a man who called himself my master;—the thoughts of this stirred up within my soul a bitter hatred and a burning indignation against the laws and the people that tolerate such things; fierce and deadly passions which tore my heart distracted and tormented me even more than my grief at the sudden separation.

But the more violent emotions ever tend to cure themselves. If the patient survive the first paroxysm, his mind speedily begins to verge towards its natural equilibrium. I found it so. The torture of furious but impotent emotions at first almost overpowered me. But my feelings softened by degrees; till, at length, they subsided into a dull, but fixed and settled misery; a misery which the impulse of temporary excitement may sometimes make me forget, but which, like the guilty man's remorse, is too deeply rooted to be ever eradicated.

CHAPTER XXVI.

AT length we arrived at Charleston, the capital of South Carolina. We spent several days in recruiting ourselves after our long journey. As soon as we had recovered from our lameness and fatigues, we were dressed up in new clothes, and fitted out to show off to the best advantage. We were then exposed for the inspection of purchasers. The women and children, pleased with their new finery, seemed to enjoy the novelty of their situation, and appeared as anxious to find a master and to bring a high price, as though the bargain were actually for their own benefit. The greater part of our company were bought up by a single purchaser, and I among the rest. We were purchased by General Carter, a man of princely fortune, indeed, one of the richest planters in South Carolina; and were immediately sent off to one of his plantations, at some distance from the city.

The lower country of South Carolina, from the Atlantic for eighty or a hundred miles inward, including more than half the state, is, with the exception I shall presently mention, one of the most barren, miserable, uninviting countries in the universe. In general, the soil is nothing but a thirsty sand, covered for miles and miles with forests of the long-leaved pine. These tracts are called, in the expressive phrase of the country, *Pine Barrens.* For a great distance inland, these Barrens preserve almost a perfect level, raised but a few feet above the surface of the sea. The tall, straight branchless trunks of the scattered pines rise like slender columns, and are crowned with a tuft of gnarly limbs and long, bristly leaves, through which the breezes murmur with a monotonous sound, much like that of falling waters, or waves breaking on a beach. There is rarely any undergrowth, and the surface is either matted with the saw-palmetto, a low evergreen, or covered with a coarse and scattered grass, on which herds of half-wild cattle feed in summer, and starve in winter. The trunks of the pines scarcely interrupt a prospect, whose tedious sameness is only varied by tracts, here and there, of almost impenetrable swamp, thickly grown up with bays, water oaks, cypresses, and other large trees, adown whose spreading branches and whitened trunks a long dusky moss hangs in melancholy festoons, drooping to the ground, the very drapery of disease and death. The rivers, which are wide and shallow, swollen with the heavy rains of spring and winter, frequently overflow their low and marshy banks, and help to increase the extent of swampy ground, the copious source of poisonous vapours and febrile exhalations. Even where the country begins to rise into hills, it preserves, for a long distance, its sterile character. It is a collection of sandy hillocks, thrown together in the strangest confusion. In several places, not even the pine will grow; and the barren and thirsty soil is clothed only with stunted bushes of the black jack, or dwarf oak. In some spots even these are wanting, and the bare sand is drifted by the winds.

Throughout this extent of country, of which, with all its barrenness, a great part might be, and by the enterprising spirit of free labour doubtless would be, brought into profitable cultivation, there are only some small tracts, principally along the water-courses, which the costly and thriftless system of slave labour has found capable of improvement. All the rest still remains a primitive wilderness, with scarcely anything to interrupt its desolate and dreary monotony.

This description does not include the tract stretching along the sea-shore, from the mouth of the Santee to that of the Savannah, and extending in some places twenty or thirty miles up the country. The coast between these rivers is a series of islands;—the famous *sea-islands* of the cotton-markets; and the main land, which is separated from these islands by innumerable narrow and winding channels, is penetrated, for some distance inland by a vast number of creeks and inlets. The islands present a bluff shore and a fine beach towards the ocean, but the opposite sides are often low and marshy. They were originally covered with a magnificent growth of the live, or ever-green oak, one of the finest trees anywhere to be seen. The soil is light; but it possesses a fertility never yet attained in the dead and barren sands of the interior. These lands are protected by embankments from the tides and floods, and the fields are divided and drained by frequent dykes and ditches. Such of them as can be most conveniently irrigated with fresh water are cultivated as rice-fields;—the remainder are employed in the production of the long staple, or sea-island cotton,—a species of vegetable wool, which excels every other in the length of its fibre, and almost rivals silk in strength and softness.

These beautiful districts present a strong contrast to the rest of the lower country of South Carolina. As far as the eye can stretch, nothing is to be seen but a smooth, level, highly-cultivated country, penetrated in every direction by creeks and rivers. The residences of the planters are often handsome buildings, placed on some fine swell, and shaded by a choice variety of trees and shrubbery. These houses are inhabited by their owners only in the winter. They are driven from home in the summer, partly by the tiresomeness of a listless and monotonous indolence, and partly by the unhealthiness of the climate, which is much aggravated by the rice cultivation. This absentee aristocracy congregates in Charleston, or dazzles and astonishes the cities and watering-places of the North, by its profuse extravagance and reckless dissipation. The plantations are left to the sole management of overseers, who, with their families, form almost the only permanent free population of these districts. The slaves are ten times as numerous as the free. The whole of

H 2

this rich and beautiful country is devoted to the support of a few hundred families in a lorldly, luxurious, dissipated indolence, which renders them useless to the world and a burden to themselves; and to contribute towards this same great end, more than a hundred thousand human beings are sunk into the very lowest depths of degradation misery.

General Carter, our new master, was one of the richest of these American grandees. The plantation to which we were sent was called Loosahachee; and though very extensive, was but one out of several which he owned. Coming as I did from Virginia, there were many things in the appearance of the country, and in the way in which things were managed, that were entirely new to me.

I and my companions, who had always been accustomed to some small quantity of meat, as a relish to our corn diet, found our mere unseasoned hominy neither so palatable nor so nourishing as we could wish. Being strangers and new-comers, we had not yet learned the customs of the country, and were quite unacquainted with many of the arts by which the Carolina slaves are enabled to eke out their scanty and insufficient allowance. Our only resource was an appeal to our master's generosity; and it happened, that about a fortnight after we were put upon the plantation, General Carter, with several of his friends, made a flying visit from Charleston to Loosahachee, to see how the crops were coming on. This we thought to be a good opportunity to get some improvement of our fare. We did not like to ask too much, lest our request should be rejected without ceremony. Indeed we determined to be as moderate as possible; and after due consultation, it was resolved to petition our master for a little salt to season our hominy—a luxury to which we had always been accustomed, but which was not included in the Loosahachee allowance, which consisted simply of corn, a peck a week to each working hand. My companions requested me to act as spokesman, and I readily undertook to do so.

When General Carter and his friends came near my task, I walked towards him. He asked me what I meant by leaving my work in that fashion, and inquired what I wanted? I told him that I was one of the servants whom he had lately purchased; that some of us were born and raised in Virginia and the rest in North Carolina; that we were not used to living upon bare hominy without anything to give it a relish; and that we should take it as a very great favour if he would be kind enough to allow us a little salt.

He seemed to be rather surprised at the boldness of this request, and inquired my name.

"Archy Moore," I answered.

"Archy Moore!" he cried with a sneer,—"and pray tell me how long it has been the fashion among you fellows to have double names? You are the first fellow I ever owned who was guilty of such a piece of impertinence; and a damned impertinent fellow you are. I see it in your eye. Let me beg leave to request of you, Mr. Archy Moore, to be satisfied with calling yourself Archy, the next time I inquire your name."

I had taken the name of Moore since leaving Spring-Meadow; an assumption not uncommon in Virginia, and which is there thought harmless enough. But the South Carolinians, who of all the Americans seem to have carried the theory and practice of tyranny to the highest perfection, are jealous of everything that may seem in any respect to raise their slaves above the level of their dogs and horses.

The words and manner of my master were sufficiently irritating, but I was not to be shuffled off in that way. I passed over his rebuke in silence; but ventured again, in the most respectful terms I could command, to renew the request, that he would be pleased to allow us a little salt to season our hominy.

"You are a damned unreasonable, dissatisfied set of fellows as ever I met with!" was the answer. "Why, boy, you eat me out of house and home already. It is as much as I can do to buy corn for you. If you want salt, isn't there plenty of sea-water within five miles? If you want it, you have nothing to do but to make it!"

So he said; and as they wheeled their horses and rode away, he and his companions joined in a loud laugh at the wit and point of his answer.

CHAPTER XXVII.

AMONG Mr. Carleton's servants, or rather the servants that had been Mr. Carleton's, but who had now become the property of General Carter, was one named Thomas. While we had lived together at Carleton-Hall, I had contracted an intimacy with him, which we still kept up. He was of unmixed African blood, with good features, a stout, muscular frame, and on several accounts a very remarkable man.

His bodily strength, and his capacity for enduring privation and fatigue, were very uncommon; but the character of his mind was still more so. His passions were strong and even violent; but what is very rare among slaves, he had them completely under his control; and in all his words and actions he was as gentle as a lamb. The truth was, that when quite young, he had been taken in hand by certain Methodists who lived and laboured in his neighbourhood; and so strong and lasting were the impressions which their teaching made upon him, and so completely had he imbibed their doctrines, that it seemed as if several of the most powerful principles of human nature had been eradicated from his bosom.

His religious teachers had thoroughly inculcated into a soul, naturally proud and high-spirited, that creed of passive obedience and patient long-suffering, which under the sacred name of religion has been often found more potent than whips or fetters, in upholding tyranny and subduing the resistance of the superstitious and trembling slave. They had taught him, and he believed, that God had made him a servant, and that it was his duty to obey his master and be contented with his lot. Whatever cruelties or indignities the unprovoked insolence of unlimited authority might inflict upon him, it was his duty to submit in humble silence; and if his master smote him on one cheek, he was to turn to him the other also. This, with Thomas, was not a mere form of words run through with and then forgotten. In all my experience, I have never known a man over whom his creed appeared to hold so powerful a control.

Nature had intended him for one of those lofty spirits who are the terror of tyrants and the bold assertors of liberty. But under the influence of his religion, he had become a passive, humble, and obedient slave. He made it a point of duty to be faithful to his master in all things. He never tasted whiskey; he would sooner starve than steal; and he perferred being whipped to telling a lie. These qualities, so very uncommon in a slave, as well as his cheerful obedience and laborious industry, had gained him the good-will even of Mr. Carleton's overseer. He was treated as a sort of confidential servant; was often trusted to keep the keys, and give out the allowance; and so scrupulously did he fulfil all that was required of him, that even the fretful caprice of an overseer had no fault to find. He had lived at Carleton-Hall more than ten years, and in all that time had never once been whipped. What was most remarkable and uncommon of all, at the same time that he obtained the confidence of the overseer, Thomas had succeeded in gaining the good-will of his fellow-servants. There never lived a kinder-hearted, better-tempered man. There was nothing he was not ready to do for a fellow-creature in distress; he was ever willing to share his provisions with the hungry, and to help the weak and tired to finish their tasks. Besides, he was the spiritual guide of the plantation, and could preach and pray almost as well as his master. I had no sympathy for his religious enthusiasm, but I loved and admired the man; and we had long been on terms of close intimacy.

Thomas had a wife, Ann by name, a pretty, sprightly, good-natured girl, whom he loved exceedingly. It was a great comfort to him—indeed he regarded it as a special interposition of Providence in his behalf—that when carried away from Carleton-Hall they had not been separated. Never was a man more grateful or more delighted than Thomas was when he found that both he and Ann had been purchased by General Carter. That they should fall into the hands of the same owner was all he desired; and he readily transferred to the service of his purchaser all that zeal and devotion which, as he had been taught to believe, a slave owes to his master. While all the rest of us, upon our first arrival at Loosahachee, had been complaining and lamenting over the hardness of our tasks, and the poor and insufficient food which our new master allowed us, Thomas said not a word; but had worked away with such zeal and vigour, that he soon gained the reputation of being one of the best hands on the place.

Thomas's wife had an infant child but a few weeks old, who, according to the Carolina fashion, was brought to her in the field to be nursed;—for the Carolina planters, spendthrifts in everything else, in all that regards their servants are wonderful economists. One hot afternoon, Ann sat down beneath a tree, and took the infant from the hands of the little child, herself scarcely able to walk, who had the care of it during the day. She had finished the maternal office, and was returning slowly, and perhaps rather unwillingly, to her task, when the overseer rode into that part of the field. The name of our overseer was Mr. Martin. He was one of those who are denominated smart fellows and good disciplinarians. He had established a rule that there was to be no loitering at Loosahachee. Walking was too lazy a pace for him; if there was any occasion to go from one part of the field to another, it was to be in a run. Ann had perhaps forgotten, at all events she was not complying with this ridiculous piece of plantation discipline. This was no sooner observed by the overseer than he rode up to her, cursed her for a lazy vagabond; and commenced beating her over the head with his whip. Thomas happened to be working close by. He felt every stroke ten times as keenly as though it had lighted upon his own shoulders. Here was a trial too strong for the artificial principles of any creed. He moved forward as though he would go to his wife's assistance. We who were by begged him to stop, and told him he would only get himself into trouble. But the cries and shrieks of his wife made him deaf to our entreaties; he rushed forward, and before the overseer was aware he seized his whip, snatched it from his hand, and demanded what he meant by beating a woman in that way for no offence whatever?

To judge from Mr. Martin's looks, this was a display of spirit, or, as he would call it, of insolence and insubordination, for which he was not at all prepared. He reined back his horse for a rod or two;—when, seeming to recollect himself, he put his hand into his coat-pocket and drew out a pistol. He cocked it and pointed it at Thomas, who dropped the whip and turned to run. Mr. Martin fired; but his hand shook too much to enable him to take a very effectual aim; and Thomas continued his flight, leaped the fence, and disappeared in the thicket by which it was bordered.

Having put the husband to flight, the overseer turned to the wife, who stood by trembling and crying. He was boiling over with rage and passion, and seemed determined to spend his fury on this helpless and unhappy woman. He called the driver of the gang and two or three other men to his assistance, and bade them strip off her clothes.

The preparations being complete, Mr. Martin commenced the torture. The lash buried itself in her flesh at every blow; and as the poor wretch threw up her gashed and gory arms, the blood ran down in streams. Her cries were dreadful. Used as I had been to similar scenes, my heart sickened and my head grew dizzy. I longed to seize the monster by the throat and dash him to the ground. How I restrained myself I do not know. Most sure I am, that nothing but the base and dastard spirit of a slave could have endured that scene of female torture and distress, and not have interfered.

Before Mr. Martin had finished, poor Ann sunk to the ground in a state of total insensibility. He ordered us to make a litter of sticks and hoe-handles, and to carry her to his house. We laid her down in the passage. The overseer brought a heavy chain, one end of which he put around her neck, and the other he fastened to one of the beams. He said her fainting was all pretence; and that if he did not chain her she would be running away and joining her husband.

We were now all ordered into the woods to hunt for Thomas. We separated and prétended to examine every place that seemed likely to conceal him; but with the exception of the drivers, and one or two base fellows who sought to curry favour with the overseer, I do not believe that any of us felt any great anxiety, or took much pains to find him. Not far from the fence was a low swampy place, thickly grown up with cane and gum-trees. As I was making my way through it, I came suddenly upon Thomas, who was leaning against the trunk of a large tree. He laid his hand upon my shoulder, and asked what the overseer had done to his wife. I concealed from him, as well as I could, the miserable torture which had been inflicted upon her; but I told him that Mr. Martin was all fire and fury, and that it would be best for him to keep out of the way till his passion could subside a little. I promised to return in the evening and to bring him food. In the mean time, if he would lie close, there would be little danger that any one would find him.

We were presently called back from our ineffectual search, and ordered to resume our tasks. I finished mine as quickly as I could; hastened home, got some food ready, and went to see poor Anne. I found her lying in the passage chained as we had left her. Her low moans showed that she had so far recovered herself as to be once more sensitive to pain. She complained that the chain about her neck hurt her and made it difficult to breathe. I stooped down and was attempting to loosen it, when Mrs. Martin made her appearance at the door; she asked what right I had to meddle with the girl; and bade me go about my business. I would have left the food I had brought, but Mrs. Martin told me to take it away again; it would learn the wench better manners, she said, to starve her for a day or two.

I took up my little basket and went away with a heavy heart. As soon as it grew dark I set off to meet Thomas; but lest my steps might be dogged by the overseer or some of his spies, I took a very roundabout course. I found him near the place where I had met him before. His earnest entreaties to know the whole drew from me the story of his poor wife's sufferings and her present situation. It moved him deeply. At intervals he wept like a child; then he strove to restrain himself, repeating half aloud some texts of scripture, and what seemed a sort of prayer. But all would not do; and carried away at last by a sudden gust of passion, forgetful of his religious scruples, he cursed the brutal overseer with all the energy of a husband's vengeance. Presently he recovered his self-command, and began to take fault to himself, ascribing all the blame to his own foolish interference. The thought that what his affection for his wife had prompted him to do had only served to aggravate her sufferings seemed to agitate him almost to distraction. Again, the tide of passion swept all before it. His countenance grew convulsed, his bosom heaved, and he only found relief in half-uttered threats and muttered execrations.

He consulted with me as to what he had better do. I knew that the overseer was terribly incensed against him. I had heard him say that if such a daring act of insolence was not most signally punished, it would be enough to corrrupt and disorder the whole neighbourhood. I was aware that Mr. Martin would not dare absolutely to put him to death. But this prohibition to commit murder is the sole and single limit to an overseer's authority; and I knew that he had both the right and the will to inflict a torture compared to which the agonies of an ordinary death-struggle would be but trifling. I therefore advised Thomas to fly, since even if he were caught at last, no severer punishment could be inflicted upon him than he would be certain of upon a voluntary surrender.

For a moment this advice seemed to please him; and an expression of daring determination appeared in his face, such as I had never seen there before. But it disappeared in an instant. "There is Ann," he said; "I cannot leave her, and she, poor, timid thing, even if she were well, I could never persuade her to fly with me. It will not do, Archy; I cannot leave my wife!"

What could I answer?

I understood him well, and knew how to sympathise with him. I could not but admit the force of his objection. Such feelings I knew it would be in vain to combat with arguments; indeed I could not make up my mind to attempt it; and as I had no other advice to give, I remained silent.

Thomas seemed lost in thought, and continued for some minutes with his eyes fixed upon the ground; presently he told me that he had made up his mind,—he was determined, he said, to go to Charleston and appeal to his master.

The little I had known of General Carter did not incline me to put much dependence on his justice or generosity; but as Thomas seemed pleased with this plan, and as it was his only chance, I applauded it. He ate the food I had brought, and determined to set off immediately. He had only been once to Charleston during all the time we had been at Loosahachee; but as he was one of those people who, if they have been once to a place, find little difficulty in going a second time, I had no doubt of his finding his way to town.

I returned to my cabin; but I was so anxious and uncertain about the success of Thomas, in the scheme he had adopted, that I could not sleep. At daylight I went to my task. My anxiety acted as a stimulus upon me, and I had finished long before any of my companions. As I was passing from the field to my cabin I saw General Carter's carriage driving up the road, and as it passed me I observed poor Thomas behind, chained to the footman's stand.

The carriage drove up to the house; General Carter got out of it, and sent off in great haste for Mr. Martin, who had taken his gun and dog early that morning, and had been beating about the woods all day in search of Thomas. In the meantime General Carter ordered all the hands on the plantation to be collected.

At last Mr. Martin arrived. The moment General Carter saw him he cried out, "Well, sir, here is a runaway I have brought back for you. Would you believe it, the fellow had the impertinence to come to Charleston with the story of his grievances! Even from his own account of the matter he was guilty of the greatest insolence I ever heard of,—snatching the whip from the hand of an overseer! Things are coming to a pretty pass indeed, when these fellows undertake to justify such insubordination. The next thing we shall hear of they will be cutting our throats. However, I stopped the scoundrel's mouth before he had said five words. I told him I would pardon anything sooner than insolence to my overseer,—I would much sooner excuse impertinence towards myself. And to let him know what I thought of his conduct, here you see I have brought him back to you, and I have done it even at the risk of being obliged to sleep here to-night and catching the country fever. Whip the rascal well, Mr. Martin! whip him well! I have had all the hands collected, that they may see the punishment, and take warning by it."

Mr. Martin, thus invited, sprung upon his prey with a tiger's ferocity. But I have no inclination to disgust myself with another description of the horrid torment of which, in America, the whip is the active and continual instrument. He who is curious in these matters will do well to spend six months upon an American plantation. He will soon discover that the rack was a superfluous invention, and that the whip, by those well skilled in the use of it, can be made to answer any purposes of torture.

Though Thomas was quite cut up with the lash, and whipped by two drivers till he fainted from pain and loss of blood, such was the nerve and vigour of his constitution, and the noble firmness of his mind, that he stood it like a hero, and disdained to utter any of those piercing screams and piteous cries for mercy which are commonly heard upon the like occasions. He soon got over the effects of this discipline, and in a few days was at work again as usual.

Not so with his wife. She was naturally of a slender constitution, and perhaps had not entirely recovered from the weakness incident upon childbirth. Either the whipping she had suffered, or her chains and starvation afterwards, or both together, had brought on a violent disorder, of which at first she seemed to get better, but which left her suffering under a dull nervous fever, without strength or appetite, or even the desire of recovery. Her poor baby seemed to sympathise with its mother, and pined from day to day,—at length it died. The mother did not long survive it; she lingered for a week or two. Sick as she was, she had no attendant except a superannuated old woman, who could neither see nor hear. Thomas of course was obliged to go to his tasks as usual. He returned one night, and found her dead.

One of the drivers, a mean-spirited fellow, and Mr. Martin's principal spy and informer, was the only person allowed to preach at Loosahachee, and to act as the leader in those mummeries to which the ignorant and superstitious slaves give the name of religion. He paid a visit to the afflicted husband, and offered his services for the funeral. Thomas had so much natural good sense, that he was not, like many persons of his way of thinking, imposed upon and taken in by every one who chose to make use of the cant of sanctity. He had long ago seen through this hypocritical fellow, and learned to despise him. He therefore declined his assistance; and pointing to me, "Himself and his friend," he said, "would be sufficient to bury the poor girl." He seemed about to add something more; but the mention of his wife had overpowered him, his voice choked, his eyes filled with tears, and he was constrained to be silent.

It was a Sunday. The preacher soon left us; and poor Thomas sat the whole day watching his wife's body. I remained with him; but I knew how useless any attempt at consolation would be, and I said but little.

Towards sunset several of our fellow-servants came in; and they were presently followed by most of the plantation people. We took up the body and carried it to the place of burial. This was a fine, smooth slope covered with tall trees. It seemed to have been long used for its present purpose. Numerous little ridges, some of them new, and others just discernible, indicated the places of the graves.

The husband leaned over the body, while we busied ourselves in the sad office of digging its last resting-place. The shallow grave was soon finished. We all remained silent, in expectation of a prayer, a hymn, or some similar ceremony. Thomas attempted once or twice to begin, but his voice rattled in his throat, and died away in an inarticulate murmur. He shook his head, and bade us place the body in the grave. We did so; and the earth was soon heaped upon it.

It was already growing dark; and the burial being finished, those who had attended at it hastened homeward. The husband still remained standing by the side of the grave. I took his arm, and with a gentle force would have drawn him away. He shook me off, and raising his hand and head, he muttered in a low whisper, "Murdered, murdered!" As he spoke these words he turned his eyes on me. There gleamed in them a spirit of passionate and indignant grief. It was plain that natural feeling was fast gaining the mastery over that system of artificial constraint in which he had been educated. I sympathised with him, and I pressed his hand to let him know I did so. He returned the pressure; and, after a short pause, he added, "Blood for blood; is it not so, Archy?" There was something terrible in the slow but firm and steady tone in which he spoke. I knew not what to answer; nor did he appear to expect a reply. Though he addressed me, the question seemed intended only for himself. I took his arm, and we walked off in silence.

CHAPTER XXVIII.

It is customary in South Carolina to allow the slaves the week from Christmas to the new year, as a sort of holiday. This indulgence is extended so far, that during that week they are, for the most part, allowed to leave the plantations, the scenes of their daily labours and sufferings, and to wander about in the neighbourhood, pretty much at their own will and pleasure. The highways present at that season a singular appearance. The slaves of every age and sex, collected from the populous plantations of the tide-waters, and dressed in the best attire they have been able to muster, assemble in great numbers, swarming along the road, and clustering about the little whisky-shops, producing a scene of bustle and confusion, witnessed only at the Christmas holidays.

Those shops are principally supported by a traffic with the slaves for stolen rice and cotton,—a traffic which all the vindictive fury of the planters, backed by an abundant legislation, has not been able to eradicate. They are the chief support, in fact, the only means of livelihood, open to a considerable portion of the lower order of the white aristocracy of the country. It is the same in Carolina as in Lower Virginia. The poor whites are extremely rude and ignorant, and acquainted with but few of the comforts of civilised life. They are idle, dissipated, and vicious, with all that vulgar brutality of vice which poverty and ignorance render so conspicuous and disgusting. Without land, or, at best, possessing some little tract of barren and exhausted soil, which they have neither skill nor industry to render productive; without any trade or handicraft art; and looking upon all manual labour as degrading to free men, and fit only for a state of servitude,—these poor white men have become the jest of the slaves, and are at once feared and hated by the select aristocracy of rich planters. It is only the right of suffrage which they possess that preserves them the show of consideration and respect with which they are yet treated. This right of suffrage, of which the select aristocracy are extremely anxious to deprive them, is the only safeguard of the poor whites. But for this, they would be trampled under foot without mercy, and by force of law and legislation would soon be reduced to a condition little superior to that of the very slaves themselves.

On the Christmas holidays which succeeded my becoming an inhabitant of Loosahachee, a great number of slaves, of whom I was one, were assembled about a little store on the neighbouring high-road, laughing, talking, drinking whisky, and making merry after our several fashions. While we were thus employed, I observed, riding along the road, a mean-looking fellow, shabbily dressed, with a face of that disagreeable cadaverous hue that makes the inferior order of whites in Lower Carolina look so much like walking corpses. He was mounted on a lean scraggy horse, whose hips seemed just bursting through the skin, and he carried in his

hand an enormous whip, which he handled with a familiar grace, seldom
acquired except by an American slave-driver. As he passed us, I
noticed that all the slaves who had hats pulled them off to him; but as
I did not see anything in the fellow's appearance that demanded any
particular respect, and as I was ignorant of the Carolina etiquette,
which requires from every slave an obsequious bearing towards every
freeman, seldom expected in Virginia, I let my hat remain upon my
head. The fellow noticed it; reined up his jaded beast, and eyed me
sharply. My complexion made him doubt whether I might not be a
freeman; my dress, and the company I was in, gave him equal grounds
for supposing me a slave. He inquired who I was, and being told that I
was one of General Carter's people, he rode towards me with his upraised
whip, demanding why I did not take off my hat to him, and, without
waiting for an answer, he began to lay the lash over my shoulders. The
fellow was evidently drunk, and my first impulse was to take the whip
away from him. Luckily, I did not yield to this impulse; for any
attempt to resist even a drunken white man, though that resistance was
only in repelling the most unprovoked attack, according to the just and
equal laws of Carolina, might have cost me my life.

I learned upon inquiry that this fellow had been an overseer; but
some time previous had been discharged by his employer for suspected
dishonesty. Not long after, he had set up a whisky shop about half a
mile distant. From what he said to the owner of the store where we
were assembled, it would seem that his shop had not been so much frequented during the holidays as he had expected, and in beating me, he
had vented his drunken spite and ill-humour on the first object that
gave him anything like a pretence to exercise it. I learned, too, that
this fellow, whose name was Christie, was a cousin of Mr. Martin, our
overseer. They had been close friends; but had lately had a violent
quarrel. Christie had stabbed Martin, and Martin had shot at Christie
with his double-barrelled gun. He had taken a still more effectual
revenge by doing the best to stop the trade from Loosahachee to Christie's
shop, which he had formerly winked at, and which had been carried on,
much to Christie's benefit, by the exchange of well-watered whisky for
General Carter's rice and cotton.

I no sooner heard this account of Mr. Christie, than it occurred to
me that I had him in my power, and, at once, I resolved to make him
smart in his turn, for the lashes he had inflicted upon me. It is true, I
was obliged to play the part of a spy and an informer; but such low
means are the only resource which the condition of servitude allows. As
soon as I got home, I hastened to the overseer, and with an abundance
of hypocritical pretences, and professions of zeal for my master's service,
I communicated to him, as a great secret, the fact that Mr. Christie was
in the habit of trading with the hands, and buying whatever they
brought him, without asking any questions.

Mr. Martin said that he was well aware of it, and he would give me
five dollars if I would help him to detect Christie in the fact.

We quickly struck up a bargain. The overseer furnished me with a
quantity of cotton, and I set off one moon-light night to pay a visit to
Mr. Christie's shop.

He recognized me at once, and jested a good deal about the whipping
he had given me. He thought it an excellent joke; and it best answered
my purpose to appear very much of the same opinion. I found him not
at all disinclined to trade, provided I would exchange my cotton for his
whisky, at the nominal price of a dollar a quart. It was not long be-

fore I paid him a second visit. That time, Mr. Martin and one of his friends were posted outside the shop, at a place where they could peep between the logs, and see and overhear the whole transaction.

To buy rice, cotton, or in fact anything else, of a slave, unless he produces a written permit from his master to sell it, according to the Carolina statute-book, is one of the most enormous crimes a man can commit. Mr. Christie was indicted at the next court. He was found guilty on the express testimony of Mr. Martin and his companion, and was fined a thousand dollars and sentenced to a year's imprisonment. The fine swept away what little property he had, and how his imprisonment ended I never heard. More than one of the jurymen who convicted him were grievously suspected of the very same practices; but the dread of incurring fresh suspicion, or perhaps the jealous rivalry of trade, made those very fellows the most clamorous for his condemnation.

Mr. Martin was so well pleased with my services in this affair—in which he fancied I had put myself forward merely to be used as his cat's paw—that he took me quite into favour, and began to employ me as one of his regular spies and informers. Tyranny, whether on the great scale or the little, can only be sustained through a system of espionage and betrayal, in which the most mean-spirited of the oppressed are turned into the tools and instruments of oppression. There are many alleviations of the wretchedness of servitude to be expected from the favour and indulgence of an overseer. Let it be remembered also, that so strong are the allurements which power holds out, that even among freemen there are hundreds of thousands always to be found, who are ready to assist in sacrificing the dearest rights of their neighbours, by volunteering to be the instruments of superior tyrants. What then can be reasonably expected from those who have been studiously and systematically degraded? What wonder if among the oppressed are found the readiest and most relentless instruments of oppression?

As I knew I could turn Mr. Martin's favour to good account, I took care not to let him suspect with what scorn and loathing I regarded the office in which he sought to employ me. But while he imagined that I was engaged heart and hand in his service, I counterworked him more than once, by communicating his plans and stratagems to those whom he sought to entrap. This same Mr. Martin, though he was absolute viceroy over more than three hundred people, was a very ignorant and a very stupid fellow. Several circumstances occurred which, with a shrewd person, would have betrayed me; but I succeeded so completely in blinding Mr. Martin's eyes, that he still continued to place an unlimited confidence in my fidelity. Of this he soon gave me a new proof, for, riding one day into the field where I was at work, and not finding matters going on just to suit him, he called out the driver of the gang, and took from him the whip, which he carried as the badge and principal instrument of his office. He then called for me; and having given me twenty or thirty lashes, according to the custom in such cases, he put the whip into my hand, appointed me driver of the gang, and bade me do the first duty of my new office upon the fellow to whose place I had succeeded.

It is under the inspection of drivers, who are appointed from among the slaves, at the will of the overseer, that the culture of a Carolina plantation is carried on. The overseers have learned too much of the airs and the luxurious indolence of their employers to be willing to be riding about all day in the hot sun looking after the labourers. The slaves are divided into gangs, and each gang is put under the charge of a driver, who is generally selected for his cowardly and mean-spirited subserviency, and his readiness to tyrannize over and to betray his companions. The driver is entrusted with all the unlimited and absolute authority of the master himself. He receives a double allowance; he has no task; his sole business is to look after his gang and see that they perform the work assigned them; and for this purpose he takes his station in the midst of them, whip in hand. When the overseer makes his appearance in the field, all the drivers collect about him to receive his orders. For the performance of the work assigned to his gang, each driver is himself responsible; and that he may perfectly understand by what means he is to enforce its performance, the overseer usually inducts him into office by giving him a severe castigation with the very whip which he afterwards puts into his hand to be used upon his companions.

The absolute power of an overseer is often, I ought rather to say always, shockingly abused; but the absolute power of drivers is yet one step higher towards the perfection of tyranny. The driver faithfully copies all the arrogance and insolence of the overseer from whom he receives his commission; and as he is always among his gang, the aggravating weight of his authority is so much the heavier. He is but one of themselves, and the slaves are naturally more impatient of his rule than they would be of the same dominion exercised by one belonging to what they have been taught to regard as a superior race, and whom, being a freeman, they are ready to acknowledge as actually their superior. Besides, the drivers are far from limiting their demands, as the overseer himself generally would do, to the performance of the field labour. They have a thousand little spites to gratify, a thousand purposes of their own to accomplish. They are, in fact, the absolute masters of everything which any of their gang may happen to possess; and the persons of the women are as much at their disposal as at that of the overseer or the master. Even if by chance a driver should happen not to be disposed to abuse his authority, the dread of losing his situation and the knowledge that all the deficiencies of any of his subordinates will be visited upon his head, makes him of necessity hasty, harsh, and cruel.

Heaven is my witness, that while I held the office of driver my great object was to use the authority which it gave me to alleviate, as far as I could, the misery of my companions. My gang consisted of the Carleton hands, with whom I had long been connected, and whom I looked upon as friends and fellow-sufferers. Many is the time when I have seen one and another fainting under his task and unable to finish it, that I have dropped the whip, seized the hoe, and instead of the stimulus of the lash have used the encouragement of aid and assistance. This I did repeatedly, though Mr. Martin more than once, when he found me so employed, expressed his disapprobation, and told me it was no way, and would only bring the station of driver into contempt.

But it is no part of my purpose to write an eulogium on myself; and I shall not hesitate to confess the whole truth. There were times that I abused my office; and I verily believe that no man ever exercised an unlimited authority who did not abuse it. The consciousness of my power made me insolent and impatient; and with all my hatred, my hearty, experimental hatred of tyranny, the whip had not long been placed in my hands before I caught myself in the act of playing the tyrant.

Power is ever dangerous and intoxicating. Human nature cannot bear it. It must be constantly checked, controlled, and limited, or it declines inevitably into tyranny. Even all the endearments of the family connection, the tenderness of connubial love, and the heart-binding ties of paternity, seconded, as they always are, by the strong influence of habit and opinion, have not made it safe to entrust the head of a family with absolute power even over his own household. What terms, then, are strong enough in which to denounce the vain, ridiculous, and wanton folly of expecting anything but abuse where power is totally unchecked by either moral or legal control?

CHAPTER XXIX.

Since the death of his wife, a remarkable change had taken place in my friend Thomas. He had lost his former air of contentment and good-nature, and had grown morose and sullen. Instead of being the most willing and industrious labourer in the field, as he used to be, he seemed to have imbibed a strong distaste for work, and he slighted and neglected his task as much as possible. Had he been under any other driver than myself, his idleness and neglect would have frequently brought him into trouble. But I loved and pitied him, and I screened him all I could.

The wrongs and injuries that had been inflicted upon him since his arrival at Loosahachee seemed to have subverted all the principles upon which he had so long acted. It was a subject on which he did not seem inclined to converse, and upon which I was unwilling to press him; but I had abundant reason to suspect that he had totally renounced the religion in which he had been so carefully instructed, and which, for so long a time, had exercised so powerful an influence over him. He had secretly returned to the practice of certain wild rites, which in his early youth he had learned from his mother, who had herself been kidnapped from the coast of Africa, and who had been, as he had often told me, zealously devoted to her country's superstitions. He would sometimes talk wildly and incoherently about having seen the spirit of his departed wife, and of some promise he had made to the apparition; and I was led to believe that he suffered under occasional fits of partial insanity.

At all events, he was in most respects an altered man. He had ceased to be the humble and obedient slave, contented with his lot, and zealously devoted to his master's service. Instead of promoting his master's interest, it seemed now to be his study and his aim to do as much mischief as possible. There were two or three artful, daring, unquiet spirits on the plantation, from whom, till lately, he had kept aloof, but whose acquaintance he now sought, and whose confidence he soon obtained. They found him bold and prudent, and what was more, trusty and magnanimous; and they soon gave place to his superiority of intellect, and acknowledged him as their leader. They were joined by some others, whose only motive was the desire of plunder, and they extended their depredations to every part of the plantation.

In this new character, Thomas still gave evidence that he was no ordinary man. He conducted his enterprises with singular address; and when all other stratagems by which to save his companions from detection proved unavailing, he had still one resource that showed the native nobleness of his soul. Such was the steady firmness of his mind, and the masculine vigour of his constitution, that he was enabled to do what few men could. He could brave even the torture of the lash—a torture, as I have said already, not less terrible than that of the rack itself. When every other resource failed him, he was ready to shield his companions by a voluntary confession, and to concentrate upon himself a punishment which he knew that some among them were too feeble and faint-hearted to endure. Magnanimity such as this is esteemed even in a freeman the highest pitch of virtue :—how then shall we sufficiently admire it in a slave ?

Thank God, tyranny is not omnipotent!

Though it crush its victims to the earth, and tread them into the dust, and brutify them by every possible invention, it cannot totally extinguish the spirit of manhood within them. Here it glimmers, and there it secretly burns, sooner or later to burst forth in a flame that will not be quenched and cannot be kept under !

So long as I was in the confidence of Mr. Martin, I was able to render Thomas essential service by informing him of the suspicions, plans, and stratagems of the overseer. It was not long, however, before I forfeited that confidence; not because Mr. Martin entertained any suspicions of my playing him false,—for it was very easy to throw dust into the eyes of so stupid a fellow,—but because I did not come up to his notions of the spirit and the duty of a driver. The season was sickly ; and as the hands who composed my gang were from a more northern climate, and not yet seasoned to the pestiferous atmosphere of a rice-plantation, they suffered a good deal from sickness, and several of them were often unable to work. I had explained this to Mr. Martin, and he seemed to be satisfied with my explanation : but riding into the field one day, in a particularly bad humour, and I believe a little excited with liquor, he got into a towering rage at finding not half my gang in the field, and more than half the tasks untouched.

He demanded the reason.

I told him that the hands were sick.

He swore they had no business to be sick ; he was tired, he said, of this talk about sickness ; he knew very well it was all sham, and he was determined to be imposed upon no longer. "If any more complaints are made of sickness, Archy, you have nothing to do but whip the scoundrels and set them to work."

"What," said I, "if they are really sick ?"

"Sick or not sick, I tell you. If they are not sick a whipping is no more than they deserve : and if they are, why nothing is so likely to do them good as a little blood-letting."

"In that case," said I, "you had better appoint another driver ; I should make a poor hand at whipping sick people."

"Hold your tongue, you damned insolent blackguard. Who gave you leave to advise me or dispute my orders? Hand me your whip, you rascal."

I did so ; and Mr. Martin thereupon administered upon me a fresh infliction of that same discipline he had bestowed when he first put the whip into my hand. So ended my drivership ; and though I now lost my double allowance, and was obliged to turn into the field again and perform my task like the other hands, I cannot say that I much regretted it. It was a pitiful and sorry office, which no one but a scoundrel ever ought to undertake.

I now united myself more closely to the party of Thomas, and joined heart and hand in all their enterprises. Our depredations became at last so considerable that Mr. Martin was obliged to establish a regular watch, consisting of his drivers and a few of their subordinates, who kept prowling about the plantation all night, and made it unsafe to venture into the fields. This arrangement was hastened by a circumstance that happened upon the plantation, about which a very strict inquiry was instituted, but which led to no definite result. On one and the same night General Carter's splendid plantation-seat and his expensive rice mills were discovered to be on fire, and notwithstanding all efforts to save them, both were totally consumed. Several of the slaves, and Thomas among the rest, were put to a sort of torture to make them acknowledge some participation in this house-burning. That cruelty availed nothing. They all stoutly denied knowing anything about it. I was, as I have said, very much in Thomas's confidence, yet he never spoke to me about that fire. As he was one of those men who know how to keep their own secrets, I always suspected that he knew much more about the matter than he chose to divulge.

At all events, it was evidently a much more potent feeling than the mere love of plunder by which Thomas was actuated. Since his wife's death he sometimes drank to excess; but this was seldom, and there never was a man more temperate in his meats and drinks or less fastidious than Thomas generally was. He had formerly dressed with much neatness; now he neglected his dress altogether. He did not love society; he had little intercourse with anybody except with me; and it was not always that he seemed to wish even for my company. Thomas had little use for his share of the plunder; and, in fact, he generally distributed it among his companions.

When the thing was first proposed, he seemed to have little inclination to extend our depredations beyond the limits of Loosahachee. But as it was no longer safe to continue them there, and as his companions had rioted too long in plunder to be willing to relinquish it, Thomas yielded at last to their urgent solicitations, and led us night after night to the neighbouring plantations. We soon pushed our proceedings so far as to attract the notice of the overseers whose domains we had invaded. At first they supposed that the thieves were to be looked for at home; and numberless were the severities they exercised upon those whom they supected. But, in spite of all their cruelties, the depredations were still continued; and such was the singular art and cunning which Thomas displayed in varying the scene and manner of our visits, that for a long time we escaped all the traps and ambushes that were planned against us.

We were one night in a rice field, and had almost filled our bags, when the watchful ear of Thomas detected a sound, as if of some one cautiously approaching. He supposed it might be the patrol, which, of late, instead of whiling away their time by the help of a fiddle and a bottle of whisky, had grown more active, and actually performed some of the duties of a night watch. Under this impression he gave a signal for us to steal off quietly, in a certain order which he had arranged beforehand. The field was bordered on one side by a deep and wide river, from which it was protected by a high embankment. We had come by water, and our canoe lay in the river, under the shade of a clump of bushes and small trees which grew upon the dike. One by one we cautiously stole over the bank, carefully keeping in the shade of the bushes, and all but Thomas were already in the boat. We were waiting for our leader, who, as usual, was the last man in the retreat, when we heard several shouts and cries, which seemed to indicate that he was discovered, if not taken. The sound of two musket shots fired in rapid succession increased our terror. We hastily shoved the boat from the shore, and pushing her into the current of the flood-tide, which was setting up the river, we were carried rapidly and silently out of sight of our landing-place. The shouts were still continued, but they grew fainter and fainter, and seemed to take a direction from the river. We now put out our paddles, and plying with all our strength we pretty soon reached a small cove or creek, the place where we kept our boat, and at which we were accustomed to embark. We drew the canoe on shore, and carefully concealed it among the high grass. Then, without taking out our rice-bags, and leaving our shoes in the boat, we ran towards Loosahachee, which we reached without any further adventure.

I was very anxious about Thomas; but I had scarcely thrown myself upon my bed before I heard a light tap at the door of my cabin, which I knew to be his. I sprang up and let him in. He was panting for breath and covered with mud. Thomas said, that just as he was going to climb the embankment, he looked behind him and saw two men rapidly approaching. They seemed to observe him just at the same moment, and called to him to stop. If he had attempted to reach the boat it would have drawn them that way, and perhaps led to the detection of the whole company. The moment they called to him he dropped his rice-bag, and stooping as low as he could, he pushed rapidly through the rice in a direction from the river. His pursuers raised a loud shout, and fired their muskets at him,—but without effect. He jumped several cross ditches, made for the high ground at a distance from the river, and drew off the patrol in that direction. They pursued him closely; but as he was very strong and active, and well acquainted with the place, he succeeded in escaping from among the ditches and embankments of the rice-field, gained the high grounds, and took a direction towards Loosahachee. But though he had distanced his pursuers, they had still kept upon his track, and he had expected that they would follow him up, and would shortly be arriving.

While Thomas was telling his adventures, he had stripped off his wet clothes, and washed off the mud with which he was covered. I furnished him with a dry suit, which he took with him to his own cabin, which was close by mine. I hastened round to the cabins of our companions and told them what visitors to except. The barking of all the plantation dogs pretty soon informed us that the patrol was coming. They had roused up the overseer, and, with torches in their hands, they entered and searched every cabin in the quarter. But we were prepared for their visit; we were roused with difficulty out of a deep sleep, and seemed to be very much astonished at this unseasonable disturbance.

The search proved to be a very useless one; but as the patrol were certain that they had traced the fugitive to Loosahachee, the overseer of the plantation upon which we had been depredating, came over the next morning to search out and punish the culprit. He was accompanied by several other men, who it seems were freeholders of the district, selected with such forms, or rather such neglect of all form, as the laws of Carolina prescribe in such cases. Five Carolina freeholders, selected at hap-hazard, constitute such a court as in most other countries would hardly be trusted with the final adjudication of any matter above the value of forty shillings at the utmost. But in that part of the world they not only have the power of judging all charges against slaves, and sentencing the accused to death, but what the Carolinians doubtless consider a much graver matter—the right of saddling the state treasury with the estimated value of the culprit. This law for refunding to the masters, nominally a part, but what by over-valuation usually amounts to the entire value of condemned slaves, deprives the poor wretches of that protection against an unjust sentence, which otherwise they might find in the pecuniary interest of their masters, and leaves them without any sort of shield against the prejudice, carelessness, or stupidity of their judges. But why should we expect anything like equity or fairness in the execution of laws which themselves are founded upon the grossest wrong? It must be confessed, that in this matter the Americans preserve throughout an admirable consistency.

A table was set out before the door of the overseer's house; some glasses and a bottle of whisky were placed upon it, and the court proceeded to business. We were all brought up and examined one after the other. The only witnesses were the patrol who had pursued Thomas, and they were ordered by the court to pick out the culprits. That was rather a difficult matter. There were between sixty and seventy men of us; the night had been cloudy and without a moon, and the patrol had only caught some hasty and uncertain glimpses of the person whom they had followed. The court seemed rather vexed at their hesitation. Yet perhaps it was not very unreasonable, since they were quite unable to agree together as to what sort of a man it was. One thought him short; the other was certain that he was quite tall. The first pronounced him a stout, well-set fellow; the other had taken him to be very slender.

By this time the first bottle of whisky was emptied, and a second was put upon the table. The court now told the witnesses that it would not do—they did not come up to the mark at all: and if they went on at that rate, the fellow would escape altogether. Just at this moment, the overseer of the plantation which had been plundered rode up: and as soon as he had dismounted, he stepped forward to the relief of the witnesses. He said, that while the court was organising, he had taken the opportunity to ride over and examine the rice-field, in which the rogue had been started up. It was much trampled in places, and there were a great many foot-prints: but they were all just alike, and seemed to have been made by the same person. He took a little stick from his pocket, on which, he said, he had carefully marked the exact length and breadth.

Now this was a trick for detecting people, which Thomas understood very well, and he had taken good care to be prepared for it. Our whole company were provided with shoes of the largest size we could get, and all exactly the same pattern; so that our tracks had the appearance of being made by a single person, and he a fellow with a very large foot.

This speech of the overseer seemed to revive the drooping hopes of the judges, and they made us all sit down upon the ground and have our feet measured. There was a man on the plantation named Billy, a harmless, stupid fellow, wholly unconnected with us; but unluckily for him, the only one of all the slaves whose foot corresponded at all with the measure. The length of this poor fellow's foot was fatal to him. The judges shouted with one voice, and in the style of condemnation to be expected from such a court, that "they would be damned if he was not the thief." It was in vain that the poor fellow denied the charge, and pleaded for

I 2

mercy. His terror, confusion, and surprise, only served to confirm the opinion of his guilt; and the more he denied and the louder he pleaded, the more positively his judges were determined against him. Without further ceremony, they pronounced him guilty, and sentenced him to be hung!

The sentence was no sooner pronounced than preparations were made for its execution. An empty barrel was brought out, and placed under a tree that stood before the door. The poor fellow was mounted upon it; the halter was put about his neck, and fastened to a limb over his head. The judges had already become so drunk as to have lost all sense of judicial decorum. One of them kicked away the barrel, and the unhappy victim of Carolina justice dropped struggling into eternity.

The execution over, the slaves were sent into the field; while Mr. Martin, with the judges and witnesses, and several others whom the fame of the trial had drawn to Loosahachee, commenced a regular drunken debauch, which they kept up all that day, and the night following.

CHAPTER XXX.

THE authority of masters over their slaves is in general a continual reign of terror. A base and dastard fear is the sole principle of human nature to which the slave-holder appeals. When it was determined to hang the poor fellow, whose fate I have described in the last chapter, his judges could not know, nor do I suppose they much cared, whether he were innocent or guilty. Their great object was to terrify the survivors; and, by an example of what they would denominate wholesome and necessary severity, to deter from any further trespasses upon the neighbouring plantations. In this they succeeded; for though Thomas endeavoured to keep up our spirits, we were thoroughly scared, and felt little inclination to second his boldness, which seemed to grow more determined, the more obstacles it encountered.

One of our confederates, in particular, was so alarmed at the fate of poor Billy, that he seemed to have lost all self-control, and we were in constant fear lest he should betray us. When the first paroxysm of his terror was at its height, the evening after he had witnessed the execution, I believe he would gladly have confessed the whole, if he could have found a white man sober enough to listen to him. After a while, he grew more calm; but in the course of the day he had dropped some hints, which were carefully treasured up by one of the drivers. He reported them, as I discovered, to the overseer; but Mr. Martin had not yet recovered from the effects of the frolic, and he was too drunk and stupid to understand a word that the driver said to him.

We had begun to get the better of our fears, when a new incident happened, which determined us to seek our safety in flight. Some persons, in passing along the river bank, had discovered our canoe, which, in the hurry of our retreat, we had taken too little care to conceal. It contained not only our bags full of rice,—for we had not yet recovered courage enough to go after them,—but our shoes also, all exactly of the same size, and corresponding with the measure which had been produced upon the trial. Here was ample proof that quite a number had been engaged in the scheme of depredation, and as one of the company had been traced to Loosahachee, it would be reasonable to look for the others upon the same plantation. Luckily, I obtained an early intimation of this discovery, by means of one of the overseer's house-servants, with whom I had the policy to keep up a pretty intimate connection. A man had arrived at the overseer's house, his horse dripping with foam, and with an appearance of great haste and impatience, he had asked to see the overseer. The moment he came in, the stranger requested to speak with him alone, and Mr. Martin took his guest into another room, and locked the door. The girl, who was my spy and informant, under an appearance of the greatest simplicity, was artful and intelligent; and she was prompted to overhear this secret conversation, as much by her own curiosity, as by the suspicion that it might possibly be something in which I would take an interest. She contrived to conceal herself in a closet, which was separated from the room in which the overseer and his visitor were conversing, only by a thin partition, and having overheard his story, the substance of which I have already mentioned,—and learned, besides, that the court would hold a new session at Loosahachee the day following.—she hastened to inform me of what she had heard. She knew nothing in particular of our affairs; but she had reason to believe that this piece of news would not be entirely uninteresting to me.

I informed Thomas of what she had told me. We agreed at once that our best chance of safety was in flight, and we immediately communicated our intention, and the cause of it, to the rest of our confederates. They were anxious to accompany us, and we all resolved to be off that very night.

As soon as evening came on we stole away from the plantation, and gained the woods in company. As we anticipated that a very diligent search would be made for us, we thought it best to separate. Thomas and myself resolved to keep together; the others scattered and took various directions. As long as the darkness lasted we travelled on as rapidly as we could; when the morning began to appear we plunged into a thick swampy piece of woods, and having broken down some branches and young trees, we made as dry a bed as we were able and lay down to sleep. We were much fatigued with our long and rapid journey, and slept soundly. It was past noon when we waked. Our appetites were sharp, but we had no provisions. Just as we were beginning to consider what course it would be best for us to pursue, we heard the distant baying of a hound. Thomas listened for a moment, and then exclaimed that he knew that cry. It was a famous dog, a cross of the bloodhound, which Mr. Martin had long had in training, and upon whose performances in tracking out runaways he very much prided himself. The place where we were was a thick swamp, in which it was difficult to move, and not easy to stand; to cross it would be impossible, and we resolved to get into the edge of it, where the ground was harder and the undergrowth thinner, and to continue our flight. We did so, but the hound gained rapidly upon us, and his baying sounded louder and louder. Thomas drew a stout sharp knife which he carried in his pocket. We were now just at the border where the dry ground came down upon the swamp, and looking behind us, across the level and open woods, we could see the hound coming on with his nose to the ground, and uttering at intervals a deep and savage cry; farther behind, but still in full view, we saw a man on horseback, whom we took to be Mr. Martin himself.

The dog was evidently upon our track, and following it to the place where we had first plunged into the swamp, he disappeared from our view; but we could still hear his clamour, which grew louder and almost constant, and we soon perceived by the rustling and cracking of the underwood that he was close upon us. At this moment we faced about and stood at bay,—Thomas in front, with his knife in hand, and I just behind, with a sharp and heavy lightwood knot, the best, indeed the only, weapon of which I could avail myself. Presently the dog emerged from the swamp. The moment he saw us he redoubled his cry, and dashed forward foaming and open-mouthed; he made a great leap directly at Thomas's throat, but only succeeded in seizing his left arm, which Thomas raised as a shield against the dog's attack. At the same instant he dealt a stroke with his knife which penetrated to the hilt, and dog and man came struggling to the ground. How the contest would have ended had Thomas been alone is very doubtful, for though the hound soon received several wounds, they only seemed to increase his ferocity, and he still struggled to get at the throat of his antagonist. My lightwood knot now did good service; two or three heavy blows upon the dog's head laid him senseless and sprawling on the ground.

While we had been awaiting the dog's attack, and during the contest, we had scarcely thought of his master, but looking up, after it was over, we discovered that Mr. Martin was already very near us. When the dog took to the swamp, his master had followed along upon its edge, and came suddenly upon us before we had expected him. He pointed his gun and called upon us to surrender. Thomas no sooner saw the overseer than he seemed to lose all his self-control, and grasping his knife he rushed directly upon him. Mr. Martin fired, but the buckshot rattled harmlessly among the trees, and as he was attempting to wheel his horse, Thomas dashed upon him, seized him by the arm, and dragged him to the ground. The horse ran frightened through the wood, and it was in vain that I attempted to stop him. We looked round in expectation of seeing some others of the huntsmen coming up; none were in sight, and we seized the opportunity to retreat, and to carry our prisoner into the covert of the swamp.

We learned from him, that by the time the court and their attendants arrived at Loosahachee, our flight had been discovered, and that it was immediately resolved to raise the neighbourhood, and to commence a general search for the runaways. All the horses, dogs, and men that could be come at were put into requisition. They were divided into parties, and immediately commenced beating through the woods and swamps in the neighbourhood.

A party of five or six men, with Mr. Martin and his bloodhound, had traced three of our companions into a thick swamp, just on the bank of a river. The pursuers dismounted, and with their guns in their hands, they followed the dog into the thicket. Our poor fellows were so overcome with fatigue, that they slept till the very moment that the hound sprang in upon them. He seized one of them by the throat, and held him to the ground. The others ran; and as they ran, the pursuers fired. One of the fugitives fell dead, horribly mangled and cut to pieces with buck-shot; the other still continued his flight. As soon as the dog could be compelled to quit his hold of the man he had seized, which was not without difficulty and delay, he was put upon the track of the surviving fugitive. He followed it to the river, where he stood at fault. The man had probably plunged in, and swam to the other side; but as the dog could not be made to take the water, and as the swamp on the opposite bank was reputed to be very soft and dangerous, no further pursuit was made; the chase in that direction was given up, and the poor fellow was suffered to escape for the present.

The pursuers now separated. Two of them undertook to carry back to Loosahachee the captive they had taken, and the other three, with Mr. Martin and his hound, were to continue the hunt in search of the rest of us. They learned from their captive the place at which we had parted company, and the directions which the several parties had taken. After beating about for some time, the hound struck upon our trail, and opened in full cry; but the horses of Mr. Martin's companions were so broken down, that when he began to spur on, to keep up with the hound, he soon left them far behind. Mr. Martin ended his story by advising us to go in and surrender ourselves; giving us his word and honour as a gentleman and an overseer, that if we would offer him no further violence or injury, he would protect us from punishment, and reward us most handsomely.

The sun was now setting. The short twilight which follows a Carolina sunset would soon be succeeded by the darkness of a cloudy and moonless night; and we felt but little apprehension of being immediately troubled by our pursuers. I looked at Thomas, as if to inquire what we had better do. He drew me aside, having first examined the fastenings of our prisoner, whom we had bound to a tree, by some cords found in his own pocket, and which were doubtless intended for a very different purpose.

Thomas paused for a moment, as if to collect his thoughts; then, pointing to Mr. Martin, "Archy," he said, "that man dies to-night."

There was a wild energy, and at the same time a steady coolness, in the tone in which he spoke. It startled me; at first I made no answer; and as meanwhile I looked Thomas in the face, I saw there an expression of stern exultation, and a fixedness of purpose not to be shaken. His eyes flashed fire as he repeated, but in a low and quiet tone, that contrasted strangely with the matter of his speech, "I tell you, Archy, that man dies to-night. She commands it; I have promised it; and now the time is come."

"Who commands it?" I hastily inquired.

"Do you ask who? Archy, that man was the murderer of my wife!"

Though Thomas and I had lived in great intimacy, this was almost the first time, since the death of his wife, that he had mentioned her to me in such plain terms. He had, it is true, now and then made some distant allusions to her; and I recollected that on several occasions before, he had dropped some strange and incoherent hints about an intercourse which he still kept up with her.

The mention of his wife brought tears into his eyes; but with his hand he wiped them hastily away, and soon recovering his former air of calm and steady determination, he again repeated, in the same low but resolute tone, "Archy, I tell you that man dies to-night."

When I called to mind all the circumstances that had attended the death of Thomas's wife, I could not but acknowledge that Mr. Martin had been her murderer. I had sympathised with Thomas then, and I sympathised with him now. The murderer was in his power; he believed himself called upon to execute justice upon him; and I could not but acknowledge that his death would be an act of righteous retribution.

Still I felt a sort of instinctive horror at the idea of shedding blood ; and, perhaps, too, there still crept about my heart some remains of that slavish fear and servile timidity which the bolder spirit of Thomas had wholly shaken off. I acknowledged that the life of the overseer was justly forfeit; but, at the same time, I reminded Thomas that Mr. Martin had promised, if we would carry him home in safety, to procure our pardon, and protect us from punishment.

A scornful smile played about the lip of my comrade while I was speaking. "Yes, Archy," he answered, "pardon and protection !—and a hundred lashes, and a hanging the next day, perhaps. No! boy, I want no such pardon ; I want no pardon such as they will give. I have been a slave too long already. I am now free ; and when they take me they are welcome to take my life. Besides, we cannot trust him ;—if we wished it, we cannot trust him. You know we cannot. They do not think themselves obliged to keep any promises they make us. They will promise anything to get us in their power, and then their promises are worthless as rotten straw. My promises are not like theirs ; and have I not told you that I have promised it ? Yes, I have sworn it ; and I now say, once for all, that man must die to-night."

There was a strength and a determination in his tone and manner which overpowered me. I could resist it no longer, and I bade him do his pleasure. He loaded the gun which he had taken from Mr. Martin, and which he had held in his hand all the time we had been talking. This done, we returned to the overseer, who was sitting at the foot of the tree to which we had bound him. He looked up anxiously at us as we approached, and inquired if we had determined to go in?

"We have determined," answered Thomas. "We allow you half an hour to prepare for death. Make the most of it. You have many sins to repent of, and the time is short."

It is impossible to describe the look of mingled terror, amazement, and incredulity with which the overseer heard these words. One moment, with a voice of authority, he bade us untie him ; the next, he forced a laugh, and affected to treat what Thomas had said as a mere jest ; then, yielding to his fears, he wept like a child, and cried and begged for mercy.

"Have you shown it ?" answered Thomas. "Did you show it to my poor wife ? You murdered her ; and for her life you must answer with your own."

Mr. Martin called God to witness that he was not guilty of this charge. He had punished Thomas's wife, he confessed ; but he did only what his duty as an overseer demanded ; and it was impossible, he said, that the few cuts he gave her could have caused her death.

"The few cuts !" cried Thomas. "Thank God, Mr. Martin, that we do not torture you as you tortured her ! Speak no more, or you will but aggravate your sufferings. Confess your crimes ! Say your prayers ! Do not spend your last moments in adding falsehood to murder !"

The overseer cowered beneath this energetic reproof. He covered his face with his hands, bent down his head, and passed a few moments in a silence which was only interrupted by an inarticulate sobbing. Perhaps he was trying to prepare himself to die. But life was too sweet to be surrendered without another effort to save it. He saw that it was useless to appeal to Thomas ; but rousing himself once more, he turned to me. He begged me to remember the confidence he had once placed in me, and the favours which, as he said, he had shown me. He pro—

mised to purchase us both, and give us our liberty, anything, everything, if we would only spare his life !

His tears and piteous lamentations moved me. My head grew dizzy, and I felt such a faintness and heart-sinking, that I was obliged to support myself against a tree. Thomas stood by, with his arms folded and resting on the gun. He made no answer to the reiterated prayers and promises of the overseer. Indeed, he did not appear to notice them. His eyes were fixed, and he seemed lost in thought.

After a considerable interval, during which the unhappy overseer continued to repeat his prayers and lamentations, Thomas roused himself. He stepped back a few paces, and raised the gun. "The half hour is out," he said ; "Mr. Martin, are you ready ? "

" No ! oh, no ! Spare me, oh, spare me !—one half hour longer,—I have much—"

He did not live to finish the sentence. The gun flashed ; the ball penetrated his brain, and he fell dead without a struggle.

CHAPTER XXXI.

WE scraped a shallow grave, in which we placed the body of the overseer. We dragged the dead hound to the same spot, and laid him with his master. They were fit companions.

We now resumed our flight,—not, as some perhaps may suppose, with the frightened and conscience-stricken haste of murderers, but with that lofty feeling of manhood vindicated and tyranny visited with a just retribution which animated the soul of the Israelitish hero whilst he fled for refuge into the country of the Midianites, and which burned in the bosoms of Wallace and of Tell as they pursued their midnight flight among the friendly cliffs and freedom-breathing summits of their native mountains.

There were no mountains to receive and shelter us. But still we fled through the swamps and barrens of Carolina, resolved to put, as soon as possible, some good miles between us and the neighbourhood of Loosahachee. It was more than twenty-four hours since we had tasted food, yet such was the excitement of our minds that we did not faint, and were hardly sensible of weakness or fatigue.

We kept a north-westerly direction, steering our course by the stars, and we must have made a good distance, for we did not once stop to rest, but pushed forward at a very rapid pace all night. Our way lay through the open "piney woods," through which we could travel almost as fast as on a road. Sometimes a swamp or the appearances of a plantation would compel us to deviate from our track, but as soon as we could we resumed our original direction.

The darkness of the night, which for the last hour or two that it lasted had been increased by a foggy mist, was just beginning to yield to the first indistinct grey dawn of the morning. We were passing along a little depression in the level of the pine barrens, now dry, but in the wet season probably the bed of a temporary stream, looking for a place in which to conceal ourselves, when we suddenly came upon a man lying, as it seemed, asleep in the midst of a clump of bushes, with his head resting on a bag of corn. We recognised him at once. He was a slave belonging to a plantation next adjoining Loosahachee, with whom we had had some slight acquaintance, but who, as we were informed, had been a runaway for some two or three months past. Thomas shook him by the shoulder, and he wakened in a terrible fright. We told him not to be alarmed, for we were runaways like himself, and very much in need of his assistance, being half dead with hunger, and in a country with which we were totally unacquainted. At first the man appeared very reserved and suspicious. He feared, it seemed, lest we might be decoys, sent out on purpose to entrap him. At last, however, we succeeded in dissipating his doubts; and no sooner was he satisfied with the account we gave of ourselves than he bade us follow him, and we should presently have food.

With his bag of corn upon his shoulder he pursued the shallow ravine in which we had found him, for a mile or more, till at length it widened into what seemed a large swamp, or rather a pond grown up with trees. We now left the ravine, and followed along on the edge of the pond for some distance, when presently our guide began wading in the water, and called to us to follow him. We plunged in; but before going far, he laid down his bag of corn upon a fallen tree, and going back he carefully effaced the marks which our footsteps had made upon the muddy edge of the pond. He now led us forward through mud and water up to our waists for near half a mile. The gigantic trees, among which we were wading, sprung up like columns from the surface of the water, with round, straight, whitish-coloured branchless trunks, their leafy tops forming a thick canopy over-head. There was scarcely any undergrowth, except a species of enormous vines, which ran twining like great cables about the bodies of the trees, and reaching to the very tops, helped with their foliage to thicken the canopy above us. So effectually was the light excluded, and so close did the trunks of the trees stand together, that one could see but a very little way into this watery forest.

The water began to grow deeper, and the wood more gloomy, and we were wondering whither our guide was leading us, when presently we came to a little island which rose a few feet from the surface of the water, so regular and mound-like, that it had quite the appearance of an artificial structure. Perhaps it was the work of the ancient inhabitants of the country, and the site of one of their forts or fastnesses. It was about an acre in extent, and was covered with a thick growth of trees, quite different, however, from those of the lake by which it was surrounded, and much inferior in size and majesty. Its edges were bordered by low shrubs and bushes, whose abundant foliage gave the islet the appearance of a mass of green. Our guide pointed out to us a little opening in the bushes, through which we ascended; and after having gained the dry land, he led us through the thicket along a narrow and winding path, till presently we came to a rude cabin built of bark and branches. He now gave a peculiar whistle, which was immediately answered, and two or three men presently made their appearance.

They seemed a good deal surprised at seeing us, and me especially, whom apparently they took for a freeman. But our guide assured them that we were friends and fellow-sufferers, and led the way into the cabin. Our new hosts received us kindly; and having heard how long we had been without food, before asking us any further questions, they hastened to satisfy our hunger. They produced beef and hominy in abundance, on which we feasted to our hearts' content.

We were then called upon to give an account of ourselves. Accordingly we made a relation of our adventures, omitting, however, any mention of the fate of the overseer; and as our guide, who knew us, could confirm a part of our story, our account was pronounced satisfactory, and we were presently admitted to the privilege of joining their fraternity.

There were six of them besides ourselves; all brave fellows, who, weary of daily task-work and the tyranny of overseers, had taken to the woods, and had succeeded in regaining a savage and stealthy freedom, which, with all its hardships and dangers, was a thousand times to be preferred to the forced labour and wretched servitude from which they had escaped. Our guide was the only one of them whom we had ever seen till now. The leader of the band had fled from his master's plantation in the neighbourhood, with a single companion, some two or three years before. They did not, then, know of the existence of this retreat; but being sharply pursued, they had attempted to cross the pond or swamp, by which it was surrounded—a thing, I suppose, which had never been tried before. In this attempt they were fortunate enough to light upon the islet, which, being unknown to any one else, had ever since served them as a secure retreat. They soon picked up a recruit or two, and had afterwards been joined by their other companions.

Our guide, it seems, had been to a neighbouring plantation to trade for corn; a traffic which our friends carried on with the slaves of several of the nearest plantations. After the business was concluded, the men with whom he had been dealing had produced a bottle of whiskey, of which our guide had drank so freely, that he had not gone far on his way home before his legs failed him. He sunk down in the place where we had found him, and fell fast asleep.

Drinking whiskey away from home, according to the prudent laws of this swamp-encircled commonwealth, was a high misdemeanor, punishable with thirty-nine lashes, which were forthwith inflicted upon our guide with a good deal of emphasis. He took it in good part though, as being the execution of a law to which he had himself assented, and which he knew was enacted as much for his own benefit as for the benefit of those who had just now carried it into execution.

The life upon which we now entered had at least the charm of novelty. In the day time we eat, slept, told stories, and recounted our escapes, or employed ourselves in dressing skins, making clothes, and curing provisions. But the night was our season of adventure and enterprise. As the autumn was coming on we made frequent visits to the neighbouring corn-fields and potato-patches, which we felt no scruples whatever in laying under severe contribution. This, however, was only for a month or two. Our regular and certain supply was in the herds of half-wild cattle, which wander through the "piney woods" and feed upon the coarse grass which they furnish. We killed as many of these cattle as we needed, and their flesh, cut into long strips, we dried in the sun. Thus cured, it is a palatable food; and we not only kept a stock on hand for our own consumption, but it furnished the principal article of a constant but cautious traffic, which, as I have already mentioned, we carried on with the slaves of several neighbouring plantations.

This wild life of the woods has its privations and its sufferings; but it has too its charms and its pleasures; and in its very worst aspect, it is a thousand and ten thousand times to be preferred to that miscalled civilization which degrades the noble savage into a cringing and broken-spirited slave;—a civilization, which purchases the indolence and luxury of a single master with the sighs and tears, the forced and unwilling labour, the degradation, misery, and despair of a hundred of his fellowmen! Yes—there is more of true manhood in the bold bosom of a single outlaw than in a whole nation of cowardly tyrants and crouching slaves!

CHAPTER XXXII.

By the end of the winter, the herds of cattle which were accustomed to frequent our neighbourhood were a good deal thinned; and the pasturage had now become so bare and withered that what remained of them were little better than walking skeletons, and in fact, scarcely worth the trouble of killing.

Moreover, the overseers of the neighbouring plantations were beginning to be very well aware that they were exposed to some pretty regular and diligent depredators. We learned from the slaves with whom we trafficked, that there was a good deal of talk about the rapid disappearance of the cattle, and that preparations were making for a grand hunt in search of the plunderers.

With the double object of disappointing these preparations, and of getting among some fresh herds of cattle, it was resolved that five of us should make an excursion to a considerable distance, while the other two remained at home and kept close.

One of our number undertook to lead us into the neighbourhood of a plantation beyond the Santee, on which he had been raised. He knew all the country about it perfectly well. There were several good hiding-places, he said, in which we could conceal ourselves in the day time; and the extensive woods and wastes furnished a good range, and abundance of cattle.

We set off under his guidance, and kept on for several days, or nights rather, in a northwardly direction. On the fifth or sixth evening of our journey, we started soon after sun-set, and having travelled till a little past midnight, through a country of abrupt and barren sand hills, our guide told us that we were now in the neighbourhood into which he intended to carry us. But as the moon had gone down, and it was cloudy and quite dark, he was rather uncertain as to the precise place we were at; and we should do best, he said, to camp where we were, till daylight, when he would lead us to some better place of concealment.

This advice was very acceptable;—for by this time we were way-worn, tired, and sleepy. We kindled a fire, cooked the last of the provisions we had brought with us, and having appointed one of our number to keep watch, the rest of us lay down and were soon fast asleep.

I, at least, was sleeping soundly, and dreaming of poor Cassy and our infant child, when my dream was interrupted, and I was roused from my slumbers by what seemed a discharge of fire-arms and a galloping of horses. I sprang upon my feet, hardly knowing whether I was awake. At the same moment my eye fell upon Thomas, who had been sleeping beside me, and I perceived that his clothes were all stained with blood. He had already gained his feet, and without stopping to hear or see anything further, we sprung together into the nearest thicket, and fled for some time, we scarcely knew where or why. At last, Thomas cried out that he could go no further. The bleeding of his wounds had weakened him much, and they were now growing stiff and painful. The morning was just beginning to dawn. We sat down upon the ground, and endeavoured to bind up his wounds the best way we were able. A ball or buck-shot had passed through the fleshy part of his arm, between the shoulder and elbow. Another shot had struck him in the side,—but as far as we could judge, had glanced on one of his ribs, and so passed off without doing any mortal injury. These wounds had bled profusely, and were now very painful. We bound them up as well as we could, and looking round we found a little stream of water with which to wash away the blood and quench our thirst.

Thus recruited and refreshed, we began to consider which way we should turn and what we were to do. We did not dare to go back to the camp where we had slept; indeed we were very doubtful whether we were able to do so, for the morning had been dark and we had fled with heedless haste, taking very little note of our direction. Our island retreat was at the distance of some seven or eight days' journey; and as we had travelled in the night and not always in precisely the same direction, it would be no very easy matter to find our way back again. However, Thomas prided himself upon his woodmanship, and though he had not observed the course of our journey quite so closely as he could have wished, he still thought that he might succeed in finding the way back.

But his wounds were too recent and he felt too weak to think of starting off immediately. Besides, it was already broad daylight, and we had the best of reasons for travelling only by night. So we sought out a thicket in which we concealed ourselves till nightfall.

As the evening came on, Thomas declared that he felt much better and stronger, and we resolved to set out at once on our return. In the first place, however, we determined to make an attempt to find the camp of the preceding night, in hopes that some of our companions might have escaped as well as ourselves, and that by some good luck we might chance to fall in with them.

After wandering about for some time, at length we found the camp. Two dead bodies, stiff and bloody, lay by the extinguished embers of the fire. They seemed to have been shot dead as they slept, and scarcely to have moved a limb. The bushes about were stained and spattered with blood; and by the moonlight we tracked the bloody flight of one of our luckless companions for a considerable distance. This must have been our sentinel, who had probably dropped asleep and thus exposed us to be surprised.

Perhaps he might be lurking somewhere in the bushes, wounded and helpless. This thought emboldened us. We shouted and called aloud; but our voices echoed through the woods, and died away unanswered. We returned again to the camp, and gazed once more upon the distorted faces of our dead companions. We could not bear to leave them unburied. I hastily scraped a shallow trench, and there we placed them. We dropped a tear upon their grave, and sad, dismayed, dejected, we set out upon our long, weary, and uncertain journey.

CHAPTER XXXIII.

WE travelled slowly all that night, and soon after the morning dawn we concealed ourselves again, and lay down to sleep. Thomas's wounds were much better, and seemed disposed to heal. The hurt in his side was far less dangerous than we had at first supposed; and as the pain had subsided, he was now able to sleep.

We slept well enough, but awoke weak and faint for want of food; for it was now some twenty-four hours since we had tasted any. The sun was not yet down; yet we resolved to set out immediately, in hopes that daylight might point out to us something with which to satisfy our hunger.

After travelling a considerable distance through the woods, just as the sun was setting, we struck into a road. This road we determined to follow, in hopes that it might presently lead us into the neighbourhood of some farm house, near which we might light upon something eatable. It was an unlucky resolve; for we had not gone above half a mile, when, just upon the crest of a short hill, we suddenly came upon three travellers on horseback, whom the undulations of the road had concealed from us till we were within a few yards of each other.

Both parties were mutually surprised. The travellers reigned up their horses and eyed us sharply. Our appearance might well attract attention. Our clothes—such as we had—were torn and ragged. Instead of shoes, we wore a kind of high moccasins, made of untanned ox-hide; we had caps of the same material; and the dresses of both of us, especially of Thomas, were spattered and stained with blood.

They took me for a freeman, and one of them called out, "Hallo, stranger, who are you, and where are you going? and whose fellow is that you have along?"

I did my best to take advantage of my colour, and to seem what they took me for. But this I soon found would not avail; for though apparently at first they did not suspect that I was a slave, yet our appearance was so strange that they questioned me very closely. As I had no definite idea where we were, and was totally unacquainted with the neighbourhood, I was not at all able to hit upon appropriate answers to the numerous questions they put me; and my statements soon grew confused and contradictory. This served to excite their suspicions; and while I was attending to the questions of the one who acted as chief spokesman, another of the company suddenly sprang from his horse, and seizing me by the collar, swore that I was either a runaway, or a negro-stealer. The other two jumped down in a moment; and while one of them caught me by the arm, the other attempted to seize Thomas.

He eluded this attempt and turned to run. He had gone but a little distance, when looking back and seeing me on the ground, he forgot at once his wounds, his weakness, and his own danger. He grasped his staff, and rushed to my rescue. They had throttled me till I was powerless and almost insensible; and while one of them still held me to the ground, the other stood up to meet Thomas, who, as as he turned short round, had struck his pursuer to the earth, and now came on to my relief, with his staff uplifted. His new antagonist was both strong and active. He succeeded in avoiding the stroke of Thomas's cudgel, and immediately closed with him. Thomas had but little use of one arm; and his strength was much reduced by loss of blood and long fasting; but he struggled hard, and was already getting the upper hand, when the fellow whom he had knocked down at the commencement of the fight regained his senses, and came to the assistance of his companion. Both together they were too much for him; and they soon got him down and bound his hands. They did the same with me; and one of them having produced a piece of rope from his saddle-bags, they made halters of it, which they put about our necks, and by the application of their whips they compelled us to keep up with their horses.

In about half an hour we came to a mean and forlorn-looking cabin by the roadside. It appeared to be a sort of inn or tavern, and here we were to lodge. The only persons about the house seemed to be the landlady herself and her little daughter, some ten or twelve years old. The whole appearance of the place bore evident marks of discomfort and poverty. Our captors had no sooner provided for their horses than they called for chains; trace-chains, they said, or, in fact, anything in the shape of a chain would answer their purpose. But much to their disappointment the landlady declared that she had nothing of the sort. However, she procured some old rope, and having secured us as effectually as they could, they made us sit down in the passage.

The landlady told them that in all probability we were runaways, for the neighbourhood had lately been much troubled by them. A company of five or six men, she said, had gone out two or three nights since on purpose to hunt up the rascals, and had unexpectedly come upon quite a party, asleep in the woods around a fire.

The gang seemed too large to be easily taken, but it was resolved that the fellows should not escape, especially as the man whose slaves they were supposed to be, and who was one of the party, openly declared that he had rather they were all shot than to have them wandering about the country, useless to him and mischievous to his neighbours.

The company separated, and each man approached from a different point. Upon a given signal all fired, and then putting spurs to their horses, they rode off and returned home each by himself. Nobody had stopped to see what execution was done, but as the men were all good shots, it was supposed that most of the runaways were either killed or desperately wounded; and as our clothes were bloody and one of us was hurt, she thought it likely, she said, that we belonged to that same gang.

It appeared in the course of the conversation between the landlady and her guests that the murderous kind of attack to which our companions had fallen victims, but which had been intended for another party of runaways, is an operation occasionally practised in Lower Carolina, when a party of slave-hunters falls in with a gang of fugitive slaves too large to be easily arrested.

The dispersion of the attacking party, and each one shooting and returning by himself, is only the effect of an ancient and traditionary prejudice. By the law of Carolina, the killing of a slave is regarded as murder; and though, probably, this law was never enforced, and would doubtless be treated by a jury of modern slaveholders as an old-fashioned and fanatical absurdity, there still linger in the breasts of the people some remains of horror at the idea of deliberate bloodshed, and a sort of superstitious apprehension of the possible enforcement of this anti-quated law. To blindfold their own consciences, and to avoid the possi-bility of a judicial investigation, each man of an attacking party takes care to see none of the others when they fire; and no one goes to the place to ascertain how many have been killed or disabled. The poor wretches who are not so fortunate as to be shot dead upon the spot are left to lingering torments of thirst, fever, starvation, and festering wounds; and when at length they die, their skeletons lie bleaching in the Carolina sun, proud proofs of slave-holding civilization and humanity.

While our captors were at supper, the little girl, the landlady's daughter, came to look at us, as we lay in the passage. She was a pretty child, and her soft blue eyes filled with tears as she looked upon us. I asked her for water. She ran to get it for us; and inquired if we did not want something to eat. I told her that we were half dead with hunger; and she no sooner heard it, than she hastened away, and soon returned with a large cake of bread.

Our arms were bound so tight that we were utterly helpless, and the little girl broke the bread, and fed us with her own hand.

Is not this one instance enough to prove that nature never intended man to be a tyrant? Avarice, a blind lust of domination, the false but specious suggestions of ignorance and passion, combine to make him so; and pity at length is banished from his soul. It then seeks refuge in the woman's heart; and when the progress of oppression drives it even thence, as sad and hesitating, it prepares to wing its way to heaven, still it lurks and lingers in the bosom of the child!

By listening closely to the conversation of the travellers—for by this time the landlady had produced a jug of whisky, and they had become very communicative—we learned that we were within a few miles of the town of Camden, and on the great northern road leading from that town to North Carolina. Our captors, it seemed, were from the upper country. They had not passed through Camden, but had struck into this road very near the place where they met us. They were travelling into Virginia to purchase slaves.

After discussing the question at considerable length, they concluded to delay their journey for a day or two, and to take us to Camden, in hopes to find our owner and obtain a reward for apprehending us; or if nobody should claim us immediately, they could lodge us in jail, adver-tise us in the newspapers, and give further attention to the business upon their return.

By this time the whisky jug was emptied, and the travellers made preparations for sleeping. There were but two rooms in the house. The landlady and her daughter had one, and some beds were prepared for the guests in the other. We were carried into their room, and after again lamenting that the landlady could not furnish them with chains, they carefully examined and re-tightened the ropes with which we were bound, and then undressed and threw themselves upon their beds. They were probably fatigued with their journey, and the whisky in-creased their drowsy inclination; so that before long they all gave evident tokens of being in a sound slumber.

I envied them that happiness, for the tightness of my bonds and the uneasy position in which I was obliged to lie prevented me from sleeping. The moonbeams shone in at the window, and made every object distinctly visible. Thomas and myself were lamenting in whispers our wretched condition, and consulting hopelessly together, when we saw the door of the room cautiously and silently opening. In a moment the landlady's little daughter made her appearance. She came towards us with noiseless steps, and one hand raised, as if motioning to us to be silent. In the other she held a knife, and stooping down, she hastily cut the cords by which we were bound.

We did not dare to speak, but our hearts beat hard, and I am sure our looks expressed the gratitude we felt. We gained our feet with as little noise as possible, and were stealing towards the door, when a new thought struck Thomas. He laid his hand upon my shoulder to draw my attention, and then began to pick up the coat, shoes, and other clothes of one of our captors. At once I understood his intention, and imitated his example. The little girl seemed astonished and displeased at this proceeding, and motioned to us to desist; but without seeming to understand her gestures, we gained the door with the clothes in our hands, and passing out of the passage, we walked slowly and cautiously for some distance, taking good heed, lest the sound of our footsteps might give an alarm. In the meantime the little girl patted the house-dog on the head and kept him quiet. When we had gained a sufficient distance, we started upon a run, which we did not give over till we were fairly out of breath.

As soon as we had recovered ourselves a little, we stripped off our ragged dresses, and hid them in the bushes. Luckily the clothes which we had brought off in our flight fitted us very tolerably, and gave us a much more respectable and less suspicious appearance. We now went on for two or three miles, till we came to a road that crossed the one upon which we were travelling, and ran off towards the south.

In all this time, Thomas had said nothing; nor did he scarcely seem to notice my remarks, or to hear the questions which from time to time I put to him. When we came to the cross road, he suddenly stopped, and took me by the arm. I supposed that he was going to consult with me as to the course which we should take, and great was my surprise to hear him say, "Archy, here I leave you."

I could not imagine what he intended, and I looked at him for an explanation.

"You are now," he said, "on the road to the north. You have good clothes, and as much learning as an overseer. You can readily pass for a freeman. It will be very easy for you to get away to those free states, of which I have heard you speak so often. If I go with you, we shall both be stopped and questioned. We shall be pursued, and if we keep together, and follow this road, we shall certainly be taken. It is a great way to the free states, and I have little chance and no hope of ever getting there, and if I did, what should I gain by it? I will try the woods again, and do as I can. I shall be able to get back to our old place; but you, Archy, you can do better. You are sure of getting away to the north. Go, my boy; go, and God bless you!"

I was deeply moved, and it was some time before I was able to reply. The thoughts of escaping from my present situation of danger and misery, to a land where I could bear the name and enjoy the rights of a freeman, flashed upon my mind with a radiant and dazzling brightness, that seemed almost to blot out every other feeling. Yet still my love for Thomas, and the gratitude I owed him, glimmered through these new hopes, and a low voice from the very centre of my heart bade me not to desert my friend. After too long a pause, and too much hesitation, I began to answer him. I spoke of his wounds, of our sworn friendship,

K

and of the risk he had so lately run in my behalf, and insisted that I would stay with him to the last.

I spoke, I fear, with too little of zeal and earnestness. At least, all that I said only seemed to confirm Thomas in his determination. He replied that his wounds were healing, and that he was already almost as strong as ever. He added, that if I stayed with him, I might do myself much harm, without the chance of doing him any good. He pointed along the road, and in an energetic and commanding voice, he bade me to follow it, while he should take the cross-road towards the south.

When Thomas had once made up his mind, there was a firmness in the tone with which he spoke, sufficient often to overawe the most unwilling. At the present moment, I was but too ready to be prevailed upon. He saw his advantage, and pursued it. "Go, Archy," he repeated, "go,—if not for your own sake, go for mine. If you stay with me, and are taken, I shall never forgive you for it."

Little by little, my better feelings yielded, and at last I consented to the separation. I took Thomas by the hand, and pressed him to my heart. A nobler spirit never breathed,—I was not worthy to call myself his friend.

"God bless you, Archy," he said, as he left me. I stood watching him as he walked rapidly away, and as I looked, I was ready to sink into the earth with shame and mortification. Once or twice, I was just starting to follow him; but selfish prudence prevailed, and I held back. I watched him till he was out of sight, and then resumed my journey. It was a base desertion, which not even the love of liberty could excuse.

CHAPTER XXXIV.

I WALKED on as fast as I was able, till after daylight, without meeting a single individual, or passing more than two or three mean and lonely houses. Just as the sun was rising, I gained the top of a considerable hill. Here there was a small house by the road-side, and a horse saddled and bridled was tied to a tree near by. The animal was sleek, and in good condition, and from the cut of the saddle-bags, I took him to belong to some doctor, who had come thus early to visit a patient. It was a tempting opportunity. I looked cautiously this way and that, and seeing nobody, I unfastened the horse, and jumped into the saddle. I walked him a little distance, but presently put him into a gallop, that soon carried me out of sight of the house.

This was a very lucky acquisition; for as I was upon the same road which the travellers from whom I had escaped would follow, as soon as they resumed their journey, I was in manifest danger of being overtaken and recognized. As I found that my horse had both spirit and bottom, I put him to his speed, and went forward at a rapid rate. My good luck did not end here; for happening to put my hand into the pocket of my new coat, I drew out a pocket-book, which, beside a parcel of musty papers, I found on examining it a little to contain quite a pretty sum of money in bank notes. This discovery gave a new impulse to my spirits, which were high enough before, and I pushed on all day without stopping, except now and then to rest my horse in the shade of a tree.

Towards evening I got a supper, and corn for my horse, at a little hedge tavern; and waiting till the moon rose, I set out again. By morning, my horse was completely broken down, and gave out entirely. Thankful for his services thus far,—for, according to my reckoning, he had carried me upwards of a hundred miles in the twenty-four hours,— I stripped off his saddle and bridle, and turned him into a wheat-field to refresh himself. I now pursued my journey on foot; for I feared if I kept the horse, the possession of him might perhaps get me into difficulty; and in fact, he was so jaded and worn out, that he would be of very little use to me. I had got a good start upon the travellers, and I did not doubt that I could get on as fast upon foot as they would on horseback.

Before sunset, I arrived at a considerable village. Here I indulged myself in a hearty meal, and a good night's sleep. Both were needed; for, what with watching, fasting, and fatigue, I was quite worn out. I slept some ten hours, and awoke with new vigour. I now resumed my journey, which I pursued without much fear of interruption; though I judged it prudent to stop but seldom, and to push forward as rapidly as possible. I kept on through North Carolina and Virginia; crossed the Potomac into Maryland; and avoiding Baltimore, I passed on into Pennsylvania, and congratulated myself that at last I trod a soil cultivated by freemen.

I had gone but a few miles before I perceived the difference. In fact, I had scarcely passed the slave-holding border, before the change became apparent. The spring was just opening, and everything was beginning to look fresh, green, and beautiful. The nicely cultivated fields, the numerous small enclosures, the neat and substantial farm-houses, thickly scattered along the way, the pretty villages and busy towns, the very roads themselves, which were covered with waggons and travellers, —all these signs of universal thrift and comfort gave abundant evidence that at length I saw a country where labour was honourable, and where every one laboured for himself. It was an exhilarating and delightful prospect, and in strong contrast with all I had seen in the former part of my journey, in which a wretched and lonely road had led me on through a vast monotonous extent of unprofitable woods, deserted fields grown over with broomsedge and mullen, or fields just ready to be deserted, gullied, barren, and with all the evidences upon them of a negligent, unwilling, and unthrifty cultivation. Here and there I had passed a mean and comfortless house; and once in fifty miles a decaying, poverty-stricken village, with a court-house, and a store or two, and a great crowd of idlers collected about a tavern-door, but without one single sign of industry or improvement.

I was desirous of seeing Philadelphia; but that city, so near the slave-holding border, I feared might be infected with something of the slave-holding spirit; for the worst plagues are the most apt to be contagious. I passed by without passing through it, and hastened on to New York. I crossed the noble Hudson, and entered the town. It was the first city I had ever seen; at least, the first one worthy to be called a city; and when I beheld the spacious harbour crowded with shipping, the long lines of warehouses, the numerous streets, the splendid shops, and the swarming crowds of busy people, I was astonished, and delighted with the new idea which all this gave to me of the resources of human art and industry. I had heard of such things before, but to feel, one ought to see.

I did nothing for several days but wander up and down the streets, looking, gazing, and examining with an almost insatiable curiosity.

New York then was far inferior to what it must by this time have become; and the commercial restrictions which then prevailed must have tended to diminish its business and its bustle. Yet, to my rustic inexperience, the city seemed almost interminable; and the rattling of the drays and carriages over the pavements, and the crowds of people in the streets, far exceeded all my previous notions of the busy confusion of a city.

I had now been in New York about a week, and was standing one forenoon by a triangular grass-plot, near the centre of the town, gazing at a fine building of white marble, which one of the passers-by told me was the City Hall, when suddenly I felt my arm rudely seized. I looked round, and with horror and dismay I found myself in the gripe of General Carter,—the man who in South Carolina had called himself my master—but who, in a country that prided itself in the title of a "free state," ought no longer to have had any claim upon me.

Let no one be deceived by the false and boastful title which the northern states of the American Union have thought fit to assume. With what justice can they pretend to call themselves free states, after having made a bargain with the slave-holders, by which they are bound to deliver back again into the hands of their oppressors, every miserable fugitive who takes refuge within their territory? The good people of the free states have no slaves themselves. Oh, no! Slave-holding, they confess, is a horrible enormity. They hold no slaves themselves; they only act as bum-bailiffs and tipstaves to the slave-holders!

My master—for so even in the free city of New York I must continue to call him,—had seized me by one arm, and a friend of his held me by the other. He called me by name; and in the hurry and confusion of this sudden surprise I forgot for a moment how impolitic it was for me to appear to know him. A crowd began to collect about us. When they heard that I was seized as a fugitive slave, some of them appeared not a little outraged at the idea that a white man should be subject to such an indignity. They seemed to think that it was only the black whom it was lawful to kidnap in that way. Such indeed is the untiring artfulness of tyranny that it is ever nestling even in the bosoms of the free: and there is not one prejudice, the offspring, as all prejudices are, of ignorance and self-conceit, of which it has not well learned how to avail itself.

Though several of the crowd did not scruple to use very strong expressions, they made no attempt to rescue me; and I was dragged along towards that very City Hall which I had just been admiring. I was carried before the sitting magistrate; some questions were put and answered; some oaths were sworn, and papers written. I had not yet recovered from the first confusion of my seizure; and this array of courts and constables was a horrid sort of danger to which I was totally unaccustomed, so that I scarcely know what was said or done. But, to the best of my recollection, the magistrate declined acting on the question; though he consented to grant a warrant for detaining me in prison till I could be taken before some other tribunal.

The warrant was made out, and I was delivered over to an officer. The court-room was filled with the crowd, who had followed us from the street. They collected close about us as we left the court-room; and I could see by the expression of their faces, and the words which some of them dropped, that they were very well inclined to favour my escape. At first, I seemed all submission to the officer; we had gone, however, but a very few steps when, with a sudden spring, I tore myself from his grasp, and darted among the crowd, which opened to give me a passage. I heard noise, confusion, and shouts behind me; but in a moment I had cleared the inclosure in which the City Hall stood, and crossing one of the streets by which it was bounded, I dashed down a narrow and crooked lane. The people stared at me as I ran, and some shouted, "Stop thief!" One or two seemed half-inclined to seize me, but I turned one short corner, and then another, and finding that I was not pursued, I soon dropped into a walk.

For this escape I return my thanks, not to the laws of New York, but to the good-will of her citizens. The secret bias and selfish interest of the law-makers often leads them wrong; the unprompted and disinterested impulses of the people are almost always right. It is true that the artful practice and cunning instigation of the purchased friends and bribed advocates of oppression, joined to the interest which the thieves and pickpockets of a great city always have in civil tumult and confusion, may now and then succeed in exciting the young, the ignorant, the thoughtless and the depraved, to acts of violence in favour of tyranny. But so congenial to the human heart is the love of freedom, that it burns not brighter in the souls of sages and of heroes, than in the bosoms even of the most ignorant and thoughtless, when not quenched by some excited prejudice, base passion, or sinister influence.

In my previous wanderings about the town, I had discovered the road that led northwardly out of it; and I soon turned in that direction, determined to shake off from my feet the very dust of a city where I had been so near falling back again into the wretched condition of servitude.

I travelled all that day, and at night the innkeeper, at whose house I lodged, told me that I was in the state of Connecticut. I now pursued my flight for several days, through a fine hilly and mountainous country, such as I had never seen before. The nobleness of the prospect, the craggy rocks and rugged hills, contrasted finely with the excellent cultivation of the valleys, and the universal thrift and industry of the inhabitants. Where freedom nerves the arm, it is in vain that rocks and hills of granite oppose the labours of the cultivator. Industrious liberty teaches him the art to extract comfort, competence, and wealth, from a soil the most unwilling and ungrateful.

I knew that Boston was the great sea-port of New England; and thither I directed my steps, resolved to leave a land, however otherwise inviting, whose laws would not acknowledge me a freeman. As I approached the town, the country lost much of its picturesque and hilly grandeur; but this was made up for by the greater beauty of its smoother and better cultivated fields; and by the pretty dwellings scattered so numerously along the road, that the environs of the town seemed almost a continued village. The city itself, seated on hills, and seen for a considerable distance, gave a noble termination to the prospect.

I crossed a broad river, by a long bridge, and soon entered the town; but I did not stop to examine it. Liberty was too precious to be sacrificed to the gratification of an idle curiosity; a New York mob had set me free; a Boston mob might perhaps delight in the opportunity of restoring me to servitude. I found my way, as soon as the crooked and irregular streets would allow me, to the wharves. Many of the ships were stripped and rotting in the docks; but after some search and inquiry, I found a vessel about to sail for Bordeaux. I offered myself as a sailor. The captain questioned me, and laughed heartily at my land-lubberly air and rustic ignorance; but, finally, he agreed to take me at half wages. He advanced me a month's pay; and the second mate, who was a fine young fellow, and who seemed to feel for my lonely and helpless ignorance, assisted me in buying such clothes as would be necessary for the voyage.

In a few days our cargo was completed, and the ship was ready for sea. We dropped off from the wharf; threaded our course among the numerous islets and headlands of Boston harbour, passed the castle and the lighthouse, sent off our pilot, and with all sail set and a smacking breeze we left the town behind.

As I stood upon the forecastle, and looked towards the land, which soon seemed but a little streak in the horizon, and was fast sinking from our sight, I seemed to feel a heavy weight drop off me. The chains were gone. I felt myself a freeman; and as I watched the fast-receding shore, my bosom heaved with a proud scorn,—a mingled feeling of safety and disdain.

"Farewell, my country!" such were the thoughts that rose upon my mind, and pressed to find an utterance from my lips. "And such a country! A land boasting to be the chosen seat of liberty and equal rights, yet holding such a portion of her people in hopeless, helpless, miserable bondage!

"Farewell, my country! Much is the gratitude and thanks I owe thee! Land of the tyrant and the slave, farewell!

"And welcome, welcome, ye bounding billows and foamy surges of the ocean! Ye are the emblems and the children of liberty—I hail ye as my brothers! for, at last, I, too, am free!—free!—free!"

CHAPTER XXXV.

THE favourable breezes with which we had set out did not last long. The weather soon became tempestuous, and we were involved in fogs, and driven about by contrary winds. Our labours and hardships were very great; but still I found a sort of pleasure in them. It was for myself that I toiled and suffered; and that thought gave me strength and vigour.

I applied myself with the greatest zeal and good-will to learn the business of my profession. At first, my companions laughed at my ignorance and awkwardness, and were full of their jokes and tricks upon me. But though rude and thoughtless, they were generous and good-natured. In the very first week of our voyage, I had a fair fight with the bully of the ship. I whipped him soundly; and the crew all agreed that there was something in me.

I was strong and active; and as I made it a point to imitate whatever I saw done by any of the crew, I was surprised to find in how short a time I was able to run over the rigging and venture upon the yards. The maze of ropes and sea-terms that at first perplexed me soon grew clear. Before we were across the ocean, I could hand, reef, and steer, with any man on board; and the crew swore with one consent that I was born to be a sailor.

But I was not satisfied with setting sails and handling ropes. I wished to understand the art of navigation. One of our crew was a young man of good education, who served before the mast, as is common with New Englanders, in expectation of presently commanding a ship himself.

He had his books and his instruments; and as he had already been one or two voyages, he understood pretty well how to apply them, and used to keep a reckoning of the ship's course. This same young sailor, Tom Turner by name, was a fine, free-hearted fellow as ever lived; but he was of slight make, and his strength was not equal to his spirit. I had gained his good-will by standing by him in some of our forecastle frolics; and seeing how anxious I was to learn, he undertook to be my instructor. He put his Navigator into my hand, and whenever it was my watch below, I was constantly poring over it. At first, the whole matter seemed mighty mysterious. It was some time before I could see into it. But Tom, who had a fluent tongue, lectured and explained; and I listened and studied; and presently I began to understand it.

All this time we were beating about in the neighbourhood of the banks of Newfoundland; and as we experienced a constant succession of storms and contrary winds, we made but little progress. We lost a couple of topsails and several of our spars, and had been out some seventy days in very rough weather.

I took it all kindly though; I was in no hurry to get ashore. I had chosen the ocean for my country; and when the winds roared, the rigging rattled, and the timbers creaked, I only wrapped my monkey-jacket a little closer, braced myself against my sea-chest, and studied my Navigator—that is, if it happened to be my watch below; for when upon deck, I was always ready at the first call, and was the first to spring into the rigging.

At last, the weather moderated, and we made sail for the coast of France. We had made the land, and were within a few leagues of our harbour, when an armed brig, with the British colours flying, bore down upon us, fired a shot a-head, and sent a boat's crew on board.

In those days, American vessels were quite accustomed to such sort of visitations; and our captain did not seem to be much alarmed. But no sooner had the boat's officer reached our deck, than laying his hand upon his sword, he told the captain that he was a prisoner.

It seemed that while we were beating about on the Grand Bank, America, at last, had screwed up her courage, and had declared war against England. The armed brig was a British privateer, and we were her prize. At first, we were all ordered below; but presently we were called up again, and offered the choice of enlisting on board the privateer, or being carried prisoners into England. Near half our crew were what the sailors call Dutchmen, that is, people from the North Sea, or the coasts of the Baltic. These adventurers readily enlisted. Tom Turner was spokesman for the Americans; and when called upon to follow this example, he answered the lieutenant, in a tone so gruff as to be little better than a growl,—"We'll see you hanged first!"

For myself, I felt no patriotic scruples. I had renounced my country; if indeed that place can be fitly called one's country, which, while it gives him birth, cuts him off, by its wicked and unjust laws, from every-thing that makes life worth having. Despite the murmurs and hisses of my companions, I stepped forward, and put my name to the shipping paper. Had they known my history, they would not have blamed me.

After cruising for some time, without success, we returned to Liver-pool to refit. Our crew was recruited, and we soon put to sea again Cruising off the coast of France, we took several prizes, but none of very great value. We now made sail for the West Indies, and in the neigh-bourhood of the Bermudas, while close hauled to the wind and under easy sail, we discovered a vessel a-head, and gave chase.

The chase slackened sail and waited for us to come up. This made us suppose that it might be a man-of-war; and as we were more anxious for plunder than for fighting, we put up the helm and bore away.

The chase now made sail in pursuit; and as she proved to be much the better sailor, she gained rapidly upon us.

When we saw that there was no chance of escaping, we took in our light canvas, brought the vessel to, ran up the British flag, and cleared for action.

The enemy was an armed and fast sailing schooner—an American privateer, as it proved, about a fair match for the brig, in point of size and armament, but in much finer trim, and most beautifully worked. She ran down upon us; her crew gave three cheers, and shooting across our bows, she gave us a broadside that did much execution. She tacked and manœuvred till she gained a favourable position, and then poured in her fire with such steadiness that she seemed all a-blaze. Her guns were well shotted, and well aimed, and did serious damage. Our captain and first lieutenant were soon wounded and disabled. We paid back the enemy as well as we could; but our men dropped fast, and our fire began to slacken. The schooner's bowsprit got fast in our main rigging, and directly we heard the cry for the boarders. We seized our pikes, and prepared to receive them; but a party of the enemy soon got a footing on board the brig, wounded the only officer on deck, and drove our men, frightened and confused, towards the forecastle.

I saw our danger, and the idea of falling again into the hands of the tyrants from whom I had escaped summoned back my ebbing courage. I seemed to feel a more than human energy spring up within me. I put myself at the head of our yielding and dispirited crew, and fought with all the frantic valour of a mad hero of romance. I struck down two or three of the foremost of the enemy; and as they quailed and shrunk before me, I cheered and encouraged my companions, and called on them to charge. My example seemed to inspire them. They rallied at once, and rushed forward with new courage. They drove the enemy before them; tumbled some into the sea, and pressed the others back into their own vessel.

Nor did our success stop here. We boarded in our turn; and the decks of the schooner saw as bloody a battle as had been fought on those of the brig. The fortune of the fight still ran in our favour, and we soon drove the enemy to take refuge on the quarter-deck. We called to them to surrender, but their captain, waving his bloody sword, sternly refused. He encouraged his men to charge once more, and rushed furiously upon us. His cutlass clashed against my pike and flew from his hand. He slipped, and fell upon the deck, and in a moment my weapon was at his breast.

He cried for quarter. I thought I knew his face.

" Your name?"

" Osborne!"

" Jonathan Osborne, late commander of the Two Sallys?"

" The same!"

" Then die;—a wretch like you deserves no mercy!" and as I spoke I plunged the weapon to his heart, and felt thrilling to the very elbow-joint the pleasurable sense of doing justice on a tyrant.

But justice ought never to be sullied by passion, and, if possible, should be unstained with blood. If in my feelings, at that moment, there was something noble, there was far too much of savage fury and passionate revenge. Yet, from what I then felt, I can well understand the fierce spirit and ferocious energy of the slave, who vindicates his liberty at the sword's point, and who looks upon the slaughter of his oppressors almost as a debt due to humanity.

The crew no sooner saw their captain slain than they threw down their arms and cried for quarter. The schooner was ours, and a finer vessel never sailed the seas.

Every officer on board the brig was wounded. All confessed that the capture of the prize was, in a great measure, due to me; and, with the approbation of all the crew, I was put on board as prize-master.

CHAPTER XXXVI.

WE had a short passage to Liverpool. The schooner was condemned as a prize, and was bought in by the owners of the brig. They fitted her out as a privateer; and as they had been informed how large a share I had in her capture, they offered me the command of her. I readily accepted it; and having selected an experienced old sailor for my first lieutenant, I soon collected a crew and set sail.

The cruising ground which I preferred was the coast of America. Off the harbour of Boston we were so lucky as to fall in with and make prize of a homeward-bound East-Indiaman, with a very valuable cargo of teas and silks. We put a prize-crew on board and sent her off for Liverpool, where she arrived safely, and produced us a very handsome sum in prize-money. We now stood to the southward, and for a month or two we cruised off the capes of Virginia. As we kept well in to the coast, we often made the land; and I never saw it without feeling a strong inclination to send a boat's crew ashore, and to kidnap from their beds such of the nearest planters as I could lay my hands upon. But I did not think it prudent to attempt to carry into execution this piece of experimental instruction, of which the Virginians stand so much in need.

My cruising adventures, chases, and escapes, would fill a volume; but they are little to my present purpose. Suffice it to say, that while the war lasted I kept the seas; and when it ended, most reluctantly I left them. My share in the prizes we had taken rendered me wealthy—at least what the moderation of my wishes made me esteem so. But what was to supply the ever-varying stimulus and excitement which till now had sustained me and prevented my mind from preying on itself, and poisoning my peace with bitter recollections? The images of my wife, my child, and of the friend to whom I owed so much, often, on my voyages, flitted mournfully across my mind; but the cry of "Sail ahead" would call off my thoughts, and dissipate my incipient melancholy in the bustle of action. But now that I was on shore, homeless, alone, a stranger, with nothing to occupy my mind,—the thoughts of those dear sufferers haunted me continually. The very first thing I did was to look up a trusty agent whom I might send in search of them. Such a one I found. I gave him all the information which might promote the object of his mission; I allowed him an unlimited credit on my banker, and stimulated his zeal by a handsome advance, and the promise of a still larger reward if he succeeded in the object of his mission.

He sailed for America by the first opportunity, and I consoled myself with the hope that his search would be successful. In the mean time, to have some occupation that might keep off anxious doubts and troublesome anxieties, I applied myself to study. When a child I had a fondness for reading and an ardent love of knowledge. This love of knowledge the accursed discipline of servitude had stifled and kept under, but had not totally extinguished. I was astonished to find it still so strong. Having once turned my attention that way, my mind drank in all sorts of information, as the thirsty earth imbibes the rain. I might rather be said to devour books than to read them. I scarcely gave myself time to sleep. No sooner had I finished one than I hurried to another with restless inquietude. I read on without selection or discrimination. It was a long time before I learned to compare, to weigh, and to judge. It happened to me as it has happened to mankind in general. In my anxiety to know, I was ready to take everything on trust; and I did not stop to distinguish between what was fact and what was fiction. But while I allowed an abundance of folly and falsehood to be palmed upon me under the sober disguise of truth, I had but little taste for writers professedly imaginative. I could not understand why they wrote, or what they aimed at. I despised the poets; but voyages, travels, histories, and narratives of every sort, I devoured with undistinguishing voracity. Time and reflection have since enabled me to extract something of truth and philosophy from these chaotic acquisitions.

For a while, my studies had much the same stimulating and exciting effect with my former activity. They raised my spirits, and enabled me to bear up under the discouraging advices which I received from America. But they palled at last,—and when my agent returned with the disastrous information, that all his searches had been unavailing, I found no support under the load of grief that overwhelmed me.

From such information as my agent had been able to obtain, it appeared that Mrs. Montgomery, Cassy's mistress, had become security to a large amount to that brother of hers, by whose advice and agency she managed her affairs. That brother was a planter, and among the American planters the passion for gambling is next to universal,—for it is one of the few excitements by which they are able to relieve the listless and wearisome indolence of their useless lives. Mrs. Montgomery's brother was a gambler, and an unsuccessful one. Having ruined himself, he began to prey upon his sister. Besides embezzling all such money of hers as he could lay his hands upon,—and as he had the entire management of her affairs, her income was much at his disposal,—he induced her, under various pretences, to put her name to bonds and notes to a large amount. On these notes and bonds suits were commenced; but this, her brother, who strove to defer the disclosure of his villanies as long as possible, took care to conceal from her; and the first thing she knew of the matter, her entire property was seized on execution.

Among her other chattels, my wife and child were sold,—for it is the law and the practice of America to sell women and children to pay the debts of a gambler !

Cassy and her infant had fallen into the hands of a gentleman,—such is the American phrase,—who followed the lucrative and respectable business of a slave-trader. My agent no sooner learnt his name than he set out in pursuit of him. But he found that the man had been dead for a year or two, and that he had left no papers behind him, from which might be traced the history of his slave-trading expeditions. Not yet discouraged, my agent travelled over the entire route which he was told the deceased slave-trader had usually followed. He even succeeded in getting some trace of the very gang of slaves which had been purchased at the sale of Mrs. Montgomery's property. He tracked them from village to village, till he arrived at Augusta, in the state of Georgia; but here he lost sight of them altogether. That town is, or was, one of the great marts of the American slave trade, and here, in all probability, the slaves were sold; but to whom, it was impossible to discover.

Thus baffled in his search, my agent had recourse to advertisements in the newspapers, in which the person of my wife was particularly described, mention was made of the name of her late owner, and a very generous reward was offered to any one who would give information where she or her child was to be found. These advertisements brought him an abundance of communications, but none to the purpose, and after having spent near two years in the search, he gave it up, at last, as unavailing.

Of Thomas, he could learn nothing, except that General Carter had never retaken him. A man of his figure and appearance had been occasionally seen traversing the woods of that neighbourhood, and lurking about the plantations, and it seemed not unlikely that he was still alive, and the leader of some band of runaways. Such was the information which my agent brought me.

While he remained in America, however little encouragement his letters gave, still I could hope; but now the last staff of consolation was plucked from under me. What availed it that I had myself shaken off the chains, which were still hanging, and perhaps with a weight so much the heavier, to the friend of my heart, to the wife of my bosom, to the dear, dear infant, the child of my love? The curse of tyranny, indeed, is multifold,—nay, infinite! It blasted me across the broad Atlantic; and when I thought of Cassy and my boy, I shrunk and trembled, as if again the irons were upon me, and the bloody lash cracking about my head! Almighty God! why hast thou created beings capable of so much misery!

I recovered slowly from the shock, which at first had quite unmanned me; but though I regained some degree of composure, it was in vain that I courted anything like enjoyment,—a worm was gnawing at my heart which would not be appeased. Never was there a bosom more inclined than mine to the simple pleasures of domestic life; but I found only torture in the recollection that I was a husband and a father. Oh, had my wife and my dear boy been with me, in what a sweet retirement I could have spent my days, ever finding a new relish for present bliss in the recollection of ills endured and miseries escaped!

The sense of loneliness which oppressed me, and the bitter thoughts and hateful images that were ever crowding on my mind, made my life an irksome burden, and drove me to seek relief in the excitements of travel. I visited every country in Europe, and sought occupation and amusement in examining their scheme of society, and studying their laws and manners. I traversed Turkey and the regions of the East, once the seats of art and opulence, but long since ruined by the heavy hand of tyranny and the ever-renewed extortions of military pillage. I crossed the Persian deserts, and saw in India a new and better civilization slowly rising upon the ruins of the old.

The interest I felt in the oppressed and unfortunate race with which upon my mother's side, I am connected, carried me again across the ocean. I have climbed the lofty crests of the Andes, and wandered among the flowery forests of Brazil.

Everywhere I have seen the hateful empire of aristocratic usurpation lording it with a high hand over the lives, the liberty, and the happiness of men; but everywhere, or almost everywhere, I have seen the bondsmen beginning to forget the base lore of traditionary subserviency, and already feeling the impulses and lisping in the language of freedom. I have seen it everywhere,—everywhere except in my native America.

There are slaves in many other countries, but nowhere else is oppression so heartless and unrelenting; nowhere else has tyranny ever assumed a shape so fiendish; nowhere else is it, of all the world beside, the open aim of the laws, and the professed purpose of the masters, to blot out the intellects of half the population, and to extinguish at once and for ever both the capacity and the hope of freedom.

In Catholic Brazil, in the Spanish islands, where one might expect to find tyranny aggravated by ignorance and superstition, the slave is still regarded as a man, and as entitled to something of human sympathies. He may kneel at the altar by his master's side, and he may hear the Catholic priest proclaiming boldly from his pulpit the sacred truth that all men are equal. He may find consolation and support in the hope of one day becoming a freeman. He may purchase his liberty with money; if barbarously and unreasonably punished, he may demand it as his legal right; he may expect it from the gratitude or the generosity of his master, or from the conscience-stricken dictates of his priest-attended deathbed. When he becomes a freeman he has a freeman's rights, and enjoys a real and practical equality, at the mere mention of which the prating and prejudiced Americans are filled with creeping horror and passionate indignation.

Slavery in those countries, by the force of causes now in operation, is fast approaching to its end; and let the African slave-trade be once totally abolished, and before the expiration of half-a-century there will not a slave be found in either Spanish or Portuguese America.

It is in the United States alone—that country so apt to claim a monopoly of freedom—that the spirit of tyranny still soars boldly triumphant, and disdains even the most distant thought of limitation,—here alone, of all the world beside, oppression riots unchecked by fear of God or sympathy for man.

To add the last security to despotism, the American slave-holders, while they fiercely refuse to relinquish the least tittle of their whip-wielding authority, have deprived themselves, by special statute, of the power of emancipation, and have thus artfully and industriously closed up the last loop-hole through which Hope might look in upon their victims!

And thou, my child! these are the mercies to which thy youth is delivered over! Perhaps already the spirit of manhood is extinguished within thee, already perhaps the frost of servitude has nipped thy budding soul, and left it blasted, worthless!

No! oh no! it ought not, must not, cannot, shall not be so! Child! thou hast yet a father,—one who has not forgotten, and who will not forsake thee. Thy need is great, and great shall be his efforts. That love is little worth which disappointment tires or danger daunts.

Yes, I have resolved it. I will revisit America, and through the length and the breadth of the land I will search out my child. I will snatch him from the oppressor's grasp, or perish in the attempt. Should I be recognized and seized! It is not in vain that I have read the history of the Romans. I know a way to disappoint the tyrants,—the guilt be on their heads! I cannot be a slave the second time.

CHAPTER XXXVII.

HAVING formed the resolve recorded at the close of the last chapter, I began immediately to make preparations to carry it into execution, and now once more I resume my pen to recount my further adventures.

I had lived for years past a life of constant uneasiness and anxiety; haunted, as it were, by the spectres of wife and child, pale, weeping, holding out imploring hands, as if calling to me for aid and deliverance. From the moment that I began to prepare for my new journey and search, I felt a lightness, an exhilaration, a relief, as if a great stone had been plucked out of my heart. Now, at last, I had again something to live and to strive for,—a shadow perhaps, one so vain and unsubstantial that ever since the failure of my former searches it had seemed idle to attempt to pursue it. Yet how much better to pursue even a shadow, if one can but prevail upon himself for the moment to think it real, than to sit still in hopeless and idle vacuity! Man was made to hope and to act.

Before leaving England, I took care to provide myself with passports as a British subject, under the name of Captain Archer Moore, by which I was known to my English acquaintances, and with letters also of introduction to the mercantile correspondents of those acquaintances in the principal commercial towns of America. It was in the character of a traveller, curious to investigate American society, that I revisited the country of my birth.

As it was from Boston that I had taken my departure, so I resolved to reland there, and thence to retrace my steps to the scenes of my youth, as the first means towards obtaining, if possible, some clue to the object of my search.

It was now more than twenty years since I had hastily fled from Boston, a panting fugitive, eager to find on the boisterous ocean, or somewhere beyond it, that freedom which the laws of America denied me there. How different from the stern and deperate spirit of defiance with which I had seen those shores fade from my sight was the tender sentiment, rising almost to hope, with which I again saw spreading out before me that same land emerging from the waters; cruel land of bondage as it had been to me, but where yet I might—O, kind Heaven, that I might!—regain a long-lost wife and child!

As we landed at the wharf and made our way into the town, we found it in a state of great confusion. A vast crowd, mostly of well-dressed people, was collected about a building, which I afterwards understood to be the City Hall; and just as we approached it, an unfortunate person, with a rope about his neck, was dragged, apparently from some neighbouring house or by-way, into the middle of the street. The shout was raised, "Hang him!" hang him!" and the gentlemen in fine broad-cloth, in whose hands he was, seemed quite ready to do the bidding of the mob, and to be looking round, as if for some lamp-post or other convenience for that purpose. Making our way with great difficulty to an adjoining street, we found it completely choked up with a well-dressed crowd, through which, amid jeers and insults, a few women, holding each other's hands, slowly made their way, retreating apparently from a neighbouring building, and for some reason or other evidently objects of very great indignation.

On reaching my hotel, called, I think, the Tremont House, I anxiously inquired into the occasion of all this tumult. The landlord informed me that it had all been caused by the obstinacy of the women whom I had seen in the streets. In spite of the remonstrances of the citizens, as expressed at a great public meeting lately held, in which all the leading merchants and lawyers had participated, these obstinate females had persisted in meeting to pray for and to plot the abolition of slavery; and what was still more provoking, to listen to the exhortations on that subject of an emissary lately sent over from England. It was the object of the gentlemanly mob I had seen, composed, as he assured me, of men of property and standing, to catch this emissary if they could, and to punish him in some fitting way for his insolence.

"And pray," said I, "as you have no slaves in Boston, nor, I believe, in this part of the country, why all this zeal against these good women? Being an Englishman myself, I must confess to some little interest in this unfortunate countryman of mine, whom your Boston gentry are so anxious to hang. Why need your lawyers and merchants play the dog in the manger—neither themselves do anything to abolish slavery, nor even allow the women to pray for it?" "As a stranger and an Englishman," said the landlord, who, though in a great state of excitement against the offending females, was evidently a person not without good feelings, "these things may seem a little strange to you. Yet allow me to suggest a word of caution. It would be an unpleasant thing for me to have one of my guests seized as a British emissary, and made to undergo the scrutiny and perhaps insults of a party of volunteer police. Suffice it to say, that just at this moment the price of cotton is very high, and southern trade a great object. New York and Philadelphia have set the example of mobbing the abolitionists, and we should be in danger of losing all our southern customers if we did not follow the example. Besides, at a public meeting held here in Boston, we have just nominated a candidate for president; and should we fail in zeal for southern interests, how are we to expect to get any southern votes?"

After this specimen of Boston, I saw nothing to detain me there, and so hastened on to New York. It was not without strong emotions that I stood again in the park, on the very spot where General Carter had seized and claimed me as a slave. The whole scene, with all its incidents, came back to my mind as fresh as at the moment of the seizure, and I walked straight to the court-room, to which I had been carried, with as little doubt, hesitation, or uncertainty as if it had all happened the day before. There were a number of prisoners at the bar, the room was crowded with spectators, and a trial or examination of evident interest was going on. It soon appeared that the prisoners were charged with having sacked and plundered a number of houses, whose occupants were suspected to be tainted with abolitionism, and having, in the same spirit, burnt down an African church. The feeling in the court-room seemed, however, altogether in favour of the prisoners, and such, as far as I could judge by the newspapers, and the conversations which I heard, was the current opinion of the city. The prevailing idea seemed to be, that the persons really guilty of the riots were those who had suffered by them, since it was their pestilent, upopular opinions which had stirred up the mob to sack and plunder their houses.

What I saw in New York and Boston served to cure me of an error, as to America, sufficiently common. I had supposed that in the free states, so called, there was really some freedom. I knew, indeed, by my own experience, that no asylum was to be found there by refugee slaves from the southern states; but I had imagined that the native-born inhabitants did enjoy a certain degree of liberty. My mistake in this respect was now very apparent. No one in New York or Boston was at liberty, at the time of my visit, to entertain, or at least publicly to express, any detestation of the system of slavery, or desire or hope for its speedy abolition, under penalty of being visited with the public indignation. Such persons, indeed, would be lucky if they escaped without insult to their persons, and destruction of their property. The leading politicians, lawyers, and merchants of those cities under whose encouragement and instigation these outrages were inflicted, seemed to stand in no less awe and terror of the anger of the southern planters than the very slaves who delved the plantations. Those slaves were held in check by the whip and superior force; the northern freemen, so called, by their own pusillanimity and base love of money. In fact, already I began to doubt whether this voluntary slavery of the nominally free—voluntary on the part of an overwhelming majority, however a virtuous and noble minority might struggle against it—was not every way a more wretched and lamentable thing than the forced slavery of the labourers of the south. Hitherto I had hated a country, from whose prison-houses I had with such difficulty escaped, and which continued to retain, if, indeed, death had not fortunately delivered them, those nearest and dearest to me. To this hatred I now began to add contempt for a mean-spirited population, in which there were more voluntary slaves than forced ones.

From New York I passed on to Philadelphia, and thence to Washington. That city had greatly expanded since, as one of a chained gang of slaves, I had been lodged in the slave-prison of Messrs. Savage, Brothers, and Company, for shipment to the south. In every village and town on my way I heard the same execrations vented against the abolitionists, with accounts of new riots in which they had suffered, or new attempts to subject them to more legal punishments. There seemed to be a general conspiracy against freedom of speech and freedom of the press. A learned judge of Massachusetts, after severely denouncing the abolitionists as incendiaries, proposed to have them indicted at common law as guilty of sedition, if not of treason. The accomplished governor of the same state said ditto to the judge, and added fresh denunciations of his own. Almost the only person in New England of any note, as I understood, who ventured to withstand this popular clamour, or to drop a word of apology for those unfortunate abolitionists, was Dr. Channing, whose writings have made him well known wherever the English language is read; but whose refusal on this occasion to become, by silence, a participator in the outrages going on around him, had very nearly destroyed, at least for the time, his weight and influence at home.

Washington I found in the greatest state of excitement. An unfortunate botanist, who had been gathering plants in the neighbourhood, had, from some cause or other, fallen under suspicion as being an abolitionist. His person, room, and trunks had been searched. He was found to have in possession a pile of newspapers, which was made to serve the purpose of an herbarium, in which to dry, press, and preserve his plants. This pile of papers, on being carefully scrutinized, was found to contain some articles bearing strongly to abolition sentiments. The whole district of Columbia was at once in commotion. The unfortunate botanist had been immediately arrested on the charge of having in his possession an incendiary publication. The alarm had reached a very high pitch; but when it was known that this botanical incendiary, this fellow who sought to entice the flowers and the herbage into a bloody conspiracy, was safely locked up in gaol, and all bail refused, the city of Washington, especially the southern members of Congress, once more breathed freely, as if delivered from impending destruction.

The high degree of excitement, alarm, and terror, which I found thus prevailing wherever I went, and which, according to all accounts, over-spread at this moment the whole United States, was much of a puzzle to me. I doubt very much whether the Stamp Act itself had caused half so much commotion. Even the sacking of Washington by the British could hardly have produced more alarm than I found prevailing in that city and neighbourhood. The mere fact that a few women of Boston had formed a society to pray for the abolition of slavery, or that a file of abolition newspapers had found its way to the district of Colum-bia, did not seem sufficient to account for so great an alarm. Even the circumstance, that a Miss Prudence Crandall, somewhere in Connecticut, had set up a school, to which she admitted coloured children on terms of equality with her white pupils, would not appear in itself so alarming a matter, since a number of the most pious and distinguished gentlemen of her state and neighbourhood, including a judge of the United States court, had taken an early opportunity to break up her school and to send her out of the town. I was assured, in fact, that this was not all. This Boston female society and Connecticut school were only small items. I was told of a grand plot formed by the abolitionists, tending to the most alarming results; no less than the cutting the throats of all the white men throughout the south, horrible indignities upon all the white women, the ruin of northern trade and commerce, the destruction of the south, and the dissolution of the Union. It was admitted by some of the more charitable persons with whom I conversed, that pos-sibly the abolitionists themselves did not distinctly contemplate all these ends. But they asked for the immediate abolition of slavery, a thing which could end in nothing but in the above-mentioned disasters and horrors.

I had a great curiosity to know who these formidable plotters, objects of so much alarm and terror, might be. I was not ignorant of affairs in America, but of these terrible abolitionists I had never heard; indeed, it would seem as if they had all at once started suddenly out of the ground. I learnt, upon inquiry, that within a short time past there had sprung up, in New England and elsewhere, several societies, delegates from which had lately met at New York, to the number of twelve men, where they had formed a national society. It was the fundamental principle of those societies, that to hold men in forced bondage was politically a wrong, socially a crime, and theologically a sin; disqualifying those guilty of it to be esteemed either good democrats, good men, or good Christians; and that, nationally and individually, this wrong, crime, and sin, ought to be at once repented of and abandoned. These fanatical persons had rapidly increased in numbers. Several wealthy merchants, several zealous and eloquent divines had joined them. A good deal of money, as much as forty or fifty thousand dollars, had been contributed and expended in the dissemination of this startling creed, partly by agents and missionaries sent forth for that purpose, partly by the publication of newspapers, of which there were already two or three devoted to the cause, and especially by the printing of tracts, setting forth the cruelties and injustice of slavery, which had been sent by mail into all parts of the country, even into the southern states.

It was these tracts that had thrown the whole south, planters, politicians, merchants, lawyers, divines, into an agony of terror, a terror with which even the people of the north so far sympathized as to be ready to trample underfoot, for the extinction of these horrible innovators, every safeguard of liberty hitherto esteemed the most sacred. Free speaking and free writing were not to be any longer tolerated. Throughout the United States, so far as related to the subject of slavery, they were to be suppressed by mob violence.

A few hundred men and women, hitherto mostly obscure and unknown, by the holding of a few public meetings and the publication of a few tracts, had thrown a whole country into commotion. Not John the Baptist, when he preached that the kingdom of heaven was at hand, had more terribly alarmed King Herod, the scribes and the pharisees; and now, as then, the murder of the innocents seemed to be thought the most feasible way of staving off the apprehended catastrophe.

As there are glens among the mountains where the faintest spoken words come back in thunder from a thousand echoes, so there are times and seasons when human hearts respond in like manner to the faintest uttered truth, testifying to the force of it, sometimes by loud responses of approbation and applause, sometimes in deafening shouts of indignation, defiance, and conscience-stricken dread.

CHAPTER XXXVIII.

HAVING reached Richmond on my southern journey, I found that city also showing the general alarm. A committee of vigilance for the suppression of incendiary publications was vigorously at work, and as we drove into the town, a great bonfire was burning in the main street, consisting of publications lately seized and condemned. One of the books thus burnt at the stake was made up, I was told, entirely of extracts from speeches delivered within a few years past in the Virginia House of Delegates, in which the evils of slavery had been pretty strongly depicted. But whatever liberty of that sort might previously have been allowed, nothing of the kind was to be tolerated for the future.

At Richmond I procured a horse and servant,—for in Lower Virginia there were no public conveyances,—and set off on a visit to Spring-Meadow, my birthplace. To satisfy inquiries,—since any traveller, a stranger and unknown, was at that time liable to suspicion,—I gave out that, on a former visit to the country, many years before, I had become acquainted with the family at Spring-Meadow, to which, indeed, I claimed a distant relationship. As I began to approach that neighbourhood, I found the aspect of desolation and desertion characteristic enough of Virginia as I remembered it, and as I now again saw it, growing more and more marked. As I rode along absorbed in thought, my eyes at length met an object which I recognized, being no other than the shop and dwelling-house of Mr. Jemmy Gordon, situated at the crotch of the roads, some six or seven miles from Spring-Meadow. It was a fine, warm summer afternoon, and on a rude bench or settle beside the door was sitting, more asleep than awake, an old gentleman, who, to the best of my recollection, could be no other than Mr. Jemmy himself. I accordingly addressed him as Mr. Gordon, when he roused himself up, did the honours of the house with a grace, and bade me walk in and refresh myself with a glass of peach brandy. He confessed, however, that I had the advantage of him, as he found it impossible to recollect my name. I endeavoured to remind him of a young Mr. Moore, an Englishman, who, some twenty years before, had passed a week or two at Spring-Meadow, and more than once had ridden by his shop; and after a good deal of nodding, thinking, and muttering to himself, he declared at last that he recollected me perfectly. When I inquired after Spring-Meadow and its occupants, Mr. Gordon shook his head mournfully. " Gone, sir, all gone to rack and ruin. Colonel Moore, in his old age, was obliged to move off somewhere, to Alabama, with such of the hands as he could save from the clutch of the sheriff; and that's the last I've heard of him. The old plantation has been abandoned these ten years; and the last time I was by there, the roof of the mansion-house was all tumbling in." As I knew there was no house nearer than Gordon's, I begged of him to entertain me for a day or two, while I took a turn round the old plantation. From my conversation with him, I learned that, with the decrease of the population in the neighbourhood, his trade had fallen off, and that he, too, had serious thoughts, old as he was, of moving off to Alabama, or somewhere else at the south-west. Early the next morning, leaving my servant and horse behind me, I set off on foot. But I was no sooner out of sight of Jemmy Gordon's house than I directed my steps, not to Spring-Meadow, but to that old deserted plantation on the higher lands above to which I had fled with Cassy, and where, in the hopefulness and thoughtlessness of youth, runaways as we were, we had passed some weeks of happy privacy, ending, indeed, in heavy tribulation. The great house had now completely fallen, and was one undistinguishable heap of ruins; but the little brick dairy, near the run below, was very much in the same condition as when we had found in it a temporary shelter. As I sat down beneath one of the great trees by which it was shaded, how all the past came rushing up before me !

After an hour or two of reverie, I made my way through the woods to Spring-Meadow, where I found another similar scene of desolation. The garden, where I had spent so many thoughtless hours in childish sports with Master James, was now overgrown with persimmons, which choked and overshadowed the few remaining shrubberies. Yet the old garden walks might be distinctly traced in several places, and there were considerable remnants of an old summer-house, where we had sat hour after hour, hid away from his brother William, and studying Master James's lessons together. Adjoining the garden was the family buryingground, and over Master James's grave I dropped a tear. My mother's grave I had to seek in another part of the plantation. What stranger, lighting on the spot could have now distinguished, from any difference in the grass and trees that waved above them, or in the wild aspect around of nature regaining her dominion, in which spot the master rested, and in which the slave? These silent graves, already half obliterated, no less than the fast-mouldering ruins of what had once been the seat of opulence and plenty, seemed plainly to testify that not by such means were families to be perpetuated, prosperous communities to be founded, or permanent triumphs over nature secured.

CHAPTER XXXIX.

RETURNING to Richmond, I found that consequential little town still in a state of the greatest alarm. The whole ordinary course of law had been set aside, and a self-constituted committee of vigilance assuming to dictate to the citizens what newspapers they should be allowed to receive, and what books to read, or to have in their houses. At such a moment, it was very easy to fall under suspicion; and, unfortunately, just before setting out on my late excursion, I had drawn attention to myself at the dinner-table, by an unlucky jest at the fright into which the great state of Virginia had been thrown by a few picture-books; for it was the cuts with which some of the abolition tracts were illustrated which seemed to inspire the greatest alarm. My coming back redoubled their suspicions. I had hardly had time to wash and dress myself, when I was waited upon by three grave-looking gentlemen, among the most respectable citizens of the town, as the landlord assured me, and in terms polite, but very peremptory, they required me to make my immediate appearance before the vigilance committee, then sitting in the Town-hall.

I had brought letters to a merchant of the place, whom I found, like most of the merchants in the southern towns, to be a northern man by birth, and from whom, on the presentation of my letters on my first arrival, I had received the usual attentions. With some difficulty, I obtained leave from the bailiffs of the vigilance committee to send for this gentleman, and also for another, whom I had met at his house at dinner, and whom I understood to be a leading lawyer. The merchant soon sent me an apology for not coming. His wife had suddenly been seized with an alarming sickness, which made it impossible for him to leave her. But when I read this note to the three volunteer bailiffs, who still remained with me, regaling themselves with mint-juleps at my expense, they heard it with an incredulous smile; and one of them exclaimed—"What more could you expect of the sneaking Yankee? He means to keep himself out of harm's way, at all events."

The lawyer soon made his appearance, and having accepted a fee, entered with great apparent, and I dare say real, zeal into my case. I begged to know whether those who had summoned me before them possessed any legal authority, and whether I was bound to pay any attention to their summons. I had supposed, I said, that the state of

Virginia was a country of laws, and that I could only be held to answer to some charge sworn against me before some magistrate. Was I obliged to submit to a personal examination before this vigilance committee? To this my friendly lawyer replied, that in the present state of alarm, the law was suspended. The necessity of self-preservation rose above all law; and in the imminent danger to which the whole southern states were exposed—the breaking out of a general slave insurrection—everything must be sacrificed to the safety of the community. The throats of the white inhabitants, the purity of their wives and daughters, were at risk. Two Yankee schoolmasters had been warned out of the town the day before, and nothing but the earnest efforts of himself and a few others, and their own prudence in not attempting the slightest resistance to this mandate, had saved them from the indignity, perhaps, of a public flogging, and a coat of tar and feathers. As it was, they had been obliged to fly, because they had not known how to hold their foolish Yankee tongues—this, perhaps, was a sly hit at my own imprudent freedom of speech—the chief witness and informant against them being a fellow whom one of them had sued the day before, to recover payment for several quarters' schooling for his children, and who, so the lawyer seemed to intimate, had taken this compendious method of squaring the account. It would be safest for me, in the present excited state of the public mind, if I wished to save myself from disagreeable personal indignities, to pay the greatest deference to the committee and their orders; and he would do his best to get me off as easily as possible.

Having found, upon inquiry, that the English consul was absent from the city, I hastened with my lawyer to wait upon the vigilance committee, and the more so as a second detachment of volunteer bailiffs had already arrived, rather ominously backed by a mob, collected before the door of the hotel, with orders to bring me by force if I delayed any longer. Those who had me in charge did their best to protect me, yet I did not entirely escape without insults from the crowd.

Having arrived in the august presence of the committee, I found myself obliged to submit to a very stringent examination on the part of the chairman, a sharp-nosed, grey-eyed gentleman, and in spectacles, deacon, I was told, of a Presbyterian church. He inquired as to my name, birthplace, occupation, and object in visiting the country; which I stated to be, to observe its manners and customs, and, in fact, as I added, I had found them very singular indeed, and well worthy of a traveller's curiosity. I might, however, as well have kept my observations to myself, for this sally brought a scowl blacker than before across the brows of the very solemn-looking committee, and a reproving shake of the head and glance of the eye from my friendly lawyer, who sat in one corner, but who was not allowed to take any part in the proceedings.

In the course of my answers, I had referred to my letter of introduction brought to the merchant, to whom a message was immediately sent, to come before the committee, and to bring that letter with him. His wife must have recruited very suddenly, for in a surprisingly short time the merchant made his appearance, with the letter in his hand; the sweat running down his face, and the poor man trembling in an agony of terror, that went far to raise grave suspicions against both him and me. The letter happened to be from Tappan, Wentworth, and Co., well-known bankers of Liverpool. No sooner had the chairman read the signature, than his face, though quite long and serious enough before, underwent a very sudden elongation; his eyebrows rising up like those

of a man who had just seen a ghost, or something else very terrible—
"Tappan! Tappan!" he repeated to himself several times, in a sharp,
quick, and snivelling tone—"Tappan! Tappan! there we have it; a
bloody emissary, no doubt! That, you know," he continued, turning to
his colleagues, "is the name of the New York silk-merchant, who is one
of the leaders in this nefarious conspiracy, and who has given I don't
know how many thousand dollars to circulate these horrid incendiary
tracts. How I wish I had the rascal here now! I should rejoice to be
one to help to put a rope round his neck. Ah, Mr. Doeface," he added,
with an ominous nod to the poor trembling merchant to whom the
letter was addressed, and a look in which indignation and commiseration
were about equally mingled, "ah, Mr. Doeface, I am very sorry to find
that you have any such correspondents."

Exclamations, threats, and oaths resounded from all sides of the
crowded hall, and before either Mr. Doeface, who seemed indeed past
speaking, or I, could get in a word, messengers were despatched to
search the merchant's house from garret to cellar, and his warehouses
also, in hopes of discovering some of the obnoxious tracts, while others
were deputed to break open and examine my trunks, which breaking
open, however, I prevented by handing out my keys. Meanwhile, with
very great difficulty, I brought the honourable chairman and his colleagues to perceive that the letter which had produced so great a commotion was dated, not at New York, but at Liverpool; and as I happened to have in my pocket-book two or three other letters of credit
from the same firm to merchants in Charleston and New Orleans, I at
length succeeded in making it understood that my letter of introduction
was not, after all, such palpable evidence of treason and sedition as had
at first been supposed.

Luckily, my friend, the Yankee merchant, had but very little of a
literary turn. After a thorough search of his premises, the committee
of inspection were able to discover nothing except a number of picture
books belonging to his children, and some twenty or thirty pamphlets,
all of which were brought in for the critical inspection of the vigilance
committee. At the sight of the picture books the committee grew very
solemn, and the chairman cast another look over the top of his spectacles, half of pity and half of reproach, at the Yankee merchant, whose
teeth began to chatter worse than ever, and who rolled up the whites of
his great eyes in as perfect an agony as if he had just been caught in the
very act of horse-stealing or forgery. But after a solemn and serious inspection, during which the whole assembled multitude held their breath,
clenched their fists, set their teeth, and looked daggers at the suspected
offender, nothing worse appeared than Jack the Giant Killer and Little
Red Riding Hood. One very fierce-looking old gentleman on the committee, with puffing cheeks and bloodshot eyes, apparently not very
familiar with juvenile literature, and a little the worse for liquor,
thought there was something rather murderous in these representations,
especially as the pictures were pretty highly coloured. But his colleagues assured him that these were very ancient books, which had been
long in circulation, and though, perhaps, considered in themselves, like
the Declaration of Independence, the History of Moses, and the
Deliverance of the Israelites, as recorded in the Bible, or the Virginia
Bill of Rights, they might seem to have rather a malign aspect, yet
they could not be set down as belonging to that class of incendiary or
abolition publications, the having which in one's possession would be
proof of conspiracy.

With myself it came near going considerably worse. As ill-luck would have it, the only book that I happened to have in my trunk was a volume of Sterne's Sentimental Journey; and that unlucky volume happened to have for a frontispiece a prisoner chained in a dungeon, and underneath, by way of motto, Sterne's celebrated exclamation, "Disguise thyself as thou wilt, still Slavery, still thou art a bitter draught, and though thousands have been made to drink thee, none the less bitter on that account!"

The production of this book, with this horrible frontispiece to it, and incendiary motto, evidently produced a profound sensation. The great eyes of my friend, the Yankee merchant, dilated almost to saucers at the sight of it. But, fortunately, several of the members of the committee were pretty well read in light literature, and were able to assure the assembled multitude that Lawrence Sterne was no abolitionist. It was not difficult to perceive, that two or three of the gentlemen on the committee, though it is by no means easy to rise above the contagion of popular passion, however absurd, were perfectly aware of the ridiculous light in which themselves, and the community to which they belonged, must appear in my eyes. But they did not dare to suggest any such idea, lest they should be suspected of lack of sensibility to the public danger, or a disposition to shield abolitionists. Indeed, it was quite enough to do away any tendency to laugh—the thought that before a less well-read committee of vigilance, as might easily happen in the rural districts, the having in a man's trunk a stray volume with an unfortunate frontispiece might subject him to summary punishment as a plotter of rebellion and murder.

Finally, after a most thorough, searching, and deliberate examination, conducted, as the Richmond newspapers of the next day had it, "with the greatest decorum, and with the strictest regard to every principle of equity," the evidence against me resolved itself into the unlucky witticism about the picture books, in which I had indulged at the hotel dinner table; a piece of personal disrespect for the commonwealth of Virginia and the institution of slavery, which it was impossible for me to deny, and which was circumstantially testified to by no less than seven witnesses.

The committee, however, wishing, as they said, to preserve, as far as possible, the ancient reputation of Virginia for hospitality, in consideration that I was a stranger and a foreigner, saw fit to dismiss me unpunished; not, however, without a long exhortation half-way between a scolding and a sermon, delivered in a rasping nasal tone, by the sharp-nosed, gray-eyed chairman, in which he dwelt with great unction, even with tears in his eyes, upon the sin and danger of jesting about sacred things; nor did he wind up without a hint, that, all things considered, I might as well leave Richmond at my earliest convenience.

CHAPTER XL.

I LOST not a moment in profiting by the kind advice of my sermonizing friend, the chairman; and by the assistance of the lawyer, who seemed really anxious for my safety, I evaded the mob collected in the street, who appeared inclined to put me on trial a second time, and as speedily as possible obtained a conveyance out of town, there to wait the approach of the great southern mail stage-coach, my legal friend promising to see that my baggage was put on at Richmond. Two or three days' ride in this conveyance, in which I was the only passenger, brought me to the little village, a court-house, jail, and tavern; in which last was the post-office, the nearest point on the route to Carleton-Hall and Poplar-Grove, which I intended next to visit. As the coach, which was little better than a sort of lumber-wagon, drove up, there were collected about the tavern-door a dozen or two of those idlers, several of them rather out at the elbows, and more than half of them decidedly tipsy, commonly to be found on that route, about the doors of such places. They were engaged in discussing, with most vehement gesticulations, what then seemed to be the only topic wherever I went—the wicked plot and conspiracy of the bloodthirsty abolitionists. One of them held in his hands a little tract, which had come directed to him through the post-office, entitled "Human Rights," the sight of which seemed to have upon him and his companions much the effect of the bite of a mad dog; for they were all more or less foaming at the mouth, and all seemed exceedingly anxious, if not to bite, at least to hang somebody. The man with the tract, as I was told, was a candidate for Congress in that district. He seemed to suspect a little that the sending him this tract on human rights was a contrivance to damage him with the people, on the part of his rival, who had a brother living in New York; but the prevailing opinion appeared to be, that the tract was a *bonâ fide* abolition emissary, a sort of bomb-shell stuffed with sedition and murder, which might at any time explode; and though some wished to preserve it as a palpable proof of the reality of the abolition conspiracy, the prevailing opinion seemed to be, that it would be safest to burn it forthwith. Accordingly, amid oaths and execrations, and wishes that a dozen or two of the abolitionists were tied to it, it was solemnly deposited in the kitchen fire. Their hand thus in, the company, headed by the would-be member of Congress, beset the coach, and insisted upon searching the mail-bags for the detection of like dangerous missives. Nor could the driver protect his charge in any other way than by the most positive asseverations that the mail-bags from the north had undergone a thorough search and purgation at Richmond. I had taken care to secure the good graces of this driver, who was a very shrewd fellow, a Yankee from Maine, and who gave me such an excellent character to the landlord, as, together with a little prudent dissimulation on my part, secured me from the danger of fresh annoyances. The old story of having, during a former tour some twenty years before, enjoyed the hospitality of Carleton-Hall and Poplar-Grove, served as an excuse for wishing to visit those plantations, and for inquiring about their former and present inhabitants. Of their former possessors, Mr. Carleton and Mrs. Montgomery, I was able to learn but little. Mr. Carleton had adopted the common resource, of emigration to the south-west. The Montgomerys were gone, it was said, to Charleston, but nobody knew anything more of them. Both plantations, I was told, belonged at present to a Mr. Mason, a very odd sort of a gentleman, who would, no doubt, be very glad to see me.

I slept that night at the tavern, or rather tried to sleep, but, disturbed as I was by the stinging of mosquitoes, the barking of dogs, and, what was infinitely worse, the sound of the hand-mills with which the slaves of the establishment were busy all night in preparing their next day's allowance of meal, with but little success. No sooner did I sink into a doze, than that well-remembered sound mingled with my dreams, and I began to imagine it was myself who was grinding.

Rising in the morning unrefreshed, I proceeded on horseback to Carleton-Hall. Having introduced myself as once the guest of the former proprietor, I received, according to the hospitable custom of the south, where the leisure of the planters makes them always eager for company, a very cordial and friendly welcome. Mr. Mason I found to be a gentleman, in manners, education, and sentiment, such as would do honour to any part of the world. In the course of the week that I remained his guest, I learnt from him that his father, a man of natural energy, who had raised himself from a humble position, after acting many years as an overseer, had become the purchaser of Carleton-Hall and Poplar-Grove, when those two plantations had passed out of the hands of their former proprietors. Having enjoyed very small advantages himself, being, in fact, hardly able to write his name, he had been the more anxious to educate his son, whom he had sent to a northern college, and afterwards to travel in Europe. Unlike a large number of the young men of the south, sent to the north for their education, the young Mason had made a good use of his opportunities; and four or five years before he had returned home, just in time to receive, under the will of his dying father, possession of the estates, and the guardianship of two young sisters,—and charming little girls they were,—joint heirs with himself of the plantations and the people.

The plantation at Carleton-Hall, instead of being worn out and just ready to be deserted, like too many others in that neighbourhood, I found to be in a much better state of cultivation than when I had formerly known it. The buildings were all in good repair, and the negro houses were so well clustered, and so neat and tidy, with little gardens about them, as, instead of an unsightly nuisance, as is usually the case, to be real ornaments to the landscape.

Under the profound dissimulation, which slaves know so well how to assume in all its varieties, from stupid indifference to appearances of the strongest emotion, whether joyful or sorrowful, it is often extremely difficult to get at their real feelings. Yet there was something hardly to be mistaken in the broad, good-natured smile with which, wherever we went, Mr. Mason's friendly greeting was looked up for and returned, by young and old, man and maiden, and especially in the joyous clamour with which the children of the plantation gathered about him. We went to see them in the school-room, as he called it, where they all assembled every day, not to be taught anything, but to be kept out of mischief, under the care of a venerable, white-haired old woman, bent half double with age, whom they called "Granny;" and a merry sight of it they were, from infants of three or four months, in the arms of little nurses just big enough to carry them, to children of twelve or fourteen, all cleanly dressed,—a thing I had never seen before on a plantation,—the larger ones having the range of an ample play-ground about the nominal school-house, where they amused themselves with sports and monkey tricks innumerable. The only thing that Granny undertook to teach was good manners, upon which subject her lectures, at least during the presence of visitors, were very incessant and sufficiently amusing. The title of "Granny" was not in her case merely nominal, so Mr. Mason told me. She was, in fact, grandmother, or great-grandmother, or great-great-grandmother, of nearly every one of the children about her. Mr. Mason himself addressed her by the title of Aunt Dolly, with almost as much kindness and affection as if she had been his own grandmother—treatment on his part to which he said she was well entitled, as being, in fact, the founder and source of the fortunes of the family. His father's first earnings had been invested, some fifty years before, in the purchase of Aunt Dolly, then a young woman with three or four children. She afterwards had others, twelve in all, and all females. The daughters had been scarcely less fruitful than the mother; and it was from this source that the whole plantation, as well as that at Poplar-Grove, had been stocked. In fact, his father, who was a man of some scruples, had never sold a servant in his life, and never bought one except Aunt Dolly, at her own special request, and a number of likely men as husbands for his superabundant females.

The system of management upon Mr. Mason's plantation, inherited, as he told me, in part from his father, but improved by himself, I found to be totally different from anything I had ever seen elsewhere, except that it reminded me, in several points, of the discipline of Major Thornton, to whom I had myself formerly belonged. Mr. Mason was, like Major Thornton, his own overseer, though he employed an assistant under him for each of the plantations,—men, like himself, of intelligence, education, and humanity, but whom, he said, it had cost him great searching to find, and great labour to train. Everything went on with the regularity of clockwork. The allowances to the people, both of food and clothing, were generous, and the tasks by which everything was done, moderate. The whip was only used on very rare occasions, and that rather for the punishment of the misdemeanors which the people committed against each other, than for those against the master; for, said Mr. Mason, "I am not only plantation manager, but judge and magistrate to settle all our internal disputes, and, in fact, to tell the truth, the very hardest worked slave in the whole establishment. How many planters in North Carolina do you suppose would accept my property on condition of managing it as I do?" The great stimulus employed to make the people work was emulation. They were divided into eight or ten classes, according to their capacity and aptitude for labour, individuals being promoted or degraded according to their merits, and each class, according to the amount of labour it performed, being distinguished by certain privileges and badges of honour. The lowest class of all was called the "lazy class," into which there was a great horror of falling, except on the part of two or three habitual sluggards, who were always in it, and who served as standing butts for all the wit of the plantation. At the close of every harvest, there was a grand fancy ball, at which the people were allowed precedence, according to their merits. The best of them had the first choice of characters, the range of which first choice was, however, rather limited, lying between General Washington, in sword and cocked hat, and old Master Mason, my host's father, till lately General Jackson, since he was chosen president, had come in as a rival. All the rest had the choice of characters, each according to his place on the list of merit; and as Mr. Mason allowed a certain moderate compensation for extra labour beyond the regular task, the buying of finery to figure at this fancy ball proved a great stimulus to many, the women especially. Some of the people were excellent mimics. Every doctor, minister, and overseer in the neighbourhood got taken off; and on the whole, Mr. Mason said, the acting was often superior to such as he had seen a good deal applauded on the New York and London boards. The idea itself he had picked up from a West-India planter with whom he had become acquainted in England.

CHAPTER XLI.

Two or three days after my arrival at Carleton-Hall, Mr. Mason and myself, who had become by this time excellent friends, rode to visit Poplar-Grove. Of the old servants' quarter, the only building standing was one quite near the great house, a neat little cottage, which Mrs. Montgomery had caused to be built on purpose for me and Cassy, and in which our child had been born. The honeysuckle which we had planted in commemoration of that event, and which she had twined with so much care over the door, was still growing there, though exhibiting many signs of age—old, bent, and gnarled, and the ends of the twigs beginning to die. The little garden around was still neatly kept, and I thought I recognized some of the very rose-bushes which she and I had planted. Little did Mr. Mason imagine my feelings as we rode together by that cottage door! O, how I longed to be alone and unobserved! It was, indeed, with the greatest difficulty that I prevented myself from springing from my saddle and rushing into the house. It seemed to me almost as if I should find Cassy there and the child!

I learnt, from conversation with Mr. Mason, that the pecuniary results of his system of management were not less satisfactory than the moral ones. Owing to his father's good-nature in indorsing the paper of a friend, the plantations, as he inherited them, had been burdened by a heavy mortgage, which was now nearly paid off. I did not fail to congratulate this worthy gentleman on having approached so near to the solution of a problem which all my observation and experience had made me believe insoluble—the making plantation life a tolerable condition of existence, as well for the slaves as for the free. But, though evidently well pleased with my compliments, Mr. Mason shook his head. "I shan't deny, sir," he said, "that I feel a certain pleasure from the approval, by a man of your experience and discernment, of my poor efforts to do the best I can in the very trying and embarrassing position in which

Providence has placed me; but after all, sir, make the very best of it, this slavery is a damnable business for whites and blacks, and all of us together." Though we had talked before with a good deal of freedom, and though I had given Mr. Mason an account of my experiences at Richmond with a pretty free expression of my own feelings and opinions, he had all along observed a certain uneasy reserve, as if doubting if it would be safe to speak out. Willing enough to draw him on, I replied, " Certainly, sir, if all masters were like you, slavery would be a very different thing from what it is, and vastly more tolerable." " Ay," said he, with a significant smile, " if all masters were like me, slavery would cease to exist to-morrow?" " What," I asked, " are you an abolitionist?" I almost regretted the question the moment I had put it, for I at once perceived that even his sound head and heart were not entirely proof against a word so terrible to every southern ear — a sort of synonyme, in fact, for rape and throat-cutting. He began in a hesitating manner to disavow that character, but soon gave his answer a different turn. " No more an abolitionist," he said, " than Washington, or Patrick Henry. This is an evil, cursed system, beyond the reach of individual effort, and only to be remedied by public action. The worst evils, I am satisfied, that could possibly arise from setting all the slaves free to-morrow would not begin to approach the amount of evil suffered, whether by blacks or whites, in every ten years that slavery continues to exist." " What," I asked, " would it be safe to set so many ignorant slaves free at once, and without any preparation for it? The general opinion among slaveholders seems to be that, if so freed, the slaves would begin by cutting the throats and taking possession of the wives and daughters of their masters, and end by dying of starvation for want of somebody to provide for them. You must begin, they say, by preparing them for freedom." " It is hardly worth while," answered Mr. Mason, " to speculate upon a contingency so improbable, just now, as the setting free of all the slaves by the spontaneous act of their owners. A deal of preparation, I fear, will be wanting before we can come to that—preparation not so much, however, on the part of the slaves as on that of the masters. The slaves, in my opinion, are quite well enough prepared for freedom already; about as much so as slaves ever will be or can be. From my observations at home and abroad, they are decidedly more intelligent, and a good deal more kind-hearted and manageable, than either the Irish or the English peasantry. The difficulty, and the only difficulty, about their working for wages is precisely the same which has defeated two or three attempts that I have known to carry on plantations by free labourers imported from Europe. While we have so much more land than inhabitants, as we still do in most of the southern states, the negroes would prefer to scatter, and, instead of working for wages, to set up like our present poorer class of free whites, each man a little plantation of his own. That is what has happened in Hayti. The sugar plantations, which require the employ-ment of numerous labourers, have been in a great measure abandoned, while the coffee cultivation, which each cottager can carry on for himself, still flourishes, and forms the staple of the island."

" If that is all," I answered, " the slaves themselves would not seem to be in any great danger of starving, however it might be with some of their late masters. But pray, sir, what do you think of the throat-cutting, and other enormities?" " These," he replied, " are bugbears inherited from our grandmothers. The wild savages, many of them prisoners of war, formerly imported from Africa, when they rose in insurrection, as they sometimes did, naturally enough began, if they could, by cutting their masters' throats. An insurrection, even now-a-days, as it is sure to be met by bullets, bowie knives, hangings and burnings, is likely enough, while it lasts, to be prosecuted by the same methods. The negro is an imitative creature, and easily adopts the example which his master sets. But to suppose that our slaves, if voluntarily set free, would take to robbing and murdering their white neighbours, instead of bestirring themselves, like other poor folks,—like the Irish emigrants, for instance, landed on our shores in no respect their superiors, except in freedom,—to earn an honest living by their labour, for themselves and their children, seems to me quite ridiculous. It is paying a very poor compliment, indeed, to the courage and superiority of us whites, to doubt whether we, superior as well in numbers as in everything else, could not inspire awe enough to maintain our natural position at the head of the community, and to keep these poor people in order without making slaves of them."

"But suppose," said I, "the emancipated slaves should prove as harmless as you imagine. Suppose they should actually labour enough to save themselves from starvation; yet, scattered upon little patches of ground, would they not live in idleness and poverty, leaving the present productive plantations abandoned, and reducing the whole south to a squalid misery, such as we see in the present villages of free blacks?"

"The present free coloured people in the United States," said Mr. Mason, "are a poor, persecuted race, placed, especially in the southern states, under very anomalous circumstances, and yet, even among them, I have known some very deserving persons. It would, however, be more reasonable to deduce the position which our supposed emancipated slaves would be likely to assume, from that at present occupied by the mass of our white people who do not own slaves. I must confess there is not much to boast of in the condition of the poor white people throughout the southern states. It is freedom which makes the chief difference between the slaves and those poor whites. Here in North Carolina a very great number of them can neither read nor write, nor tell their own age; nor are they, in any intellectual or moral respect (except that consciousness of being their own masters, which goes so far towards making a man), superior to the generality of the plantation slaves. Yet however there may be some among our rich planters who would think it a very good thing to reduce these poor white men to slavery, he would be a bold fellow indeed who would dare to propose, much more to undertake it. That, indeed, would seem scarcely necessary, for already the operation of our system is terribly depressing to them, as well as to the slaves. It hangs like a millstone about their necks, since it makes almost every kind of manual labour disgraceful; and apart from manual labour, how few other chances have the poor to acquire that capital necessary to give them a start in the world! And yet, with all these drawbacks and impediments, it is still this class of the poor free whites which forms the substratum and basis of our southern civilization, such as it is. My father began life a poor man. He has often told me that he came the first time to Carleton-Hall barefooted, not being, in fact, the owner of a pair of shoes. The fathers or grandfathers of almost all my neighbours were poor men also. It is a common saying that a plantation seldom remains in the same family beyond the third generation. It is out of this class of the poor that the new proprietors spring up, and it is into this class of the poor that the families of the former proprietors subside. But consider how this class of the poor is sunk, deteriorated, and weighed down by slavery! No wonder that in wealth, industry, intelligence, everything that makes a community respectable, we are so far behind the free states. Not only have our poor free people vastly less chance to rise than the people of the same class at the north, but by holding the bulk of our labourers in perpetual slavery we cut off the very main source whence fresh energy and strength ought to flow in upon us. Here, in my opinion, is the great evil which this system inflicts upon the community, as well as the greatest wrong which it inflicts on the individuals. It is very easy to say, that compare my slaves with as many families of poor white people within a range of ten miles about, and they are better fed, better clothed, better lodged, and vastly freer from care and anxiety. That is true; but there goes a man now——. Ah, Peter, how'dy, my good fellow?" Such were the words with which Mr. Mason nodded to an immense brawny black man, who passed us just at this moment driving a cart. "There goes a man, now, who, if he was his own master, and in a country where his colour did not deprive him of equal rights, would, before he died, have a plantation of his own, and one worth owning, too. That fellow has a'head; his opinion upon any question of cultivation, or upon any application of plantation labour, is worth more, any day, than mine and that of my two overseers put together. And do you suppose that slavery under any form can agree with such a man as that? There is a considerable class who seem to be born to be the mere instruments of others; and if only such persons were born slaves, it might not be of so much consequence." "But among those born in servitude there are all sorts of characters. Why, Mr. Mason, it might have happened to me or to you to be born a slave. There are slaves here in North Carolina quite as white as either of us; and do you suppose that under any circumstances we should have rested content under such a fate? We might have submitted, rather than jump out of the frying-pan into the fire, and yet have found the frying-pan not by any means our natural element."

CHAPTER XLII.

RETURNING the next day to Carleton-Hall, we found, sitting in the porch, a gentleman whom, from his dress and manner, I at once perceived to belong to the clerical profession. My host, who met him with great cordiality, introduced him to me as the Reverend Paul Telfair, rector of the Episcopal church of St. Stephen's.

There was something in Mr. Telfair's presence which strongly impressed me the moment I set my eyes upon him. He was a slight but rather tall young man, not, I should judge, above three or four-and-twenty. His pale but handsome features lightened up, when he spoke, with a radiant smile, which seemed to spread around him a serene halo. His address was perfectly simple and unpretending, and yet it had in it at once such dignity and winning sweetness, as to put one in mind of a real minister of grace and messenger from heaven.

"This," said Mr. Mason, "is the son of that Miss Montgomery, now Mrs. Telfair, whose mother was once the owner of Poplar-Grove, and at not finding whom still resident upon it you seemed so much disappointed. I never saw that lady," he continued; "but knowing the son as I do, I am not surprised that you should so much have missed the presence of the mother."

It appeared, in the course of our subsequent conversation, that the Montgomerys, having removed, after the loss of their property, to Charleston, had endeavoured to support themselves, though much to the scandal of some of their relations, by setting up a female school. It was not long, however, before Miss Montmongery attracted the admiration of a wealthy gentleman of that city, a Mr. Telfair, whose wife she became, and by whom she had an only son,—the young clergyman who had so favourably impressed me, and in whose face, striking as it was, there had yet appeared something familiar, which I now traced back to my recollection of the mother.

"Besides," added Mr. Mason, "since you take so much interest in my system of plantation arrangements, let me tell you that Mr. Telfair is a main spoke in the wheel. Not only does he do all the marrying and christening, services thought, both at Carleton-Hall and Poplar Grove, to be quite indispensable, but the keeping those who misbehave at home on Sunday is one of the most effective punishments which I can inflict. It is a great proof," he added, "of my young friend's gifts, not only that he has so completely eclipsed the itinerant Methodists, and the vinegar-visaged Presbyterian exhorters, who used formerly to predominate in this neighbourhood, but that even black parson Tom himself, for a long time the admiration, not only of my two plantations, but I may say of the whole county, has been content to restrain his gifts, and to subside into the humble position of clerk and catechist."

Mr. Telfair, as I afterwards learnt, had, through the influence of his mother, upon whom, during her state of poverty, religious ideas had made a deep impression, been devoted from an early age to the work of the Christian ministry. From a child he had esteemed himself set aside for that service; and having been admitted to holy orders, had given himself up, without stint, to religious labours the greater part of the time, as rector of St. Stephen's, a few miles distant.

One of the old parish churches of colonial times, when the Church of England was the established religion of North Carolina, and, indeed, of all the southern states, St. Stephen's, since the revolution, had gone into a state of great decay and dilapidation. But, though the roof had fallen, and the doors and windows had disappeared, the solid brick walls of the old church had yet remained standing. Mr. Telfair, having chosen this neighbourhood as a sort of missionary ground, had caused the old church to be repaired, mainly at his own expense, and had with untiring zeal gathered together a congregation, and revived the almost forgotten worship, according to the decent ceremonies of the Church of England.

As was well befitting the disciple of one who had especially addressed himself to the poor and lowly, the despised and the rejected, the moral and religious condition of the slaves had been from the beginning a subject of very great interest with Mr. Telfair. In Mr. Mason he had found a zealous co-operator and active churchwarden, and the example of the one, and the bland and persuasive exhortations of the other, had not been without a marked influence in the neighbourhood on the conduct of the masters and the condition of the servants.

But whatever amelioration the system of slavery might be capable of, it was impossible for Mr. Telfair, or any other man of observation and humanity, to regard it with any patience as a permanent condition of things. The intimate relations into which he was brought, both with the masters and the slaves, made him thoroughly aware of the false position in which both were placed by it, and for want of any other apparent method of getting rid of so great an evil, he had entered with very great eagerness into the scheme of colonization. He was himself the president of a county colonization society; his personal exhortation had led to the emancipation of several favourite slaves, with the view of sending them to Liberia, and his glowing imagination, overleaping, in the eagerness of benevolent hope, all bounds of time and space, seemed to regard as an event almost at hand the removal of the black and coloured population from the United States, and the civilization and Christianization of Africa. So thoroughly did he seem himself convinced, and so did he warm and light up with the subject, that, however visionary his hopes might appear, nothing could be more agreeable than to hear him give utterance to them.

. These brilliant hopes, however, we found for the moment obscured by an ominous shadow. Mr. Telfair spoke without bitterness, yet not without indications of the most poignant regret, of the late doings of the northern abolitionists, as having put back the cause of emancipation, he feared, for many, many years. He himself had just been made personally to feel their effects. He had established, in connection with his church, a Sunday school for the slaves, in which, besides oral instruction, some of them had been taught to read. A committee of planters had just waited upon him to require him to discontinue this course of instruction,—in fact, during the present state of excitement, and, until further notice, to discontinue his slave Sunday school altogether. "Ah, Captain Moore," said Mr. Telfair, addressing himself to me, "this is but an unfavourable time for you to visit the southern states. You see what it is to have slavery in a country. In fact, it makes slaves of the whole of us. It now appears that the liberty of the press and the freedom of speech, about which we have made so many boasts, cannot be allowed, consistently with the public safety, in countries where slavery prevails. There is, at this moment, no more liberty of speech or of writing in any slave state,—and from the accounts we get of mobs and riots in Boston, New York, Philadelphia, and elsewhere, the case does not seem to be much better in the free states,—than there is at Rome, Vienna, or Warsaw. I suppose that, in either of those cities, a man is at full liberty to express his opinion, in words or print, of domestic slavery as it exists in America. The only questions forbidden to be discussed there are those relating to the domestic policy of those cities and countries. So here you may denounce Popery and Russian despotism as loudly as you please; but pray be very careful what you say about domestic slavery. In any mixed company I should not think it safe, just now, to say what I have said here. In fact, I find myself already a marked man. A printed letter of mine to a friend, on behalf of the colonization scheme, in which, in proof of the evils of slavery, I had quoted from Washington, Jefferson, Patrick Henry, and other distinguished patriots, when just ready for publication, was seized the other day at Richmond, by the committee there, and ordered to be burnt as an incendiary publication."

"Indeed," said I, "then that unfortunate letter of yours was probably part of the bonfire that lighted my entrance into Richmond;"

and I went on to give him an account of my adventures in that city. "Not content with burning my letter," so the good clergyman continued, "if, in fact, it was not rather Washington and Jefferson for whom the burning was meant, the Richmond committee have reported me to our county committee as a suspected person, on whom an eye is to be kept; and these good gentlemen, besides putting a stop to my Sunday school, have also taken my newspaper reading under their supervision. For some months past I had received through the postoffice a newspaper, printed at New York, called the '*Emancipator.*' It is, I understand, the chief organ of the new society of abolitionists there. It had been sent to me gratuitously, and I had read it with a good deal of interest, wishing to discover what its conductors would be at. But this my good friends, or rather masters, of the committee of vigilance, consider altogether too dangerous. They cannot allow the peace of the country to be so perilled. They have forbidden the postmaster to give out the paper any more, and they have forbidden me to take it out or to read it. This is the degree of liberty that exists at present in North Carolina!"—words spoken with an indignant emphasis, and some little bitterness, in spite of the serene self-control which Mr. Telfair in general exhibited.

"And how does it happen, gentlemen," said I, "that the evils of slavery, which it would appear have been not only pretty largely felt, but pretty freely discussed among you, from the time of Jefferson downward, and nowhere, as I have been told, more fully and freely than in some recent debates in the Virginia legislature, how does it happen that this subject has become all at once prohibited? Pray, I should like to learn, what is the mighty difference, after all, between colonizationists, like our good friend Mr. Telfair here, and these northern abolitionists, whose interference, he seems to think, is likely to prove so serious a damage to the cause of emancipation? Isn't it slavery that you are both alike hostile to? Isn't it emancipation that you are both alike aiming at?" "The difference between us," replied Mr. Telfair, "is sufficiently palpable, though I don't so much wonder at your asking the question; for I can perceive, especially since the late excitement broke out, a growing disposition to confound us together, and to set down as incendiary, and as hostile to the welfare of the south, the bare sentiment of dislike to slavery. But with respect to] us colonizationists, the case is this: we admit the evils of slavery to be very great, so great, that duty to ourselves, our children, to the entire population, black and white, requires from us the greatest efforts to get rid of them. But we do not see how it is possible to get rid of these evils so long as the black population remains among us. It is a very common opinion in America, that it is impossible for two distinct races of men to live together, at least two races so distinct as the whites and the negroes, on anything approaching to terms of equality. It seems to be believed that, so long as the blacks remain among us, we must either make slaves of them, or they will turn about and make slaves of us. The late president Jefferson gave expression to this common opinion, by his remark that we hold the slaves like a wolf by the ear, whom it is neither safe to hold nor to let go. I must confess that I, for one, and a considerable number of our colonization friends would probably concur with me, do not exactly assent to this view of the case. It seems to me that we whites are the wolf, and the unfortunate negroes the lamb whom we have caught by the ear, and whom, if we only had the will, we might let go without any sort of danger. Why can't we allow freedom to the negroes as well as to the Irish or the Germans? But with the inveterate prejudices of our people, it seems useless to preach that doctrine. The poorest, meanest, and most degraded of our whites would be all up in arms at the very idea of it. The more low, brutal, and degraded a white man is, the more strenuously does he insist on the natural superiority of the white men, and the more he is shocked at the idea of allowing freedom to the 'niggers.' Our colonization system of emancipation yields to this invincible feeling. Before emancipating the slaves, or simultaneously with their emancipation, we propose to remove them out of the country. Regarded by the larger number as completely visionary, and even by us who believe in it, expected to operate, at least at first, only by very slow degrees, this scheme has not been calculated to produce much alarm. Even very vivid pictures of the evils of slavery, and strong declamations against it, have been permitted, so long as they have been regarded only as the expression of speculative opinions and of individual sentiment, accompanied, as they generally are, by the admission, more or less distinct, that, however great these evils may be, there is no hope or means of their removal so long as the two races remain in juxtaposition.

"But the new sect of the abolitionists has broken through all these limits. In the first place, they begin with denouncing the holding of slaves as a sin inconsistent with any just pretensions to the character of a Christian. Now, there was a time, and that not many years ago, when the great body of the southern slave-holders would have laughed at this denunciation, because only a small portion of them made any pretension to be Christians, while with large numbers the open avowal of infidel opinions was not uncommon. But by the multiplied labours of the various sects within the last twenty-five years, the profession of Christianity, and in some respects, too, I hope, the practice of it, has very greatly increased among us; and for our good slave-holding people to be told that they are no Christians, touches them in a very sensitive point. In fact, from our excessive squirming at the charge, I cannot but suspect myself that we feel a little as though there was some truth in it.

"Then again, these abolitionists say your slaves have a right to be free, and it is your duty to set them free at once. You need not trouble yourselves about the consequences of doing your duty; do it, and leave the consequences to God.

"What a difference it makes whether a thing is said in earnest, or only by way of flourish and clap-trap! What a difference when a maxim is to be applied to our own case, and when to that of others! Our good southern democrats have been preaching for half a century, more or less, that all men are born free and equal—a maxim which they have set forth as the very basis of their political system; but now, when they are asked, not in flourish, in jest merely, but in real earnest, themselves to carry their own doctrine into practice, you see how the wolf shows his teeth!

"You will judge from all this," added Mr. Telfair, "that I do not share the ferocious prejudices against the abolitionists, of which you have seen already, since you came among us, so many specimens. They have done me the honour to send me, by the mail, quite a number of their publications, besides the newspaper that I spoke of. I have read them all attentively, and I can safely say, that the vulgar and current charge against them of stimulating the slaves to revolt is totally unfounded. The revolt which they have attempted to stimulate, and the revolt, I am very much inclined to think, of which our committees of vigilance are most afraid, is, a revolt of Christian consciences against the evils and enormities of slavery.

"But, although I admit the rectitude of their motives, I do not any the less on that account condemn their conduct. You can judge from my own case the awkward position in which they have placed every southern well-wisher of the negroes. The only result, I am afraid, will be to tighten the bonds of the slaves, to check all efforts that have been making for their mental and moral improvement, and to put the most serious obstacles in the way of that scheme of colonization, which is the only remedy for the sore evils of slavery which the south seems in the least to tolerate."

CHAPTER XLIII.

MR. TELFAIR, perhaps from professional habit, seemed to run upon such subjects as occupied his mind, into a sort of lengthened discourse, and I let him go on without interruption. Mr. Mason, I had observed during this conversation, had not let drop a single word; and after Mr. Telfair had left us, I felt some curiosity to draw him out. I accordingly put to him several questions, by way of getting at his opinion of the colonization scheme. "I am a member," he said, "of the Colonization Society—secretary, in fact, of the same branch of which Mr. Telfair is president; one of my servants, a superior man, who evinced a disposition to go, I set free, and sent to Liberia; but I am sorry to say he died of the seasoning fever within a month or two after his arrival. I always thought the Colonization Society a good thing, as a sort of brooding hen, under whose wings the callow humane sentiment of the south might take shelter, and be cherished and kept alive against a time of more efficient action. I never expected anything important from what it might do directly, but a good deal from its keeping the evils of slavery, and the necessity of some remedy for them, constantly before the public mind. The best thing it has done yet certainly is, its having hatched out of its northern eggs these same abolition societies, which are making so much stir just at this moment."

"Indeed," I asked, "and is that the fact?"

"So far as I am informed," said Mr. Mason, "all the most active persons in these abolition societies first had their intention drawn to the subject by the colonization scheme. Of that scheme several of them were originally warm champions. But on further consideration, it seemed too much like carrying coals to Newcastle, the transporting some two or three millions of people from their homes, where their labour is greatly needed, and is capable of being productively applied, across the ocean to an uncultivated wilderness, where the native supply of labour already far exceeds the demand. As the slaves must be emancipated before they can be colonized, it seemed quite effort enough to emancipate them here, without being obliged to provide in addition for their transportation out of the country, at immense and ruinous expense, depriving the southern states of that productive labour which is the very thing they stand most in need of. It was these ideas, combined with those of the sin and wrong of slavery, a wrong and sin to be abandoned, not gradually, but at once, that no doubt gave rise to the abolition societies."

"But," I asked, "in view of such results as those mentioned by Mr. Telfair, how can you speak of the springing up of these societies as a good thing?"

"I hope," said Mr. Mason, looking round with an air of some uneasiness, but whether real or assumed I could hardly tell—"I hope there are no lurking members of the committee of vigilance within ear-shot. Our overseers have a habit of playing the evesdropper among the negro cabins, and how soon the same system may be extended to us masters is more than I can tell. But to answer your question,"—and here he sunk his voice almost to a whisper,—"the first step towards the cure of any serious disorder is to understand the real nature of it, and especially to bring the patient himself to a true sense of his own con-dition. And that is a result which these abolition societies are already beginning to produce. Even those who have thought most about it have never hitherto been fully aware of the real nature and extent of the evil we had to deal with. We knew, indeed, that our American goddess of liberty lay asleep and dreaming, like Milton's Eve, with a foul toad at her ear; yet we thought that, after all, it was but a toad, which, however ugly and venemous, the growing light of day, as the sun was getting towards high noon, would drive to skulk into some hole or other. But these northern abolitionists having undertaken to poke the creature a little by way of hastening his progress, choosing for that purpose the famous national declaration of ours that all men are created free, with certain unalienable rights,—see how this, as we thought comparatively harmless thing, starts up a horrible and blood-thirsty monster, threaten-ing to swallow down the poor trembling goddess of American liberty at a single gulp! I do not mean the liberty of black men or coloured men, —for here in America they never had any,—but the liberty of us white men, us masters.

"The pretended danger of slave-insurrection is made occasion for suppressing all liberty of thought, speech, or writing, derogatory to the institution of slavery. That danger does very well to frighten fools with, and it is by frightening fools that knaves generally get themselves entrusted with power. But the insurrection, as Mr. Telfair very well remarked, which the leaders in this business are most afraid of, is not an insurrection of slaves, but an insurrection of conscience—an insur-rection which they intend to find the means, if they can, to anticipate and prevent.

"Here now," he added, taking up a newspaper, "here it is openly con-fessed and stated in so many words by the *Washington Telegraph*, a leading champion of the rights and interests of the slave-holder, and a chief promoter of all the prevailing alarm: 'We hold'—here he read from the paper—'that we have most to fear from the gradual operation of public opinion among ourselves, and that those are the most insidious and dangerous invaders of our rights and interests, who, coming to us in the guise of friendship, endeavour to persuade us that slavery is a sin, a curse, and an evil. Our greatest cause of apprehension is from the operation of the morbid sensibility which appeals to the consciences of our people, and would make them the voluntary instruments of their own destruction.' And the way in which it is proposed to prevent these

M 2

appeals to the morbid sensibility of conscience is pretty distinctly set forth in another paragraph, which I find quoted from the *Columbia Telescope*, a South Carolina paper: 'Let us declare that the question of slavery is not, and shall not be, open to discussion; that the system is deep-rooted among us, and must remain for ever; that the very moment any private individual attempts to lecture us upon its evil and immorality, and the necessity of putting means in operation to secure us from them, in the same moment his tongue shall be cut out and cast upon the dunghill.'

"This appeal to southern consciences, which it is proposed to put down by this summary process, has revealed the true state of the case. The great mass of our people, whether at the south or the north, even those who speak of slavery as an evil, do not really regard it so. Compared with the emancipation of the slaves, they regard it as a positive good. They may possibly admit that slavery is bad, but they are quite certain that freedom would be much worse. Then again, there appears to be among us a vastly larger class than anybody supposed, who hold that slavery is no evil at all in any sense, but a positive good; a good thing for the slaves, who are thus enabled to live free from care, in sleek and happy contentment, and a good thing for the masters, who, in being raised above the necessity of base and servile employments, are thus enabled to preserve the dignity of freedom. This romantic view of the case might not, perhaps, so well bear discussion, but you see they do not intend to allow any. Yet, without a full and free discussion of our existing system, in all its bearings and operations, how can we reasonably hope or expect to bring about any beneficial change? The struggle which you now see beginning, and which this northern appeal to southern consciences has provoked, is plainly, to my mind, the final and decisive struggle between the extension and perpetuation of slavery on the one hand and emancipation on the other. The institution of slavery in this country is vastly more potent than anybody had supposed. It not only has complete control of the governments of all the southern states, so as to be enabled to enact whatever laws it pleases, but, by means of its vigilance committees and its system of lynchings, it completely overrides both laws and constitutions in the exercise of a despotic and arbitrary power, derived from the discretionary discipline of the plantation, but totally inconsistent with all established ideas of English or American liberty. Not content with this, it is eagerly clutching at all the powers and patronage of the general government, which it seeks to transform from a bulwark of freedom to a bulwark of slavery; and not content with this, it seeks to dictate to the northern states a course of action in conformity with this same view. Having completely suppressed, at least for the time being, all liberty at the south, of speech, writing, or reading on this forbidden subject, it is endeavouring to accomplish the same thing at the north. Northern politicians are stimulated, by hopes of currying southern favour, to put themselves at the head of anti-abolition mobs, and northern merchants, by the hope of securing southern customers, to hold public meetings to call upon the state legislatures to pass laws to restrict the liberty of the press. That very thing I see has just been done in the degenerate city of Philadelphia; and Boston and New York are very loudly called upon to imitate the disgraceful example. Yes, Mr. Moore, seasonably or unseasonably, the great battle has begun,—the great struggle on which the future fate of America is to depend. The slavery or the freedom of our coloured inhabitants is an interesting question: that, however, has already become but a merely subordinate one. The first great question is, shall not merely the political, but the intellectual, moral, and religious control of this country pass into the hands of the upholders of perpetual slavery? or shall our old American notions that all men are equal before God, and ought to be equal before the law, continue to circulate? Shall the control, not only of our politics and legislation, but of our newspapers, our churches, our literature, our public sentiment, pass into the hands of the hard, the cruel, the tyrants by nature, the mercenary, the scoffers at justice and human rights, the sleek, comfortable time-servers, equally ready, for a consideration, to read prayers to God or to the devil? or shall the votaries of human advancement, the friends of man, the true servants of the God of love, have liberty to live, speak, and labour among us? The first question is about our own liberty, and that not alone the liberty of acting, but the mere liberty even of writing, reading, talking, and thinking."

Warming with his subject, and striding up and down the room, Mr. Mason had uttered all the latter part of this long discourse, not without many gesticulations, and in a tone of voice rising at times a little above the ordinary key. But he suddenly checked himself, and added, in a subdued tone, "I, for my part, had rather have been born the most miserable negro in North Carolina, than, having enjoyed, as I have, the advantages of education and the privileges of freedom, to find myself, from being the master, as I had imagined, of my own slaves, my own thoughts, and my own course of conversation and reading, all at once converted into a deputy slave-driver, under a committee of vigilance, composed, as those committees generally are, of the greatest fools and the greatest scoundrels among us, and obliged to read, talk, and think under their inquisitorial jurisdiction."

"Pardon me," said I, "Mr. Mason, if I take the liberty of putting one question. How is it possible that, entertaining the opinions which, since I have enjoyed the pleasure of your hospitality, I have heard you so freely express—how is it possible that you can continue a slaveholder?" "As to that," answered Mr. Mason, "you must have observed before now that the opinions and practices of men do not always run in parallel channels. A man's own opinion and his own choice have often very little to do with the position which he occupies. The people on this and the other plantation came to me by inheritance. You certainly would not have me, to escape from a position personally disagreeable, sell out my interest in slaves, pocket the money, move off to the north, and leave them to their fate."

"No, certainly," I replied; "if they are to remain slaves, I hardly think they would gain anything by a change of masters."

"Their remaining slaves," said Mr. Mason, "is not at present a thing within my control. In the first place, there exists still an undischarged mortgage, in which they are included. But that I hope to pay off within the next six months. Then the portions of these two young sisters of mine are a lien upon the estate, for the discharge of which I have yet made only a partial provision. Then, again, here in North Carolina, a master cannot set his slaves free at his own will and pleasure. He must first have the consent of the county court, and now-a-days that is not a thing so easy to be obtained.

"However," he added, "since I have gone so far in making a confidant of you, I will tell you yet another secret. I do not mean to remain a slaveholder except just so long as is necessary, to escape from that position with honour to myself and benefit to all the parties concerned. All my arrangements are made with that view. To give me any freedom of action in this matter, it is necessary first to clear off the encumbrances, the [debts due, and the portions of my sisters. Those sisters are to set off in a few days for the north, there to be placed for their education. I mean to invest their money at the north. I hope they will marry and settle at the north. They shall have no slave-holding husbands if I can help it, and that for more reasons than one. I don't want my sisters to be the mere heads of a seraglio, with some black or brown favourite, perhaps quite carrying the day over them in real preference. Their poor mother—you are to observe they are only half-sisters of mine—suffered quite enough in that way. The poor woman actually fretted herself to death with jealousy and vexation, for which, I am sorry to say, my honoured father gave her too much cause. In fact, he had very patriarchal ideas. You may easily perceive, from the variety of complexion, that, among the servants here and at Poplar-Grove, there is a considerable infusion of Anglo-Saxon blood. I don't doubt that a large part of the lighter coloured among them can claim more or less of blood relationship to myself; and therefore I feel the more called upon to act the part, not of a mean, selfish despot, but of the head of a family, the chief of a tribe, whose clansmen are his poor relations, who have a family claim upon him for the judicious conduct of their joint affairs.

" My plan is this : As soon as the debts are paid, and I have laid by enough money to purchase a good tract of land in Ohio or Indiana, I mean to emigrate with the whole family. To set them free here, even if there were no legal obstacles in the way, would not, in the present state of feeling towards free coloured people, and the little chance they can have to rise in the world, be much of a favour. It would be too much like setting them free as the 'coons are, as one of them once said to me, making a sort of free vermin of them, rather than free men. And with the ignorance and incapacity which a life of slavery has engendered, and the prejudices and obstacles they would have to encounter in any of the free states,—in some respects more violent and oppressive than those felt here,—it would hardly be much of a favour to send them out by them-selves, to seek their fortune at the north. To give them a fair chance, to prevent them from bringing a disgrace on the idea of emancipation, I intend to go with them, and to be the leader and founder of the colony. That is the work for which I reserve myself. I live a bachelor, as you see ; nor do I ever mean to marry, so long as I live in a slave state. With all these people to settle and provide for, I have quite family enough, quite encumbrances enough on my hands, without that."

What an honest glow of enthusiasm, confidence, and self-respect kindled in Mr. Mason's face as he spoke! How the nobleness of the man grew upon me as he thus detailed his plans and intentions ! Here, indeed, was the spirit of genuine Christianity. Here was a man indeed. How small a number of such men would suffice to save the southern Sodom from perdition ! to make it truly a land of joy, of justice, of peace, plenty, and of hope, instead of what it now is—the stumbling-block of freedom, the opprobrium of civilization and Christianity !

CHAPTER XLIV.

In leaving Mr. Mason's hospitable mansion, where I had protracted my stay beyond all reason, I felt like parting with an old friend. As he pressed my hand and said farewell, he bade me remember that much had passed between us in confidence; and that any hint, dropped incautiously, as to his opinions and intentions, might affect him most injuriously, endangering his peaceful residence in the country, and it might be his life.

Returning to the stage tavern, whence I had made this agreeable side visit, I prepared to pursue my southern journey. I resolved, however, while forwarding my baggage to Charleston by the stage-coach, to proceed myself leisurely on horseback; for I had some curiosity to strike upon, if I could, and to retrace the road which I had followed in my escape from slavery. It being made known that I wished to purchase a horse, I soon found myself beset by a dozen jockeys or more, who did their best to impose upon me, one after the other, animals lame, halt, blind, and broken-winded. But I succeeded, by the aid and assistance of my friend, the Yankee stage-driver, whom I found very knowing on the subject of horse flesh, and who, to explain the fact that so many broken-down animals were offered, observed to me aside, and with a knowing wink, that these southern folks treated their horses almost as bad as they did their niggers,—in mounting myself to my satisfaction; and with a few shirts and other necessaries stuffed into my saddle-bags, I started afresh on my journey.

A few days' travelling, without the occurrence of anything remarkable, brought me into the vicinity of Camden; and as I carefully scrutinized the road, I did not fail presently to recognize that very same little hedge-tavern where Thomas and myself had been taken as prisoners, and whence, by the aid of the blue-eyed little girl, we had effected our escape, carrying with us the spoils of Egypt, in the shape of the clothes and money of our captors. With mind excited as mine had been by the incidents of that eventful escape, the whole scene, with all its surroundings, stamps itself wonderfully on the memory. I could recall exactly the general appearance of the road, as we had been dragged along, fastened to the saddles of our captors, and of the little hedge-tavern, as it had first appeared in sight, and no sooner did I again see it than I recognised it at once for the very same; indeed, there was the less difficulty in doing that, since, in the whole of my horseback journey I had not found a single house which had any appearance of newness about it, nor were houses of such frequent occurrence as to tend much to confuse one's recollection. Twenty years had made very little change in that part of the country. As the house still had the external appearance of a tavern, or at least of a whisky-shop, I determined to stop a while to reconnoitre.

A stout and rather good-looking boy of twelve or fourteen, without hat or shoes, and with no other clothes than a shirt, not lately washed, and the tattered fragments of a pair of pantaloons, so much too large for him as probably to have been his father's, took my horse as I dismounted at the door, and promised to provide him with water and corn. Walking into the single room which served for kitchen, barroom, dining and sleeping room for the family, the only other room in the house being reserved for guests, I observed an old crone of a woman sitting by the window, zealously plying a loom, in which she was weaving a piece of coarse homespun. Two small children, who were rolling and tumbling on the floor, spoke to her as "granny." She might doubtless have once been the mistress of the family, but seemed now to have resigned the more immediate charge of matters to a younger woman, probably a daughter of hers, as the children, while calling the old woman "granny," called the younger one "mammy." This younger woman stood at a table, mixing corn cakes in a great wooden tray. She was very poorly dressed, and without shoes or stockings, but with an expression of good-nature on her face, and an expressive, soft blue eye, which marked her, however rude and poverty-stricken, as one of those tender-hearted females who can never look upon distress without doing what they can to remove it. Entering into conversation with the women about the weather, crops, distance to Camden, and whether they could give me anything for dinner, and so forth, I presently inquired, as if incidently, whether they had long lived at this place. "O, law, yes," said the old woman at the loom. "Why, my Susy, there, who, you see, has already a family growing up about her,—she was born in this house, and three or four more children, too, older than she, and as many more younger; but they are all gone now, except only her that stays by her old mother."

"Not dead, I hope?" I asked, in a sympathizing tone.

"O, no! not dead," said the old woman, "but as good as dead to me; all gone, all moved off, some to Florida, and some to Alabama, and some to Texas, and that's the last I shall ever hear of them." And here followed a deep sigh.

"But don't you sometimes get a letter?" I inquired.

"Get a letter!" said the old woman, with a toss of the head, such as left little doubt in my mind that she had been a smart piece in her day, very different from her good-natured daughter—"get a letter! And which of my sons and daughters, do you suppose, knows how to write, or to read either, for that matter? Poor people here in Carolina don't have any chance at learning; no schools, and nothing to pay the teacher with, if we had any. That's what has made them all move off to seek a living elsewhere. Susy here knows how to read; I reckon you must have heard of it somewhere; but how do you suppose it happened? When she was a young girl, there was a Yankee pedler stopped once at our house, one of those fellows as goes travelling with a horse and waggon, selling wooden clocks,—and there's one of them now" (here she pointed to the corner where the machine hung), "only it hasn't gone any this ten years,—and pins and needles, and tin-ware, and they do say wooden nutmegs, though I don't know as this one that I am speaking of ever sold any. Awful cheats, though, some of those Yankee pedlers are—awful!" said the old lady, dropping her shuttle, and holding up both hands, and looking at me with a very woe-begone expression. "That's one reason our folks are all so poor, and that even those who own slaves have to keep moving off to Alabama, because these cheating Yankee pedlers carry off all the money out of the country; at least, that's what I heard Colonel Thomas, the member of Congress, say, the last time he was round this way electioneering. Howsomever, I don't know any harm of this particular Yankee that I was speaking of. He used to come round about once a year; and he sold his things a good deal cheaper, and I can't say but that they were just as good as you can buy in Camden-Town. Well, one time this pedler came to our house, sick with a mighty smart fever. I thought he would die, sure enough; and I rather reckon he would, if Susy, there, though she was then only twelve or fourteen years old, had not looked after him just as if he had been her own father. And so, you see, when he began to get well, as it was a good while before he was able to travel again, he took to teaching the child to read, as he said, out of gratitude. He put her on the track, and gave her a spelling-book out of those he carried round to sell; and a nice new Bible,—get it, Susy, and show it to the stranger,—which he said his mother gave him just before he set out from Connecticut; and so, you see, whenever any pedler, or Methodist minister, or other person of learning that wasn't too proud, came along, Susy would get a lesson from them, till she learnt to read as glib as could be; and now she teaches her children too. You wouldn't believe it, but that boy Jim there," pointing to the boy who had taken my horse, "knows how to read! All his mother's doings; and if he can only now and then get hold of a newspaper, he is as proud as a peacock."

All this long history of her daughter, on the part of the old lady, served to confirm me in the conjecture I had formed, that the bare-footed matron before me, distinguished by such remarkable literary accomplishments and motherly tenderness, and to the first-rate excellency of whose corn-cakes I was myself shortly after able to testify, must be the identical little girl to whom Thomas and myself had owed our escape on that night, so memorable to me, on which I had started on my northern travels in pursuit of freedom.

To make matters sure, while she was setting a table for my dinner in the other room, I inquired of her if she could recollect how, a great many years ago,—it must have been before the time that the pedler taught her to read,—two men, one black, the other white, had been brought prisoners to her mother's house, and confined for the night in this very room. As I went into the matter somewhat in detail, I could easily perceive, as the circumstances were recalled to her memory, though she said nothing, a gleam of wondering recognition lighting up a face, which, though it could not be called handsome, more especially as the uncombed hair hanging about her head gave her a sort of wild appearance, had yet upon it an unmistakeable stamp of good-heartedness, which did not fail to make a very agreeable impression. But when, in the course of the story, I came to speak of the little girl who stole in at night, and, while their keepers slept, cut the bonds of the prisoners, alarm and anxiety spread over her before smiling features; and though she strove hard to preserve an unconscious self-composure, it was easy to perceive that she experienced no little terror, as if she were now in danger of being called to account for that act of childish generosity. However, I very soon quieted her fears on that score. Great, indeed, was her astonishment, when I informed her that I was the self-same white prisoner whom she had released, and what was more, that I was both ready and able to make some return to her for the favour she had then done me.

Upon taking the liberty after this introduction, and the assurance that I wished to befriend her, to inquire a little into her domestic affairs, I learnt, chiefly indeed from this old woman, who insisted upon doing pretty much all the talking, that her husband, though a good sort of a man enough, was shiftless and idle, and that the support of the family devolved pretty much on the women. The husband, indeed, wanted to emigrate, but the old woman, with a degree of home feeling not very usual, so far as I have noticed, with that class of the American people, was unwilling to go, and the daughter would not without the mother. It seemed to be the great object of the daughter's ambition to send her eldest boy, Tom, to school. She had already taught him all she knew, and he was presently called in to give a specimen of his accomplishments by reading a chapter from the pedler's Bible, which the good mother produced from a closet, and which, carefully covered with cloth, was evidently preserved with great care.

There was, it seemed, in that neighbournood, what was called a manual-labour boarding-school, lately set up by the Methodists, of which religious sect the boy's mother was a zealous member. This school was principally designed for the instruction of those of limited means, who, by labouring a certain number of hours in the day, might acquire, along with their learning, some mechanical trade, and at the same time diminish the cost of their board and instruction. This cost, even without such reduction, did not much exceed the moderate sum of a hundred dollars a year. But though, by great economy, my bene-factress had already laid aside, as she told me, about thirty-seven dollars, where the rest of the hundred was to come from—and she wanted the boy to have at least a year's schooling—she did not know; and besides, it would take about the whole of her present savings to fit him out with clothes, books, and other necessaries.

I bade the good woman make herself easy on that score, and the boy having washed and dressed himself, and caught a scrubby pony belong-ing to the family, we set out together that same afternoon to visit the school, which was at no great distance.

The founder and chief teacher of it, lately a travelling minister of the Methodist connection, but who had now devoted himself entirely to this new work, was, I found, originally from the north. He had been bred a shoemaker, but feeling a call to preach, had quitted his original vocation, and after many wanderings had finally reached South Carolina, of which circuit he had become one of the preachers. In point of education and manners, the contrast was very marked indeed between this good man (for such I soon satisfied myself he was) and my late clerical acquaintance, Mr. Telfair; but in zeal, enthusiasm, and the desire of benefiting those about him, both physically and spiritually, there were strong points of resemblance between them. On the whole, I was well satisfied that my young *protégé* should be trusted in such good hands. I paid down for him his board and tuition for a year, and in case it should be thought best for him to remain a second year, I left with the teacher an order on the merchant in Charleston, on whom I had letters of credit. I also desired to be informed by letter, through the same source, of the boy's progress and promise, with a view, if he proved deserving, of doing something more for him. Having sent him home with money enough to fit him out, without intrenching on his mother's little store, I turned my horse's head towards Charleston, resolved to take my route as nearly as I could in the general direction of my former travels in that region.

CHAPTER XLV.

As I began to approach the neighbourhood of Loosahachee, I perceived, at a distance on the road, a group of men on horseback, upon whom, as they moved at a very slow pace, I gained rapidly. As I drew nearer, the group presented a very striking appearance. There were twelve or fifteen fierce-looking white men, very variously mounted, with rifles in their hands, and well provided with pistols and bowie knives, their dresses bedaubed with half-dry mud, as though they had been engaged in some aquatic expedition. A negro fellow, who followed on foot, and by the side of whom, with a sharp eye upon him, rode a white man armed to the teeth, held in leash some four or five savage-looking dogs, which I easily recognized as of the breed usually trained and employed for hunting runaway slaves. But the most remarkable objects, and those upon which the attention of the white men of the company seemed to be fixed with looks gloomy and ferocious, though not unmingled with triumph, were near the centre of the group, a little in front. Here I perceived the apparently lifeless body of a white man, whose pale features bore still a scowl of brutal rage upon them, that contrasted strangely with their death-like fixedness. The clothes, muddy and torn, as if in some recent struggle, were all dabbled with blood, which seemed still to ooze from a fatal wound in the breast. The body had been secured on the back of a horse, which was led by a negro man, whose blank and stolid features, upon which, however, I thought I could trace a certain obscure gleam of repressed satisfaction, presented a curious contrast, as did that of the black man who led the hounds, to the fierce, furious, and indignant looks of the white men.

Side by side with this dead body rode a black man, wounded and bleeding, and evidently a prisoner, for his feet were tied together under the horse's belly, and his hands bound behind him. He was a man of most powerful and athletic frame, verging on old age, with an enormous bushy beard, weak, apparently from his wounds, and almost fainting, so that it seemed with great difficulty that he kept erect; yet, in spite of his feebleness and captivity, and the vengeful glances, mixed with occasional curses, which his captors directed at him, still preserving, in a certain haughty and dogged aspect of defiance, the look of one who had been long accustomed to liberty.

There was another captive in the company on foot, with a rope round his neck fastened to the saddle of one of the white men, of a lighter colour than the mounted prisoner, barefoot and bareheaded, as was the other, and with very scanty clothing. He did not appear to be wounded; but his back was all cut and bleeding, as if he had just undergone a most severe flagellation, and his woful, supplicating, subdued look made the sullen, defiant air of his fellow-captive on horseback the more remarkable.

Riding up by the side of the mounted master of the hounds, who brought up the rear of this strange cavalcade, I inquired what had happened. It was apparent from his manner and language, notwithstanding the rude company in which I found him, that he was a person of cultivation, not unaccustomed to civilized society. Indeed, it soon appeared that he was the owner of a neighbouring plantation, who, with some of his friends and neighbours, and other rougher professional assistants, engaged for the occasion, had been out on a grand slave-hunt. The dead man they were bringing back was, he told me, no other than his own overseer.

This overseer was, he said, a very smart, driving fellow, a Yankee, who had first visited that part of the country as a pedler, but who had afterwards turned schoolmaster, and then overseer. It was generally observed, that these Yankee overseers would contrive to get the most work out of the people, and being somewhat in debt, he had employed him on that very account. But in the great ambition of Mr. Jonathan Snapdragon—for such was his name—to sustain the reputation of the section of the country from which he came, he had rather overdone the matter. The price of cotton was unusually high, and in hope of making an extraordinary crop, this Yankee overseer had resolved to work a couple more acres to the hand than had ever before been attempted on that plantation. What made the matter worse, the corn, of which the crop in all that section of the country had been light the preceding year, fell short, and it became necessary, in addition to the increased tasks, to put the people on half allowance. However, by means of a pretty liberal use of the whip, in which the Yankee overseer was a great adept, and which he seemed to take a real delight in, things had worried along till just at the pinch of the season, when it all depended upon three or four weeks of most assiduous labour, whether the weeds or the cotton should gain the ultimate ascendancy. Just at this crisis of the fate of the crop, when their services were most wanted, all the prime male hands had scurvily skulked off a few nights since into the woods, leaving the overseer with the women, children, and sick, to contend against the weeds as best he could; and that, too, said my communicative planter, looking at me with the air of a most ill-treated man, and as if sure of my sympathy, with cotton at sixteen cents the pound, and promising to be higher yet by the time the crop was ready for the market.

There had, he told me, been prowling about in that neighbourhood, for a great many years past, perhaps twenty or more, to the infinite annoyance of the whole country, a runaway negro, known commonly among the people as Wild Tom. He was believed to belong to old General Carter, a rich planter, of Charleston, who had long ago offered a standing reward of a thousand dollars for his capture, dead or alive. The story was, that he had run away from Loosahachee, one of General Carter's rice plantations some distance below, after having first killed the overseer in some quarrel about whipping his wife; and the burning down of the expensive rice-mills at Loosahachee, which had happened no less than five or six times within the last twenty years, had been commonly ascribed to his artful and daring malice and revenge.

Great efforts had been made at times to take this dangerous outlaw, and many ingenious plans had been formed to entrap him, but all had hitherto failed, not without the desperate wounding of several persons who had met him in personal encounter. He seemed to have various lurking-places, scattered over a considerable range of country, from one to another of which he fled, as occasion required, thus eluding all attempts at his capture. Sometimes, when the pursuit after him had been very hot, he would seem to disappear for months, or even a year or two, but was pretty certain to make his re-appearance when least expected and least welcome. Had he merely confined himself to the petty depredations necessary to support himself and his band of confederates, the matter would have been of less consequence; but he was believed to keep up an underhand communication with almost every plantation in the neighbourhood, and to be a general instructor in mischief and insubordination, an aider and abettor of runaways, and harbourer of fugitives.

This same Wild Tom had been seen, within a short time past, lurking about in the neighbourhood; and it was suspected that the late stampede had not taken place without his aid and assistance. It was deemed a much easier thing to find and to take him encumbered by a dozen or twenty raw recruits than if alone, or only attended, as he generally was, or at least was generally supposed to be,—for in all that was commonly reported of him, there was a great deal more of conjecture than of knowledge,—by one or two trusty, tried, and experienced companions. With my new acquaintance, the planter, — from whom I was deriving all this information, in which, since he had made mention of Wild Tom, I began to feel the deepest interest, — the recovery of his people was a matter almost of life and death, pecuniarily speaking, since, unless they were recovered, it would be necessary for him to abandon half or more of his crop, and that too with cotton at sixteen cents the pound, and promising to be higher; for hired free labourers were things unknown in that part of the country, nor could even slave labour be hired at that season of the year, when everybody was straining for dear life against the weeds, and when the ordinary supply of almost every plantation was expected to be diminished by the absence of a certain number of incorrigible fellows, who make it a rule, just at that season, to absent themselves for a summer vacation in the woods, being willing to risk the severest punishment they might encounter when taken, for the sake, at that particular season of the year and the crop, of a few weeks of agreeable woodland retirement. And here, indeed, a strong resemblance might be traced between them and very many of their masters, who, as the hot weather and unhealthy season came on, were accustomed to abandon their plantations, and to figure away for a few weeks, as grand as runaway Cuffee himself, at Philadelphia, New York, or Saratoga, to the astonishment of admiring and curious Yankees, in the assumed character of millionaires and nabobs; though sure to pay for it by pinching at home all the rest of the year, and living in almost as much terror of duns, writs, and executions, as their unhappy slaves do of the lash. In this extremity, therefore, my new acquaintance had offered a large reward for the recovery of his people; to which inducement was added the standing reward for Wild Tom; also other rewards which had been offered for other runaways from other plantations in the neighbourhood, more numerous this year than usual on account of the short supply of corn, and the greater breadth of cotton, which the prevailing high price had caused to be planted. A grand hunt had accordingly been proclaimed, and at short notice a company of near a hundred men had been collected, planters, overseers, loafers, poor whites, with four or five professional slave-catchers, and several packs of hounds, armed to the teeth, and prepared to make a search of the neighbouring swamps, in which it was customary for the runaways to take refuge, lying hid by day, and coming out by night to supply themselves by killing cattle and otherwise, and to communicate with their wives and friends who remained behind. The season, indeed, was very favourable to this operation, an uncommonly long drought having dried up the swamps to a considerable extent, and made them much more accessible than usual.

The entire company had been accordingly divided into five or six divisions, each to carry on operations by itself, and each provided with its pack of dogs, that into whose company I had fallen—I speak here not so much of the dogs as of the men—being one of them. What had been the success of the other parties my informant could not tell. What I saw before me indicated, in a general way, the mixed fortune which his party had encountered.

It had been appointed to them as their duty, to search a swamp of no great extent, but very inaccessible on account of the unusual depth of the mud and water, in many places over a man's head, in the centre of which was a small island of firm land, believed to be a favourite lurking-place of Wild Tom's, who was supposed to know better than anybody else the most convenient approaches to it.

Within half a mile from the swamp the dogs had started the lighter-coloured of the two prisoners, upon whom they came suddenly as he lay concealed in the long grass, hoping to escape observation. As the party were close by, the dogs were prevented from tearing him, and he was made prisoner without trouble. The mud on his feet and legs, and the wetness of the scanty fragments of clothing that he wore, afforded pretty strong indications that he had lately come from the swamp island, which it was the object of the party to search. He was charged with this, but affected the most stolid ignorance of the existence of any such island, or swamp either. When questioned whence he came, and whom he belonged to, he acknowledged himself a runaway from a rice-plantation below, who had lately wandered into this vicinity, of which he professed an entire ignorance, declaring himself to be dying of hunger, and not to have eaten anything hardly for a week—a story to which his plump and comfortable aspect did not give much credit. He acknowledged having heard of Wild Tom, who indeed figured largely in the current legends, white and negro, of all that region; but denied most positively ever having seen him, or knowing anything of any other runaways.

These protestations, however, did not satisfy, and to make him confess, he was tied up and whipped till he fainted; but while begging for mercy he still insisted on the truth of his story, and that he had nothing further to tell.

This experiment having failed, he was placed on the stump of a fallen tree, and a rope being put round his neck and fastened to a branch above, he was threatened with instant hanging if he did not confess. Still he continued dogged as ever, when one of the company pushed him off the stump, and allowed him to swing till he grew black in the face. He was then placed back upon the stump, the rope loosened, and himself supported by the two or three slaves who accompanied the party. At length, beginning to recover himself, whether out of terror of death, or the confusion of his ideas and the destruction of his self-control by the pressure of blood upon the brain, he began to confess freely enough that he had just come from the swamp island, and that Wild Tom was there; but he denied all knowledge of any other runaways, or that Wild Tom had anybody with him.

The prospect of capturing this celebrated outlaw, the glory thus to be gained, and the public service to be rendered—not to mention the thousand dollars reward—produced a great sensation in the company; though, till it had first been ascertained by further inquiries from the confessing prisoner, that his formidable chief had neither rifle, pistol, nor fire-arms of any sort, no arms in fact but a knife, there did seem to be some little lack of vigour in proceeding with the business; so my planter informant told me, lowering his voice, and casting a knowing glance, with a significant smile, at two or three of the fiercest looking fellows in the cavalcade before us—one in particular, who bestowed every now and then very savage looks on the mounted prisoner, and seemed with difficulty to keep his hands off him.

To make all sure, eight or ten of the company were sent to patrol on horseback round the edges of the swamp, together with all the dogs but one, while five or six of the strongest and most resolute proposed to penetrate the interior, and to storm the island retreat. The prisoner, with the rope still about his neck, the other end made fast to the waist of one of the stoutest of the company, was required to serve as guide; and though he protested that he knew nothing in particular of the approaches to the island, he was threatened with instant death in case he did not conduct them safely and expeditiously across. The fellow, however, whether through ignorance or design, led them into very deep water, in some places fairly up to their necks, through which they were obliged to wade, holding their rifles and powder horns over their heads; and, in spite of every effort to keep him quiet, as the party drew near the island, he would insist on crying, as if giving directions as to the passage, but, as was strongly suspected, with the real design of alarming his confederate. And, indeed, before the party could make good their footing on the island, he had already taken the alarm, and had plunged into the water on the other side. He had gained a considerable distance before he was seen, and as he dodged behind the great trees of the swamp, several rifle shots fired at him failed to take effect. In plunged the others in fresh pursuit, while the fugitive, engrossed by this danger behind, made the best of his way through the mud and water till he gained the firm land on the other side of the swamp, where he encountered a new danger; being seen by one of the scouts patrolling along the edge. As he bounded through the piny woods like a deer, a rifle shot grazed his side, and though it did not bring him down, yet it materially checked the swiftness of his flight. Four or five horsemen were soon upon his track. Snapdragon, the overseer, leading in the chase, soon came up with the flying negro; and after vainly calling to him to yield, and firing his pistols with only partial effect, sprang from his horse and attempted to seize him. Snapdragon was a powerful man, but he had now found his match. Wild Tom, if indeed it were really he, exhausted and wounded as he was, caught his assailant in his arms, and as they rolled upon the ground, the negro's knife was not long finding its way to the overseer's heart. But already the dogs and the other pursuers were upon him, and before he could disengage himself he was made a prisoner, and securely bound. It was not long before the whole party was assembled, when some of the more violent proposed to revenge the dead overseer by putting the new prisoner to death on the spot. But the pleasure and glory of making a parade and exhibition of their prize, and the necessity, too, in order to secure the promised reward, to identify him as General Carter's runaway, had stayed this summary procedure; and it had been resolved forthwith to hasten to the village, which served as seat of justice for the county, to commit the prisoners to jail.

We were already in the near vicinity of the county seat, which proved to be a more considerable village than usual, and from which, as if by some premonition of our coming, issued to meet us a most miscellaneous multitude; of all colours, white, brown, and black; of every age, from infants scarcely able to go alone to old negroes with heads perfectly white, making their way staff in hand; and of almost every variety of equipment, from the well-dressed and well-mounted planters to little negro boys, perfectly naked, riding on sticks by way of horses, and shouting and screaming like so many witch urchins.

Great time it was at the village of Eglinton, to which three or four other parties of the grand hunt had lately returned not unsuccessful. As we approached the jail—a little wretched brick building, containing a single room of ten or twelve feet square, with one little grated window, whence proceeded a steam and stench perceptible at a considerable distance—we found it crammed completely full of recaptured negroes, some of them severely wounded, tumbled pellmell into this black hole, which contained also two white women, committed on some charge of theft; the slaves to be detained until their masters should come forward and pay the promised reward for their capture, together with certain fees and charges which the law allows in such cases.

By way of refreshment after their fatigues, and in commemoration of their prowess, these successful men-hunters had indulged in pretty copious draughts of peach brandy and whisky, and the dead body of the overseer, conveyed to the tavern and laid out upon the table, soon wrought up those who gazed at it into a state of furious indignation.

As it was absolutely impossible to thrust any more prisoners into the jail, the two taken by the company to which I had attached myself, after being fettered and handcuffed, had been fastened by heavy chains to the iron bars of the prison window-grating.

It was only by the greatest efforts that I mastered my emotions, as making my way among the crowd of blacks and whites that gathered around him, I approached the one supposed to be Wild Tom. I bent upon him a scrutinising eye. He was greatly altered; yet I did not fail to recognize the features, too strongly impressed upon my mind ever to be forgotten, of my old friend and compatriot of twenty years before. I had expected it; yet what an agony shot through my heart to know it! It was necessary, however, to control myself, and I did. I spoke a few words, when, satisfied by my tone and look that I felt a sympathy for him, he laid aside, for a moment, that air of proud defiance with which, like a lion in the toils, he had glanced round on the crowd, and with a tone of entreaty begged me for a drink of water. By the promise of half a dollar, I induced one of the negroes to bring me a large gourd full; but just as the wounded prisoner was slowly raising it with his manacled arms to his lips, a well-dressed white man struck it with a stick which he held in his hand, and dashed it to the ground. I could not refrain from some words of protest against this piece of wanton cruelty; but the man with the stick turned upon me with a volley of oaths, inquired who I was, that dared to comfort this infernal negro murderer, and by drawing the eyes of the company upon me as a stranger, began to make my position very uncomfortable.

Just at this moment we heard a loud shout at the tavern door, at no great distance, followed up by a vigorous fight and a great uproar, as it seemed, between two parties into which the crowd assembled there had become divided. This drew off all those who had collected about the prisoners except the negro man who had brought the water, and who still stuck by, to keep me in remembrance of the half dollar; and by the promise to double it, I succeeded in obtaining another gourd-full, from which my poor captured friend was enabled without interruption to quench his feverish thirst. As he dropped the empty gourd, he turned to me an eye of acknowledgment. Thank Heaven, that in his distress and extremity I was enabled to do for him even so much as this!

Incapable as I was of affording any succour, I felt an invincible desire to make myself known to him. I felt, indeed, that to his noble and generous soul it would afford a glow of satisfaction, even in the depth of his own distress, to know of the welfare of his old friend and confederate. I stepped close to him, and placing my hand on his arm, I said, in a whisper, "Thomas, do you know me? Remember Loosahachee! Remember Ann, how she was murdered, and how you vowed vengeance over her grave! Remember Martin, the overseer, and how we buried him and the bloodhound together! Remember our parting, when I went north and you went south! I am Archy; do you know me?"

How keenly he fixed his eyes upon me as I began! With what devouring glances he gazed at me as I went on! I, too, was greatly altered—far more than he; but before I had spoken my name, I saw that he knew me. But in an instant, his eye glancing from me, that momentary gleam of joyous surprise which had lighted up his face passed suddenly away, and his features again resumed that sullen look of defiance, which seemed to say to his captors, "Do your worst; I am ready."

I felt at that same moment a hand rudely laid on my shoulder, while a voice, which I recognized as that of the same man who had dashed the calabash of water from Thomas's grasp, exclaimed, with a volley of oaths, "What the devil are you doing here in close confab with this murderer? I tell you, stranger, you don't leave here without giving an account of yourself!"

At the same time a number of men, rushing up to Thomas, began to unfasten the chains from the prison bars, and to conduct him towards the door of the tavern.

The fight had been between the more drunken and infuriated portion of the company, who, enraged at the sight of the dead overseer, wished to try and execute Thomas at once, and those who had wished to await the arrival of General Carter, for whom a messenger had been sent, and to delay final proceedings till the prisoner had first been identified as the veritable Wild Tom, and General Carter's property, lest otherwise there might be some difficulty in recovering the promised reward.

The more violent and drunken party had, however, prevailed; a court of three freeholders had been organized on the spot, and Thomas, again surrounded by a rabble of blacks and whites, was now brought before this august tribunal. I was myself, at the same time, taken into custody as a suspected person, with an intimation that my case should be attended to as soon as that of the negro was disposed of.

"Whom do you belong to?" Such was the first question which the honourable court addressed to the prisoner.

"I belong," answered Thomas, with much solemnity, "to the God who made us all!" A reply so unusual was received by some with a stare, by others with a laugh, redoubled at the repartee by one of the judges, "To God! Ah, I rather reckon you belong to the devil! Anyhow, he'll very soon have you."

N

To reiterated demands as to whose property he was, Thomas steadily replied that he was a freeman, when the same witty judge raised a new laugh by requesting him to show his free papers.

The court, after hearing a witness or two, pronounced him guilty of the murder of the overseer, after which he was asked, with a sort of mock solemnity, if he had anything to say why sentence of death should not be passed upon him.

"Go on," said the indignant culprit; "hang me, kill me, do your will! I was held a slave for the best years of my life. My wife was flogged to death before my eyes. As a freeman, you have hunted me with blood-hounds, and shot at me with rifles, and placed a price upon my head. Long have I fooled you, and paid you back in your own coin. That white man to-day was not the first who has found me too much for him. One by one, two by two, three by three, I defy, and would whip the whole of you, but the whole dozen mounted and armed, with dogs to boot, were too much for one poor black man, with nothing but his feet, his hands, and his knife. They have not always been too much; but I am getting old. Better die now, while I have strength and courage to defy your worst, than fall into your hands a broken-down old man."

These words of defiance wrought up the assembled mob of planters and overseers to a fury perfectly devilish. "Hanging is too good for him," some of them cried out, and presently the awful cry was raised, "Burn him! burn him!" No sooner was the horrible idea suggested, than volunteers were found to prepare to carry it into execution. It was in vain that I, and indeed two or three of those who had been engaged in the capture of Thomas, and among them the planter by whose side I had ridden, and from whom I had heard the story of it, remonstrated against this horrible and illegal cruelty. The same brutal scoundrel who had dashed the water from Thomas's lips now stood forward as the leader and manager in this new atrocity. It was necessary, he said, with the country agitated by abolition incendiaries, some of them, he repeated, —and here he cast a malignant glance at me,—in communication with this very outlaw, now that they had him in their power, to make an example of him. This Wild Tom had been the terror of the whole neighbourhood for years. The stories of his exploits, circulating among the negroes, had done infinite damage, and might make many imitators. It was necessary, therefore, to counteract this impression by having his career terminate in a way to inspire awe and terror.

A pile of light wood was soon collected, and the victim of slaveholding vengeance was placed in the midst of it.

The pile was then lighted, and the smoke and flames began to wreathe above his head. But even yet unsubdued, he looked round on his shouting tormentors with a smile of contemptuous defiance.

Unable to endure the horrid spectacle, I attempted to rush from among the crowd; but I found myself watched, and directly I was seized, and, by orders of the self-appointed master of the ceremonies of this horrible scene, conveyed close to the burning pile, as one on whom the spectacle of such an execution might make a salutary impression.

Thomas recognized me,—at least I thought so,—from amid the flames, and he lifted up his arm, as if to bid me farewell.

O, the horrible agony of that moment! Had I myself been in the place of my friend, could I have suffered more? My heart-strings seemed to crack; the blood rushed in a torrent to my brain. Nature could not endure it. I dropped fainting and senseless to the ground.

CHAPTER XLVI.

When I recovered my senses, I found myself on a bed, with four or five black women about me, applying various restoratives; and, as I opened my eyes, they burst out with great shouts of delight.

I found afterwards that, during my fainting fit, my pockets, as well as my saddle-bags, had been thoroughly searched, in hopes of obtaining some proofs to corroborate the suspicions raised against me by the sympathy I had exhibited.

But the only papers found were some letters of credit and introduction addressed from Liverpool to mercantile houses of established character in Charleston and New Orleans, in which I was described as an English traveller, on a tour partly of business and partly of pleasure.

Upon the production and public reading of these letters, a great difference of opinion had sprung up among the sovereigns assembled at Eglinton, acting in my case as a committee of vigilance with full powers, of the extent of which so terrible an instance had just been exhibited before my eyes.

The mere fact that I was an Englishman went very far with many of the ruder sort to confirm the supposition that I must be an abolitionist and a conspirator. The draught of water which I had persisted in procuring for Thomas was regarded by several as a very suspicious circumstance. The words I had privately addressed to him, and the appearance of some understanding between him and myself, weighed very heavily against me. The remonstrances I had made against the cruel death to which he had just been subjected, were set down as, at the very best, a great piece of impertinent interference—especially coming from an Englishman.

The same ruffian who had already twice interfered between Thomas and myself, and who had caused my seizure as a suspected person, now assumed the part of chief prosecutor. He argued with great zeal that I must be an emissary of the English abolitionists, and perhaps of the English government, sent out on purpose to stir up a slave revolt, and, from what had passed between me and Wild Tom, apparently in correspondence with that dangerous outlaw, and the least that could be done, in his opinion, with any proper regard for the public safety, was to give me a sound flogging, and to ride me on a rail out of the county.

This proposal was very favourably received; and nothing but the strenuous exertions of the planter whose acquaintance I had made on the road saved me from falling a victim to it. As I had entered Eglinton in his company, he seemed to consider me, in some sort, as under his protection; and he accordingly took up my cause with no little zeal. My overtaking him on the road, so he argued, was a matter of pure accident; my interference on behalf of the bloody murderer, upon whom such just, proper, and signal vengeance had been taken, was only a piece of misjudged humanity. It was not to be supposed that a stranger, and an Englishman, could enter into all of their feelings. While adopting all proper means promptly to suppress and punish all interference with the domestic institutions of the south, for which nobody was more zealous than he, they ought to be careful how they overstripped the limits of reason and prudence. If I had been only a northerner, it would be safe enough to maltreat me to any extent, even to burn me alive, as they just had done the "nigger." Those pitiful Yankees might be whipped, kicked, and otherwise punished, to any extent, with reason or without, and there would not be the least danger of any rumpus about it, for fear it might diminish the trade with the south. But to meddle with an Englishman was quite another affair. England did not allow any of her people to be maltreated with impunity. It was apparent from my letters that I was a person who had money and friends, and those concerned in any irregular violence inflicted upon me might find themselves called upon to answer for it. To be sure, the United States could whip the British again, as they had done in the last war. But still, in the present excited state of the slave population, a war with England was not exactly desirable. Such, as he afterwards informed me, was the general tenor of the argument by which my planter friend had saved me from the clutches of the vigilance committee. Had he or they suspected my true history, how different the result might have been!

While this discussion had been going on, I had been conveyed to the tavern, still in a senseless condition, where the negro women, with their usual good nature, had exerted themselves, as I have mentioned already, for my recovery. My planter friend soon made his appearance. He saw that I was not yet in a condition to resume my journey; and as the village, and especially the tavern and its neighbourhood, still continued a scene of drunken uproar, such as made my further stay there neither conducive to my health nor perhaps compatible with my safety, he insisted upon taking me to his own house. This invitation, under the circumstances, I was glad to accept; and keeping my room for three or four days, I gradually recovered, and grew strong again.

My host, who of course was without any clue to the special interest which I had in the death of Thomas, seemed rather surprised at the serious effect which that incident had produced upon me; nor could he otherwise explain it except by supposing that alarm for my own personal safety had a great share in it. He therefore exerted all his eloquence, as well to reassure me personally as to vindicate the reputation of the southern states against any conclusions which I might hastily draw. He assured me, upon his honour, that such scenes as I had witnessed were not by any means common. Once in a while the indignation of the people, roused to the highest pitch by some atrocious villany on the part of some negro, did vent itself in the way I had witnessed. But this burning alive was quite an exceptional circumstance. He had never known more than two or three other instances of it, and those provoked by some horrible misdemeanor, such as the murder of a white man, or the rape of a white woman. He hoped I should be candid enough to admit that a few such instances could not be considered as seriously detracting from the claims of the southern states to stand in the highest ranks of civilization and Christianity. The fact was, the negroes were such a set of unmitigated savages, that occasional examples were necessary to inspire them with a wholesome degree of dread.

I was not at present in a state of mind to conduct an argument with much advantage. Besides, notwithstanding my host's personal kindness towards me, I very soon discovered—what the circumstances under which I had first met him might have given me sufficient assurance of, that upon the subject of the evils or wrongs of slavery, he was perfectly impenetrable. Remembering, therefore, the evangelical injunction of not casting pearls before swine's feet, I contented myself with letting him understand that, however it might be in America, which I freely admitted to be a great country, the practices of slave hunts and negro burning were wholly incompatible with my English ideas of civilization or Christianity. This statement of my sentiment was received by my host with a gracious smile, a condescending wave of the hand, and the observation—evidently intended to be apologetical for my heresies, and exculpatory of them—that the prejudices of John Bull, upon some points, were unaccountable.

These mutual explanations occurred very soon after reaching the planter's house. As hopeless, apparently, of convicting me, as I was of making any impression upon him, he allowed the subject to drop; and during the remainder of my stay with him we conversed upon indifferent matters only. As soon as I felt able to ride, I hastened to resume my journey—not without a friendly warning from my host to be cautious how I gave utterance to my English prejudices. When travelling in Turkey,—so he remarked, without seeming to be aware how little creditable the comparison was to his state of South Carolina,—it was best to do as they did in Turkey, or, at least, to let the Turks do as they chose, without interference or observation.

CHAPTER XLVII.

SHORTLY after arriving at Charleston, which I reached without any further adventure worthy of note, I waited upon the mercantile gentlemen to whom I had letters of credit. Upon entering the counting-house, I found another stranger there, whom, from his bearing and appearance, I recognised at once as the master of some merchant-ship. He was speaking with great vehemence, and apparently complaining of some injury.

I gathered from what he said that his vessel belonged to Boston, in the state of Massachusetts, and that, having encountered a severe storm while on a voyage to the Havana, he had been obliged to put into Charleston to refit. Not only was his cook a coloured man, but of the eight sailors, by whom the brig was manned, no less than five were coloured, all, as the captain said, natives of Massachusetts, born on Cape Cod, and as able seamen as ever trod a deck.

These coloured men—so the captain was complaining in pretty hard terms—had just been taken out of his ship and carried off to jail; and he wished to know of the Charleston merchants, who it seemed were the correspondents of his owners, whether there was no security against this outrage, as inconvenient to him as it was injurious to the men.

"Why," said the merchant, to whom he addressed himself, with a significant glance at his partner, and a mischievous sort of look at the captain, "there has just arrived here, I understand, a commissioner from Massachusetts, appointed by the governor of that state, under a resolve of the legislature, to bring this very question of the imprisonment of coloured seamen of that state to a legal issue. The commissioner is staying at such a hotel," naming the very one at which I had put up; "that is, unless he has been turned away, for notice has already been issued to all the hotel-keepers not to harbour him. You had better apply to him, and quick too, or you may not find him. He is the very man for you, and yours is the very case for him. Try and see what he and the United States laws, and the state of Massachusetts, will do for you."

The ironical, sneering tone in which this was said, was evident enough to me; but the honest sea captain, to whom it was addressed, seemed to take it all in good earnest, and hastily started off in pursuit of the commissioner.

Having arranged my business matters with these merchants, and provided for meeting such drafts as might be made on behalf of my North Carolina *protégé*, I ventured to inquire whether the arrest of which I had just heard the captain complaining was really made under any law.

"O, yes, certainly," was the answer. "All negroes and coloured people who arrive here on shipboard are taken at once to jail, and kept there till the ship is ready to depart, when, by paying their board, jail fees, and costs, they are allowed to go in her."

"And suppose they can't pay?" said I.

"O, the captain, you know, must have his men, and he pays for them."

"But suppose the captain does not choose to pay?"

"Why, in that case, the fees are raised by selling the men at auction."

"Sell free men at auction," said I, "driven into your ports by stress of weather, and imprisoned merely for not being white!"

There was something in the tone in which I spoke that brought a slight tinge of colour into the merchant's cheek. He endeavoured to apologise for this law by suggesting the great danger of insurrection, if free coloured men, from the north or elsewhere, should be permitted to come in contact with a slave population far exceeding the whites in number, as was the case in Charleston and the neighbourhood.

"But what is it," I asked, "about this Massachusetts commissioner, to whom you referred the captain?"

"Why," said the merchant, with a contemptuous sort of a smile, "the Boston ship-owners, finding these prison fees and expenses a charge upon their ships, have all at once been seized with a mighty strong sympathy for negroes' rights,—if you want to stir a Boston man up, just touch him in the pocket,—and so they have got this commissioner sent on here to try this question in the courts. They pretend that South Carolina has no right to make a law for the imprisonment of free persons from Massachusetts, not charged with any crime, but merely from a general suspicion on account of their colour."

"And when is the case likely to come to trial?" I asked.

"Come to trial!" said the Carolina merchant, rolling up the whites of his eyes; "and do you suppose we are going to allow the case to be tried?"

"And why not?" I asked; "and how can you help it?"

"Ten to one," he answered, "the cause, if tried, would go against us. The law in question has already been pronounced unconstitutional by one of the United States judges, and he, too, a South Carolina man; but whether unconstitutional or not, we think it necessary, and the niggers and the Yankee merchants must learn to put up with it. As to helping it, that is a very simple matter. The commissioner from Massachusetts has already had notice to take himself off, and all the hotel keepers, as I mentioned to the captain, not to entertain him, at their peril. We shan't tolerate any such abolutionist spies and conspirators here in Charleston. In fact, if the old gentleman had not had the Yankee shrewdness to bring a daughter of his along with him by way of protector, he might before this time have found himself tumbled out of the city, neck and heels, comfortably dressed in a coat of tar and feathers. There is not a lawyer here who would dare bring a suit for him. Most of our merchants are northern men,—I am one myself," said my informant,—"but we are all Carolinians in feeling; in fact, if we expect to live here, we have to be so, and I shall be on hand to do my part, and if the old gentleman hesitates about it, to help him in finding his way out of the city. The matter has been settled at a public meeting. He is not to be allowed to sleep here another night."

"And what do you imagine the state of Massachusetts and the Boston merchants will say at being so unceremoniously kicked out of the courthouse doorway?"

"O, as to the merchants, they will probably do like a well-bred Carolina negro, who takes off his hat when he gets a kick for his insolence, and grins out, with a low bow, a 'Thank ye, master.' Kicking agrees quite as well with Yankee merchants as with niggers; and both niggers and merchants are quite used to it! As to the state of Massachusetts, so long as that state continues to be controlled, as at present, by the mercantile and manufacturing influence, there is no danger of any trouble from her. She will pocket the insult very quietly. The political leaders in Massachusetts, of both parties, are exceedingly anxious to hire themselves out as negro drivers to the south. What would become of Boston or Massachusetts without the southern trade? As the poor Yankees live on the crumbs which fall from our table, they are not to be particular about the terms on which they are allowed to pick them up. Of course, if they are allowed to pick up the crumbs, they must expect now and then to eat a little dirt."

My Carolina acquaintance seemed to make a rather low estimate of the spirit of Massachusetts; yet when I recollected what I had myself seen and heard in passing through Boston a few weeks before, I could not but admit that this calculation upon mercantile servility and cupidity was a pretty safe one.

As I reached the hotel, on my return from the merchant's, I found a great crowd collected in the streets. A carriage stood at the door, and presently, a tall, white-haired old gentleman appeared, with a lady leaning on his arm, very ceremoniously attended by half-a-dozen gentlemen, in white kid gloves, whom I afterwards understood to be a detachment of the vigilance committee, specially appointed to escort the Massachusetts commissioner out of the city. The commissioner and his daughter were placed in the carriage, which drove off amid the shouts, jeers, and execrations of the assembled multitude; and so far as I have heard, this is the last that Massachusetts has ever done towards vindicating the rights of her imprisoned seamen.

English seamen, as I have been told, sometimes suffer under the same law. If such are the facts, Great Britain will no doubt find the means of bringing these insolent slaveholders to reason; and perhaps, through her agency, the timid and trembling northern states may sooner or later regain a free entry into the port of Charleston. It would indeed be a curious circumstance if British aid and interference should be found the only means of securing to the northern merchants and seamen, as against the domineering influence of their southern masters, their rights under the constitution of the United States. Such an interference on behalf of humanity and sailors' rights might almost pass for an offset to the wrongs formerly inflicted by Great Britain in the impressment of American seamen.

CHAPTER XLVIII.

HITHERTO, during my journey southward, the excitement of the various adventures through which I had passed, as well as the occupation which I had found for my thoughts in revisiting the scenes of my youth, under circumstances so changed, had kept my mind from dwelling upon the hopelessness of the search which I had undertaken. Augusta, in the state of Georgia, was the last point to which, in my researches many years before, I had been able to trace my wife and child. It was now some twenty years since they had entered that town as part of a slave coffle destined for the south-western market. This was the last trace I had of them. To Augusta, therefore, I now directed my course, not, however, without the most depressing feelings, and a painful consciousness that when I reached that place I should be without the slightest clue to guide me any farther.

I left Charleston in the stage-coach for Augusta, long before daylight. As the day began to dawn, I found myself one of four passengers. At first we were pretty silent, each trying to sleep in his corner, or else eyeing his fellow passengers, as if wishing to ascertain their character before making any advances towards acquaintance. At breakfast we began to thaw out a little, and by dinner time we were quite sociable.

It presently appeared that two of the passengers were northern men; one of them the editor of a New York newspaper, the other a Boston agent, employed in the purchase of cotton for some mercantile houses or manufacturing companies of that city. The third passenger was a person of very striking appearance, with a face of great intelligence, a dark eye that seemed to penetrate you at a glance, a captivating smile, manners exceedingly soft and winning, and something in his whole bearing that indicated a man accustomed to mingle freely in society.

He was evidently taken by the other two for a wealthy planter, and he neither did nor said anything to contradict the assumption, receiving with an air of gracious condescension the court which they paid to him.

After a variety of topics, the conversation, as is common in America, settled down upon politics, and especially upon the nomination lately made for president and vice-president by a convention of the democratic or Jackson party assembled at Baltimore. Mr. Van Buren, the nominee of that convention for the presidency, was very sharply criticized by the two northern men, on the ground, principally, that in a convention for revising the state constitution of New York, he had been in favour of allowing the blacks to vote. The planter, or supposed planter, adopted, in the course of the conversation, a non-committal course, which, according to the criticisms made on Mr. Van Buren's character, might almost have rivalled the adroitness of that gentleman himself. The nomination of Mr. Richard M. Johnson for the vice-presidency seemed to give still less satisfaction; indeed, it was mentioned that a portion of the members of the convention by which it was made had been greatly dis-satisfied at it, and had refused to give it their support. Some hints that were dropped excited my curiosity as to the grounds of their opposition, and I followed up the matter by a good many questions. The opposition to Mr. Johnson was made, I was told, by the delegation from Virginia. They did not object to the political orthodoxy of Mr. Johnson, who, indeed, was a democrat of the first water,—to say the truth, so the New York editor told me, considerably too much of a democrat to suit the tastes of the Virginians. He was not respectable enough for them; quite too vulgar in his tastes and habits; and they had insisted upon nominating a certain Mr. Rives in his place.

Upon my inquiring more specifically in what the vulgarity of Mr. Johnson consisted, it came out that he entertained in his house a number of black and brown wives, and was the father of a family of coloured children.

Very much to the surprise of my two northern fellow-passengers, who exhausted all their rhetoric in condemnation of Mr. Johnson's coarseness and vulgarity,—a practical amalgamator for vice-president!—the supposed planter avowed himself a supporter of the Van Buren-Johnson nomination; and he undertook to offer some apologies for the latter gentleman.

" The horror of you northern people," he said, nodding his head to the Boston cotton-broker, "and the hue and cry you have lately raised on the subject of amalgamation and the intermixture of the races, may be all very sincere, but for us in the south, with so many living evidences of our frailty multiplying about us in every direction, to attempt to make a bugbear of amalgamation, or to wink it into non-existence, by any ostrich-like process of sticking our heads into the sand, and refusing to recognize as a fact what everybody knows, and what is testified to by the varying complexion of every considerable family of slaves in the country, is certainly a very great absurdity.

" For my part, I like to see a little consistency. We southerners defend slavery because, as we say, it is a law of nature that when two races are brought together in the same community, the stronger and nobler race should predominate over the weaker. But if, in such a case, it is the law of nature that the men of the weaker race should be made slaves of by those of the stronger, is it not just as much also a law of nature that the women of the weaker race should become concubines to the men of the stronger? Does not it always so operate? and is not that the means which nature takes gradually to extinguish the inferior race, and to substitute an improved, mixed race in the place of it?

" Some of us undertake to defend slavery out of the Bible, and to justify it by the example of the patriarchs. Very well; if the example of the patriarchs is to justify me in holding slaves, will it not also justify our democratic candidate for the vice-presidency in raising up to himself a family by the help of his maid-servants?

"In fact, sir," turning to me, who had taken an early opportunity to avow myself an Englishman, "it is precisely because our democratic candidate for the vice-presidency follows the example of the patriarchs a little too closely, that all this hue and cry is raised against him. It is not his taste for black women, it is not his family of coloured children, —perhaps these innocent gentlemen here from the north know nothing about the matter, but, if so, any white boy in the city of Charleston of sixteen years old and upwards could enlighten them,—it is not these little peccadilloes that reflect anything upon Mr. Johnson's character. They are as much parts of our domestic institutions here at the south as the use of the cow-hide; just as natural to us southerners as chewing tobacco; just about as common, and just as little thought of. But the pinch is here. Mr. Johnson, being a bachelor, with no white wife or white children to control him, and, withal, one of the best-natured men in the world, must needs so far imitate the example of the patriarchs as actually to recognize a number of coloured daughters as his own children. He has raised and educated them in his own house. He has even made efforts to introduce them into respectable society. The spirit of the Kentucky women—the women, you know, are all natural aristocrats— defeated him in that; but he has procured white husbands for them, and their children, under the law of Kentucky, will be legally white, and entitled to all the rights and privileges of white persons. It is this in which the scandal of Mr. Johnson's conduct consists. If, instead of acting the affectionate father by his daughters, he had quietly shipped them all off to New Orleans to be sold at auction, to be made concubines of by the purchasers, instead of marrying them respectably, and securing for their children the full privileges of Kentucky citizenship, we should never have heard that brought against him, either north or south, as a reason why he ought not to be vice-president. I do not imagine that either of our northern friends here would have made the least objection to him on that score!"

"But you don't undertake to say," stammered out the Boston cotton-broker, "that any respectable man at the south does that? That, I thought, was one of the slanders of the abolitionists."

"I do undertake to say," was the answer, "that a man may do it without any tarnish to his respectability, and if he should apply the next day after to be admitted a member of any of our most pious Christian churches, that would never be made a ground for refusing him. Church discipline is mighty strict in some matters. I once knew a man excommunicated from a Presbyterian church for sending his children to a dancing-school, but I never yet heard of any southern church that ventured to inquire into the paternity of slave children, or the relations of female slaves towards their owners. The violent death of a slave by the hand of the owner may, under certain circumstances, lead to a judicial investigation more or less strict; but, short of that, a Turkish harem is not more safe from impertinent intrusions and in-quiries, whether civil or ecclesiastical, than one of our slave-holding families. If honest Dick Johnson had not acknowledged those children to be his, do you suppose that anybody—unless, perhaps, by way of joke—would have ventured to charge them upon him? His offence consists not in having the children, but in owning them."

"I am afraid," said the New York editor, "you will give our English friend here," nodding at me, "rather a low idea of southern morals.

There are some little family secrets that ought not to be spoken of before everybody."

"Pity," said the other, " you had not thought of that before. In that case, you might have let Dick Johnson alone. All I insist upon is, that, bating the lack of a little hypocrisy and grimace, and making due allowance for a little extra goodnature, he is not so very much worse than his neighbours."

"But," retorted the New York editor, " as a southern man and a slave-holder, can you undertake to say that such conduct as his—this attempt to put blacks and whites on an equality—is not dangerous to the insti-tutions of the country ?"

"Not so dangerous by half," was the prompt reply, " as the attempt-ing to commingle and confound with the mass of the slaves the children of free fathers, inheriting from the father's side a spirit not very consistent with the condition of servitude. What do you think is likely to be the consequence of having among our slaves the descendants of such men, for instance, as Thomas Jefferson ?"

"Thomas Jefferson ! nonsense !" exclaimed the New Yorker.

"Nonsense or not, I can only say, that I once saw a very decent, bright mulatto woman, at least three-quarters white, sold at auction, who claimed to be a granddaughter of that famous ex-president, and, as far as resemblance goes, her face and figure sustained her pretensions. At any rate, the woman brought an extra hundred dollars or so beyond her otherwise market value, as the purchaser facetiously observed, on account of the goodness of the breed."

The two northern passengers seemed a little shocked at this story, the force of which they attempted to evade by insisting that the woman must have been an impostor, and that perhaps this idea was got up for the very purpose of enlivening the sale.

"Well," said the other with a laugh, " that certainly is very possible. Gouge and McGrab were unquestionably shrewd fellows, and in the way of trade, up to almost anything."

My interest in the conversation was here redoubled. Gouge and McGrab! McGrab was the name of the slave-trader by whom my wife and child had been purchased and transported to Augusta, and it was as his property that my agent formerly employed in that business had obtained the last trace of them.

I hastened to inquire when and where it was that my fellow-passenger had witnessed this sale of Jefferson's alleged granddaughter.

"O, at Augusta, in Georgia, some twenty years since," was the answer.

"And pray," I asked, " who is this McGrab that you speak of ? I have an interest in getting some trace of a slave-dealer of that name."

He readily replied that McGrab was a Scotchman by birth, but a South Carolinian by education, engaged some years ago, along with his partner Gouge, in the supply of the southern market with slaves. The head-quarters of their traffic was at Augusta. McGrab scoured the more northern slave-states, attending sheriffs' and executors' sales, and driving such private bargains as he could to keep up the supply, which he forwarded from time to time to his partner Gouge, who attended chiefly to the business of selling at Augusta. But the partnership had been many years dissolved, and McGrab himself a long time dead. Gouge was still living at Augusta, retired from business, and one of the wealthiest men in the place.

"I ought to know something," he added, aside to me, " of these men and their business, for in my younger days I was three or four years their clerk and bookkeeper, and for a while their partner. I owe old Gouge a grudge, and if you have any claim against them, and I can any way assist you, you shall be welcome to my services."

CHAPTER XLIX.

THE stage coach stopped for dinner at a dirty, uncomfortable tavern, the management of which seemed to be altogether in the hands of the slaves, of whom there was a great superabundance, the landlord being a sort of gentleman guest in his own house. The head servant of the establishment, a large, portly, soft-spoken mulatto, but very shabbily and dirtily dressed, seemed, for some reason or other—perhaps from my politeness to him—to take quite a fancy to me. After dinner he called me aside, and inquired if I was acquainted with the gentleman who had sat opposite to me at the table. This was the supposed planter, my stage companion, in his younger days, as he had informed us, clerk and book-keeper, and afterwards partner, of Gouge and McGrab. "No," I answered, "I did not know him, except as my fellow-traveller from Charleston; I should like very well to know his name."

"As to his name," said my mulatto friend, "it would not be so easy to tell that. He goes by a good many names. Most every time he comes this way he has a new one. Have a care of him, master; he's a gambler. I thought I'd tell you, lest you might get cheated by him."

As this information seemed to come from pure good-will on the part of my informant, I had no reason to distrust its correctness. I knew very well that gambling was not only practised in these southern slave states, as it is in the overgrown capitals of Europe, as a means of re-lieving the ennui of idleness, but that here, as there, a regular class of professional gamblers had sprung into existence, who lived by fleecing the unskilful and unwary. It was by no means unusual for members of that fraternity to have all the external marks of gentlemen; nor was there any improbability in the suggestion that my new acquaintance belonged to it.

Though he had inclined to differ, in the course of the morning, from our two northern companions on some questions of politics and mo-rality, I could not but admire the grace and art with which he con-trived, in the course of the afternoon, to worm himself into their confi-dence. When the stage coach stopped for the night at another tavern, still more dirty, uncomfortable, and every way untidy—if that could well be—than the one at which we had dined, he proposed, after supper, a game of cards by way of whiling away the time. The other two were ready enough for it, and the three were soon busy at the game, in which they were joined by one or two planters of the vicinity, who happened to be lounging about the house. For myself, I positively declined to join them, declaring that I never touched a card, and never played at any game for money; and perceiving from my manner that I was quite inflexible on that point, the alleged gambler remarked, with some significance, that I had taken a very wise and safe resolution for a stranger travelling through the southern states.

After watching the game for some time, I retired to bed; and rising pretty early the next morning, since the journey was to be renewed at five o'clock, I found them still at it: the two northern dupes haggard with want of sleep, and their very lengthened faces, distorted with ill-suppressed anxiety and suffering, seeming to have grown ten years older in that single night. They bore, in fact, but a distant resemblance to the two spruce, sleek gentlemen with whom I had ridden the day before. The other seemed as fresh and self-possessed as at the moment he had sat down; and as I entered the room, he took up and pocketed, with a graceful nonchalance that was quite admirable, the last stakes, and as it proved too, the last money, of his two companions.

Having sat down, as I afterwards learnt, with only ten dollars in his pocket, as his whole means and stock in trade, he had made a good night of it. In the morning he had not less than two thousand, besides a fine mulatto boy of fifteen or sixteen, whom one of the planters had made over to him by way of squaring accounts.

Finding our two companions quite drained, he insisted upon paying their tavern bills himself, and upon lending each of them fifty dollars, as a fund to go upon till they could obtain further remittances; and this he did with as unconscious an air of sympathy and commiseration as if they had lost their money by some accident, instead of his having himself been the agent of their loss, by means, not merely of his superior coolness and skill, but probably also by some other tricks of his profession. Not the master, who tosses a dollar to his slave by way of Christmas present, could do it with a greater air of generosity.

It was curious to remark the crestfallen air of the Boston cotton-broker and the New York editor, after the loss of their money. The day before, they had held up their heads; they had had their opinions, and pretty positive ones, too; nor had they been at all slow or modest in asserting them. To-day they seemed quite sunk into nobodies, the stiffening all taken out of them, moody and silent, with nothing to say about anything, eyeing the person to whom their money had been transferred, and to whom, the day before, they had paid such court as a rich planter, with a singular mixture of dislike and terror, much like that with which I had often seen an unfortunate slave eye a master whom he feared and hated, but from whom he felt it impossible to escape.

Indeed I could not but think, that strip those two northern gentlemen of their fine clothes, and set them up in their present crest-fallen and disconsolate condition on the auction-block of Messrs. Gouge and McGrab, or some other slave-dealers, especially with the cool, keen eye of their late depredator upon them, and they might very easily have passed muster as two "white niggers," born and bred in servitude, and stupid fellows at that, easily to be kept in order, and from whom very little mischief or trouble need be apprehended.

Finding these two disconsolate individuals sad, solemn, and as dry as a squeezed lemon, and quite insensible to all his efforts to amuse them, the gambler, whose victims they had become, directed his conversation to me. I cannot say but that I decidedly enjoyed their predicament. "O, my fine fellows," said I to myself, "you now have a little experience what a nice thing it is, this being stripped and plundered! You think it mighty hard to part with a few hundred dollars, the earnings, by means I don't know how particularly honest, of perhaps only a few weeks—money lost, too, not less by your own consenting folly, than by the skill and tricks of a man more knowing and adroit than yourselves. Now learn to sympathize with multitudes of poor fellows in natural gifts and endowments not so very much, if at all, your inferiors—some of them, indeed, vastly your superiors—regularly stripped and plundered, minute by minute, hour by hour, day by day, week by week, month by month, year by year, through a whole lifetime; and that, too, by pure fraud and force, without any consenting folly on their part; plundered, too, not only of the earnings of their hands, but, it may be, of the very wives of their affections, and children of their love, sent off to a slave-auction to suit the convenience, or to meet the necessities, of the men that call themselves their owners; and with just about as much right and title of ownership as this gambler has in you—the right of the weak over the strong, and of the crafty over the simple!"

CHAPTER L.

As the late clerk, book-keeper, and partner of Gouge and McGrab, now, as it seemed, professional blackleg and gambler, might be able, from his former connection with that respectable slave-trading firm, to afford me information essential to the search in which I was engaged, I received his advances very graciously. In fact, the manliness of sentiment which he had evinced the day before in the defence of his favourite candidate for the vice-presidency had inclined me in his favour; and as to his present pursuits, I was disposed to think them quite as honest and respectable as the slave-trading business in which he had formerly been engaged, or as the slave-breeding business, by which so many southern gentlemen of unquestioned respectability gained at least a part of their livelihood.

I found him, indeed, a very agreeable companion, free, in a great measure, from those local provincialisms and narrownesses almost universal among even the best educated and most liberal-minded Americans; keen in his observations, acute in his judgments (a vein of sly satire running through his conversation), but good-natured rather than bitter.

Such was the beginning of a companionship which gradually ripened into something of a confidential intimacy. I did not conceal from Mr. John Colter (for that was the name by which he chose to be known to me) my knowledge of his rather dubious profession; at the same time, I was willing to accept, at their full value, his graces, talents, agreeable parts, and the frequent indications which he gave, at least in words, of a naturally generous and kindly disposition. Why not make allowance for his position and circumstances? Why not regard him with as much charity as is asked generally for slave-holders?

As if to confirm me in this toleration, by which he was evidently not a little flattered, and to which he did not seem much accustomed, in the course of a second night's stoppage, in a ramble by moonlight, Mr.

Colter having at hand no more pigeons to pluck, let me pretty fully into his history.

It appeared that he was the son of a wealthy planter, or of one who had once been wealthy, and who, while he lived, had maintained the reputation of being so. He had, of course, been brought up in habits of great profusion and extravagance. His literary instruction had not been neglected, and he had been sent to travel a year or two in Europe, where he spent a great deal of money, and fell into very dissipated habits, and whence he was recalled by the death of his father, whose estate, when it came to be settled, proved insolvent, the plantations and slaves being covered by mortgages, and a large family of children left wholly unprovided for.

Thus thrown entirely on his own resources, he had great difficulty in finding means to live. The general resource of decayed families was to emigrate to the new lands of the west; but this was hardly possible, unless one could take a few slaves with him, and he had none, nor the means of procuring any, his character for profusion and extravagance being too well established for any of his father's old friends to be willing to trust him. Indeed, since the estate had turned out insolvent, it was curious to remark, notwithstanding his father's numerous acquaintance, and the ostentatious hospitality with which for so many years he had kept open doors, how very few friends the family had.

Being a good scholar, he might have found occupation as tutor in some family; but this was looked upon as a servile position, incompatible with the dignity of a southerner, and only fit to be filled by fellows from the north. " The Romans, you know"—so he remarked to me—" intrusted the education of their children to slave pedagogues; we generally get ours from New England." As to going into mercantile business, that would require capital; and that business, too, was mostly engrossed by adventurers from the north, who generally procured their clerks and assistants from the same quarter.

At length, unable to do any better, he had obtained employment from the rich slave-trading firm of Gouge and McGrab, rising presently to be their first clerk and bookkeeper, and being finally admitted as a partner.

But this kind of business he had found objectionable on several accounts. In the first place, it was not considered respectable, though on what grounds he was puzzled to tell. He could well understand how I, an Englishman, and even how one of these Yankee fellows—if it were possible to find one, which might be doubted, with courage enough to say that his soul was his own—might find something objectionable in this business of trading in human muscles and sinews, buying and selling men, women, and children, at auction or otherwise. For himself, he did not pretend to any great piety or morality, he left that to the other members of the firm. McGrab was not actually a Methodist, but his wife and children were devoutly so, and as the old man himself frequently attended their meetings, the Methodists expected to get him, too, at last. Gouge was a very devout Baptist, who had been regularly converted and dipped, and had built a church at Augusta, almost entirely at his own expense; but with all his piety he had never been able to see any harm in the business, buying and selling fellow church members with as little scruple as the mere unconverted heathen. Indeed, Gouge thought slavery and slave-trading a very good thing every way, not only in the concrete, but in the abstract also. Didn't St. Paul say, " Slaves, obey your masters ?" And didn't that settle the question that some were to be slaves, and some were to be masters, and that the slaves had nothing to do but to obey? Such was the way that Gouge reasoned, putting the matter with wonderful force and unction; so much so, that once—when on a visit to New York in search of three or four prime house-servants, who had been purchased in Baltimore, but had broken prison the night after, and whom Gouge had traced to that city—falling into an argument on the subject at the hotel where he was stopping, and having a very grave address and clerical aspect, he had been mistaken by a clergyman, who happened to be present, for a D.D., and had been invited to preach on the divine origin of slavery, in one of the most fashionable churches of that city.

"Still," said Colter, "in spite of the reasoning and the texts of my pious partner, I never have been able to approve either of slavery or the slave trade in the abstract. What, indeed, could be more contemptible, than for a parcel of intelligent and able-bodied white folks to employ their whole time, pains, and ingenuity, in partly forcing, partly teasing, and partly coaxing a set of reluctant, unwilling negroes into half-doing, in the most slovenly, slouchy, deceptive, and unprofitable manner, what those same white people might do fifty times better, and with fifty times less care and trouble, for themselves? Viewed thus in the abstract, the whole system, I must say, seems to me a very pitiful affair. But in what respect the slave traders are less respectable than the slave raisers, or the slave buyers, I am unable to see; and yet it is a fact that Mr. A. B., of Virginia, who only saves himself from emigration and a sheriff's sale by selling every year a half a dozen or so of prime young hands, male and female, for the southern market, pretends to look with a certain contempt on the trader to whom he sells them, while Mr. C. D., of Georgia, who invests all his surplus cash, and all that he can borrow besides, in the purchase of fresh slaves, pretends to look with a similar contempt on the trader of whom he buys them." For some reason or other,—so Mr. Colter humorously remarked,—the old maxim, that the receiver is as bad as the thief, did not seem to hold good of the slave trading business; for what reason, except that it is so much easier to see the mote in a neighbour's eye, than the beam in one's own, he was quite unable to tell.

Then, again, there were things about the trade very unpleasant. To be sure, with the worst part of it he had little to do. The buying up the slaves in the more northern states was principally managed by McGrab. The getting them away from their homes, and the separation of families, was often a troublesome and disagreeable business; at least it would have been to him, though McGrab never complained of it. The principal management of the sales at Augusta had been in the hands of Gouge, who understood, as well as anybody, showing off the stock to the best advantage. Very few persons could out-do him in passing off a consumptive or scrofulous hand as every way sound, or a woman of forty-five for a woman of thirty. His (Colter's) share of the business had chiefly consisted in having charge of the slave pen at Augusta, where the stock was kept to be fatted and put in order for market. Indulgence and plenty were the order of the day at the pen, the object being to keep the people as cheerful, and to put them into as good plight as possible. Yet some scenes would occur there—such as the separation of mothers and children hitherto kept together—rather distressing to a man of sensibility, like himself; so said Colter, laying his hand upon his heart, with a sort of theatrical, mocking air, which made it difficult to tell whether he was in jest or earnest. "To confess the truth," he added, "I always had a foolish susceptibility about me to the tears of women and children, which a little unsuited me for the business. Not being by any means pious, I've tried my hand at several things, first and last, but have had too much respect for the memory of my mother, who instilled into my youthful mind a great veneration for religion, to make any pretensions to that,—I was not able, like my partner Gouge, to shelter myself behind St. Paul and the patriarchs; and my natural, carnal, unconverted heart, as Gouge said, would sometimes betray me into very bad bargains.

"In fact, the first serious quarrel that I had with my partners—and which led to my going out of the concern—grew out of an incident of that sort. McGrab had brought in a superior lot of people from North Carolina, and among them an uncommonly fine young woman, with a nice little boy, just old enough to talk—very light mulattoes; in fact they might have passed for white. The deep melancholy of her great black eyes, and, in spite of a sadness which no smile ever enlivened, the sweet expression of her face, made an impression on my susceptible heart the very first moment that I saw her. I should have desired to retain her as my own, but this I knew was a piece of extravagance to which my partners would never consent, especially as I was already indebted to the firm for two other girls selected from the stock. She had evidently been raised very delicately, the body servant of a lady whose goods had been sold on execution; and McGrab, relaxing into a grim smile, chuckled over her as about the finest piece he had ever purchased—and such a bargain too! He had bought her and her boy for five hundred and fifty dollars, while she alone was worth at least two thousand, and the boy might sell for a hundred more. She understood needlework very well, and would fetch a thousand dollars any day as seamstress or body servant; but at least twice as much, said McGrab—winking with one eye at Gouge,' whose solemn face lighted up into a sort of smile at the anticipation—at least twice as much in the New Orleans market as a fancy article!"

Struggle as I might, it was impossible for me, at these cruel words, to suppress a deep sigh. The keen eye and quick observation of Colter had not failed to perceive that the mention of the young woman and her child from North Carolina had touched me in some tender point, and he seemed to have dwelt with more detail on the incident, as if with design to probe me.

"What is the matter?" he exclaimed, coming to a stop, and looking me full in the face. "You seem to be strangely affected. If you are going to sigh and mourn over every handsome young woman sold as a fancy article in the New Orleans market, you will have a pretty sad time of it."

It was only by the greatest effort that I controlled my voice, to inquire if he remembered the young woman's name.

"O, yes," he replied; it was some time ago,—twenty years, I dare say; but names and faces I very seldom forget. The girl, I think, was called 'Cassy.'"

At the sound of that dear name my heart beat violently; but supporting myself against a tree under which we stood, "Can you recollect," I asked, "the name of the child?"

"Let us see," said my companion, reflecting for a moment. "O, yes, I have it. I think she called the child 'Montgomery.'"

That was the name we had given to our boy, out of compliment to Cassy's kind mistress; and I no longer doubted that it was of my wife and my child that he spoke.

O

CHAPTER LI.

MASTERING my emotion as well as I could, I begged Colter to go on with his story. But this he was in no hurry to do.

"You seem," he said, eyeing me closely, "to have some more than ordinary interest in this affair. You mentioned, I recollect, this not being your first visit to America, but that you had formerly travelled here, some twenty years ago. Twenty years ago you must have been a young man, and young men are easily captivated; and you young Englishmen, when you get among us, notwithstanding all we hear about English virtue and decorum, are no more anchorites than the rest of us. But even the chaste Joseph, or Scipio, or the Pope of Rome himself, might readily be pardoned for melting a little before such attractions. There is a soft, winning, captivating way about some of those girls that makes them perfectly irresistible. I don't wonder at the envy, rage, and jealousy of our white women; they can't help being conscious of their own inferiority in these respects. Of course, it makes them cross and fractious,—natural enough; but that does not help the matter, nor render them any the more agreeable. So they have to be content with being mistresses of the house and the servants, while some slave girl, black, yellow, or white, as the case may be, is mistress of their husbands' affections.

"There are a good many of these girls whom it is quite enough to spoil the temper of the best-natured woman in the world to have in the house with them.

"As to this Cassy, in whom you seem to take such a particular interest, she would do credit to anybody's choice. I say this as both connoisseur and amateur in these matters, and indeed professionally, as a dealer in the article,—in all which respects I reckon my opinion to be worth something. The boy was a fine boy, too. I wonder who his father was! Fact," said he, looking me full in the face, with a comical sort of an air, "I shouldn't be surprised if there was some resemblance!"

Perceiving, however, that his attempted jocularity did not suit the temper of my mind, and his keen glance detecting, probably, the tear that stood in my eye, he modified his tone a little.

"They do, sometimes, get a tight hold of our hearts. It is all very well for us to lord it over the men, as if they were brutes, monkeys, inferior animals; but the women are very often too much for us. Why, I have known, before now, the most fierce, brutal, savage fellow, who feared neither God nor man, made a complete baby of—as manageable as a tame bear who dances to order—by some little black or yellow girl of fifteen or twenty, who has thus contrived to play the Queen Esther on the plantation, and to stand often between the fury of her lord and master and the backs of her dingy kindred. This is one of its alleviations not much dwelt upon by those who undertake to apologise for slavery, but which, perhaps, does more than everything else put together to infuse a certain modicum of kindly feeling into the relation of master and slave. That is the way that nature takes to bring both master and slave to their natural equality. Cupid, with his bow and arrows, is the sworn enemy of all castes and patrician distinctions.

"Pray, sir, did you ever read *Edwards's History of the West Indies?*"

"Yes, I have."

"Then, perhaps, you recollect an ode inserted in it, addressed to the Sable Venus. Edwards, you know, was a Jamaica planter, a grave historian, an advocate of the slave trade, perfectly orthodox on that whole subject, but a man of sense and observation, experience and sensibility, who had both seen and felt too much to undertake to found an argument for slavery, such as we hear now-a-days, on the pretended antipathy between the races, and who, in wishing to give a correct view of the state of things in the West Indies, thought it best to assume the disguise of verse and allegory. Happening to meet with the book, lately, at Charleston, the ode quite struck my fancy, and, by way of joke, I wrote off several copies, and sent them to a number of our leading southern statesmen at Washington. I dare say I can repeat it, preserving the ideas at least, if not always the words, and changing, as I did in my copies, the scene from Jamaica, where Edwards lays it, to this meridian, which it suits just about as well."

So saying, he repeated, with a sort of mock earnestness suited to their tone, the following stanzas, of which he afterwards gave me a copy:—

THE SABLE VENUS.

AN ODE.

Come to my bosom, genial fire,
Soft sounds and lively thoughts inspire;
　　Unusual is my theme;
Not such dissolving Ovid sung,
Nor melting Sappho's glowing tongue—
　　More dainty mine I deem.

Sweet is the beam of morning bright,
Yet sweet the sober shade of night,
　　From rich Angola's shores;
While beauty, clad in sable dye,
Enchanting fires the wondering eye,
　　Farewell, ye Paphian bowers!

O, sable queen! thy wild domain
I seek, and court thy gentle reign,
　　So soothing, soft, and sweet;
Where melting love, sincere delight,
Fond pleasure ready joys invite,
　　And unpriced raptures meet.

O 2

The prating French, the Spaniard proud,
The double Scot, Hibernian loud,
  And sullen English own
The pleasing softness of thy sway,
And here transferred allegiance pay,
  For gracious is thy throne.

From east to west, o'er either Ind,
Thy sceptre sways : thy power, we find,
  Beyond the tropics felt;
The blazing sun, that gilds the zone,
Waits but the triumphs of thy throne,
  Quite round the burning belt.

When thou, America to view,
That vast domain, thy conquest new,
  First left thy native shore,
Bright was the morn and soft the breeze ;
With wanton joy the curling seas
  The beauteous burden bore.

Thy skin excelled the raven's plume,
Thy breath the fragrant orange bloom,
  Thy eye the tropic's beam ;
Soft was thy lip as silken down,
And mild thy look as evening sun,
  That gilds the mountain stream.

The loveliest limbs thy form compose,
Such as thy sister-Venus chose
  In Florence, where she's seen :
Both just alike, except the white—
No difference at all at night
  The beauteous dames between.

O, when thy ship had touched the strand,
What raptures seized the ravished land !
  From every side they came ;
Each mountain, valley, plain, and grove,
Haste eagerly to show their love ;
  Right welcome was the dame.

Virginia's shouts were heard aloud,
Gay Carolina sent a crowd,
  Grave Georgia not a few ;
No rabble rout. I heard it said
Some great ones joined the cavalcade;
  The muse will not say who.

Gay goddess of the sable band,
Propitious still this grateful land
  With thy sweet presence bless :
Here fix secure thy constant throne ;
We all adore, and thee alone,
  The queen of love confess.

For me, if I no longer pay
Allegiance to thy sister's sway,
  I act no fickle part:
It were ingratitude to slight
Superior kindness. I delight
  To feel a grateful heart.

Then, playful goddess, cease to change,
Nor in new beauties vainly range;
    For whatso'er thy hue,
Try every form thou canst put on,
I'll follow thee through every one;
    So staunch I am, so true.

Do thou in gentle Phibia smile,
In artful Beneba beguile,
    In wanton Mimba pout,
In sprightly Cuba's eyes look gay,
Or grave in sober Quashaba,
    I still should find thee out.

"There," said he, repeating the last stanza, and giving to it all the benefit of a very graceful elocution, "that's a chorus equal to anything in Tom Moore, in which three quarters of our young men, and a good many of the old ones, too, for that matter, might join, and yet half of them, perhaps just fresh from love-making to some sable inamorata, will talk to you about the antipathy of the races, and just as likely as not, wind up with a discourse on the horrors of amalgamation! What a world of cant, humbug, and hypocrisy, we do live in!"

As I remained silent, he still went on,—"Supposing, though, this Cassy to have been a sweetheart of yours,—and I can't conceive why else you show so much interest in her,—still I can hardly set you down as a votary of the sable Venus. She rather belonged to the white race; but, you know, here at the south, we reckon all slaves as 'niggers,' whatever their colour. Just catch a stray Irish or German girl, and sell her, —a thing sometimes done,—and she turns a nigger at once, and makes just as good a slave as if there were African blood in her veins."

"If," I said, commanding myself as well as I could, "you really suppose I have any such interest as you speak of in the girl and her child, you might as well leave off this fooling, and tell me what became of them. We will, if you please, discuss these matters of antipathies, and amalgamation and the sable Venus, which you seem so fond of, at some other more convenient opportunity."

"Well," said he, "so far as I personally am concerned, I stand quite clear. If I had actually foreseen that, twenty years after, I was to be hauled over the coals by yourself in person,—and, having been watching your eye for the last half hour, I judge you to be one I should not care about quarrelling with,—I could not, on the whole, have done better by the girl than I did.

"Should I say that I made no amorous advances to her, you would scarcely believe me. I did; but she replied with such a mere agony of tears and entreaty, as quite extinguished all my passion, and converted it into pity.

"I soon found that her most immediate and pressing source of suffering was the apprehension lest she might be separated from her boy, and, indeed, there was some occasion for it. A New Orleans trader, with whom we had often dealt, had evinced a great disposition to buy her. After a careful examination of her person, taking more liberties than I shall care to mention to you, he pronounced her a prime wench, a first-rate article, A number one, extremely well adapted to the New Orleans market, and he offered to pay two thousand dollars for her, cash, which Gouge agreed to take, provided he would give an additional hundred dollars for the boy. But the trader did not want the boy, who would only be a drawback upon the value of the woman when he came to sell her: at least, so he pretended, and he insisted that the boy ought to be thrown into the bargain. A lady of Augusta, in search of a small boy to bring up as body servant to her infant son, offered to give seventy-five dollars for him. The chance seemed to be that the boy would be sold to the Augusta woman, and the mother to the New Orleans trader. Aware of this, in the greatest distress she appealed to me to save her from this separation. It so happened that during Gouge's absence at a sheriff's sale some ten miles in the country, where he thought some bargains might be picked up, a lady and gentleman called at the pen in search of a female attendant for the lady. The gentleman was a Mississippi planter, resident somewhere in the neighbourhood of Vicksburg, returning home with his new wife, whom he had lately married at the north. I pointed out this Cassy to their notice, and she besieged them with pressing entreaties, making the little boy kneel, and put his tiny hands together, and pray first the lady, and then the gentleman, to buy him and his mother, and not to let the New Orleans trader take his mother away from him.

"The lady, after due inquiries of Cassy as to her accomplishments and capabilities, declared her to be just the person she wanted. She had been bred up at the north, did not like niggers, and could not bear to have a black wench about her; whereas this one, she said, was as nice and as white almost as a New England girl, and the boy might soon be taught to clean the knives, wait at table, and make himself otherwise useful.

"I offered to take, for the two, two thousand and fifty dollars; a price which the husband thought enormous. He could buy three first-rate field hands for that. Somebody that was not quite so young and good-looking would answer his wife's purpose just as well, and might perhaps, too, be a safer bargain all round—an intimation clear enough to me, but which the wife did not seem to understand. She still insisted upon buying Cassy; and being yet in the honeymoon, she carried the day; and the bill of sale was signed, the money paid, and the mother and child delivered to their new owners, just as Gouge rode up to the pen.

"When the hard-hearted old rascal found out that I had sold the mother and child together for twenty-five dollars less than he could have got by selling them separately, you can't imagine what a fuss he made. This pious Baptist church member, who had been mistaken in New York, as I have told you, for a doctor of divinity, thrown quite off his balance, cursed and swore like a pirate. If I had fairly given them away he would not have been more abusive. I should have thought that for the moment at least he had fallen from grace, only that was no part of his creed. He was no Methodist; he and McGrab used to have some warm disputes sometimes on that head. McGrab thought that even the best man might sometimes fall away; but Gouge insisted very positively upon the perseverance of the saints, of whom he did not doubt himself to be one.

"I dwelt upon the hardship of separating the mother and her child, and told Gouge he ought to be satisfied, as we made a handsome profit on the transaction as it was. I had ascertained—so I told him—that the woman was pious, and that, apart from her dread of being separated from her child, she had a great horror of being sold for the New Orleans market; and I insisted, that as a matter of religion and conscience it was better to dispose of her, as I had done, to a private family, and most probably a kind mistress, than to sell her to the New Orleans slave-trader. Here I thought I had my pious partner at advantage, and I followed it up by quoting the text, 'Thou shalt not oppress the widow and the fatherless.' Though I was not so well read in the Scriptures as Gouge, it came into my mind as quite to the purpose. But highly indignant that such a graceless fellow as I, who belonged to no church, and made no pretensions to have any religion, should presume to dictate to him on that subject, Gouge turned upon me with a perfect fury. The text, he said, did not apply. He had once had a long talk on that very subject with Parson Softwords. As slaves could not be married, there could be—so the parson thought—no widows among them; and as to the children, not being born in lawful wedlock, they could not become fatherless —for they had no fathers—being in the eye of the law, as he had heard the learned Judge Hallett observe from the bench, the children of nobody. As to pious niggers, that was all moonshine; he did not believe in any such thing. He belonged, in fact, to 'a pretty numerous sect in these parts, called Anti-mission Baptists, or Hard Shells, who don't think the Lord ever intended the heathen to be converted, or negroes to be anything but slaves, or anybody to be saved except their own precious selves, and that entirely by faith and grace, wholly independent of works. As to the girl's making such a fuss about parting from her child, that, Gouge said, was a piece of great nonsense. Wasn't she young enough to have a dozen more?

"The upshot of the matter was, what with Gouge's brutality and purse-proud insolence, and my hot temper, which I had not then learned so well how to command, that we soon got into a violent quarrel, which ended in my giving him a caning on the spot, and of course in the breaking up of the partnership.

"I was, indeed, quite too soft for that business. As to the men, I should have done well enough with them; but the women, old and young, were always getting up such scenes, and were always so full of complaints about being separated from their daughters, and their mothers, and their babies, and their husbands, that to a man who had the least of a tender spot in his heart it was perfectly intolerable.

"Thus ousted from the slave-trading business, it became necessary for me to find some other occupation; but that was not so easy. The occupations that a southern gentleman can adopt without degradation are very few indeed. My manners, address, the good songs I could sing, and good stories I could tell, had made me rather a favourite in society; and as I never drank, and understood a thing or two about cards and dice, billiards and faro tables, I was able to replenish my pockets in that way; and finally, for want of a better, that became my regular profession."

"And," said I, wishing to pay him off a little for his late tantalisings, "is this one of those few occupations which a southern gentleman can adopt without degradation?"

"The gentility of gambling can't be denied," he said, "since it is very freely practised by the larger part of southern gentlemen. Once in a while the legislatures are seized with a fit of penitence or virtue, and pass laws to break it up: but nobody ever thinks of paying any attention to those laws, or attempting to enforce them, except, now and then, some poor plucked pigeon, who undertakes to revenge himself in that way. But though gambling is just as genteel as slave-holding, somehow or other, by an inconsistency like that in the case of the slave-traders, we who make a profession of it, though we associate constantly with gentlemen, are not, I must confess, reckoned to belong precisely to that class, except, indeed, we get money enough to buy a plantation and retire."

"It is charged," said I, "upon those of your profession, that, not content with the fair chances of the game, you contrive to take undue advantages."

"Yes; and so do half of the gentlemen players, as far as they know how, and have the opportunity. There is always a tendency, in games of chance, to run a little into games of skill. Suppose we do plunder the planters—don't they live by plundering the negroes? What right have they to complain? Isn't sauce for the goose sauce for the gander? I tell you, our whole system here is a system of plunder from beginning to end. 'Tis only the slaves, and some of the poor whites who own no slaves, who can be said to earn an honest living. The planters live on the plunder of the slaves, whom they force to labour for them. The slaves steal all they can from the planters, and a good many of the poor whites connive at and help them in it. A parcel of blood-sucking Yankee pedlers and New York agents overrun our country, and carry off their share of the spoils; and we who have cool heads and dexterous hands enough to overreach the whole set—planters, Yankees, and New Yorkers—we stand, for aught I see, upon just as sound a moral basis as the rest of them. Everything belongs to the strong, the wise, and the cunning; that is the foundation-stone of our southern system of society. The living upon the plunder of others is one of the organic sins of this community; and the doctrine, I believe, has been advanced by a celebrated northern divine, that for the organic sins of a community, nobody is individually responsible. Now, if this good-natured sort of doctrine, which, for my part, I don't find any fault with, is going to save the souls and the characters of Gouge and McGrab, or of the planters who patronise and support them, shan't we professional gentlemen also have the benefit of it?"

CHAPTER LII.

IT was not very difficult to discover under the volubility and vivacity, a little forced, of this philosophical blackleg, into whose intimacy I had been so suddenly introduced, a deep-seated and bitter chagrin, and even shame, at living as he did; however he might urge, by way of apology, that it was only one of the applications of the fundamental principle of every slave-holding community. This, indeed, was an idea upon which he seemed to pride himself, and upon which he dwelt with a good deal of pertinacious ingenuity. To gain a living by the plunder of the weak and simple was, he admitted, in the abstract, not to be defended. Yet, if he did not do it, somebody else would. His abstinence would not save them. The weak and simple were destined to be plundered; and plundered they would be by somebody. Bred up as he had been to extravagant habits, could he be expected to renounce an employment—

liable indeed to some fluctuations and uncertainties, as well as to some moral objections, but, on the whole, one that paid—and to run the risk of starving, just to gratify his conscientious scruples? He trusted, he said, that, though a professional gambler, he had a conscience. His quarrel with Gouge and McGrab, and his abandonment of the slave-trading business, at which he might have made a fortune, was, he thought, evidence enough of that. But there was a limit to all things. A man must live, and live by such means, too, as his position and gifts allow him to adopt; and, all things considered, he did not see that he could be expected to give up his profession any more than the slave-holders their slaves. Nor can I say that I did, either.

On the whole, besides the necessity I was under of using him, and the additional information he might give me in the search in which I was engaged, there was something in his straightforward, downright way of looking at things, as well as in his lively conversation and agreeable manners, which rather pleased me.

I therefore proceeded to make a return of his confidence, at which he seemed to be a good deal flattered. Complimenting his sagacity, I admitted my intimacy with a female slave, many years ago, whom, from his description of her, and the circumstances he had mentioned, I believed to be the very one whom McGrab had purchased in North Carolina, and whom he had sold to the Mississippi planter; and I added, that I believed her boy to be my child. What was the name of the planter, and could he aid me any further in finding them out?

"And suppose you find them," he asked, "what do you intend to do?"

"Buy them," I answered, "if I can, and set them free."

"Better think twice," he replied, "before you set out on any such adventure. Time, you know, makes changes. You can't expect to get back the young girl you left in North Carolina. O, the deceitful baggage! Didn't she tell me, with tears streaming down those great black eyes of hers, and such an air of truth that I couldn't help believing her, that she had a husband, the only man she had ever known anything about, who was the father of her child, and who had been carried off by the slave-traders a year or two before, and whom she expected yet to meet, by some good providence, somewhere in the south! Don't flatter yourself with the idea of any constancy to you. Even had she wished it, it could hardly have been in her power. Like as not you will find her, if at all, grown as plump as a beer-barrel, housekeeper, and something else besides, to her master; or may be, by this time, cook or washerwoman, and the mother, as Gouge said she might be, of a dozen additional children, and perhaps with an agreeable variety of complexions; though, for that matter, slave-women of her colour are in general mighty squeamish and particular—quite as much so as the white women—as to any connection with men of a darker hue than themselves."

Painful to me as these suggestions were, I could not but admit their high degree of probability. To what might not twenty years of servitude have reduced the wife of my heart! To what humiliations, dishonours, miserable degradations, corrupting connections, might she not have been subjected, tempting as she was by her innocence, beauty, and gentleness, and exposed, without the least shield of law, religion, or public opinion, to the unbridled appetite, I do not say of any lecherous debauchee, but of any polygamous patriarch, amorous youth, or luxurious respectability who might have the fancy or the means to purchase her!

It made my heart grow sick and my brain spin to think of it.

"And then the boy," continued my tormenter. "If you had him as I saw him; a bright little fellow, just able to speak, full of life and joy, and unable to understand what made his mother cry so, you might hope to make something of him. He was a child such as nobody need be ashamed of. But what do you suppose he is by this time, with the benefit of a slave education? If, my dear sir, you intended to act the father by him, or the friend by her, you should not have left them all this time in slavery."

I hastened to explain, in general terms, that my leaving them as they were was, at the time of my separation from them, a thing entirely beyond my control; it was not in my power to do otherwise; but that, so soon as I became possessed of the means, I had made every effort to discover and to purchase them; that I had traced them to Augusta, where all clue to them had been lost; but that the clue which he had so unexpectedly and accidentally put into my hands, had recalled all the past, and, as I was unmarried, childless, and with nothing else in particular to occupy my thoughts, had inspired me with fresh desire to find them out, and, if possible, to make them free.

"Quite a romantic fellow, I see," rejoined my companion; "quite another Dick Johnson. True enough, the idea is not very agreeable of of having one's children kicked, cuffed, and lashed through the world at the discretion of brutal overseers, peevish mistresses, or drunken, cross-grained masters, with no possible opening to rise if they would, and with no chance before them but to propagate a race of slaves. I dare say it seems so to you, with your English education, and especially as you have not any lawful children for your affections to fix upon. But here we don't mind it. A man is expected to sacrifice his own private paternal feelings, if he has any, for the good of the class to which he belongs. I dare say, in the course of time, the only representatives of many of our most distinguished southern statesmen and wealthiest families will be found among their slave descendants.

"Take my advice, and give over a ridiculous, Quixotic expedition. However, if you will persist in it, I will help you what little I can. The Mississippi planter, to whom the girl and her child were sold, was named Thomas. I have seen him several times since in my travels. Indeed, some handsome sums of money have before now passed from his pocket to mine. He still lives, or did lately, at no great distance from Vicksburg. I have friends in that town to whom I will give you letters, and by whose assistance you can find him out. Perhaps your girl and her boy are still living in his family. But have a care that you don't catch a Tartar."

CHAPTER LIII.

LEAVING my new acquaintance behind at Augusta, where, as he said, he had business to attend to, and provided with the letters which he had promised me, I set out for Vicksburg.

Great was my joy at once more getting on the track of the lost ones; yet I could not but be harassed with many distressing doubts and uncertainties as to what, even if I found them, might be the results of my search.

The first part of my journey from Augusta led me through a district worn out and partially abandoned; a fac simile,—and from the same causes,—of what I had seen so much of in Virginia and the Carolinas. Crossing the Oconee, and presently the Oakmulgee, I reached a new country, of which the earliest settlements did not date back more than twenty years; but which already presented, here and there, specimens of the destructive agricultural system of the south, in gullied fields, especially on the hill sides, from which the soil had been completely washed away, over which still stood erect the blackened trunks of the tenants of the original forest, killed by the process of girdling, but which, though dead and blasted, remained yet firmly rooted in the soil, sternly smiling, as it were, over the scene of destruction; the virgin soil, at first so fertile, having been washed into the neighbouring hollows, and leaving exposed nothing but a barren surface of red and arid clay. Can there be a more striking symbol than one of these abandoned fields,—the dead, giant trunks still towering over it, as if by way of memento of what it once was,—of the natural effects of the plundering system upon which the whole organization of the slave-holding states is based, and which extends even to the land itself, rifled of its virgin strength by a shiftless system of ignorant haste to be rich,—and then abandoned to hopeless sterility?

Having crossed the Flint, I entered then upon the primitive forests, the hunting-grounds of the Creeks, but from which the insatiable cupidity of the greedy Georgians, backed by the power of the federal government, was already preparing forcibly to expel them,—a thing soon after effected,—in order to replace the wild, free tenants of the forest by gangs of miserable slaves purchased up and transferred from the worn-out fields of Virginia and the Carolinas.

Upon presently reaching the banks of the Alabama, I emerged from these soon-to-be-violated solitudes, and thence to the banks of the Mississippi, traversed a country which the Indians had been already compelled to resign, and which was rapidly filling up with a most miscellaneous population from the more northern slave states; scions of the "first families" of Virginia, with such numbers of slaves as by some hocus-pocus they could save from the grasp of their creditors, coming to refound their fortunes in this new country; gangs of slaves sent out under overseers by the wealthier slaveholders of the old states, to open new plantations, where their labour might be more productive; Georgia "Crackers," with their pale, tallow-coloured visages; with other wretched specimens of white poverty, ignorance, and degradation, coming from North Carolina, squatters on these new lands; Yankee traders, and doctors, and lawyers, quacks, and pettifoggers, with land speculators, slave-traders, gamblers, horse thieves, and all kinds of adventurers, including a reasonable mixture of Baptist and Methodist preachers,—all, except the preachers, and not all of them, with but one idea in their heads, the growing rich suddenly; and with but two words in their mouths, namely, "niggers" and cotton.

It was, indeed, in these new settlements, had one leisure and curiosity for the purpose, that the slave-holding system of the United States might be seen operating unrestrained, and exhibiting its true character and richest development. All the old slave states had been originally planted as free communities on the British model, slavery having been superinduced thereupon as an excrescence or accessory; and, by tradition and habit, there still remain in those states,—though fast dying out, under the influence of the slave-breeding business,—some good old wholesome English ideas. But the states of Alabama and Mississippi have been thoroughly slave states from the beginning, filled up by a colluvium of immigrants from the older slave states, mostly young men who, in leaving their homes, would seem to have left behind them, as mere prejudices, every principle of humanity, justice, or moderation, ready, like so many ferocious sharks, to devour everything and everybody, and even each other. Nowhere[1] in any part of the globe calling itself civilized, I doubt very much if anywhere, at any time, have ferocious enormities, and cold-blooded murders, with pistols, rifles, and bowie-knives, been so much a matter of every-day occurrence. Nowhere, between Lynch law committees on the one hand, and private murderers on the other, has life been so utterly insecure. As to the security of property, let the New York merchants who have traded to those states, let the English holders of Mississippi bonds, answer. Not that the holders of those bonds deserve any commiseration. Those securities were created,—and the purchasers of them knew it, or ought to have known it,—to raise funds with which to enable the Mississippi planters to increase their stock of slaves; and it is but a righteous retribution, that Englishmen who lent their money for so nefarious a purpose should be cheated out of every penny of it.

In the older slave states, the slaves living often on plantations on which they were born, and the connection between them and their owners being frequently hereditary, they cannot but establish certain ties of sympathy with those owners more or less strong, and customs of indulgence, and especially family relations among themselves, which have a partial operation to alleviate their condition. But in the migration southward, accomplished to a great extent through the agency of slave-traders, all these ties and connections are broken up; all the horrors of the African slave-trade are renewed; all the rudiments of ideas previously existing in Maryland and Virginia, and North Carolina, Kentucky, and Tennessee, that the negroes, after all, though they be slaves, are still men, and as such entitled to a certain degree of human sympathy and regard, and even to be looked upon as capable of improvement, of religious instruction, and perhaps, sometime or other, of liberty; these shoots of the sentiment of humanity, which, though tender, and, as it were, scarcely daring to show themselves, and nipped, of late, by disastrous frosts, yet give promise and hope of a rich future harvest,—all these germs of consolation, in the transfer of the wretched slaves to the states of which I now speak, are assiduously plucked up as pernicious weeds in the nettle-bed of slavery. Every better sentiment, every voice of sympathy, is carefully extinguished, the idea being sedulously inculcated by courts, and legislatures, and politicians, and newspapers, and by at least half or more of those who call themselves ministers of the Gospel, that the negroes are in nature, what they are treated as being—mere merchandise, mere property, mere animals, intended to be used like horses and oxen, in making cotton, and like horses and oxen, to be kept for ever under the yoke, the bridle, the goad, and the whip, never fit for or capable of being anything but slaves.

The old English idea that liberty is to be favoured,—that idea which abolished slavery in Europe, and which once had considerable influence on the courts and legislatures of the more northern slave states,—has, in these new hotbeds of cotton and despotism, been totally extinguished. Once a slave, a slave for ever,—black father or white father, whatever the complexion,—beyond the possibility even that the slave-owning parent shall be able to emancipate his own children. Such is the diabolical doctrine of despotism, announced by Chief Justice Sharkey,—and never was judge more significantly named,—from the bench of the Supreme Court of Mississippi. And already this doctrine begins to find many advocates among the inhabitants of the new slave-breeding Guinea, into which Virginia and Maryland have degenerated; nor, when the pinch comes, will there be wanting northern merchants eager to please their southern customers; northern politicians, for the prospect of office, ready to worship Satan himself; northern editors, who publish papers for circulation at the south; northern doctors of divinity, ready to yield up, if not their own mothers,—for though he might say it in the heat of the moment, not even the famous Dr. Dewey is quite brave enough to stick to that,—yet, at all events, ready to surrender their own brothers into servitude, to keep the slaveholders quiet and good-natured : plenty of such supple tools will not be wanting to preach, throughout the pretended free states, subscription to the perpetuity of servitude as the corner-stone of the American Union !

Let those who would trace the onward march of American slavery, since the time of Washington and Jefferson, call to mind the difference between the principles avowed by them and those set up at the present day by the Mississippi Sharkeys and Virginia slave-breeders for the market, who nominate the presidents, dictate the legislation, make tools of the politicians, and aspire, not unsuccessfully, to control the moral and religious sentiment of America !

CHAPTER LIV.

As I entered the town of Vicksburg, an appalling prospect met my eyes: five men hanging by the neck, just swung off, as it would seem, from an extempore gallows, and struggling in the agonies of death; a military company drawn up in arms; a band of black musicians playing "Yankee Doodle;" a crowd of by-standers, of all ages and colours, apparently in the greatest state of excitement; and a frantic woman, with a young child in either hand, addressing herself, with vehement gesticulations, to a man who seemed to have the direction of the proceedings, and whom I took—though I did not perceive that he wore any official dress or badge—to be the high sheriff of the county.

On reaching the hotel, I learnt, however, to my great astonishment, that this was no regular execution by process of law, but entirely an amateur performance, got up by a committee of citizens, headed by the cashier of the Planters' Bank,—one of those institutions whose bonds are not unknown in England, though I believe they bear no particular price at the present moment,—the very person, in fact, whom, from the office he had assumed, I had supposed to be the high sheriff. I learnt all this with astonishment, because the victims had appeared to be white men. Had they been black or coloured, their being hung in some paroxysm of popular passion or fear would not in the least have surprised me.

Inquiring a little further into the history of this singular proceeding, I was told that the men who had been hung were gamblers, part of a gang of cheats and desperadoes by whom that town had long been infested; that the citizens, determined to tolerate such a nuisance no longer, had ordered them to depart, and, when they refused to do so, had proceeded to force their houses and destroy their gambling tools,—an operation which the gamblers resisted by force, firing upon their assailants, and having actually shot dead a leading and very estimable citizen, in the act of forcing his way into one of the houses.

The gamblers, however, had all been taken, except two or three, who had managed to escape. The blood of the company was up. The sight of their slaughtered leader, copious draughts of brandy, the recollection of their own losses at the gaming-table, and the dread of being challenged and shot, or shot without being challenged by the gamblers, two or three of whom were known as very desperate fellows,—all these motives co-operating, and it being very doubtful whether, if the matter was referred to the legal tribunals, those who had riotously broken into the houses of other people, even with the professed object of destroying roulette-tables, might not run quite as much risk of condemnation as those who had fired, even with fatal effect, upon their burglarious assailants. All these things considered, it had finally been determined, as the shortest and most expedient method of settling the business, to take the gamblers to the skirts of the town, and to hang them there on the instant.

To those, indeed, accustomed to the curt proceedings of the slave code, under which suspicion serves for evidence, and power usurps the place of judicial discrimination, all the delays and formalities of the ordinary administration of penal jurisprudence must seem tedious and absurd; and hence the constantly increasing tendency in the south to substitute, in the place of that administration, in the case of white men as well as of slaves, the summary process of Lynch law. It is vain, indeed, to expect that men constantly hardened and brutalized in the struggle to extort from their slaves the utmost driblet of unwilling labour, and accustomed freely to indulge, as against these unresisting victims, every caprice of brutal fury, should retain any very delicate sense of the proprieties of justice as among themselves.

Before I had yet learnt more than a general outline of the story, the principal actors in this affair, finding it necessary to sustain their dignity and to recruit their self-reliance by fresh draughts of brandy, reached the hotel at which I was stopping. They were followed by the woman, with the two little children, whom I had noticed as I passed the place of execution, and whom I now found to be the wife of one of the victims. It was in vain that she besought permission to take down and to bury the body of her husband. This was denied, with brutal threats that any person who dared to cut them down till they had hung there twenty-four hours, by way of example, should be made to share their fate. Such, indeed, was the passionate fury of the multitude, that the poor woman, in alarm for her own life, fled to the river bank, and, placing her two children in a skiff, entered herself, and pushed off, thinking this a safer course than to remain longer at Vicksburg.

After the tumult had subsided a little, I showed the bar-keeper the direction of the letter of introduction I had brought, and inquired if he knew such a person.

No sooner had he read the name than his face assumed an expression of horror and alarm. "Do you know that person?" he eagerly inquired.

I told him I did not. This was my first visit to this part of the country. The letter had been given me by a gentleman whom I had met at Augusta.

"Pray don't mention the name," he replied; "say nothing of it to anybody. This letter is addressed to one of the persons whom you saw hung as you came into the town. He kept a roulette table, no doubt, and understood a thing or two; but was a generous-hearted soul for all that; and every way quite as much a gentleman as half those concerned in hanging him. Should you mention his name, you might yourself be seized as one of the gang, and hung with the rest."

Congratulating myself on this lucky escape, I then ventured to inquire of the bar-keeper if he knew a planter in that vicinity of the name of Thomas.

There had been, he told me, a planter of that name,—and from the account he gave of him, I was satisfied it was the one of whom I was in search,—who lived formerly a few miles off; but within two or three years past he had moved to a distance of some fifty miles, in Madison county, up the Big Black.

The friendly bar-keeper aided me the next day in procuring a horse, and I set out for Madison county, again passing, as I left the town, the five murdered gamblers still swinging from the gallows.

Proceeding up the Big Black, I presently found that the spirit of extempore hanging was by no means confined to Vicksburg, but raged as a sort of epidemic in all that part of the state of Mississippi.

The counties of Hinds and Madison were excited to a pitch of terror bordering on madness, by the rumour of a slave insurrection. Some overseers, lurking among the negro cabins, had obtained some hint of a conspiracy; and two white steam-doctors from Tennessee, through the instigation of two or three of the regular craft,—who regarded these "steamers," with no little jealousy and indignation, and who insisted that they were nothing but horse thieves in disguise,—had been arrested, along with two or three negroes, as concerned in the plot.

A vigilance committee and volunteer courts had been speedily organized, and the black and white prisoners condemned to death. Brought out to be hanged, they had been urged to confess, which they had done very extensively, in the hope, probably, of saving their lives; and from their confessions, dressed up by the lively imagination of the court and the bystanders, the plot, whether real or imaginary, had been made to assume a most alarming shape.

According to these confessions, it was not a mere negro or servile plot, but had been got up by a gang of white desperadoes, negro thieves, horse thieves, gamblers, and other ingenious gentlemen who lived by their wits, to whom were ascribed ideas as to the rights of the cunningest and the strongest—precisely those to be expected in a slave-holding community. They were to put themselves at the head of the insurgent negroes, were to rob the banks, and thus, like so many Catalines, to make themselves masters of the country.

Unable to reach my destination the first day, I sought hospitality for the night at the house of a planter, one of the most respectable men, as I was afterwards told, in all that vicinity, but who, instead of putting himself forward, as was expected of him, to take the lead in unravelling the plot and punishing its authors, had chosen to remain quietly at home.

He had great doubts, I found, whether there was, in fact, any plot, and whether the whole thing was not a chimera of the imagination. Alarms of negro plots, founded on alleged overheard conversations, and throwing everybody, especially the women and children, into the most horrible panics, were as much epidemics, he told me, all through the south, as the autumn bilious fevers. He was too much accustomed to those alarms, which had always, so far as he knew, ended in smoke, or the hanging of a few negroes on suspicion, to pay much attention to them. Yet he admitted that the increasing number, at the south, of desperate and uneasy white men, without property or the means to acquire any, might be likely, as the present resource failed of helping one's self to a plantation by squatting on Government lands, to lead hereafter to frightful commotions.

We were quietly discussing this subject over a cup of tea, when two or three truculent-looking white men rode up to the house; and one of them, dismounting, handed a dirty and rumpled piece of paper to my host.

As he read it, his brows began to lower. It was, in fact, a summons or requisition from the committee of vigilance for his speedy personal appearance before them, bringing with him, also, the stranger—meaning me—who had been traced to his house.

Upon his inquiring of the bearer what the committee of vigilance wanted of him, the answer was, that his not taking any part in the proceedings had been thought very strange, and that some of the confessing prisoners had stated something by which he was implicated.

To all this he coolly replied, that he was ready to answer for his conduct before any regular court, but he did not recognise the authority of the committee of vigilance. "As to this gentleman, my guest," he continued, "I am a justice of the peace, and if you will bring proof against him of any violation of the laws, I will issue a warrant for his arrest; but, except on some lawful warrant, I shall not suffer him to be taken from my house."

The only ground of suspicion against me seemed to be, that I was a stranger, who ought not to be allowed to traverse the country, in its present state of alarm, without giving an account of myself. But as my host did not think this a sufficient ground for the issue of a warrant, the messengers of the vigilance committee shortly departed; not without furious threats of returning soon with men enough to take us both by force, and pretty plain intimations that after this resistance to the authority of the committee, which could be looked upon in no other light than as plain proof of our concern in the plot, we could reasonably expect nothing short of hanging. Six white men and eighteen negroes, they added, had been hung already, and many more had been arrested.

No sooner had these fellows gone, than I turned to my host to thank him for his protection; but almost before replying to me, he ordered two horses to be saddled. "I wish I could protect you," he added: "but though I mean to stand a siege myself, and shall rely, if compelled to surrender, upon my numerous friends and connections to shield me, it would not be safe for you to remain.

"Your horse is hardly fit for a new start; but I will give you a fresh one, and will send yours back to Vicksburg. You shall have my negro man Sambo for a guide. He knows the country well, and, if anybody can, will carry you safe to the banks of the Mississippi, for which you had better make by the shortest cut. Steamboats are passing continually up and down. Get on board the first that comes along, and forego your travels in these parts for the present."

No sooner said than done. In fifteen minutes I was again on the road; and travelling all night, under the skilful guidance of Sambo, following unfrequented paths, swimming creeks and rivers, and fording swamps, by morning we reached a lonely wood-yard on the banks of the river, where the steamers were accustomed to stop for fuel. Before long, a boat bound to New Orleans made its appearance, and, upon a signal for that purpose, she checked her course for the moment, and sent a skiff to take me on board.

A few days after arriving in New Orleans, I read in the newspapers how the house of Mr. Hooper—for that was the name of my generous host—had been attacked; how he had barricaded his doors and windows; had wrapped his infant child in a feather bed, and, not venturing to employ any of his slaves to assist him, had alone defended the house, keeping the assailants at bay for some time, and dangerously wounding one of their number; nor had he surrendered till the breaking of his arm by a musket-ball had made it impossible for him any longer to load and fire. His case—as I afterwards learned, when he was brought before the vigilance committee—had been a subject of vehement controversy; but as his connections were numerous and powerful, the committee did not dare to proceed to extremities against him.

P

CHAPTER LV.

HAVING written a letter of inquiry to Mr. Thomas, since the disturbed state of the country had interrupted my personal visit, while waiting an answer, passing in one of my walks through a principal street of New Orleans, I was attracted to enter a large warehouse, where a sale of slaves was going on at auction.

The auctioneer was engaged at the moment in the sale of plantation hands and mechanics. There stood on the block a blacksmith, a first-rate hand, as the auctioneer described him, who had paid his master, as rent for himself, twenty dollars a month, clear of all expenses, for the last five years; and upon whom the bid had already risen to fifteen hundred dollars. A report, indeed, circulated in the room, that he had already paid that sum, out of his extra earnings, to purchase his liberty; which amount his master, a Bostonian, settled in New Orleans, had coolly pocketed, and had then sent the man to be sold at auction. The circulation of this story checked the bidding, since this breach of faith, it was thought, might provoke the man to run away. The auctioneer steadily denied the truth of it; but being called upon to ask the man himself, he refused to do so, observing, with a laugh, that the evidence of a slave would not be received against his master.

My attention was presently attracted to a group of female slaves, apparently of a superior class, and most of them very light-coloured. One woman, in particular, soon fixed and absorbed all my attention. Those eyes! That mouth! Her figure was more plump, and fuller; the face was older than I remembered it; but her raven hair, and pearl-like teeth perfectly preserved, still gave her a youthful aspect. Her height was the same, and there was the same grace in every gesture and movement. I watched her with the intensest interest. Was it possible that I could be mistaken? No; 'twas she,—'twas Cassy.—'twas the long-lost wife I sought; found at last; but where?

Press, reader, to thy heart the wife of thy bosom, and thank God that you were both born free! After twenty years' separation, I had again found mine, ripe in womanly beauty, exposed for sale in a slave auction room! Yet even there, reduced to that depth of degradation and misery, she was still calm and self-collected; evidently, by her manner, imposing a certain restraint on the crowd of licentious idlers, callous speculators, and anxious inquirers after human conveniences, to whose inspection, and now gross, now rude, and now teasing inquisition, she, in common with the rest, was subjected.

The present, however, was not a moment to give way to feeling. It was necessary to act. Summoning up all my energies, I rapidly considered with myself what course I best might adopt. To draw Cassy's attention to myself in any way would be a hazardous operation; for I felt certain that as I had recognised her, so she would not fail to recognise me; and so public and peculiar a place as a slave auction room was hardly a desirable spot for our first interview, which, coming upon her with even greater surprise than upon myself, might have led to a scene very embarrassing, if not hazardous.

Looking round the room, as these thoughts ran through my mind, whom should I see, as if fortune or providence had determined to favour me, but my late acquaintance, Mr. John Colter, who was walking about the room examining the various groups of slaves, especially the females, with the air, to use his own expression, of both connoisseur and amateur, and with pretty evident indications of his own opinion as to his special competency to pass judgment as to the value of the article.

Catching my eye almost at the same instant that mine rested on him, he approached me with an air of much interest, and inquired what I did there, and what had been the success of my Mississippi travels? "I feared," he added, in a low tone, "when I read the account of that hanging affair in the newspapers, that I had got you into a scrape. I am glad to find you know how to take care of yourself. Here in the south-west it is pretty necessary to have one's eye-teeth cut, and one's eyes open."

"You are just the man," I answered, "whom I wanted to see. Your assistance may now be invaluable to me. I have found her! She's here!"

"Here! The deuce she is! Where? Offered for sale? Have you bought her?"

I pointed out Cassy as she stood with the other women, with downcast eyes, and apparently absorbed in thought. Colter prided himself on the strength of his memory, never forgetting, as he said, a face which he had once seen; but what could his memory be, in this case, compared to mine? After two or three glances at her, he admitted that likely enough I might be correct; but, to make all sure, while I walked in another direction, he approached her, called her by name, reminded her of Augusta and the slave prison there, and fully satisfied himself, in a short conversation, that she was in fact the same person about whose sale he had quarrelled with Gouge; and that person, from circumstances already mentioned, I was satisfied was my Cassy.

Upon his inquiring of her why she was here, and if she was now to be sold? she answered, that she was brought here for that purpose; but that they had no right to sell her, for she was free. Her former owner, a Mr. Curtis, had given her free papers many years ago; but he was lately dead, and certain persons, claiming to be his heirs, were now attempting to sell her.

Colter promised to inquire into the case, and to befriend her in the matter; for which she expressed great gratitude, adding that she had all along felt confident that heaven would send her aid in some shape.

He then hastened to report to me; and while he and I were still discussing the subject, and considering what was best to be done, the auctioneer, having finished the sale of the plantation slaves, began upon the group of females in which Cassy stood.

The one first placed upon the auction block was a finely-formed black girl, neatly dressed, her good-humoured face well set off by a bright-coloured handkerchief twisted turban-fashion about her head. Though apparently very young, she held in her arms, and caressed with much fondness, a sprightly infant of seven or eight months, quite richly dressed, and of a colour a good deal lighter than the mother's.

"Jemima," shouted the auctioneer, "first-rate chambermaid; hold your head up, my dear, and let the gentlemen see you; brought up in one of the first families of Virginia, a good seamstress, too"—reading from a paper or list containing the names and descriptions of the articles on sale—" only fifteen years of age, warranted sound and healthy in every particular!"

"And do you sell the pappoose too, mother and child in one lot ?" asked a thin, squint-eyed, hard-featured fellow.

"You know the law don't allow us," said the auctioneer with a wink, " to offer the mother and child separately. Whoever buys the girl has the privilege to take the child, if he chooses, at the usual rate—a dollar a pound for sucklings, that's the regular price everywhere; that you know, old fellow, as well as I. You've bought 'em before now, I reckon."

This drew out a laugh at the expense of the questioner, who, however, did not seem to notice it; and the auctioneer having nodded assent to his inquiry, whether, if not so taken, the child might be had separately, the sale went on.

"Only three hundred dollars offered," cried the auctioneer; " only three hundred dollars for this first-rate chambermaid and seamstress, raised in one of the first families of Virginia, sold for no fault, only to raise the wind."

"Pretty common case with those first Virginian families," said a voice from among the crowd; " they only live by eating their niggers ———"

"Warranted"—so the auctioneer went on, without noticing the interruption, which raised another laugh among some of the company—" warranted healthy, sound, and honest."

"But no virgin," responded the voice from the crowd—a sally which provoked another and still more violent explosion of laughter.

"With privilege to take the child at a dollar a pound," continued the auctioneer. "Three hundred and fifty! Four hundred! Thank you, sir," with a bow and a bland smile to the bidder. "Four hundred and fifty? Did I hear it? Four hundred and fifty! Five hundred! Can't pause, gentlemen; great heap of 'em here to sell to-day. All done at five hundred? Five hundred! Going! Five hundred dollars for a prime Virginia wench, who begins young, and promises to be a great breeder; only five hundred dollars! Why, upon my honour, gentlemen," pausing, and laying his hammer across his breast,—" upon my honour,"—this with a very decided emphasis,—" she's worth seven hundred and fifty for anybody's use; a handsome, young, good-natured, stout, and healthy chambermaid and seamstress, raised in one of the first families of Virginia, and sold for only five hundred dollars! We shall be obliged to stop the sale, gentlemen, if you don't bid better. All done at five hundred dollars? Going at five hundred dollars! Gone!" And the hammer fell. "Gone for five hundred dollars, and mighty cheap at that, to Mr. Charles Parker." Here a fat, jolly-looking, youngish gentleman stepped forward, and the black girl, looking intently at him, and as if pleased with his appearance, smiled confidingly on her new purchaser. "Mr. Parker, of course, takes the child," the auctioneer continued, addressing his clerk; " add thirty-five dollars for the child, at a dollar a pound."

"Not at all!"—so the purchaser interposed; and as he spoke, how suddenly and sadly the girl's countenance fell! "I've bought her for a wet-nurse; I don't want the brat—wouldn't take it as a gift."

I could see, as he spoke, how the mother's arms closed on the child, as if with a convulsive grasp. I expected a scene, but the same little squint-eyed, hard-featured fellow, whom I had noticed before, stepped up to the purchaser, saying in a whisper, "Take it—take it! I'll take it off your hands, and give a dollar to boot."

As the purchaser cast a doubting sort of a look at him, some one in the crowd remarked, "O, that's old Stubbings, the nigger baby broker; he makes a business of buying nigger babies; he's good!" And so, accepting the offer, Mr. Parker took possession of his new purchase, the young mother's smiles returning, with a profusion of thanks and "God bless ye's," when she found she was to take the child with her; wholly unaware, as she seemed to be, of the understanding by which the infant was to become the property of Stubbings, the speculator in that line, who promised Parker, in a few whispered words, to arrange matters so as to take the brat off quietly the next day, without giving the girl a chance to make a fuss.

"And now, gentlemen," said the auctioneer, well satisfied, apparently, that the affair just disposed of had ended so quietly, "I have now to offer you a most rare chance for a housekeeper." Here he read from the list,—"Cassy; understands housekeeping in all its branches; perfectly trustworthy, and warranted a member of the Methodist church! I can't exactly say, gentlemen, that she's young, but she's in excellent preservation for all that. Answers to the English description of 'fair ——.' You needn't laugh; she's next door to white—she answers, I say, to the English description of 'fair, fat, and forty.' Step up, Cassy, girl, and show yourself!"

O, my God! What did I not suffer at that moment! Yet it was necessary to be quiet.

Cassy had been separated from the group where I had first seen her, and brought forward by some of the assistants of the auction-room, towards the place of sale. But instead of mounting the block, as directed, she stood still beside it; and as all eyes were drawn towards her, she spoke out in a gentle, but very firm and steady tone. How that voice, as familiar to my ear as if I had heard it every day for the last twenty years, instead of hearing it now for the first time after a twenty years' interval,—how it went through my heart! "No?" she said, "I am free. By what right do you pretend to sell me?"

This exclamation, as may well be supposed, produced quite an excitement in the auction-room. As I glanced my eye rapidly over the company, it was easy to discover several who seemed to sympathize with this claim of freedom, and the auctioneer was loudly called upon for explanations.

"A very common case, gentlemen," replied the auctioneer, "very common. The woman, no doubt, thought herself free; no doubt she has lived as free for several years past: but that was all by the mere indulgence of her late owner. He's dead, and now the heirs have taken possession, and offer her for sale. That's all. Step up, Cassy, step on the block; you see there is no help for it. Gentlemen, who bids?"

"Stop a moment!" said Mr. Colter, who now quitted my side and stepped forward—"not quite so fast, sir, if you please. I appear here as this woman's friend. She is a free woman. Gentlemen will please to take warning: anybody who buys her, buys a lawsuit."

The peremptory manner in which this was spoken seemed to throw cold water upon the sale. Nobody made an offer, and the auctioneer, to shield himself from the charge of attempting to sell a free woman, found it necessary to go into further explanations.

This woman, he stated, had formerly belonged to Mr. James Curtis, a very worthy citizen, lately deceased, and well known to many of the company. He had allowed her, for several years past, to live as a free woman, and no doubt the gentleman—it was Colter he alluded to— might have every reason for supposing her to be so; but the fact was, she had no free papers, or if she had any, they were not in due and proper form; and Mr. James Curtis having died suddenly without a will, his brother, Mr. Agrippa Curtis, of the well-known Boston firm of Curtis, Sawin, Byrne, and Co., had succeeded to all his property; and finding his ownership of this woman unquestionable, had directed her to be sold; "and here comes the owner himself," said the auctioneer, "and his Boston lawyer with him; no doubt they can satisfy you as to the title."

As he spoke I observed two individuals entering the room, one a very small man, with a head about as large as that of a respectable tabby cat, and with little wandering unquiet eyes, and a compressed, pursed-up mouth, that might call to mind the said tabby, caught in the act of stealing cream, but while seeming to anticipate a box on the ear for her villany, still licking her chops all the while, as though the cream was all the sweeter for having been stolen. This I afterwards understood was Thomas Littlebody, Esq., of Boston, counsellor at law and legal adviser of Mr. Agrippa Curtis, or Grip Curtis, as he was more commonly called among his familiars—the principal in this business, a bald-headed man about forty, the impenetrable and immovable stolidity of whose features made it difficult to form any conjecture, from that source, as to his character, beyond the probability of his not being likely to be carried away by any great excess of sensibility.

"A very pretty story," said Colter, stepping up to these two worthies as they entered the room and approached the auctioneer, and eyeing them with a look that seemed to make them rather uncomfortable. "The company see how it is. I am glad to find no Louisianian is concerned in this pitiful, kidnapping business. The woman is as free as you or I. This story about the flaw in the papers is all a humbug; nothing in the world but one of your scurvy, low-lived Yankee tricks, to put a few hundred dollars into the pocket of a scoundrel. Yet, to save trouble, I'm willing to buy off this pretence of claim for a hundred dollars. Come, Mr. Auctioneer, go ahead with your sale. One hundred dollars —that's my bid."

"One hundred dollars!" repeated the auctioneer, as if mechanically— "gentlemen, I'm offered one hundred dollars!"

"I offer this," said Colter, looking proudly round on the company, "to buy off these Yankee blood-suckers, and to secure the freedom of a free woman. We shall see," he added, "whether, under these circumstances, any southern gentleman will bid against me, or"—brushing by Mr. Curtis and his lawyer, and darting at them a malign scowl, such as I hardly thought possible from so handsome a face—"any swindling Yankee either."

Thomas Littlebody, Esq., the Boston lawyer, started back some three or four paces, as if this must have certainly been meant for him. Mr. Grip Curtis, with that gravity and immobility which seemed to be a part of his nature, stood his ground better; and opening his great owl-like eyes, observed, with a drawl, "I hope you don't intend to insinuate anything against my moral character!"

"I shall, though," rejoined Colter, "if you undertake to bid at your own auction. It's quite enough to palm off a free woman upon this respectable company, without turning buy-bidder at the sale!"

"One hundred dollars is offered, gentlemen—one hundred dollars!" repeated the auctioneer; but there was no further bid.

The little squint-eyed baby-broker, who had watched the whole proceeding with keen interest, as if here might be a chance for him to turn an honest penny, once opened his mouth, as if going to bid; but at a look from Colter, he shut it as suddenly up as if his tongue had been pricked with a bowie-knife; and I think Colter showed him the handle of one from under his vest. At all events, the apparently intended bid died away inaudible.

"As gentlemen don't seem inclined to purchase," said Mr. Grip Curtis, stepping forward to the auctioneer's side, "I withdraw this woman from the sale."

These words filled me with lively alarm; but Colter's practice, I found, had made him a match for any Yankee of the lot. He coolly produced the advertisement, closing with these words, "To be sold without reserve," and insisted that the sale should go on. In this, the company and the auctioneer sustained him; and as no other bids were made, presently the auctioneer's hammer fell. "Sold," he said, "for one hundred dollars, to Mr. —— ?"

"Cash," answered Colter, handing out one of the very hundred dollar bills which he had won a few weeks before from the Boston cotton-broker. "Make out a receipted bill of this Boston man's claim to this woman, as sold to Mr. Archer Moore, of London."

The bill was speedily made out, and, in spite of a certain degree of dissatisfaction visible meanwhile even through the solemn stolidity of the foiled Bostonian, Colter motioning to Cassy to come with us, to which she responded with all alacrity, and we three left the sale-room together; but not before the laughing and good-natured auctioneer had another woman on the auction-block, a lady's maid of sixteen, raised in a good Maryland family, warranted intact, and title unquestionable, upon whom he solicited a generous bid.

I shall not undertake to describe the scene between myself and Cassy, when she came to recognise in me, as she speedily did, her long-lost husband. Her joy at the meeting was no less exalted than mine; but her surprise was greatly diminished by a confident expectation which, it seemed, she had all along entertained, and which had formed with her a settled article of belief—the hope of sanguine souls easily transforming itself into faith—that sooner or later she should certainly again find me. And so, like a true wife and lover, she had kept, in all this long absence, the best place in her heart empty, swept, and garnished, and waiting to receive me; and now she clasped me to it, rather as him whose return from a long wandering she had day by day and night by night patiently expected and waited for, than as one irretrievably lost, and unexpectedly, however welcomely, found.

O, tie of love, and natural bond of marriage, union of hearts, which laws and priestly benedictions may sanction if they choose, but cannot make; so neither can time, nor separation, nor prosperity, nor suffering nor all that unbridled power may inflict, or helplessness submit to, nor aught save death, nor death itself, undo thee!

CHAPTER LVI.

THE new mistress—into whose hands, by the humane interference of Mr. Colter, Cassy had passed from the slave-pen of those pious and respectable gentlemen, Gouge and McGrab—was, as I knew already, from Colter's account of the matter, the newly-married New England wife of Mr. Thomas, a Mississippi cotton-planter.

Born on a little New Hampshire farm, the child of poor parents, but, like so many other New England girls, anxious to do something for herself, the new Mrs. Thomas, when she first became acquainted with her future husband, had been employed as one of the teachers at a fashion-able boarding-school, at which he had placed, for their education, two young daughters of his by a former wife.

The current idea in New England of a southern cotton-planter is very much that which prevails, or used to prevail, in Great Britain of a West Indian. He is imagined to be a fine, bold, dashing young fellow, elegant and accomplished, amiable and charming, with plenty of money, and nothing to do but to amuse himself and his friends—an idea formed from a few specimens to be seen at watering-places, who, for the sake of dashing away for a few weeks at the north, run after by all the young women, and old ones too, with marriageable daughters on their hands, and stared at by all the greenhorns—are willing to starve, pinch, and be dunned at home, with now and then a visit from the sheriff, for all the rest of the year.

The young Mrs. Thomas that was to be, as yet Miss Jemima Devens, delighted at the idea of having captivated a southern planter, and of passing suddenly from poverty to riches, hastened to accept the offer of his heart and fortune, which Mr. Thomas made her after a week's acquaintance, in the course of which they had met three times. Un-fortunately, she did not stop to consider that, southern planter or not, Mr. Thomas was old enough to be her father, had a vulgar, stupid, sleepy look, could not speak English grammatically, and was an enor-mous consumer of tobacco and brandy; his affection, even during his courtship, divided pretty equally, to all appearances, between chewing, smoking, mint juleps, and Miss Devens, notwithstanding his frequent protestations that he cared for nothing in the world but her.

That he was really in love with her, so far as it was possible for such an oyster to be in love, was no doubt true; and for a young lady without connections or money, dependent on her own efforts, with no charms or accomplishments beyond those possessed by a thousand other compe-titors, and beginning also to verge to the age when the sinking into old maidhood comes to be considered as a possible, however awful contin-gency,—for such a young lady to be fallen in love with, even though it be by an oyster in the similitude of a man, is a thing not to be despised; and the said human oyster having the reputation of being rich, and able to support her in idleness and luxury, what proportion of girls of the age and in the position of Miss Devens, whether in New England or Old, or elsewhere, would refuse to accept him for a husband?

Miss Devens did confess to some littte misgiving on one point. She had a great horror of negroes—a natural antipathy, as she thought; though she did remember, that when a very little girl, they used to frighten her into good behaviour by threatening to give her away to an old black woman, the only black person anywhere in the neighbourhood of the village in which she was born, who lived all alone by herself, in a little hut surrounded by woods, where she sold root beer in the summer-time to the passers-by, dealt in all sorts of herbs, as to which she was reported to be wondrous knowing, and had, besides, at least among the children, the reputation of being a witch.

The idea of going to live upon a plantation where she would have nobody about her hardly but black people did stagger her resolution a little; till Mr. Thomas reassured her by suggesting how comfortable it was to own one's own servants, whom one could make do just as one pleased, and by the information that there were plenty of light-coloured people among the slaves, and that she should have a maid of her own as near white as possible—a promise on the strength of which Cassy had been bought for her, as already mentioned.

The new Mrs. Thomas had pictured to herself, as her destined future home, an elegant villa, splendidly furnished, surrounded with beautiful and fragrant tropical shrubbery, except the inevitable nuisance of the negroes,—to which she hoped to accustom herself in time, or for which she was willing to accept the orange blossoms as an antidote,—a perfect southern paradise. Mr. Thomas, it is true, good, easy man, had never promised her anything of the sort; but as young ladies often will, she had taken it all for granted as a matter of course. Judge, then, of her disappointment, when, on reaching Mount Flat,—for that was the name which Mr. Thomas had given to his plantation, determined, as he said, to stick to the truth, and yet not to be out-done by any of the Mount Pleasants, Monticellos, and other high-sounding names of the neighbourhood,—judge of her surprise to find her expected villa in the shape of four log houses, connected together by a floored and covered passage, without carpets, paper-hangings, or even plaster, and with roofs so imperfect that in every heavy storm of rain, every room of the four, except only that used as her bed-room, was completely afloat. Some detached log-houses, at a little distance on either side, served as additional sleeping-rooms, and others, a little in the rear, as kitchen and storehouses; and still farther back, but still in sight of the principal mansion, was a long string of miserable little huts, the town, as they called it, occupied by the plantation slaves. As to shrubbery, there were no enclosures at all about the house, except one, half decayed, of what seemed to have been intended as a garden, but which was now quite grown up with weeds and bushes. The hogs, the mules, a few half-starved cows, and a whole bevy of naked negro children, ranged freely about the house; and though there seemed once to have been some attempts at shrubbery, that was now all ruined and destroyed.

The former Mrs. Thomas, belonging, as she always took pains to let the company know, to one of the first families of Virginia, was in fact a very notable woman, whose masculine temper and active spirit had counterbalanced, so far as domestic affairs were concerned, the dozy disposition of her husband. By dint of bustling, scolding, and the free use of the cowhide, which she wielded with a grace and dexterity hardly to be attained except by those females who have had the advantage of a thoroughly southern education in the best families, she had contrived to keep things in tolerable order; but shortly after her death, some six years before, the man whom she had employed to keep the garden and the grounds about the house had been taken off and placed in the cotton field, and everything in the house and around it had since been left to take care of itself; and with the results that might have been expected, there not being in the house a whole piece of furniture of any description, and the entire aspect of things as untidy, uncomfortable, neglected, and dilapidated as can well be imagined.

To complete the dismay of Mrs. Thomas, and what gave a good deal of a shock to her New England ideas, among the black children whom she found running and romping in front of the house at the moment of her arrival—the whole group having, in fact, assembled to welcome home master and the new mistress—were quite a number of boys and girls eight or ten years old, naked as they were born, or with only some fragment of a tattered and filthy shirt hanging about them, begrimed with dirt, and shouting and chattering, as she said to Cassy, like so many imps of the evil one himself.

But within the house a still more disagreeable reception awaited her. She found the keys and the general direction of affairs under the management of a tall, portly, middle-aged black woman, commonly called aunt Emma, of formidable size and strength, who, having been a favourite upper servant, and sort of prime minister, of the late Mrs. Thomas, had succeeded, on her death, to the general control of the household. In the kitchen ruled supreme aunt Dinah, another big black woman, whose face plainly enough betrayed the irritability of her temper, stimulated from time to time by pretty free draughts of whisky. It is not necessary to mention the other servants, who were in complete subordination to those two, but all of whom, with aunts Emma and Dinah at their head, it soon appeared, were parties to a conspiracy to set at nought the authority of the new Mrs. Thomas, and to make her a mere cipher in her own house.

By some means or other, probably from one of Mr. Thomas's daughters, whom the new-married pair had brought home with them, they soon got hold of the information that the new mistress was nothing but the daughter of a poor man, who worked for his living with his own hands, and herself only a poor schoolma'am; nor could a contempt more sovereign of such humble, plebeian, pitiful origin be evinced by the daintiest female aristocrat that ever wore white kid slippers, than by the black housekeeper and the black cook.

"Pretty times these, indeed! very fine times, certainly!" exclaimed aunt Emma, with a most ominous shake of the head, and imitating with great exactness the tone, manner, and words of her deceased mistress, the first Mrs. Thomas, whose representative and successor she seemed to consider herself to be, and equally bound to look out for the honour of the family,—"fine times these, aunt Dinah! that you and I, raised in one of the first families of Virginia, should have one of these good-for-nothing, no account, poor folks put over our heads,—and a Yankee too! O, aunt Dinah, who would a-thought it, that two quality niggers like you and I, raised in one of the first families of Virginia, and always accustomed to decent society, should have to take up with a Yankee mistress? What in heavens and earth could possess poor Massa Thomas, that, having once had such a wife as old mistress was, belonging to one of the first families of Virginia, he must needs go and bring home this little Yankee nobody, to disgrace us and him too?" Such was one of a great number of similar outbursts, which Cassy, and indeed Mrs. Thomas herself, could hardly fail to overhear, since the discontented housekeeper made very little privacy of her griefs.

So far, indeed, did she carry it, that when the new Mrs. Thomas, after being in the house for three or four weeks, intimated to aunt Emma her intention to assume in person the position of housekeeper, and called upon her to give up the keys, she snapped her fingers with significant contempt in the face of her new mistress, and absolutely refused. Her old mistress—no poor body but born of one the first families of Virginia—had brought her into Massa Thomas's family, and had made her housekeeper, and on her death-bed had made her husband promise that he would never sell her, but that she always should be housekeeper; and housekeeper she meant to be in spite of all the Yankee women and poor white folks in creation.

Missis might be content to manage those servants she had brought in herself. She had brought in one, to be sure, though, according to all accounts, poor dear Massa Thomas had to buy her with his own money, and to pay a pretty round price, too. But what right had she to come in and undertake to domineer over old mistress's servants? And here aunt Emma burst out into a loud laugh, partly in defiance, and partly in derision, at being called upon to give up the keys by such a poverty-stricken Yankee interloper,—she,—so she wound up, folding her arms, and drawing herself up to her full height, exactly as the late Mrs. Thomas used to do,—she who had been raised in one of the first families in Virginia! But aunt Emma soon sunk down from this high pitch, subsiding into a flood of tears at the thought, as she expressed it, of what poor dear, dead mistress would say, she, born in one of the first families of Virginia, who hated a Yankee as she did a toad or a snake, always speaking of them as in fact no better than a set of free niggers, —an opinion in which aunt Emma seemed very cordially to join,—to come back, and find her turned out, and the keys in the hands of a Yankee!

There is nothing like a strong will, and by virtue of it the slave may sometimes usurp the place of the master. The new Mrs. Thomas made grievous complaints to her husband, insisting that aunt Emma should be whipped and sent into the field. But the good-natured, easy old gentleman was so accustomed to be himself managed by her, and so tickled at the idea of aunt Emma's contempt for the Yankees, which he himself more than half shared, that he showed a strong disposition to take her part; nor was it till after a six months' struggle, and a long series of curtain lectures, in which particular the wife had the advantage of the housekeeper, that she finally succeeded in getting possession of the keys, and aunt Emma fairly out of the house. She insisted very strenuously upon having her sent down the river and sold; or at least that she should be set to work in the field, and especially that she should have a sound flogging for her insolence; but Mr. Thomas would consent to neither. Mrs. Thomas was welcome to flog aunt Emma as much as she pleased. The late Mrs. Thomas did sometimes use the cowskin on her, he believed; but during the six years that she had been housekeeper for him, he never had had occasion to do it, and he shouldn't begin now. The most he could be persuaded to do, was to put her out of Mrs. Thomas's sight, by hiring her out somewhere in the neighbour-hood,—poor Mrs. Thomas complaining, in a sort of prophetic spirit, that he wanted to keep her near by, when she, his poor wife, was dead and gone, as she soon should be, to have her for his housekeeper again.

But, though the black housekeeper was thus at last got rid of, the black cook proved a more formidable enemy. Aunt Dinah's skill in cookery was by no means contemptible, and Mr. Thomas, who was something of an epicure, had become so accustomed to her particular dishes, that nobody else could suit him. All poor Mrs. Thomas's efforts to dislodge aunt Dinah from the kitchen proved, in consequence, unavailing. She had nothing to do,—so Mr. Thomas told her,—but to keep out of the kitchen, and let aunt Dinah alone. But that Mrs. Thomas could not do. She had a great passion for bustling, managing, meddling, fretting, and scolding, and scarcely a day passed without an encounter between her and aunt Dinah, whom she accused, not altogether without reason, of not having the slightest idea either of order or neatness, —accusations which aunt Dinah was accustomed to retort by a sort of growling observations to herself, that poor folks couldn't be expected to understand or duly value the kitchen management of quality cooks.

So far did this feud go, that Mrs. Thomas declared at last her apprehension of being poisoned, and for some months would eat nothing except what Cassy prepared for her with her own hands; though whether it was aunt Dinah's dirt, or something more fatal, that she dreaded, Cassy could never clearly make out.

In the midst of all these tribulations, which, as she complained, were wearing her out by inches, and bringing her fast to the grave, aggravating the fever and ague by which she constantly suffered, poor Mrs. Thomas had no confidant or consoler except only Cassy. The nearest neighbours were three or four miles off. The ladies of these establishments—where there were any, for several of the neighbouring planters preferred a slave housekeeper to a white wife — were from Virginia and Kentucky, holding Yankees in almost as much contempt as aunt Dinah did—a prejudice which Mrs. Thomas had too little force of character, or power of making herself either useful or agreeable, to be able to overcome. Her husband was pretty poor company at best. However it might have been in the days of his courtship, his wife had long since ceased to compete, in his affections, with his more favourite cigar, mint julep, and chaw of tobacco; and to get rid, as he said, of her eternal complaints about nothing, he kept out of her way as much as possible. Her step-daughter, a girl of fourteen, seemed to be in the conspiracy with aunt Dinah against her, as were the washer-woman, seamstress, and all the rest of the house-servants: and such was the state of nervous uneasiness in which they kept her, breaking out occasionally into exhibitions by no means very lovely, that she expressed one day to Cassy her apprehensions, lest these ugly black creatures would not only be the destruction of her health and good looks, which suffered a good deal under the effects of the ague, but the ruin of her soul also. She was sure that living on a plantation was no place to fit folks for heaven.

Cassy was impressed with a strong feeling of gratitude towards her unfortunate mistress. She greatly pitied, as well the infirmities of her temper, soured by sickness and disappointment, and failure in everything, as the miserable loneliness and substantial state of slavery into which she had sold herself; a state all the more disagreeable to her naturally busy and bustling temperament, since the post assigned her seemed to be, though bearing the name of mistress, to do nothing and to be nobody. Exerting herself by every means to calm, comfort, and divert her—an office for which she was well fitted by her own uniform, sweet, and sunny disposition—Cassy became entirely indispensable to her suffering mistress. This placed her in a rather delicate position as to the other servants, who were inclined to include her in their hostility and antipathy to Mrs. Thomas. But her sweet temper and friendly disposition soon overcame all that. Some little favours and judicious compliments—since she always took a decided pleasure in making others happy — secured for her even the good-will of the formidable aunt Dinah herself, into whose dominions she was thus able to venture with an impunity never vouchsafed to the mistress.

Little as there was, any way, of Mrs. Thomas, either of intellect or heart, this assiduity and good-will on the part of Cassy, though even she was not safe from occasional bursts of impatience and ill temper, were by no means thrown away upon her. Finding that Cassy had never been taught to read—an accomplishment which none of her former kind mistresses had thought necessary—she volunteered to teach her, and her little boy also; and she persevered in it, notwithstanding the occasional jocular threats of Mr. Thomas to have her prosecuted under the act against teaching slaves to read. Indeed, she seemed to take so much consolation in having at last found something to do, that, besides teaching Cassy various kinds of needlework, in which she was an adept, she also gave her lessons on a piano, which Mr. Thomas had bought at the north, at the time of his marriage, and which came round by water. Nor was it long before Cassy's correct ear for music made her a greater proficient than her mistress, which, indeed, was not saying much.

So things passed away during three or four years, till a bilious fever, which carried off Mrs. Thomas, exposed Cassy to new vicissitudes. She was no longer needed at Mount Flat, and in hopes to get back the large sum he had paid for her, Mr. Thomas sent her off with her child to New Orleans to be sold.

Among the purchasers who there presented themselves was a Mr. Curtis, as Cassy afterwards learned, a native of Boston, and well connected there. Like many others from the same city, he had come to New Orleans while still quite young. Afterwards entering into business himself, and succeeding in it, instead of marrying, he had, as is customary enough with the northern adventurers in that city, fallen into the habits of the place, and formed a connection with a handsome, young, light-coloured slave, whom he had purchased, and for whom he entertained so strong an affection, as to have felt very seriously her recent death, leaving behind her a little daughter some three or four years younger than our boy Montgomery.

Being of a domestic disposition, and desirous of filling up this break in his household establishment, Mr. Curtis, when his grief was a little assuaged, had become a visitant, with that view, of the slave-warehouses; and Cassy having at once very decidedly struck his fancy, he made a purchase of her and of her child. I relate all this very coolly; but imagine, reader, if you can, how I must have felt, when, ignorant of the event, I first heard the story from Cassy's own lips!

Duly installed in the superintendence of Mr. Curtis's household, which at this time was on a small and modest scale, and in the care of his little daughter, it was not long before Mr. Curtis intimated to her, in a very delicate way,—for he was thoroughly amiable, and in every respect a gentleman,—his disposition to place the relation between them on a more intimate footing.

He appeared a good deal surprised, contrasting, it is probable, Cassy's behaviour with his former experience, at the coolness with which his advances were received, and her attempts to seem not to understand them; but as he prided himself—and not without reason—on his personal attractions and winning ways with the women, and was, besides, so much more a man of sentiment than of passion, as to prize the possession of a woman's heart, however humble, far beyond that of her person, this only piqued his vanity, and made him the more resolved to make a conquest of her.

Nor, indeed, when the master condescends to make love to the slave, the man of the superior class to the woman of the inferior one, a king to a subject, a nobleman to a peasant, or even, if he takes the fancy, to the wife of a citizen, are such conquests in general very difficult. In the case of the slave woman, however transient the connection, it still for the moment elevates her from her own humble level to that of her lover; and in so doing does more to raise her in her own eyes, and those of her class, than any connection she can possibly form within that class,— a connection called marriage, perhaps, but only by courtesy; since it is not so any more than the other, being, like that other, in the eye of the law, but a transient cohabitation, creating no rights of any sort, giving no paternity to the children, and dissoluble not only at the caprice of the man, but at that also of the master and his creditors.

That very same pride, in fact, which impels the woman of the superior class to shrink with a horror, which seems to her instinctive, from any connection with the men of the inferior class, as a degradation from her own level, a sentiment not regulated by colour, but by condition, since a white woman of refinement and education would just as soon think of marrying a negro as one of your newly-imported Irish clod-hoppers, even though he might be an Apollo in figure, and, when the dirt was washed off, a perfect Adonis in complexion,—that same pride impels the slave woman readily to throw herself into the arms of any man of the superior class who condescends to honour her with his notice; that very desire for a standing in the world which makes the free woman so coy and reserved, making the slave woman yielding and easy,—since, looked at merely with that eye of prudence, by which, more than by choice, sentiment, or passion, the conduct of women in this behalf is everywhere regulated, a left-handed marriage with any man of the superior rank is every way more advantageous than anything to be hoped from any right-handed marriage—even if that were possible, which it is not—with a person of her own degraded condition.

There was, indeed, nothing but Cassy's affection for me—exposed now to a test such as female constancy, in civilized countries, is seldom tried by—and a romantic idea which she had taken up that, sooner or later, we should certainly again find each other, that could have made her proof against the efforts of Mr. Curtis to win her affections; efforts, as he laughingly told her, enough to have made him husband of half the white girls in New Orleans or Boston either.

Besides being a man of sentiment, of a delicacy not to be extinguished even by a residence in an atmosphere so corrupt as that of New Orleans, Mr. Curtis had also a good deal of romance in his composition. He could not but applaud a constancy and tenderness of which he desired himself to become the object; but he begged Cassy not to throw away her youth and her charms in an unavailing widowhood—since the separation between her and me was in all respects equivalent to death— nor, out of a mere fancy, to persist in refusing a position for herself and her child the best that she could hope; since he promised, in fact, to reward her compliance by a gift of freedom, in due time, to herself and the boy.

If she had any repugnance or dislike to him, he would not push the matter; but ought she, out of a mere fanciful caprice, to refuse this gratification to him, and provision for herself?

Finding that she was a Methodist, he even promised to call in a minister of that persuasion to consecrate their union, if she had scruples on that score; and he strongly advised her to ask the counsel of the one at whose chapel she usually attended.

Though the Methodists hold that a marriage between two slaves, celebrated by one of their ministers, is, in the eye of God, every way complete and binding on the .parties—who, according to Methodist ideas, have souls to be saved as well as white people—yet, notwithstanding the famous text, "Whom God hath joined together let not man put asunder," they have been obliged, in the slave states of America, to concede the supremacy of man; and to admit that parties separated by the command of a master, or the operation of the slave-trade, may rightly enough marry again, even though they know their former partners to be living. They excuse this by saying, that they do it of necessity; since the people, having little taste for celibacy, will form new connections: and they may as well sanction what they cannot help; the same excuse which they give for allowing their church members to hold slaves—the pious brethren will do it whether or no; a policy, in both cases, seeming to look rather to the numbers than to the purity of the church, and, perhaps, partaking something more of the wisdom of the serpent than of the harmlessness of the dove. But upon this high point of ecclesiastical policy I shall not venture to express a decided opinion.

The Methodist clergyman, whom Cassy consulted on this occasion, strongly urged her to accept of Mr. Curtis's offers, which he assured her she might do—considering all the circumstances of the case—with a perfectly safe conscience, especially if he was called in to consecrate this new connection, which would thus become a perfect marriage in the eye of Heaven, however human laws might not so regard it.

But spite of the urgency of Mr. Curtis, and the advice of the minister, still, every time that she pressed our boy to her bosom, the image of her lost husband rose up before her, and something said in her heart, He lives! he loves you! do not give him up!

So things went on for a year or more, Mr. Curtis still patiently waiting the effects of time and perseverance, when he was seized by a violent attack of yellow fever, which brought him to death's door, and from which he recovered only after a tedious and protracted convalescence. It was now Cassy's turn to show her sense of the kindness and delicacy with which she had been treated, and of the favour with which her master had regarded her. Night and day she was his constant and most assiduous nurse; and the physicians, of whom, at different times, three or four had been called in, all agreed that it was nothing but her tender care—all that a sister, a mother, a wife could have bestowed—to which he was indebted for his life.

Having been religiously educated in his childhood, the near prospect of death and the leisure and solitude of his tedious and painful recovery served to recall many ideas which the tumult of business, the gaiety of youth, the gross, sensual, worldly atmosphere in which he had so long lived, had well-nigh extinguished. It was plain, indeed, that Mr. Curtis

rose from his sick bed—whether from the effect of physical or moral
causes, or of both combined—in many respects an altered man, as if
indeed twenty years or more had suddenly been added to his age: not
less amiable or genial, but graver, and with thoughts less bent on himself: though he could never, at any time, have been accused of being
a selfish man.

One of the first things he did, when he was recovered enough to sit
up, was to execute a duplicate deed of manumission for Cassy and her
child, to go into effect as soon as the law would allow, she meanwhile
to superintend his household, receiving a certain monthly allowance.
He also, as Cassy understood, executed at the same time a deed of manumission of his little daughter Eliza, who still remained under Cassy's
care, growing up a nice companion and playmate for our little Montgomery.

When the children arrived at the proper age, Mr. Curtis had sent
them to New England for an education; first Montgomery, and afterwards Eliza, who was sent on to the care of Mr. Curtis's brother
Agrippa, and placed by him, at Boston, in a select, fashionable, aristocratic female school.

Montgomery, having spent two or three years at a New England
academy, had been afterwards placed in a counting-house in New
York, and had lately, through the patronage of his kind benefactor,
been established there in a business for himself connected with the New
Orleans trade.

Cassy's monthly allowance in the way of wages having, in the course
years, and with the addition of interest, which Mr. Curtis scrupulously
allowed her, accumulated to a considerable sum, he had lately invested
it for her in the purchase of a small house and garden, in the suburbs
of the city, to which,—as Mr. Curtis contemplated travelling at the
north and in Europe for his health—she had some time before removed.

Everything thus, she said, had gone well with her, as if she had been
a chosen favourite of Providence; except, indeed, the long-deferred
fulfilment of her still cherished hope of again finding me. But this long
course of singular prosperity had at length been suddenly and most
frightfully overcast.

News came that Mr. Curtis, while on his way to Boston, in ascend-
ing the Ohio river, had been seriously injured by the bursting of a
boiler; and this was followed, not long after, by information of his
death. When this occurred, which was only a few weeks previous,
Montgomery was employed in his business at New York, and Eliza
was still at school at Boston. She was a beautiful and elegant girl;
her liquid dark eyes, long black hair, and brunette complexion, in
strong contrast to the prevailing type of beauty in those regions in
which light hair, light eyes, and blond complexions so generally predominate. She had, besides, a grace and elegance of movement very
seldom seen in New England,—where everybody is more or less awkward,—and all the freedom and vivacity of a bird, without the least
touch either of that blunt, masculine rudeness, or of that embarrassed
self-consciousness which spoils the address of so many of the Boston
women. These, by the way, are Eliza's criticisms, not mine; and I
shall, therefore, not hold myself answerable for their correctness.

She passed for the only daughter of Mr. Curtis, the rich merchant of
New Orleans, by a Spanish creole wife of his who had died many years
ago; and as the reputation of an heiress was thus added to her personal
attractions, you may be sure that she received a great many attentions;

nor was she without offers even of marriage from some young sprigs of the Boston aristocracy; but to these she paid no sort of attention, as she and Montgomery had been promised to each other from early childhood.

On receiving information of the accident to his brother, Mr. Agrippa Curtis had set off for Pittsburg, where he was; and in three or four weeks he returned with the news of his brother's death.

While mourning with all the energetic grief natural to her age and origin over this sad news, Eliza found herself strangely neglected by her late fond school companions, not one of whom came near her; and while she was wondering what the matter could be, she received a note from the teacher, with the information that he could not allow her in his school any longer. It seems that a report had suddenly spread, that Eliza had African blood in her veins; that she was not Mr. Curtis's lawful child, nor his heir, but only the daughter of a slave woman.

Most fierce was the indignation expressed by the mothers of Eliza's school companions, especially by the daughter of a drunken tallow-chandler, who had married in her youth the keeper of a small grocery and grog-shop, but whose husband, having gone into the business of distilling, had acquired a great fortune, had bought a house in Beacon-street, and being, like his wife, of a pushing and aspiring disposition, had, by a liberal expenditure of money, placed her at the head of the fashion in Boston. This aristocratic lady thought it a most scandalous shame,—and she found many sympathizers,—that people of good family should be so shockingly imposed upon, as to have such a coloured trollop insinuated into the same school with their well-born daughters. Wasn't there a school down in Belknap-street especially intended for coloured folks, and why hadn't she been sent there? This sketch of this Mrs. Highflyer,—for that was the name of this fashionable Boston lady,—I must also credit to Eliza, who, to confess the truth, was a good deal of a rogue and a mimic, with an eye to the ridiculous, and a little tendency to caricature.

Nobody seemed to sympathize more completely with Mrs. Highflyer than Mr. Agrippa Curtis himself, though he had known perfectly well Eliza's origin from the beginning, and had been himself the person to introduce her into Boston society, and the fashionable school she had attended. His relation to his deceased brother, of whose property he gave himself out as the heir, made it improper for him, he said, to express himself freely as to his singular conduct, in the introduction into the fashionable society and respectable families of Boston of such a low person; though, in fact, his brother was a strange, unaccountable man in many respects, and to him quite unfathomable. But he did not hesitate to express himself in the most decided terms to poor Eliza, when she called upon him for protection and advice, going so far as actually to order her out of his house, as a vile cheat and impostor.

The keeper of the fashionable boarding-house where she lodged was prompt to imitate these aristocratic examples; in fact, the boarders themselves were all up in arms, especially the women,—for the men did not seem to have so much objection to her,—threatening to leave if she were not turned out; and the poor girl might, perhaps, have been obliged to sleep in the street, had not a little milliner, to whom she had formerly shown some kindnesses, taken her home, even at the risk of offending all her fashionable customers.

She wrote at once to Montgomery, at New York, who came on im-

Q

mediately to her assistance. Happening to meet Mr. Agrippa Curtis in State-street, about the time of high change, he expressed to him, in pretty plain terms, his sense of his conduct. That gentleman—he passed for such in Boston, notwithstanding a prevailing rumour that the mercantile firm of Curtis, Sawin, Byrne, and Co., to which he belonged, had laid the foundation of their fortune by an underhand connection with the Brazilian slave-trade—retorted, in great dudgeon, that he was not to be lectured by any cursed runaway nigger, the son of a ———; a polite allusion to Montgomery's descent, a circumstance with which Mr. Grip Curtis had become well acquainted in visits to his brother at New Orleans. Montgomery replied by knocking the scoundrel down on the spot; and one of the bystanders having the good nature to hand him a stick,—for Mr. Agrippa Curtis, though highly respectable, was not very popular,—as the fellow rose up, my boy proceeded to give him a severe caning, to the great apparent satisfaction of at least half of the assembled merchants, some of whom made a ring around them, in order, as they said, to have fair play; perhaps, too, for the better chance of enjoying Mr. Grip's capers and contortions, which, as Montgomery wrote to his mother, were highly ridiculous.

Mr. Agrippa Curtis immediately made a complaint at the police court, before which Montgomery was had up and fined twenty dollars. He also commenced a private suit, laying his damages at ten thousand dollars, in hopes to prevent Montgomery's getting bail; in which, however, he did not succeed.

As Montgomery, so soon as he had got bail in Mr. Grip Curtis's suit, was preparing to take Eliza with him to New York, a letter to her arrived from a Mr. Gilmore, a lawyer in New Orleans, who had all along been the confidential adviser and law agent of Mr. Curtis, informing her of Mr. Curtis's death, and that certain business affairs indispensably required her immediate presence at New Orleans, and enclosing a draft to pay her passage and expenses. On reaching New York a similar letter was found there for Montgomery. Neither of the young people had any reason to imagine that these letters were not written in perfect good faith. They knew Mr. Gilmore as a portly, round-faced, smiling, benevolent-looking, white-haired, oldish gentleman, of whom Mr. James Curtis thought very highly; and as they had abundant reasons for supposing that he had made some provision for them by will, it seemed reasonable enough that their presence at New Orleans might be necessary. But some business arrangements required Montgomery's previous attention, and sending on Eliza by packet, he proposed to follow himself as soon as he could.

Arriving safely at New Orleans much about the same time that I did, Eliza had gone directly to Cassy's house, who, in a day or two, had waited on Mr. Gilmore to inform him of her arrival. The deceased Mr. Curtis had several times assured Cassy, and particularly just before he left New Orleans the last time, that he had in his will remembered her and Montgomery, and had provided handsomely for Eliza. She made some inquiries of Mr. Gilmore on this subject; but the lawyer answered her evasively, telling her that it would be necessary for Eliza to call at his house at a certain hour the next day.

She went; but did not return. Cassy passed a sleepless night of anxiety and alarm, and was preparing the next morning to go to Mr. Gilmore's in pursuit of her, when, by the hand of a black boy, she received a little crumpled note from Eliza, written, apparently in great haste, with a pencil on a blank leaf torn from some book, stating that she was held as prisoner in Mr. Gilmore's house, as his slave, bought, as he pretended, of Mr. Agrippa Curtis, who had just arrived from Boston, claiming the entire inheritance of his brother's property, and herself as a part of it! Cassy was horror-struck at this terrible news; but while she was considering whom to apply to, and what could be done, Mr. Agrippa Curtis, accompanied by his Boston lawyer, by Mr. Gilmore, and two or three black servants, entered her house, claiming to take possession of that and her, as his property; and it was as a sequel to this seizure that she had been exposed for sale in the auction-room where I had so providentially found her, and but for which, spite of her protestations to claims of freedom,—which she had no means to substantiate, since the very person in whose hands her free-papers were, had proved traitor and kidnapper,—she would doubtless have been sold into some new bondage.

Such was the story of which, at our first interview, Cassy gave me a brief and hasty outline, the particulars of which I afterwards learnt more at length.

Thank God, I pressed her to my heart once more,—my own, my own true wife!

But my boy, my son, and her whom Cassy claimed and wept for as her dear, dear daughter,—what should be done for Eliza and Montgomery, the one already betrayed and entrapped, the other in great danger to be so?

Again I called Colter into our council, and again I found him prompt to sympathize, and ready to act; quite delighted, indeed, as he said, to help in counter-working these two Yankee scoundrels, who had no doubt conspired together to destroy Mr. Curtis's will, and to divide the estate between them; seeking to reduce Cassy and Eliza, and probably Montgomery too, to slavery; not so much for the sake of what they would sell for,—he didn't suppose that even these cursed skinflint Boston kidnappers, mean opinion as he had of Yankees generally, from what he had seen of them at the south, were quite mean enough for that,—but because that would be the most convenient way to dispose of them; for if allowed to retain their freedom, they might yet make trouble, especially if some unexpected duplicate of the will should ever happen to turn up.

As to Montgomery, indeed, it seemed that Mr. Grip Curtis had a special grudge against him. In fact, as we afterwards heard, he had bought, immediately after his arrival at New Orleans, an immense cowhide, in order, when the young man was once in his power, and securely tied up, to take satisfactory revenge upon him for his State-street beating.

With respect to Eliza, it afterwards turned out, that the very respectable and pious Mr. Gilmore had been so captivated at first sight by her personal charms and Boston accomplishments, as to have come at once to the conclusion to appropriate her and them to his own use, under pretence of ownership, and by the rights which the law gives a master. I say pious Mr. Gilmore, for during a visit to New York some two or three years before, he had been converted to Unitarian Christianity by the preaching of that same eloquent Dr. Dewey, whose patriotic zeal I have already had occasion to refer to; and he had since exerted himself with so much zeal to get up a Unitarian society at New Orleans, as to have acquired the nickname of the Deacon, by which he was generally known among his lighter-minded acquaintances.

CHAPTER LVII.

On Mr. Colter's suggestion, and in order to have the assistance of the law, if we could get any from that quarter, I proceeded with him to ask the advice of an eminent counsellor.

With respect to Cassy, as I had bought up Mr. Grip Curtis's pretended claim to her, she seemed safe enough; especially as, by the law of Louisiana, more humane and reasonable in this particular than that of any other slave-state, a master, after allowing his slave to live as free for ten years, even without any formal emancipation, cannot after that renew his claim of ownership; and it would not be difficult to prove that Cassy had for more than ten years past been recognised as free by the deceased Mr. Curtis. But the case of Eliza, and especially of Montgomery, appeared to be surrounded by many legal difficulties.

No one in Louisiana, as appeared by an extract which the lawyer read to us from the *Code Noir*, or Slave Code, can emancipate a slave, except by special act of the legislature, unless that slave has attained the age of thirty years, and has behaved well for at least four years preceding his emancipation. Nor, according to the decision of the courts, are any emancipations, in case of slaves under thirty, to be established by the mere allowance of freedom. By another provision of the same code, children born of a mother then in a state of slavery, follow the condition of their mother, and are consequently slaves, and belong to the master of the mother; or as the civil code of Louisiana expresses it, "the children of slaves and the young of animals belong to the proprietor of the mother of them by right of accession." Such unquestionably was the fact as to both Montgomery and Eliza; indeed it was by purchase as a slave that Montgomery had originally come into the possession of the deceased Mr. Curtis; and as neither he nor Eliza were yet thirty years of age, nor near it, it did not seem possible that Mr. Curtis could have executed in their behalf any valid act of emancipation. They, therefore, remained a part of his estate; and in default of any testamentary provision, they passed to Mr. Agrippa Curtis, who, as his only brother, his father and mother being dead, was his sole heir. There was, indeed, a provision by which slaves under thirty years of age might be emancipated, provided the owner, upon explaining his motives for it to the judge of the parish and the police jury, could obtain the assent of the judge, and of three-fourths of the jury, to the sufficiency of those motives; but as this could only be done in case of slaves born in the state, even if Mr. Curtis had taken advantage of it in Eliza's case, it could not have afforded any benefit to Montgomery.

The law of Louisiana, following the civil law, from which it is mainly derived, and more humane in this respect than the English common law, which prevails in the rest of the states, in case a father, by acts or words, recognises and acknowledges as such children of his born out of wedlock, gives to them, under the name of "natural children," a claim upon him for sustenance, support, and education in some means of earning a. livelihood. But on the other hand, the right of a person, having lawful relations, to dispose of his property by gift, either during his life or after his death, is very much restricted. In England, and in all the United States except Louisiana, a man may give or will his property to whom he pleases; but there, if he have lawful children, he can give or will nothing to his natural children, though acknowledged to be such, beyond a bare subsistence; and though he have no lawful children, yet if he have parents, brothers, or sisters, he cannot alienate by gift or will above one-fourth of his property at the utmost; the palpable object of which departure from the civil and Spanish law formerly in force is to prevent the mixed race from acquiring property by inheritance through paternal affection; while the provision restricting emancipation is evidently intended to keep as many of them as possible in the condition of slavery.

It might be, the lawyer told us, that Mr. Curtis, in sending the two children to a free state, had in so doing made them free; and perhaps that was one of his objects in sending them. Had they remained at the north, they could not have been reclaimed; but it was not yet a settled question, whether, by returning back to Louisiana, they did not revert to slavery. The Supreme Court of that state had, indeed, once decided, as had been done in several other of the slave-states, that a slave once carried or sent into a free state became free beyond all power of reclamation; but that decision was made under the influence of old-fashioned ideas, which were fast passing into oblivion; and whether the present court would stick to that opinion was more than he could venture to say.

As possession was nine points of the law, and in all questions relating to slavery, as the lawyer facetiously added, very nearly ten points, Mr. Gilmore, in having Eliza in his hands, had decidedly the advantage; and the lawyer informed us, in passing, that he had long known Mr. Gilmore as a cunning, deceitful, cheating rogue; very smooth and plausible, and full of Yankee cant about duty, justice, and religion, and willingness to do what was right; but who seemed to have very little concern for any duty or justice that did not tend to feather his own nest.

We ought, he told us, if possible, to prevent Montgomery's falling into the same trap. In case of any attempt to seize him as a slave, even though he should ultimately sustain his right to freedom, he might still get into great difficulty. By the Slave Code, according to an extract that he read, "free people of colour ought never to insult or strike white people, nor presume to conceive themselves equal to the whites; but on the contrary, they ought to yield to them on every occasion, and never speak to or answer them but with respect, under penalty of imprisonment, according to the nature of the offence."

Now, the best we could make of it was, that Montgomery was a free coloured person. In Virginia and Kentucky, in the fourth descent from a negro, all the other ancestors being white, the African taint, in the eye of the law, is extinguished; and those thus descended pass into the mass of white inhabitants, all the rights of whom they attain, even though one of their great-grandathers or great-grandmothers had been a pure negro. But in several other of the states, and Louisiana among them, the African taint never can be got rid of. The most minute and imperceptible drop of African blood, however diluted by the best white blood of the nation, still suffices to degrade him in whose veins it runs into the class of the free coloured, who "are not to presume to conceive themselves equal to the whites," but who are specially required "to yield to them on every occasion, and never speak to or answer them but with respect, under penalty of imprisonment." If, therefore, Montgomery, being seized as a slave, should, in vindication of his liberty, speak disrespectfully to any of the catchpoles, and especially should he venture to repeat the knocking-down process, which he had once tried already on the person of Mr. Grip Curtis, even though we should succeed in maintaining his right to freedom, he might still find himself exposed to very disagreeable consequences.

The first thing, therefore, to be done in Montgomery's case was, to prevent his falling into the hands of his claimants. As to Eliza, if we could contrive some way of getting her out of Gilmore's hands, we should then be in a much better position for maintaining her claim to freedom.

Montgomery, as it fortunately happened, had written to his mother just at leaving New York, mentioning, among other things, the name of the packet in which he was to sail; and this letter, by the like good luck, we found in the post-office on leaving the lawyer's office.

Colter immediately employed a boat to proceed down the river, carrying a note to Montgomery from his mother. The passage of the packet from New York had been unusually short. She was found a few miles below the city, and according to the recommendation in the note, Montgomery immediately left her, and being set on shore by the boat, came up by land; and late that same evening he arrived at a retired and quiet house in the suburbs, indicated in the letter, at which Colter had procured lodgings for myself and Cassy.

The precaution we had taken was fortunate indeed. Mr. Grip Curtis, as we afterwards found out, had employed some agent in New York to watch Montgomery's movements, and being informed of the vessel in which he came, soon after Montgomery had left, he boarded her, with a gang of assistants, on purpose to seize him.

My son, I have thee too! Snatched from the grasp—saved for the moment at least, from the already purchased cowhide of an infuriated and vindictive scoundrel, claiming to own thee!—Claiming to own my son, my boy, my child!—no longer, as I left him, a prattling infant, but now full-grown in figure, features, every youthful grace and manly beauty, fit to compare with anybody's son.

Never for me can the high ecstasy again be equalled of that moment in which I pressed my long-lost boy to my bosom! But for his youthful heart, how choked with agony the pleasure of this, to me so joyous meeting! What was it to find even a father, whom, though he had heard so often of him from his mother, he had no personal remembrance of, when at the same time he learnt the dreadful situation of Eliza, his playmate, his girl-friend and confidant, his lover now and promised wife!

How the blood mantled into his cheeks! How his dark eyes—his mother's, but without their downcast mildness—flashed fire at the thought of her danger and distress! It was with much difficulty that we detained him for a moment; and that only by assurances that Colter already had spies about the house, so that if Eliza were removed, we should be able to trace her. He knew, he said, Mr. Gilmore's house, and the adjoining premises, thoroughly. He knew also the servants in the family, having been, as a boy, a decided favourite of Mr. Gilmore's black housekeeper. He would contrive some means to enter the house that very night, and, at all personal risks, to effect Eliza's rescue.

Of the thorough scoundrelism of Mr. Grip Curtis, and his confederate Mr. Gilmore, all doubts were now removed. At Montgomery's last departure from New Orleans, a year or so before, to establish himself in business at New York, the deceased Mr. Curtis had placed in his hands a sealed packet, with written directions that it should be opened whenever his will was produced and proved in court, or within thirty days after his death, in case no will should be produced. It did not appear that Mr. Curtis entertained any suspicions of the possible ill-faith of his brother, or of Mr. Gilmore, or that they would conspire together to defeat his intentions, and to misappropriate his property. It was only to guard against accidents that he had taken this precaution.

On opening this package, which Montgomery now produced, we found it to contain a duplicate of Mr. Curtis's will, executed in due form, by which he bestowed upon Eliza, whom he acknowledged and named in it as his natural daughter, one-fourth part of his entire property, which consisted principally in houses in the city of New Orleans, estimated in the will to be worth two hundred thousand dollars. This one-fourth was all which, by the laws of Louisiana, he could give; the other three quarters going to his brother, who, with Mr. Gilmore, was made his executor. But not content with even this large inheritance, this unworthy brother had conspired, it seems, with Mr. Gilmore, not only to cheat his brother's orphan daughter out of her portion, but, by way of effectually stopping her mouth, and preventing all reclamations, to reduce her to slavery and concubinage; Gilmore, besides his part of her portion, to have her person also for his share of the spoils.

The will, after reciting that Mr. Curtis had vainly several times attempted to obtain the assent of the parish judge and three-fourths of the police jury to the manumission of Eliza, as the law required in case of slaves under thirty years of age (that respectable body not thinking the circumstance that she was his only daughter and child a sufficient motive to justify it), proceeded to state that he had sent her to be educated at Boston, with the hope, intention, and desire thereby to make her free; which he declared her to be, so far as it was lawfully in his power to make her so. But in case the law should, notwithstanding his anxiety to divest himself of it, reserve to him and his estate any property in, or right to, the services of Eliza until her attaining to thirty years of age, then, in that case, he devised and bequeathed those services to Cassy—describing her as a free woman, manumitted many years since by himself, and since employed as his housekeeper—in full confidence that, as she had so long acted the part of a mother towards Eliza, she would continue to do the same.

This was all the mention made of Cassy in the will; nor was there any mention of Montgomery, beyond a declaration of his freedom; but from a separate paper, contained in the parcel, it appeared that Mr. Curtis had deposited the sum of twenty thousand dollars with a London banker, payable, in case of his death, to Montgomery, for the joint benefit of himself and his mother—a contrivance resorted to, apparently, for defeating the stringent restrictions of the Louisiana law on the power of devising property by will in the case of persons leaving near relations.

The parcel also contained an official copy of a formal act of emancipation, executed many years ago, in favour of Cassy, before a notary public; Mr. Gilmore being one of the witnesses.

The will wound up with a most solemn adjuration to the two executors to watch sedulously over the welfare of the testator's daughter, whose guardians, during the continuance of her minority, they were declared to be.

What attention they had paid to this adjuration we have seen. They were infamous scoundrels, no doubt. Who questions it? Yet they had their temptations. Twenty-five thousand dollars apiece; to Gilmore the possession of a beautiful girl; to Grip Curtis, the gratification of his furious revenge, as well upon the mother as on the son. And it was only three persons that they sought to reduce to slavery. Pray how much worse were they than so many other of your northern Gilmores and Curtises, who—without any direct and positive temptation at all, beyond the uncertain hope of office, or of currying favour with southern customers—are ready to do their best towards the making and keeping of three millions of slaves; even to the hunting down and delivering up to the pretended claimants—without stopping to inquire whether the claim is any better founded than that set up by Gilmore and Curtis to Eliza—any panting fugitive, man, woman, or child, who may take refuge among them? Any man ready to do that—any man who does not blush at the very thought of it—what is he but a Gilmore and Grip Curtis in his soul?

CHAPTER LVIII.

POOR Eliza! Poor child indeed! Even at that distance, separated by the whole length of the city, Montgomery's heart felt the wild beating of hers, knew that it was her hour of need, and would allow us to detain him no longer. Rescue her he must and would.

Imagine, you who can, the terror and misery of that young girl, going trustingly to the house of her father's friend, and there meeting a man like Mr. Grip Curtis, of whose faithlessness and brutality she had already had some experience in Boston, and being told by him—which statement Mr. Gilmore confirmed—that she was a slave, Mr. Gilmore's slave, sold to him by Mr. Grip Curtis, to whom she had come by inheritance from his brother and her father!

" And, my dear," said Mr. Gilmore, chucking her familiarly under the chin, with the leer of an old reprobate as he was, " that you may fully comprehend the precise legal condition in which you stand, just hear what the law of Louisiana says upon the subject." Here he took down a book from a shelf. " This, my girl," he continued, "is the *Code Noir*, or Black Code, of this state, and thus it lays down the law: ' The condition of a slave being merely a passive one, his subordination to his master'—it reads *his*, child, but it means *her* too—' is not susceptible of any modification or restriction, in such a manner that he owes to his master, and to all his family, a respect without bounds, and an absolute obedience; and he is, consequently, to execute all the orders which he receives from him, his said master, or from them.' "

"The civil code," so this learned lawyer continued, "lays it down much in the same way." Here he read from another and a larger book. "'A slave is one who is in the power of a master to whom he belongs. The master may sell him, *dispose of his person*, his industry, and his labour; he can do nothing, possess nothing, and acquire nothing, but what must belong to his master.' That, my girl, is the law of Louisiana, and under that law you are my slave. I hope you will see the necessity of conforming yourself to your condition and to my wishes. We must all submit," he added, with a snuffle, "to the decrees of Providence, and the law of the land."

Many young ladies in Eliza's situation would have screamed; many would have gone into hysterics; many would have fainted; some would have gone mad. She did neither. She merely expressed her fixed determination never, by any act or consent of hers, to give the smallest countenance to anybody's pretension to make a slave of her.

Locked up for the night in an attic of the house, the next morning she persuaded a black girl, who brought her a crust of bread, to take charge of the note to Cassy, of which mention has been made. Mr. Gilmore had directed that nothing should be given to her but bread and water, in hopes to bring down her spirit. Judging others by himself, the luxurious old villain had imagined that this putting her on short allowance would be the surest way of bringing her to terms. As there seemed but little prospect of human deliverance, fallen as she had into the hands of wolves in sheep's clothing, it only remained for her to invoke the God of the fatherless to guard and protect her. During her second night's solitary imprisonment, her dead father seemed to stand beside her, and, with the same kind smile so familiar to her memory, to say, with his finger pointing to the distance, "Fear not, daughter, a deliverer comes;" and as her eyes followed in the direction of the finger, she seemed to see Montgomery emerging from the darkness, and rushing towards her with outstretched arms. In her effort to rise to meet him, she awoke and found it but a dream. And yet, how much it consoled her! In the failure of realities, how much, indeed, of human happiness has to be found in hopes, wishes, and aspirations embodied into dreams and visions!

Hitherto she had seen nothing more of Mr. Gilmore, nor of anybody but the same black girl who once a day brought her bread and water, and who, though shy of any communication with her, as she seemed to be watched from the passage, yet managed to hand her a note from Cassy, conveyed by Colter's assistance, bidding her escape from the house if she could, telling her where to go, and assuring her that friends were watching for her in the neighbourhood.

About the very hour, on the third evening of Eliza's imprisonment, that Montgomery—whom I followed, not willing to be separated from him, or to trust him alone in so hazardous an enterprise—left our lodgings to seek her out, Mr. Gilmore, having fortified his courage with wine, turned the key of the door, and entered her solitary chamber. She had heard his footstep on the stair, and had prepared to meet him, retreating into a corner behind a small table, which, with a chair and an old mattress on the floor, formed the entire furniture of her prison. As he came directly towards her, she bade him stand off, at the same time drawing and holding up a small stiletto, which Montgomery, in a playful mood, had hung around her neck by a gold chain, just as she was leaving New York, telling her that as she was to make the passage alone to New Orleans, she must have some weapon with which to defend herself; and, as it happened, she had worn it when she went by appointment to call on Mr. Gilmore.

He laughed at the sight of the tiny dagger; but stopped, drew the only chair towards him, sat down upon it, and began to read her a lecture, one half law and the other half divinity, on the folly and wickedness of resistance to legal authority, and the necessity of submission to the divine ordinances. Thomas Littlebody, Esq. the distinguished Boston lawyer, or even the Reverend Dr. Dewey himself, could not have done it better.

He told her that resistance and opposition were as useless as they would be sinful and criminal; that it was in vain to hope assistance or relief from any quarter; that Cassy, no better off than herself, had been sold into slavery the day before; and that Montgomery, having arrived that very evening from New York, was by this time in the hands of Mr. Agrippa Curtis, who, having punished him sufficiently for his insolence, intended to hire him out to work on a plantation up the Red River. She never need expect to see him more.

At these cruel words, the falsehood of which she had no means of knowing, poor Eliza turned deadly pale, alarmed more for her lover than herself, and the stiletto was just dropping from her hand, when Montgomery, pushing open the door, which stood ajar, himself entered the room.

On reaching the street, before Mr. Gilmore's door, we had found the faithful Colter on the watch. He had obtained from the servants a knowledge of the room in which Eliza was imprisoned. The whole three of us, late as it was, on pretence of urgent business with Mr. Gilmore, gained entrance into the house, and while Colter and myself waited by the door below to secure an egress, Montgomery, who knew the house, proceeded directly to the room where Eliza was. As he trod lightly, he had approached the door, and pushed it open without attracting the attention of Mr. Gilmore, who sat with his back towards it, quite engrossed in watching the effects on poor Eliza of the falsehoods he was telling, and of the law and theology which he was endeavouring to impress upon her.

As she saw Montgomery, she uttered a slight scream, and as Mr. Gilmore turned his head to see what might be the matter, he found himself seized by the throat. Montgomery pitched him head foremost into the corner where the mattress lay, and tumbling the chair and table upon him, caught Eliza by the hand, and in the twinkling of an eye, had her down the stairs, and out at the door. We followed in the rear; the whole thing being done in the briefest, most quiet, and most orderly manner, and without the slightest noise or confusion.

In half an hour our whole rescued, happy family were united,—Eliza, Montgomery, Cassy, and myself. But we were still in New Orleans; and neither in that city, nor elsewhere in the United States of America, that country meanly boasting to be free, but sunk beneath the dark flood of despotism, was there any olive-tree rising above the waters, any rest to be found for the soles of our feet.

CHAPTER LIX.

THE very next morning, by Colter's assistance, kind and zealous to the last, we were on a steamboat bound up the river, in which we reached Pittsburg without accident or adventure. Thence we crossed the mountains to Baltimore, and hastening to New York, took passage in one of the Liverpool packets, feeling no security, night nor day, till the good, blue, deep water of the ocean at length rolled beneath us; nor indeed hardly then, so long as the significant stripes of the American flag waved above our heads.

When we touched the British shore we felt safe. Thank God, there is a land that impartially shelters fugitives alike from European and from American tyranny—Hungarian exiles and American slaves!

Before leaving New Orleans, Eliza had executed a power of attorney to Mr. Colter,—to whom the copy of Mr. Curtis's will, entrusted to Montgomery, was delivered,—to proceed under it at law for the recovery of her share of her father's inheritance, with an agreement for an equal division between them of whatever might be got.

Colter encountered all the obstacles which the practised chicanery of Gilmore could place in his way; but he entered into the contest with great spirit; indeed, it seemed to have for him all the excitement of the games to which [he was accustomed. He studied the law himself, the better to push it; and whether or not his experience in his former profession was any help to him in his new one, he presently made himself known as a very shrewd and managing member of the bar. Pursuing Gilmore up and down, through every quirk and turning, to aid in which we sent occasional supplies of money, he finally established the validity of the will, and after a contest of five years, remitted to Eliza her half of the proceeds, having well earned the other half for himself. He still continues to enjoy a good practice at the New Orleans bar, and has even been talked of as a candidate for Congress; but is not thought to be southern enough in his opinions.

Mr. Grip Curtis's action against Montgomery for assault and battery, after lingering along in the Boston courts for three or four years, at last came on for trial. Mr. Agrippa Curtis had retained on his side three or four celebrated Boston lawyers, and the one who closed the case argued, with great energy, that the Union would certainly be dissolved, and society uprooted from its foundations, if the jury did not visit with signal damages such an instance of coloured insolence towards a citizen every way so amiable and highly respectable, and such a stanch supporter of the Union, as Mr. Agrippa Curtis. But all this grave, weighty argument, though aided by a most flowing oration, full, as the newspapers had it, of the most brilliant and beautiful tropes and figures, from the junior counsel, resulted, much to their disappointment, only in a verdict of twenty-five cents damages, which, with costs to one quarter part of that amount, were duly paid over to Mr. Agrippa Curtis's attorney. The jury, by some fortunate accident, happened to be composed of very low people, mechanics and others; there was only a single wholesale merchant upon it, and he not engaged in the southern trade.

As to Messrs. Gilmore and Curtis, they had a fate common with those who get their money over the devil's shoulder. Mr. Curtis settled in New Orleans, engaged in great speculations; had at one time the reputation of a millionaire; but failed, carried down Mr. Gilmore with him, and a goodly number of his Boston friends, including the old firm of Curtis, Sawin, Byrne, and Co. The establishment of his brother's will, and the consequent necessity of disgorging, gave him the finishing blow. For several years he lived a disgraced and ruined man, very much under the weather-board. Some of Gilmore's trickeries towards white clients coming to light,—for cheating coloured people, whether out of their liberty or their property, hurts no man's reputation at New Orleans,—he lost his practice, and sunk pretty much to Mr. Grip Curtis's level.

But within a year or two past, since the passage of the new fugitive slave act, by which the American Union has recently been saved from total destruction, these two worthy gentlemen having turned patriots and Union-saviours, have quite recovered themselves. Under the firm of Gilmore and Curtis,—and Mr. Colter writes me that it is privately whispered that they have a judge as a secret partner,—they have established themselves at Philadelphia in a general slave-catching and kidnapping business. Gilmore has obtained the appointment of a slave-catching commissioner for the eastern district of Pennsylvania, and Mr. Grip Curtis that of assistant to a deputy marshal, appointed for slave cases exclusively; and, of course, all three, commissioner, catchpole, and judge, play beautifully into each other's hands.

I need only add, that Montgomery follows with profit, at Liverpool, the mercantile pursuits to which he had been educated, and that a family of five beautiful and promising children, of which he and Eliza are the happy parents, does not afford much countenance to the non-sensical physiological theory that the mixed race is hybrid and sterile, under which certain American statesmen are endeavouring to find shelter against the growing inevitable danger by which their favourite system of slavery is threatened.

In vain, Americans, do you seek to make nature a party to your detestable conspiracy against the rights of humanity, and your own flesh and blood. In vain do your laws proclaim that the children shall follow the condition of the mother. The children of free fathers are not thus to be cheated of their birthright. Day by day, and hour by hour, as the chain becomes weaker, so the disposition and the power to snap it become stronger. Day by day, and hour by hour, throughout the civilized world, sympathy diminishes for you, the oppressors, and sympathy increases for your oppressed victims, becoming, as they do, day by day, not by a figure of speech merely, or by a pedigree derived from Adam, but as a matter of notorious and contemporary fact, more and more your brethren, flesh of your flesh, and blood of your blood.

Can you stand the finger of scorn pointed at you by all the civilized world?

Can you stand the still small voice of conscience, day by day, and hour by hour, reëchoing in your own hearts those uncomfortable epithets—slave-driver, slave-breeder, slave-hunter, dough-face?

As to you, graybeards in iniquity, with hearts seared, faith blighted, hope withered, and love dried up, continue, if you will, you and your Aaron, to bow down to the golden calf that first seduced you!

It is your sin, your weakness, your want of faith, that have kept your nation wandering this forty years in the wilderness. With imaginations too dull and gross to raise you to the height of any mental Mount Pisgah; incapable to see, even in your mind's eye, the distant prospect of good things to come; longing secretly in your hearts to return to the flesh-pots of Egypt; well content to make bricks for the Pharoahs; yourselves slaves hardly less than those whom you oppress; cowardly souls, frightened by tales of giants and lions, it were vain to expect that you should ever enter the promised land; cravens, fit only to die and to rot in the wilderness!

But already is coming forward a new generation, to whom justice will be something more than a mere empty sound; something as imperiously forced upon them by their own sense of right, as by the clamours and demands of those who suffer. In vain do your priests and your politicians labour to extinguish, in the minds of the rising generation, the idea of any law higher than their own wicked bargains and disgraceful enactments. When to uphold slavery it becomes necessary to preach atheism, we may be certain that the day of its downfall is nigh. This must surely be the darkness which precedes the dawn; for what greater darkness than this is possible?

To you, then, uncontaminated children, I appeal; and in mine speak the cries of millions. That which hath been hidden from the wise and the prudent, the voice of love and mercy shall reveal unto you.

Love and mercy did I say? There hardly needs that; a decent self-respect, a regard for yourselves only, might suffice.

The whip flourishes also over your heads. The white slaves in America are far more numerous than the black ones; not white slaves such as I was, pronounced so by the law, but white slaves such as you are, made such by a base hereditary servility, which, methinks, it is time to shake off.

The question is raised, and can be blinked no longer: Shall America be what the fathers and founders of her independence wished and hoped—a free democracy, based upon the foundation of human rights, or shall she degenerate into a miserable republic of Algerines, domineered over by a little self-constituted autocracy of slave-holding lynchers and blackguards, utterly disregardful of all law, except their own will and pleasure?

Yes, my young friends, it is to this destiny that you are called. Upon you the decision of this question—no longer to be staved off by any political temporizing—is devolved. Those who would be free themselves —so it now plainly appears—cannot safely be parties to any scheme of oppression. The dead and the living cannot be chained together. Those chains which you have helped to rivet on the limbs of others, you now find, have imperceptibly been twined about yourselves; and drawn so tightly, too, that even your hearts are no longer to beat freely.

Take courage, then, and do as I did. Throw off the chains! And stop not there; others are also to be freed. It seems a doubtful thing; but courage, trust, and perseverance, proof against delay and disappointment, faith and hope, will do it. I am old, and may not live to see it; but my five grandchildren, born, thank God, in free England, surely will.

PRINTED BY COX (BROTHERS) AND WYMAN, GREAT QUEEN STREET.

In 1 vol. Price 7s. cloth lettered.

THE HISTORY OF BRITISH INDIA. By CHARLES MAC-FARLANE. From the Earliest Period to the Present Time. With Copious Notes.

"The book is well written, like all Mr. MacFarlane's works."—*Globe.*

"Is clever and vigorously written."—*Daily News.*

"Is a pattern of cheapness as well as of literary merit."—*Naval and Military Gazette.*

In 2 vols. Fcap. 8vo, Price 5s. cloth lettered.

BANCROFT'S HISTORY OF AMERICA; from the Discovery of the American Continent, and its Earliest Colonization, to the War of Independence.

"Among the historians of the United States, we give to Mr. Bancroft the first place."—*Westminster Review.*

"Bancroft's Colonial History has established for himself a title to a place among the great historical writers of the age. The reader will find the pages filled with interesting and important matter; he will meet with a brilliant and daring style, acute reasoning, and picturesque sketches of character."—*Prescott's Essays.*

In 1 vol. Royal 8vo, Price 9s. cloth extra.

HISTORY OF THE POPES. By LEOPOLD RANKE. Including their Church and State, the Reorganization of the Inquisition, the Rise, Progress, and Consolidation of the Jesuits, and the means taken to effect the Counter-reformation in Germany, to revive Romanism in France, and to suppress Protestant Principles in the South of Europe. Translated from the last edition of the German by WALTER J. KELLY, of Trinity College, Dublin.

"This translation of Ranke we consider to be very superior to any other in the English language."—*Dublin Review.*

"A work singularly interesting at the present time."

"One of the most valuable contributions that have been made to history during the present century."—*Monthly Review.*

In 2 vols. Post 8vo, Price 7s. cloth lettered.

CHANNING'S (DR.) LIFE AND CORRESPONDENCE. Edited by his Nephew, WILLIAM HENRY CHANNING. A new Edition, with a Portrait.

"His nephew has compiled his biography with singular judgment. He has followed the method of Lockhart in his Life of Scott. As far as possible, the narrative is woven with letters and diaries; the subject speaks for himself, and only such intermediate observations of the editor are given as are necessary to form a connected whole . . . . . . They are interesting as revelations of the progress of culture, the means and purposes of one whose words have winged their way, bearing emphatic messages over both hemispheres — who, for many years, successfully advocated important truths, and whose memory is one of the most honoured of New England's gifted divines."

In 3 handsome vols. 8vo, cloth gilt, Price 15s. (originally published in 4to, at 5l. 5s.)

WALPOLE'S MEMOIRS OF THE REIGN OF GEORGE II. Edited, with an Introduction and Notes, by the late LORD HOLLAND. With numerous Portraits. Second edition, revised.

" We are glad to see an octavo edition of this work. The publisher has conferred a boon on the public by the republication."—*Britannia.*

" A work of greater interest than has been placed before the public for a considerable time. The memoirs abound in matter which is both useful and amusing. The political portions of the work are of undoubted value and interest, and embody a considerable amount of very curious historical information, hitherto inaccessible, even to the most determined and persevering student."—*Morning Post.*

In 3 vols. 8vo, cloth lettered, Price 1l. 1s.

RUSSELL'S (DR.) MODERN EUROPE. The History of Modern Europe, with a view to the Progress of Society, from the Rise of the Modern Kingdoms, with a Continuation to the Death of the Emperor Alexander. By WILLIAM JONES.

" Although the space of time that has elapsed since the termination of Dr. Russell's labours is comparatively short, yet such are the stupendous events which are crowded into it, and such their extraordinary importance, as to render a succinct and luminous exhibition of them a matter of general interest. Nor is it possible that they should ever cease to interest the inhabitants of Europe. Posterity will find in a faithful record of them not merely matter of surprise and astonishment, but materials of instruction to the statesman, the philosopher, and the philanthropist. In this hope the continuation of Dr. Russell's History of Modern Europe, a work of great merit and of deserved popularity, has been drawn up in a manner which the publishers trust will meet with the approbation of the reader."

In 4 vols. Square 8vo, cloth gilt, Price 15s.; or in 2 vols. 12s. 6d.

MACFARLANE'S FRENCH REVOLUTION. Being the History of the French Revolution from 1781 to the Coronation of Napoleon in 1804. By CHARLES MACFARLANE. Illustrated with numerous Woodcuts.

" They are very well narrated in Mr. MacFarlane's History of the French Revolution, lately published by Knight & Co., in four small but comprehensive volumes, which is much the truest, and therefore the best book we have seen on the subject. Mr. MacFarlane has not only consulted, but weighed and compared all preceding writers, and, of course, has arrived at the same conclusion as we have, as to the equivocating, mystifying, falsifying Jesuitism of M. Thiers, though he does not seem to have suspected the peculiar influence under which he wrote. He is not quite so well on his guard against the deeper deception of Mignet, whom, even after refuting him, he treats with more respect than his shallow philosophy and solemn insincerity deserve."—*Quarterly Review.*

In 1 thick vol. Medium 8vo, cloth lettered, reduced to 7s.
(Published at 22s.)

HISTORY OF FRANCE. By MICHELET. Translated from the French by G. H. SMITH, Esq.

" Michelet's great work contains the growth of feudalism, and develops the religious, philosophical, and artistic spirit of the middle age, until we arrive, to use M. Michelet's own language, at 'the great work of equality and of civil order slowly prepared by the monarchy, consummated by the republic, and crowned and proclaimed in Europe by the victories of Napoleon.'"

Medium 8vo, cloth lettered, reduced to 3s. 6d. (Published at 7s.)

PROCTOR'S HISTORY OF ITALY, from the Fall of the Western Empire to the Commencement of the Wars of the Revolution.

" This history has been greatly esteemed, and it is the only complete History of Italy in our language; it combines all that is valuable in Sismondi's histories, and the latest authorities on the subject."

In 1 vol. cloth gilt, Price 2s. 6d.

MACFARLANE'S LIFE OF THE DUKE OF MARLBOROUGH, with Illustrations.

" The object proposed in the above volume is to place in the hands of, or render accessible to, all classes of the community, a cheap and compendious account of the doings and sayings of one of the greatest of English warriors and statesmen."

In 1 vol. cloth gilt, Price 2s. 6d.

MACFARLANE'S LIFE OF THE DUKE OF WELLINGTON, with Illustrations.

" The times in which we live seem to call for an animated revival of our military prowess, and of the science, skill, valour, and achievements of our fathers, as well on the battle-field as on the ocean."

In 1 vol. cloth gilt, price 2s. 6d.

FRANKLIN (SIR JOHN) AND THE ARCTIC REGIONS. Being an Account of the various Expeditions sent for the Discovery of the North-West Passage, and more detailed particulars of those sent out to Discover the Fate of Sir John Franklin, and the vessels under his command. By P. L. SIMMONDS. With an Illustration and Maps.

KIRKE WHITE'S REMAINS.   BY SOUTHEY.

In 1 vol. cloth gilt, Price 4s. 6d.; or 5s. gilt edges.

KIRKE WHITE'S POETICAL WORKS; to which are added his REMAINS, FRAGMENTS, and many pieces not usually included in previous editions of his works, with Life. By ROBERT SOUTHEY. With Illustrations, by Birket Foster. And Portrait of the Author, by W. Harvey. Beautifully printed on a superfine paper.

LONGFELLOW'S POETICAL WORKS, ILLUSTRATED.

In 1 vol. cloth gilt, Price 6s. 6d.; or 7s. 6d. gilt edges.

LONGFELLOW'S POETICAL WORKS, beautifully illustrated with upwards of Thirty-four Engravings, from designs by John Gilbert; and Steel Plates, executed in the first style of art, from designs by Thomas. Printed on a superfine paper.

" The greatest care has been taken, and no expense spared, to produce the most complete and best edition of this most popular poet; it contains many pieces not contained in any other edition, and the illustrations are equal, if not superior to any work of the kind.

In 2 vols. 8vo, cloth, emblematically gilt, reduced to 12s. 6d.
(Published at 1l. 8s.)

CARLETON'S TRAITS AND STORIES OF THE IRISH PEASANTRY. A new Pictorial edition, with an Autobiographical Introduction, Explanatory Notes, and numerous Illustrations on Wood and Steel, by Phiz, &c.

The following Tales and Sketches are comprised in this edition :—

Ned M'Keown.	The Donah, or the Horse Stealers.
The Three Tasks.	Phil Purcel, the Pig-driver.
Shane Fadh's Wedding.	Geography of an Irish Oath.
Larry M'Farland's Wake.	The Llanham Shee.
The Battle of the Factions.	Going to Maynooth.
The Station.	Phelim O'Toole's Courtship.
The Party Fight and Funeral.	The Poor Scholar.
The Lough Derry Pilgrim.	Wildgoose Lodge.
The Hedge School.	Tubber Derg, or the Red Well.
The Midnight Mass.	Neal Malone.

" Mr. Carleton has caught most accurately the lights and shades of Irish life; his tales are full of vigorous picturesque description and genuine pathos. They may be referred to as furnishing a very correct portrait of Irish peasantry."—*Quarterly Review.*

" Truly—intensely Irish."—*Blackwood.*

NEW EDITION OF SHAKSPEARE'S WORKS. BY W. HAZLITT.

In 4 vols. Fcap. 8vo, cloth, emblematically gilt, plain edges, Price 10s.

SHAKSPEARE'S DRAMATIC WORKS. A new edition, with Notes and Life, printed in a new type, from the text of Johnson, Steevens, and Reed, and edited by W. HAZLITT.

The same edition, bound in calf, marbled edges, Price 24s.

" This edition, now complete, has our hearty approval; its cheapness is not to be excelled, and the binding, printing, and paper, are unexceptionable. In these days of reprints, this Shakspeare is behind no book yet offered to the public."—*Morning Herald.*

In 1 vol. Fcap. 8vo, cloth gilt, Price 2s. 6d.

SHAKSPEARE'S DOUBTFUL PLAYS AND POEMS. Printed uniform with his Dramatic Works, to which it forms a Supplemental volume.

" The Doubtful Plays of Shakspeare are printed uniform with Hazlitt's edition of his undoubted works, because the mere fact of their having been repeatedly printed as his productions, entitles them to popular perpetuation, and because there is a fair presumption that, in great or less proportion, several of them at least actually passed through his hands."

In 1 vol. Price 6s. 6d. or gilt edges, 7s.

LONGFELLOW'S COMPLETE POETICAL WORKS.
(The Liverpool Edition.)   An entire new Edition, with numerous Woodcuts.   One vol. Square Fcap. cloth, with an emblematical binding.

In 1 vol. Price 4s. 6d. cloth lettered.

COUNTRY HOUSE (The).   Containing—The Poultry Yard,
The Piggery, The Ox, and The Dairy.   Complete in 1 Vol.   Illustrated with numerous Woodcuts.

" Railroads, steam-boats, and other rapid conveyances, which have added so largely to urban populations, have at the same time afforded the means to a numerous body, whose industry is carried forward in towns, of seeking health and amusement in rural pursuits; to these, as well as to the settled country residents, this book can be confidently recommended."

THE BEST STANDARD ENGLISH DICTIONARY.

In 2 vols. Royal 8vo, 1,000 pages each vol. cloth extra, Price 2l. 2s.; half morocco, cloth sides, 2l. 10s.

CRAIG'S UNIVERSAL ETYMOLOGICAL TECHNOLO-
GICAL, AND PRONOUNCING DICTIONARY OF THE ENGLISH LANGUAGE, embracing all the terms used in Science, Literature, and Art.

The rapid strides made of late years in the arts and manufactures, as well as in science, has occasioned the introduction into our language of a vast number of new words, some of them of foreign extraction, others the invention of new theorists or scientific discoverers. This extension of our language has, to a certain degree, made all the Standard Dictionaries extant imperfect. A new and entirely complete work was therefore considered a great desideratum, and it has lately been completed, after seven years of hard and laborious mental exertion, under the superintendence of JOHN CRAIG, Esq., F.G.S., and Geological Lecturer at the Glasgow University.

From numerous literary critiques, the undermentioned are selected as giving a fair and impartial character to this important publication.

"We have withheld our opinion of this work until its rapid progress has enabled us to give it our full and perfect attention. We now unhesitatingly pronounce it as one of the best and most complete works it has fallen to our duty to criticise for many years."—Glasgow Citizen.

" This Dictionary is the only one that gives the pronunciation and derivation of all words."

" The work before us fills up a decided desideratum in the English language. He would indeed be most unreasonable who did not own the debt due to the author in giving us the singular information of the traveller, the deep learning of the divine, the curious play of the philologist, the succinct definitions of the mathematician, the technical terms of the manufacturer, the terminology of the naturalist, the newly-formed instruments of the musician, the gentle science of the herald, and the abstruse information of the physiologist."—New Quarterly Review.

For the convenience of many parties, an edition of the above is issued in One Shilling Parts, publishe   monthly.

In 1 vol. Fcap. Price 3s. 6d. cloth lettered.

LONGFELLOW'S COMPLETE PROSE WORKS. Containing his Hyperion, Kavanagh, and Outré Mer.

"One of the most pleasing characteristics of Longfellow's works is their intense humanity. A man's heart beats in every line; he loves, pities, and feels with, as well as for, his fellow 'human mortals.' He is a brother, speaking to men as brothers, and as brothers are they responding to his voice."—*Gilfillan.*

In 1 vol. Price 2s. 6d. cloth lettered, or 3s. gilt edges.

PALMYRA (The Fall of), and Rome and the Early Christians. A New Edition, with Engravings. Emblematically gilt.

"This work seems to be rapidly gaining the reputation which it so well deserves. Piso, the imagined author of the Letters, is supposed to have visited Palmyra towards the close of the third century, to have become acquainted with Zenobia and her court, to have seen the city in its glory, and to have witnessed its destruction by Aurelian (A.D. 273). It is not a work of an ordinary character—it is a production of a thoughtful, able, imaginative, and above all, a pure and right-minded author, of clear thoughts and sound sense."—*North American Review.*

In 1 vol. Price 3s. cloth, or 3s. 6d. gilt edges.

HOMER'S ILIAD. Translated by Pope. A new Edition, printed in a superior manner, on superfine paper. With Illustrations. Royal 32mo.

In 1 vol. Price 3s. cloth, or 3s. 6d. gilt edges.

HOMER'S ODYSSEY. Translated by Pope. A new Edition, printed in a superior manner, on superfine paper. With Illustrations. Royal 32mo.

In 1 vol. Price 2s. 6d. cloth, or 3s. gilt edges.

WASHINGTON IRVING'S MAHOMET AND HIS SUCCESSORS. A new Edition in one Volume. With an Illustration. Foolscap 8vo.

"As a piece of literary work, we can award high praise to this Life of Mahomet; the narrative flows on without interruption from the first page to the last, and occasionally it is brightened by passages of unusual beauty, diction, and pictorial effect in the grouping of ideas and of situations."—*Athenæum.*

In 5 vols. Royal 8vo, Price 21s. cloth lettered.

PENNY MAGAZINE (New Series). The New Series of this Popular Work (the forerunner of the numerous Illustrated Publications that have appeared of late years) contains about 2,600 pages of letter-press, and upwards of 1,100 wood engravings, executed in the first style of art.

"The work is a perfect library in itself; is particularly adapted to all going abroad, Public Libraries, Mechanics' Institutions, Naval and Military Schools, as a cheap and excellent medium to convey and disseminate sound and substantial knowledge."

In 1 vol. Price 3s. 6d. cloth, gilt edges.

QUEEN OF FLOWERS; or Memoirs of the Rose. Beautifully Illustrated with Coloured Engravings of this Celebrated Flower.

"This work has received many additions and corrections, and it is hoped that this new and illustrated edition will be deemed worthy of general approbation."

In 1 vol. Royal 8vo, Price 10s. cloth gilt.

POPE'S COMPLETE POETICAL WORKS; including his Translations. Edited by H. P. CARY, M.A. With a Biographical Notice of the Author.

"Pope's works, however often perused, afford fresh delight, and may be considered as one of the books best adapted to excite a love of literature."—Warton.

In 1 vol. Price 2s. 6d. or 3s. gilt edges.

OLIVER GOLDSMITH, a Biography. By WASHINGTON IRVING. The Vicar of Wakefield, the Deserted Village, the Traveller, and the Minor Poems. Complete in one Volume, and Illustrated with an Engraving. Foolscap 8vo.

"We read the 'Vicar of Wakefield' in youth and in age: we return to it again and again, and bless the memory of an author who contrives so well to reconcile us to human nature."—Sir Walter Scott.

In 1 vol. Price 2s. 6d. or 3s. gilt edges.

KALOOLAH; or, Journeyings in the Djebel Kumri. A book of Romantic Adventure. Illustrated by four Beautifully Coloured Engravings. Fcap. 8vo.

"The most singular and captivating narrative since Robinson Crusoe."—Home Journal.

UNIFORM SERIES OF THE AMERICAN POETS.

Price 2s. each, gilt edges.

LOWELL'S (JAMES RUSSELL) COMPLETE POEMS. With a Short Memoir.

"His works, be they as widely read as they deserve, should be in every dwelling of the land."—*Literary World.*

"His celebrity is daily increasing. Mr. Lowell never writes without thought, or publishes for the sake of praise or profit."—*Philadelphia Gazette.*

LONGFELLOW'S COMPLETE POETICAL WORKS. Including his Translations, "The Spanish Student," and his new poem, "The Sea-side and Fire-side." Royal 24mo.

"Longfellow's Works are eminently picturesque, and are distinguished for nicety of epithet and elaborate scholarly finish. He has feeling, a rich imagination, and a cultivated taste."—*R. W. Griswold.*

WHITTIER'S POETICAL WORKS. Reprinted from the Last American edition. Royal 24mo.

"His productions are all distinguished for manly vigour of thought and language."—*R. W. Griswold.*

SIGOURNEY'S POETICAL WORKS. With Introductory Preface by F. W. N. BAYLEY, Esq.

"Her writings have endeared her name to the lovers of virtue and of song everywhere; as a writer of verse she has high moral aims, and though this circumstance, with ordinary talent, might entitle her to consideration, she can add the effectual claim of literary excellence. The poetry is characterized by ease, tenderness, a chastened fancy, and a delicate susceptibility of whatever is beautiful in nature or charming in truth."—*Chambers.*

WILLIS'S POETICAL WORKS. Reprinted from the Last Revised American Edition, in which the Author has embodied Poems never before Published.

"The poetry of Mr. Willis is distinguished for exquisite finish and melody: his language is pure, varied, and rich; his imagination brilliant, and his wit of the finest description."—*R. W. Griswold.*

BRYANT'S COMPLETE POETICAL WORKS. With Life by Griswold, and Preface by F. W. N. BAYLEY, Esq. Royal 24mo.

HOLMES' POETICAL WORKS. With an Introduction by SCOBLE.

In Royal 24mo, Price 2s. each, cloth gilt edges.

CAMPBELL'S PLEASURES OF HOPE, Gertrude of Wyoming, and Miscellaneous Poems; to which are added, COLLINS'S and GRAY'S POETICAL WORKS.

"Had Gray written nothing but his Elegy, high as he stands, I am not sure that he would not stand higher—it is the corner-stone of his glory."—*Lord Byron.*

LONGFELLOW'S HYPERION AND KAVANAGH. Printed in Large Type.

LONGFELLOW'S OUTRE MER; or, a Pilgrimage beyond the Sea.

ROUTLEDGE'S ILLUSTRATED STANDARD JUVENILE BOOKS.

The greatest care has been taken in producing the present series. They have been carefully edited; but, at the same time, no liberty has been taken with the Author's meaning, or form of expression. They are printed in a large type, on superfine paper, and illustrated in the first style of art, by H. K. Browne, John Gilbert, W. Harvey, H. Warren, Corbould, &c., and are, without exception, the Cheapest, Best, and Most Complete Editions of these Universally Popular Works :—

		s.	d.	
Bound in Cloth, extra Gilt Back........		3	6	each.
Ditto	Gilt Edges	4	0	,,
Ditto	Coloured Plates	5	0	,,
Or in Morocco, extra.................		8	6	,,

CONTENTS OF THE SERIES.

SWISS FAMILY ROBINSON; or Adventures on a Desert Island. A New Edition. The Two Series complete in One Volume, entirely Revised and Improved. Eight Illustrations, by John Gilbert.

EVENINGS AT HOME; or, The Juvenile Budget Opened. By L. Aiken and Mrs. Barbauld; a New and Revised Edition. Eight Engravings, 416 pages.

SANDFORD AND MERTON. By Thomas Day. A New Edition, entirely Revised and Corrected. Eight Illustrations, 416 pages.

ROBINSON CRUSOE; including His Farther Adventures. Complete Edition, with Life of De Foe. Illustrated by Phiz. 432 pages.

GUIZOT'S (Madame), MORAL TALES FOR YOUNG PEOPLE. Translated from the latest French Edition, by Mrs. L. Burke. Illustrated by Campbell.

HANS ANDERSEN'S FAIRY TALES AND LEGENDS. Complete Edition. Illustrated by H. Warren. Translated by MADAME DE CHATELAIN.

TRAVELS OF ROLANDO; or, A Tour Round the World. By LUCY AIKEN. Newly Corrected and Revised by CECIL HARTLEY, A.M. Illustrated by Harvey. 502 pages.

ROMANCE OF ADVENTURE; or, True Tales of Enterprise, for the Instruction and Amusement of the Young. Illustrated by Campbell.

MISS M'INTOSH'S WORKS.

In Fcap. 8vo, Price 2s. each, cloth lettered; 2s 6d cloth, gilt edges.

EVENINGS AT DONALDSON MANOR. Illustrated with Beautiful Steel Engravings, executed in the First Style of Art.

CONQUEST AND SELF-CONQUEST; or, Which Makes the Hero? With Illustrations.

PRAISE OR PRINCIPLE; or, For What Shall I Live? With Illustrations from designs by John Gilbert.

CHARMS AND COUNTER-CHARMS. With Illustrations.

GRACE AND ISABEL; or, To Seem and To Be. With Illustrations from Designs by John Gilbert.

JUVENILE TALES FOR ALL SEASONS; or, Blind Alice, Jessie Graham, Florence Arnott, and other tales. Illustrated by Kenny Meadows.

" The works of Miss M'Intosh have become popular in the best sense of the word. The simple beauty of her narratives, combining pure sentiment with high principle, and noble views of life and duties, ought to win for them a hearing at every fireside in our land. They place her beside the Edgeworths and the Barbaulds, and the Opies, who have so long delighted and instructed us; and as there is little doubt that, as she becomes known, so will her works be valued as highly as any of the most popular works of the above justly famed authors, causing her name to become a household word, as a pleasing and instructive writer."

Uniform in size with Dean and Darton's Large Coloured Books for Children, with greatly improved Illustrations, New Types, and Well-Coloured pictures, an entirely New Series of Thirteen different Books.

PRICE 6d. EACH.

AUNT MAVOR'S PICTURE BOOKS FOR LITTLE READERS :—

1	The Old Cornish Woman	8 large cuts.
2	Alphabet of Foreign Things	26 cuts.
3	Uncle Nimrod's First Visit	24 cuts.
4	Story of Reynard the Fox	8 large cuts.
5	Old Mother Bunch	8 large cuts.
6	Alphabet of the Exhibition	16 cuts.
7	Uncle Nimrod's Second Visit	18 plates.
8	Alphabet of English Things	26 cuts.
9	Ploucquet's Stuffed Birds and Animals	8 cuts.
10	The Exhibition and Grand London Sights	16 cuts.
11	Uncle Nimrod's Third Visit	8 cuts.
12	Dolls and Sights of the Crystal Palace	15 cuts.
13	The Cat's Tea Party	8 large plates.

Such Pictures as are here given will gladden the eyes of our Juvenile Friends, and make them remember the wonderful sight now passed away.

In 1 vol. Price 3s. 6d. cloth lettered.

LOUDON'S (MRS.) YOUNG NATURALIST'S JOURNEY; or, the Travels of Agnes Merton and her Mamma. Second Edition, Revised and Corrected. Illustrated with numerous Engravings.

" Our young readers are assured that all the anecdotes here related of the animals are strictly true, though the incidents of the journey and the persons introduced are partly imaginary."

Price 2s. 6d. each, cloth lettered.

MYRTLE'S MAN OF SNOW; and other Tales. Wit m any Illustrations. Square, cloth gilt.

MYRTLE'S THE PET LAMB, Bertha and the Bird, &c. Illustrated by Absolon. Cloth gilt.

MYRTLE'S LITTLE AMY'S BIRTHDAY, and other Tales. Illustrated by Absolon. Square, cloth gilt.

MYRTLE'S STORY BOOK OF COUNTRY SCENES. Illustrated by Absolon. Square, cloth gilt.

MYRTLE'S LITTLE FOUNDLING, and other Tales. With Plates by Absolon. Square, cloth.

The above, with Plates Beautifully Coloured, and Gilt Edges, 3s. 6d. each.

⁎ These stories were invented, at different times, for the amusement of a little girl six years old. The pleasure she took in them induced their collection into a series, and has led to their publication.

In 1 vol. Price 3s. 6d. cloth lettered.

THE BOY'S OWN STORY BOOK. With numerous Illustrations by Wm. Harvey.

"It has been the design of the editor of the above volumes to present to his reader some of the best stories that adorn our literature, in a form peculiarly attractive to the eyes of youth."

In 1 vol. Price 4s. cloth, emblematically gilt, or 4s. 6d. gilt edges.

THE ANCIENT CITIES OF THE WORLD, in their Glory and their Desolation. By Rev. T. A. Buckley, M.A. Illustrated with numerous Engravings.

"This is a very good work, presenting such a life-stirring and picturesque series of panoramas as will impress the mind powerfully, and excite a desire to learn more of the great countries of which these renowned cities were the capitals. Neatly Illustrated and carefully written, it is 'the book' to put into the hands of every one."

CHEAP EDITIONS OF STANDARD RELIGIOUS WORKS.

In 1 vol. Price 4s. 6d. cloth lettered.

CALMET'S BIBLICAL DICTIONARY, Abridged, Modernized and Re-edited, according to the Most Recent Biblical Researches, by Theodore Alois Buckley, B.A. The volume contains upwards of 700 pages, and is printed in a New, Beautiful, and Clear Type.

"The present work is not designed to compete with the many learned and voluminous cyclopædias, and other books of reference, already in circulation, but simply to place in the hands of the great mass of the people some sounder and more extensive information than the cheap biblical dictionaries hitherto published could furnish. The advantage of making an established book the groundwork of such a publication, at the same time modernising its whole character, is too obvious to need discussion."

In 1 vol. Price 4s. 6d. cloth lettered.

LIFE OF CHRIST, OUR GREAT EXEMPLAR. By Jeremy Taylor, being the History of the Life and Death of Our Saviour, Jesus Christ, Revised and Edited, with a Life of the Author, by Theodore A. Buckley, M.A. With a Portrait, 750 pages.

"I am acquainted with no work of Taylor's (I may say with no work of any other author) in which more practical wisdom may be found, a greater knowledge of the human heart, and a more dexterous application, not only of the solemn truths of Christianity, but of even the least important circumstances related in the Life of Our Saviour, in the development of sound principles of action, and to the correction and guidance of our daily conduct."—Extract from Life by Bishop Heber.

"When the name of Jeremy Taylor is no longer remembered with reverence, genius will have become a mockery, and virtue an empty shade."—Hazlitt.

In 1 vol. Price 5s. cloth.

PICTORIAL LIFE OF OUR SAVIOUR. By DR. KITTO. In one Handsome Volume, with many Illustrations.

"To meet the demand which is happily increasing for subjects connected with Sacred History, this work of sterling value has been produced by one of our most learned students of Bible Literature. The 'Life of Our Saviour' is drawn from a close examination and comparison of the Four Gospels, and elucidated by an accurate and extensive knowledge, on the part of Dr. Kitto, of all those habits and customs of the East which are so necessary to be understood in order fully to comprehend the Scripture narrative. It is illustrated with a large number of beautiful engravings, copied by our first artists from the most celebrated productions of antiquity."

In 1 vol. Price 2s. cloth, or 2s. 6d. gilt edges.

FAMILY PICTURES FROM THE BIBLE. Edited by DR. CUMMING. And an Introduction. Illustrated with Frontispiece and Vignette by George Measom. Foolscap 8vo.

"This work is a gallery of portraits of Scripture Families—a studio full of groups and models—worthy of our study, because they are casts from perfect originals; where flaws and defects exist in any family, they are clearly marked for our avoidance; where excellency and beauty are, these are presented clear and voluminous; and, at the same time, the elements that compose and generate them are indicated with unmistakeable precision."—Extract from Dr Cumming's Preface.

In 1 vol. Fcap. 8vo, cloth lettered, Price 2s.

CHEEVER'S (DR.) MEMORIALS OF THE LIFE AND TRIALS OF A YOUTHFUL CHRISTIAN in Pursuit of Health, as developed in the Biography of NATHANIEL CHEEVER.

The same Edition, cloth extra, gilt edges, Price 2s. 6d.

"The subject of this memoir died at sea while in pursuit of health. There is a valuable account of a medical examination at Cuba, but the book is mainly occupied with religious journals and experiences. The well-known names of the editors certify and distinguish its claims upon the community."—Literary World.

In 1 vol. Price 7s. cloth lettered.

KITTO'S (DR.) BIBLE HISTORY OF THE HOLY LAND. Being an Account of the Physical Geography, Natural History, Arts and Antiquities, of the Holy Land. With numerous Illustrations.

"The object of this work is to furnish a trustworthy analysis of the interesting results of Eastern travel. The facilities of modern communication have wonderfully increased our desire to learn more of these lands, which possess the deepest interest for all Christian readers."

In Fcap. 8vo, cloth lettered, Price 2s.

ELIJAH THE TISHBITE. Translated from the German of DR. F. W. KRUMMACHER. A new edition with Portrait of the Author.

In Fcap. 8vo, cloth lettered, Price 2s.

HAWKER'S (DR.) MORNING PORTION. The Poor Man's Morning Portion, being a selection of a verse of Scripture, with Short Observations for every day in the Year. A new edition.

In Fcap. 8vo, cloth lettered, Price 2s.

HAWKER's (DR.) EVENING PORTION. The Poor Man's Evening Portion, being a selection of a verse of Scripture, with Short Observations for every Day in the Year. A new edition.

In Fcap. 8vo, cloth lettered, Price 3s. 6d.

HAWKER'S (DR.) DAILY PORTION. Being the above two works bound together.

In 1 vol. 12mo, cloth lettered, Price 3s.

ROMAINE'S LIFE, WALK, AND TRIUMPH OF FAITH. A new edition, with the Life of the Author.

In 1 vol. Fcap. 8vo, cloth lettered, Price 2s.

BOGATSKY'S GOLDEN TREASURY FOR THE CHILDREN OF GOD, consisting of Devotional and Practical Observations for every Day in the Year. A new edition, printed in large type.

In 1 vol. cloth lettered, Fcap. 8vo, Price 2s.

JENK'S PRAYERS, and Offices of Devotion for Families and for particular persons on most occasions. A new edition. By the Rev. CHARLES SIMEON. With a Preface by the Rev. Albert Barnes.

In 1 vol. Price 2s. cloth, or 2s. 6d. gilt edges.

DODDRIDGE'S RISE AND PROGRESS OF RELIGION IN THE SOUL. A New Edition, Just Published, printed in a Large Type, on Good Paper.

"Is a body of practical divinity and Christian experience that has never been surpassed by any work of the same nature."—Cleveland.

"And first, as a universal storehouse, I recommend 'Doddridge's Lectures' as necessary in the conduct of theological pursuits."—Bishop of Durham's Charge.

BARNES' NOTES, BY DR. CUMMING.

Now Published, the Entire Series of Dr. Cumming's Complete and Accurate Edition of

THE REV. ALBERT BARNES' NOTES (Explanatory and Practical) designed for the Heads of Families, Students, Bible Classes, and Sunday Schools. Edited, and carefully Revised by the Rev. JOHN CUMMING, D.D., Minister of the Scotch Church, Crown Court.

"Mr. Barnes is one of the soundest and most accomplished scholars and biblical commentators living, and his various works have been received with the most cordial favour wherever they have been read. His volumes are a most valuable contribution to the biblical literature of the country."

New Volume, now ready.

In 1 vol. Price 4s. 6d. cloth lettered.

BARNES' (ALBERT), NOTES ON THE BOOK OF REVE-LATION. Map and Woodcuts, 512 pages, cloth extra. Uniform in binding with the 10 vols. New Testament, and 4 vols. Old Testament.

THE EDITION MAY BE HAD BOTH IN SINGLE AND DOUBLE VOLUMES.

The Edition in Single Volumes contains :—

The Notes on the New Testament, in 11 vols.	1	8	0
———— Book of Isaiah, in 3 vols. without abridgment	0	7	6
———— Book of Job, in 2 vols.	0	5	0
THE COMPLETE COMMENTARY, IN THIS FORM	2	0	6

Any of these Volumes will be sold separately, as follows:—

The Notes on the Gospels of Matthew and Mark, 1 vol.	0	2	6
———— Luke and John, 1 vol.	0	2	6
———— Acts of the Apostles, 1 vol.	0	2	6
———— Romans, 1 vol.	0	2	0
———— First Corinthians, 1 vol.	0	2	0
———— Second Corinthians and Galatians, 1 vol.	0	2	6
———— Thessalonians, Timothy, Titus, and Philemon, 1 vol.	0	2	0
———— Hebrews, 1 vol.	0	2	0
———— James, Peter, John, and Jude, 1 vol.	0	3	6
———— REVELATIONS	0	4	6

The Edition in Double Volumes contains :—

The Notes on the New Testament, in 6 vols.	1	5	0
———— Book of Isaiah, in 3 vols.	0	7	6
———— Book of Job, in 1 vol.	0	4	6
THE COMPLETE COMMENTARY, IN THIS FORM	1	17	0

Any Volume may be had separately, as follows :—

The Four Gospels,	in 1 vol. containing 900 pages		0	4	0
Acts and Romans,	in 1 vol.	"	736	"	0	4	0
Corinthians and Galatians,	in 1 vol.	"	786	"	0	4	0
Ephesians to Philemon,	in 1 vol.	"	626	"	0	3	6
Hebrews and General Epistles,	in 1 vol.	"	788	"	0	5	0
THE REVELATIONS,	in 1 vol.	"	512	"	0	4	6
The Book of Isaiah,	in 3 vols.	"	1220	"	0	7	6
The Book of Job,	in 1 vol.	"	788	"	0	4	6

⁎ In ordering the above it is particularly necessary to specify "CUMMING'S EDITION."

LONDON: GEO. ROUTLEDGE & CO., FARRINGDON ST.

3629980